C Averil Clegg, a child development. She began writing ublished three non-fiction books, with Anne Woollett, about twins and their families. Fulfilling a lifelong ambition, in 1988 she began to write fiction under the name Christine Thomas.

Born in Essex in 1943 she was educated at grammar school, London University and the Polytechnic of East London. A varied career, haphazardly arranged around four children, has included being a social worker, running a PhD research project for several years, and in default of any other employment at the time, an invaluable spell in a Sainsbury's megastore which taught her a lot of things about life that don't appear in textbooks. She enjoys writing about people and many of her characters spring from her experiences as a psychologist and supermarket assistant. She is divorced and lives with her three sons in Surrey.

Also by Christine Thomas

Bridie
April
Hannah

Blessings And Sorrows

Christine Thomas

KNIGHT

First published in 1992
by HEADLINE BOOK PUBLISHING PLC

First published in paperback in 1992
by HEADLINE BOOK PUBLISHING PLC

This edition published 2000 by
Knight an imprint of Caxton Publishing Group

10 9 8 7 6 5 4 3 2 1

ISBN 1 84067 263 3

Printed and bound in Great Britain by
J. H. Haynes & Co. Ltd., Sparkford, Somerset

Caxton Publishing Group
20 Bloomsbury Street
London
WC1B 3QA

This book is for
Anne

ACKNOWLEDGEMENTS

The author wishes to acknowledge *The Experience of Infertility* by Naomi Pfeffer and Anne Woollett (Virago Press, 1983); and *Mermaid on Wheels* by June Epstein (Herbert Jenkins, 1968) whose story of Margaret Lester was an inspiration.

Also, special thanks to Nick Markwick, of the Disability Information Service, Surrey, for his help.

Prologue

'I think,' said Sister Bridges one busy Tuesday morning just after the last really warm days of the summer of 1982, 'our new ladies are all booked in, so I'll go and make them say hullo to each other.' Molly Bridges, sister of St Martha's gynaecological and obstetrics ward, in what was once a Victorian workhouse in London's East End, marched off on legs that would have done credit to a rugger player. The new ladies were half-way up her long, shabby ward, with its high ceiling, long, dusty, seldom-opened windows and green walls that flaked in places. It had a shiny brown floor, polished to a high sheen by a cleaner who banged up and down every day and got on everyone's nerves. Two straight rows of pink coverlets on iron bedsteads covered twenty-four women in varying stages of surgical treatment. The ward smelled of floor polish and clean linen and disinfectant and flowers. Shabby Victorian it undoubtedly was, and due for closure when a new district hospital was finished, but Bridges' ward was spick and span, and run with real affection for her patients. She came to a halt by the first new patient's bed.

'I bet she trained with Florence Nightingale,' said a new student nurse, watching her from down by the office, near swing doors that led out to the lifts, and benches where relatives waited and the few patients with enough strength and courage went out to smoke a fag.

'She reminds me of one of those things they carve on the front of ships, all bosoms and jutting chin, cutting up a bow wave,' the girl went on.

'Underneath that prow is the kindest heart you'll ever

come across, and one of the sweetest natures,' snapped the staff nurse. 'Unless and until you do something she considers less than perfect care for her ladies, and then she'll sail into you like the bloody Spanish Armada.'

'Does she always go and introduce the patients to each other?' the student asked, intrigued. 'They never told us to do that, in school.'

'Bridges says, make them be friends before their operations, and in five cases out of ten you've got friends for life. She says there's nothing better than a nice bit of surgery for binding women together, so she reasons that if she breaks the ice when they come in, so they don't go all British and can't speak to each other until they know each other, then when they've had their operations they all muck in and jolly each other along and get better quicker.'

'How funny.'

'It works, I can tell you.'

'I'll keep an eye on them and see,' said the student nurse with a grin.

'Make it your project, why don't you?'

'Hypothesis, a friend in the next bed is a friend in need?'

'You'll discover you can't muck around with women's insides and take their most precious bits out, and not change them in other ways, too,' said the staff nurse sternly.

'I hadn't thought of it like that.'

'Well, start thinking of it like that, because Bridges does, and it's like a cross between a hothouse and a psychiatric department and a school dormitory in here half the time. You'll see. Go and do the obs, before Bridges catches you doing nothing.'

'I thought I was learning things,' answered the girl pertly.

'You'll learn things, all right,' said the staff nurse, handing her a tray of thermometers.

'Oh, my,' murmured the girl, ambling off with the little metal tray, scuttling to a bedside when Sister Bridges bore back down the ward at speed. 'At least perhaps this ward won't be boring.'

'That's that,' Sister Bridges said with satisfaction as she steamed past. 'I think they'll get on, they're a nice bunch.'

The new ladies sat on their beds in carefully pressed nighties and dressing gowns, and regarded Bridges' progress between the beds, twelve on either side.

'Well,' offered Daphne Salmon, cleric's wife, conscious of her Christian duty, prepared to take up her rightful burden of leadership and counsel. Sitting on the side of her bed, patting a tight pepper-and-salt perm, she drew her small features together in an anxious frown resembling a worried mouse, and took the plunge.

'She doesn't leave us much choice, does she? How do you all do?' Several pairs of eyes shifted to various points of the ward, nonplussed.

Blossom Woodruff, directly opposite, sat in the middle of her bed, crossed her long, thin legs in a lotus position, craned her peroxide crew cut round, stared with bright blue eyes at Sister Bridges' receding back and murmured, 'Wow.' Daphne followed her gaze, riveted to the rise and fall of Bridges' ample buttocks, drew her knees together in an involuntary gesture of self-defence, and offered them her diagnosis as a distraction.

'I'm a repair.' She hugged her knees with scrawny middle-aged arms.

'Sounds like a car,' remarked Blossom. 'Big end gone? Shame.' Daphne flushed.

'Take no notice of my tongue,' said Blossom. 'What about you, Sarah Monroe?' Blossom read the label on the head of a bed, above the unruly black curls of the slight, dark-grey-eyed woman who sat on it, tipping a jigsaw on to her bedtable, beginning to sort pieces. They regarded the top of her dark head and waited. Sadie prodded pieces of jigsaw with square, practical hands and answered, absorbed in the fragments, 'Fibroids. Call me Sadie.'

'Me too,' said Blossom cheerfully, 'Big as a grapefruit. I bleed like a stuck pig.'

The mouse winced and twitched her whiskers nervously, unused to plain speaking.

'And you?' demanded Blossom of the waif next door to Sadie.

'A growth,' said Gabriella Miller shyly, pulling the belt of her pink candlewick dressing gown tighter, pinned down by Blossom's gaze. 'On . . .' She was young and shy and couldn't bring herself to say *bowel*. Blossom took in the bunches of fine fair hair held back by coloured elastic and an Alice band from a childlike face, all cornflower-blue eyes and transparent blue skin over jutting, delicate bones. Gabriella felt as if the challenging blue eyes opposite saw straight through her, and shivered.

'I might have cancer,' she said in a very small voice.

Sadie found all the edge pieces of her jigsaw and began to line them up. 'Growths aren't always cancer,' she said quietly. 'I should think especially not in someone as young as you.'

'I'm nineteen,' said Gabriella defensively.

'I've got cancer. It isn't the end of the world.' Lowering *Woman's Own* as if lowering a shield, a very elderly woman met their embarrassment with perfect composure.

'It is a nuisance, but you just mustn't let it get you down.'

Daphne snatched a canvas knitting bag from her locker and began clicking furiously, lips pursed into a button.

'I'm eighty years old,' Mrs Hargreaves creaked, 'and they think I don't know I'm going to die. I'm not a fool. I thought, I've never seen my grandchildren in Christchurch, and I never will at this rate, so I went straight out and booked my ticket. As soon as this lot's over, I'm going to New Zealand.'

'Brilliant,' breathed Blossom.

Mrs Hargreaves disappeared back into *Woman's Own*. Gabriella stared with bruised, shadowed eyes, and chewed her thumb.

'Perhaps you could go and talk to her,' whispered Sadie, sifting blue jigsaw pieces into a pile, leaning confidingly towards the young girl.

Gabriella shook her head sullenly.

'All right,' Sadie put her hand on the pieces and slid the bedtable away, in order to stretch her legs. 'It's giving me cramp, doing this, but I thought it would be something to do, to take my mind off coming in here.'

A very fat woman in a flowered nightie, the far side of Gabriella, turned, a pear in one pudgy pink hand.

'To tell you the truth, dear,' confided Alice Penn triumphantly, piling fruit out of paper bags into a bowl on her locker, 'I've bin on at them to get me in 'ere for months, and so 'as my doctor. I couldn't tell you all the trouble 'e's been to, and now I'm 'ere, I'm jolly well making the most of it. 'E'd be wasting 'is time, otherwise.'

She bent and rummaged in her locker, wheezing.

'You like being in hospital?' asked Sadie, surprised.

Alice's wide mouth split in a grin, showing gaps where two teeth were missing. 'I wouldn't 'ave said no to Butlins,' she said cheerfully, 'but they wasn't offering. I ain't bothered it's hospital, so long as it's a nice break. I ain't fussy, duck.'

Sadie had pulled the table back and started sorting red and green pieces.

''E was always difficult,' Alice went on, pulling the cellophane off a box of Black Magic and taking out the menu. ''E was difficult at the best of times, and then when 'e 'ad 'is first stroke, poor soul, he was terrible the way 'e carried on. Now 'e's had another one and 'e's downright bloody impossible. He can't talk, see, just shouts noises, and drives me mad. 'E carried on something dreadful when the doctor told 'im I 'ad to come in here. He's jealous, see? 'E don't want me to go away. Forty years we've bin married and 'e thinks 'e can't do without me. I thought 'e'd hit the doctor, but 'e never.'

'He?' said Sadie, bemused.

'Me 'usband.'

Curious, Blossom unwound from her lotus position and slid off her bed. 'What have you done with your husband?' she asked, crossing the ward to stand by Sadie's bed.

Alice grinned gleefully. 'The council took 'im. They've

put 'im in a home, just while I come in here. 'E carries on shocking, but in there they don't take no notice and it'll do 'im good. I'm going to enjoy myself, nice and comfy.'

She settled back against her pillows, picked up a *Mirror* and popped a coffee cream into her mouth.

'You know,' said Sadie, staring at Blossom, 'I'm sure I've seen you before.'

'Once seen, never forgotten. Shop in Sainsbury's?'

'Yes.'

'Customer Services, madam. The groveller in the brown coat. Yes, madam, no, madam, three carrier bags full, madam.' She laughed and sat down on Sadie's chair. 'Bloody customers. The shop's all right except for them.'

'I hate that place.'

'Why?' asked Blossom.

Sadie shrugged narrow shoulders. 'It's a rugger scrum. Those trolleys come hurtling down the aisles at you and you're lucky to get away with both kneecaps intact. Then you get to the checkout and the girl changes the till roll. She mangles it up, looks really pleased with herself and rings for a supervisor who takes hours to come. Then she tries to weigh kiwi fruits or something, and that machine goes beeping mad until after a quarter of an hour she finds out they're sold per piece, and then someone has to come and tell her the price of a yoghurt, and they're all martyred and shoving and bickering . . . How do you stand it?'

'You obviously wouldn't last five minutes in there,' chuckled Blossom. 'It's all right. Sometimes I hate it and sometimes I like it, but I can't afford not to do it.'

'There is *always*,' said Sadie, getting into the spirit of the thing, 'a newborn baby in there, screaming its head off. You want to strangle its mother for not picking it up. It rolls around in the top of a trolley, howling, and no one takes a blind bit of notice of it.'

'You can't start letting 'em bring in prams and pushchairs and feeding bottles,' said Blossom, scandalised. 'Just imagine, all those frustrated women in a baby-friendly environment . . . brrrm, brrrm, in for the kill. Roll over, Robocop. No *knowing* where it'd end.'

'What about somewhere to feed babies,' suggested Sadie. 'They have singles' shopping in America, why not mothers' shopping?'

'Don't be daft. Bodies in the aisles, and breastfeeding?' Blossom snorted with laughter. 'Think of those poor men, bored stiff and bad-tempered, trailing round behind some bossy wife, desperate to get to the booze department, and then falling over some woman with her jumper pulled up . . . Oooh, very bad for profits.' She wagged a finger and grinned.

Sadie laughed and said one of the Mrs Sainsburyses ought to set an example.

'Anyway,' Blossom went on cheerfully, 'I've heard a million customers swear never to come inside the place again, but when you have to, you have to. Can't be doing without the soap powder and Liebfraumilch. Swear all you like, but that's life.' She gazed at the thick green-painted walls and long grubby windows of the old building and said, 'Like here. You get sent, like prison.'

'*Prison?*' squeaked Sadie. 'Have you been in prison?'

'Catch Sainsbury's employing someone who's been in prison,' said Blossom scornfully. 'No, I mean hospital's like prison. My mother was in hospital. Multiple sclerosis. They used to string her up on traction for weeks and weeks, to take the pressure off, but she got worse and worse. I wanted her to die, because I loved her, and then when she did . . .'

'I'm terribly sorry,' Sadie said. 'I once knew someone whose wife had that. I didn't mean to . . .'

'It's all right. You been in here before?'

Sadie twisted her wedding ring and tried to laugh, but it came out as a dry sound and a shrug.

'Never mind,' said Blossom kindly.

'Not here. I was in another hospital, off and on, for years.'

'You've been ill for years?' Blossom put her head back and looked Sadie over carefully. 'You look well on it, I must say, but then we all do, don't we? Except her,' she muttered under her breath, meaning Gabriella.

'I wasn't ill. I was infertile.'

'Oh, babies,' Blossom remarked dismissively.

'Oh, no babies,' corrected Sadie, surprised at her tongue running away with her. 'No babies, not for me and Dougal. Your body lets you down and you don't know why. You get desperate for it to happen, and it doesn't. You pray for a baby and when you don't have one it comes as the cruellest let-down of them all. I'm barely over thirty and there was still time, perhaps, if they'd found out what was wrong with us, but instead of growing babies, I've grown growths, and that's that.' Sadie stopped suddenly. It was the first time she had told a stranger that she couldn't have a child, and it shook her. Somehow, though, Blossom seemed a safe person to tell.

Blossom's short nose wrinkled, as she heard the long, untold story behind Sadie's words, and accepted it without comment.

'We thought about using a syringe,' she said, sharing confidences, 'but it was me that'd have to have squirted it up, because Asia wouldn't even consider it, and when it came down to it, I just couldn't fancy it, not even for her to have a baby to look after. So we said, let's leave it.'

'Pardon?' squeaked Sadie, astounded.

'Syringe,' repeated Blossom as though stating the obvious. 'Go on, you know all about using syringes and stuff, you must do after what you just said.'

'Artificial insemination?' croaked Sadie. 'What on earth are you doing with that?'

'How else do you get it inside you?' demanded Blossom.

'Get it inside . . . ?' Sadie tailed off, speechless, began to laugh.

'Well, usually . . .'

'Oh, no, never.' Blossom shook her head vehemently.

'Why do you . . . ?' Sadie took in Blossom's crew cut and the little hole in her nose where it had been pierced, dark-green cotton pyjamas under a St Michael paisley dressing gown. She'd seen them when she was shopping for Dougal in Marks and Sparks, upstairs in the menswear department. 'Er . . .'

'I'm gay.' Blossom, used to the performance, helped her out cheerfully. 'Several men offered to help me out, but it's no good, I can't face it. So when I get broody, I do a lot of overtime. I get over it. You get too tired to bother.'

Sadie stirred her abandoned jigsaw with one finger and considered this revelation.

'I wanted to die sometimes, for a baby,' she said simply.

Blossom pulled her gown firmly round her and said nothing was worth dying about.

'Tomorrow,' Sadie went on, ignoring her, 'I'll wake up and it'll be over. All those years and years of trying, and thinking that if I could just get something about myself right . . . it would all be all right. Eve's made it anything but all right,' she added gloomily.

'Who is Eve?' asked Blossom.

'My adopted baby.'

'I thought you said you hadn't got a baby.'

'It's complicated.'

'It sounds it.'

'My husband is going to leave me because of Eve, and because he has a mistress,' Sadie continued, thinking that perhaps if she said it out loud to this stranger, it would at last be real.

Blossom, unperturbed and unsurprised, gave it careful thought. 'Tell him to go screw himself if he isn't nice to you.'

'And then?' asked Sadie anxiously.

'Depends what you want.'

'If I really knew what I wanted, and could have what I wanted, it'd be easy.'

'Sounds like you'd better find out,' said Blossom unsympathetically. Her watchful eyes sharpened. 'What does that one want now?'

The student nurse came bowling down the ward with a brown glass bottle in one hand and a roll of cotton wool under her elbow. 'Nail polish off, please, ladies, fingers and toes.'

Daphne Salmon held up blood-red nails, manicured

for suffering with elegance. She'd made the manicure appointment ages before, when she knew she'd have to come in, and paid for it out of her all-too-meagre housekeeping. 'Why?' she demanded.

'So we can see if you're turning blue and dying.' The student grinned happily.

'Give me that bottle,' said Daphne grimly.

'My, we're uptight,' murmured Blossom.

Daphne's locker was crowded with plastic bottles of miracle creams, cleansers, toners, moisturisers, perfumes, make-up and a set of heated rollers. She had nowhere to set the brown bottle down. The student, enjoying herself, added, 'It used to be scented, but these days you get basic chemical, ladies, and it doesn't half stink.'

Daphne scrubbed at her perfect nails, which the girl in the beauty salon had done with so much care.

'It's that Thatcher. She'll have you doubled up next, her and her cuts. Three to a bed and they all roll over . . .' The student sniggered, and Daphne, who voted Conservative, pretended not to hear.

'Oh, Lord,' sighed Blossom, 'look at that lot on her locker. She looks like a pious rodent. What did you do when you weren't trying to get pregnant?'

'I'm a social worker trying to think what else to do with my life other than go on and on being a social worker.'

Blossom looked startled, and then burst out laughing.

'That's funny?' snapped Sadie.

'Doing good and all that trying,' hiccuped Blossom, not apologising. 'You ought to come and work for Sainsbury's, they'd love you.'

The student thrust cotton wool at Blossom and produced a second, smaller bottle from her pale-blue overall pocket.

'I don't use varnish,' said Blossom. 'Give it to her.'

Sadie snatched nail polish remover and cotton wool and began to scrub pearly lacquer from her fingernails.

Blossom laughed. 'Try and get it all off, so they can see you turning a nice shade of navy.'

'Try, try, try,' snarled Sadie. 'I never meant to tell you all that. Forget it and leave me alone.'

Alice Penn lowered her paper and looked over curiously, fat cheeks full of chocolate-coated pink Turkish delight.

'I'm scared, too, you know,' Blossom said evenly.

Sadie held the nail polish remover in her lap and a bright flush ran up her neck under her thick curls.

'I'm sorry,' she said. 'I don't know you, and I've been talking too much. I don't know anything. Nothing in my life has been like I expected, and this operation feels like all my failures rolled into one. You don't know what that feels like.'

'How would you know what I know?' demanded Blossom.

Sadie put the top on the varnish remover and put the wad of cotton wool into the waste bag pinned by her locker.

'I don't,' she said tiredly. 'I'm assuming things. I'm sorry.'

'You said he's leaving you,' Blossom ventured. 'This seems a mean time to do it.'

'I never meant to mention it,' snapped Sadie.

'All right, already, I can take a hint,' said Blossom, rolling her eyes theatrically, and wandered off back to her own bed.

'Visiting time in a minute, ladies.'

Bridges patrolled the far end of her ward, seeing that all the new patients were present, correct and on their beds.

Daphne peered into a pocket mirror propped against her heated rollers, setting rigid curls in a concrete cover of hairspray.

'Seems funny to sit here being visited when you're not ill, doesn't it?' observed Blossom to everyone.

Gabriella's mother, an ageing, carefully made-up, bleached and rinsed, delicately wrinkled version of her fragile daughter, tottered down the ward on impossibly high Italian heels, trailing flowers, new nighties, and bright, silvery helium balloons bobbing on long ribbons, which she tied to the rail of her daughter's bed. 'Get Well Soon', the balloons shouted in fluorescent pink letters, straining towards the ceiling.

'Poppet!' she cried, throwing her arms around her child, who looked crushed.

Sadie, watching the performance, sighed, and caught sight of her husband coming towards her with a pot plant in one hand, lie-back Mothercare pushchair in the other.

We are in such a tangle, thought Sadie desperately, longing for him to come, frightened now that he was here, pushing sleeping Eve ahead of him, his hand firm on the handle, no hint of that distaste he betrayed in so many ways he could not help. Involuntarily her eyes filled.

'She looks like a little girl,' thought Dougal, wishing, now that it was too late, that he had bought the red roses bunched prettily in the florist's pail and hang the expense. That afternoon he'd taken a dozen of them to Pauline. He knew how sorely he had betrayed his wife, but he also knew he must hang on to the last shreds of his integrity. Red roses would imply things he did not mean. Better the honest understatement of a small cyclamen.

Sadie eyed him, knowing him inside out, able to read him. He didn't deceive her for one moment. 'He's still tanned from that absurd trip,' she thought, 'and he hasn't brought roses. Couldn't do it. Well, that's something to his credit.'

In the Caribbean the previous month, ninety computer salesmen, one or two wives, and a few secretaries pretending to be wives had sailed around on a boat, pretending to work. It had carried the drunken, uproarious gang in a circle for three days, then Dougal's computer company's main supplier flew them home, ferociously hungover. A conference, Dougal had said. *His* supplier's conference. It couldn't be missed. Dougal, insisting on being at home to look after her after her operation, although Sadie knew that events would surely overtake that plan, found cancelling the conference beyond him. His unselfishness did not live up to it. Nor, he pointed out, would his and Philip's reputation and profits look good if he cancelled. Philip, lifelong friend, owned the company Dougal worked for.

'Once in a lifetime,' he'd pleaded. 'Surely another three

weeks won't harm? It's the Caribbean, for God's sake. A one-off, we'll never do it again.'

'A hysterectomy is a once-in-a-lifetime,' Sadie said quietly, but without saying anything to him, persuaded the hospital to change her date.

'I thought it was a pretty red,' said Dougal, putting the cyclamen down on her locker. 'It'll last longer than flowers.'

'Cut flowers wilt quickly in here,' said Sadie, thus forgiving the absence of roses. 'Pull the chair up.'

'She's asleep. Rosalie stuffed her full of milk and some sort of goo, and said it'd keep her quiet,' he said, parking the pushchair at the end of her bed.

Sadie could see the handle poking up, Eve quite out of sight. 'She is very asleep,' she said sadly.

'You look all right,' Dougal said heartily.

'I haven't gone downhill since breakfast,' she snapped.

'I brought you this, as well,' he said hopefully, trying to please.

Sadie watched him grope in his jacket. He did *try* to get things right. He just wasn't very good at it. Perhaps he did better with Pauline. Perhaps it was partly Sadie's own fault. Of course it was; it was never entirely one-sided when things went wrong. Dougal interrupted her train of thought by pulling a bag of plums and two big rosy apples out of his pocket and putting them on her locker.

'Is there anything special you want?' he asked, at a loss how to talk to her in this place full of women.

'You could put some mineral water in the fridge in the ward kitchen and tell them it's there. I'm always sick after anaesthetics, and it's nice to drink something ice cold.' She was making an effort, helping find things he could do, to cover his guilt. They trod warily, trying not to hurt . . . there had been enough hurting.

I wonder, thought Sadie, fingering the glossy skin of the apples, what he talked about when he visited Pauline when she had the baby. Were they polite, like this? Did he sit, leaning slightly away, like he was now, as though they were strangers in a railway carriage, forced into each other's company, or did he put his warm hand on Pauline's full, ripe flesh, eyeing swollen, milky breasts through some thin nightdress, nipples hard at the subtle excitement of having her baby in her cot, her baby's father bending down, saying, 'Oh, her tiny mouth . . .'

'Like you,' Pauline would say, loving him.

Sadie leaned over and put the ripe fruit on top of her locker to hide the bright flush of misery heating her cheeks. There was a kind of roar from the far end of the ward and doors banged.

'Good God, what's that?' Dougal turned in his chair, and she wiped her hand over her face, as if to scrub off the overbright colour.

'Someone to visit, I expect,' she said.

'Well,' said Dougal indignantly, looking into the pushchair, but Eve slept, undisturbed, her curved eyelids flickering, dreaming.

Alice Penn sat up straight, put the Black Magic box on her locker, folded her arms and waited. Lurching down the ward came her husband, purple-faced, shouting slurred, incoherent words at the top of his voice.

'He's violent,' protested Dougal audibly, pulling the pushchair round beside his chair. 'Or drunk.'

'He ain't violent, and he ain't drunk, 'e's confused,' said Alice calmly. ''E'll shut up in a minute, when 'e sees me. 'E makes an awful lot of noise but 'e don't mean it.'

'*Dougal*,' hissed Sadie, ashamed.

Daphne's leonine husband ran a finger round his dog collar, sweating in the overheated ward; having long ago discovered he lacked any talent for ministration to the sick, he was clumsily embarrassed by their helplessness. Daphne confused him by being not at all helpless, sitting bolt upright, plastered with make-up and perfume. He sat speechless, weighed down by a disagreeable feeling that she expected him to find this whole affair somehow romantic. Mr Penn unnerved him, banging his way to the end of his wife's bed where he stood breathing heavily.

'Do you think I should . . . help?' the cleric suggested reluctantly.

'No,' said Daphne firmly.

'Hullo, duck,' Alice said.

'They said 'e could come if I came with 'im,' panted her sister, hurrying up as fast as she could with seventeen stone and varicose veins. ''E's been driving them mad.'

'It's all right, duck,' said Alice. 'I'm all right.'

She reached to take one of his hands and he collapsed on to a hard plastic chair close to her side, his mouth working.

'It's all right,' repeated Alice, holding his hand. 'Don't start goin' on.'

Like a great sad baby, he clutched her fingers, bowing his head, quiet.

'Oh, dear,' whispered Sadie, 'how terribly sad. She said she'd come in for a holiday, and I see what she meant. He's had two strokes.'

'They're holding hands,' said Dougal sadly. 'Perhaps I should have a stroke and you'd hold my hand.'

Alice's sister patted Mr Penn's broad back and chattered nineteen to the dozen.

'Who's that?' asked Dougal, trying to distract both of them. He gazed at Blossom, who was sitting cross-legged, unpacking a sandwich box, propping up a thermos flask so it didn't spill.

'That's Blossom,' said Sadie.

'Smoked salmon,' called Blossom, hearing her name, holding up delicately cut brown sandwiches with the crusts off. 'Out of dates. Cheap. Asia's made lovely sandwiches.'

A girl watched eagerly as Blossom ate the picnic, shy black eyes gleaming in her milky Indian face. Blue-black hair cascaded down her back in a thick twist, so long she could have sat on it, but she parked her thin little leggings-clad bottom carefully on the edge of her chair and drew the fabulous hair over her shoulder.

Eve hiccuped in her sleep and brushed her fist over her small mouth, mumbling through pale pink gums. Sadie watched her but made no effort to touch her. If she did, she'd cry and beg and blurt out the whole dull pain that lay heavy where tomorrow the surgeon would knife, most literally.

'I always wanted to be really skinny like that,' she said wistfully.

'It's not attractive, not that thin,' said Dougal.

'It depends who you want to attract, I would have thought,' said Sadie. Blossom licked her fingers with enjoyment, bent over and kissed her lover tenderly. 'I was starving, pet,' she said.

'Good Lord,' said Dougal, going brick-red, fascinated.

Mr Penn was trying to say something, to squeeze words out from a mouth beyond his control.

'Aah, aah,' he struggled, loud as a wounded bull, bellowing helplessly. 'Uuurgh.'

'There, there, duck, I know you mean me,' said Alice, squeezing his fingers. 'Uuurgh is Alice, isn't it, pet?'

Her sister said, 'We won't stay long.'

'It's a madhouse,' said Dougal. 'Are you going to be all right?'

'You're a one to talk,' muttered his wife. Dougal's tan flushed.

I bet Pauline Cookham won't have a tan, she thought maliciously, because it would give her away. She must have sat on that stupid boat absolutely lathered in sunblock with silver foil on her nose, in case his wife sees the pair of them tanned in May and puts two and two together.

The only angry kind of pleasure left was knowing that they thought she didn't know, when she did.

Mr Penn made a choking sound and stood up.

'I think it's probably time for you all to go,' said Sadie, suddenly exhausted. 'Eve will need feeding again as soon as you get back. Kiss her for me, lots and lots, and give Rosalie and Maria my love.'

'I'll see you tomorrow,' he said, pushing back his chair, leaving the kissing unacknowledged.

'Tomorrow it'll all be over,' his wife said brightly.

He fingered the cyclamen.

'I thought it would cheer you up. It's a lovely colour.'

Eve lay between them like a porcelain doll, wrapped in a lacy shawl.

'It has. Goodbye, Dougal,' said Sadie.

He kissed her cheek. Mr Penn followed Alice's waddling sister past the row of beds, past quickly averted, curious eyes. Michael Salmon prised Daphne's fingers off his own, and brushed invisible crumbs from his black trousers. By some unspoken consent they all tidied chairs away and headed for the double doors, and the real, outside world, looking back and waving, then hurrying away. Visiting was over.

'That's better,' said Blossom, wiping her mouth with a tissue.

'It's kind of him to make the effort, but I'm rather glad he's gone, to tell the truth,' said Daphne with unexpected honesty, going pink, fluttering her eyelids.

'Huh,' murmured Mrs Hargreaves shrewdly to herself; she had watched them all with interest, her own bedside empty.

'Being in hospital is a bit like boarding school – you belong and they don't. Two worlds, so you have nothing to talk about,' said Sadie.

'I don't know what you all mean,' whispered Gabriella Miller, missing her mother already. Her father was dead.

'You will, darling, one day,' called Blossom.

If she's got much more than one day left in her, thought Mrs Hargreaves bluntly.

Tomorrow, thought Sadie, we'll all be flat on our backs and with bits of ourselves missing. Not quite the same. How strange.

Alice looked into her Black Magic but there weren't enough left to share. She opened a packet of chocolate digestives and began to hand them round.

'I just had a funny thought,' said Sadie.

The women looked at her. Alice stood in the middle of the five beds wiping crumbs from her lips.

'Go on, have one while you can,' she urged, holding out the packet. 'They start starving us soon.'

'No, thanks. I was thinking,' Sadie went on, 'that if anyone except doctors did to us what the surgeons are going to do tomorrow, they'd go to prison. For grievous bodily harm. Isn't that a strange thought?'

Daphne pursed her little mouth grimly, ready to defend doctors. But Sadie knelt on her bed, turning her back without inviting an answer. She set out her jigsaw, and, staring at it with unfocused eyes, lost in thought, began fitting the pieces together.

Chapter One

One bitter January day in 1954, Siberian winds swept frostbound East Anglia, bringing heavy snow, and four-year-old Sadie Carswell's parents went skating. Young solicitors from King's Lynn, they came to visit Andrew Carswell's aunts in their tiny old stone cottage tucked between village and sea on an isolated headland on the north Norfolk coast. The two old women were their only family on either side, crusty, impossible and much loved. Impassable roads, ice and drifting snow forced the Carswells to stay longer than the one night they intended, sleeping uncomfortably on the put-u-up in their friend Mary Llewellyn's sitting room. She lived half a mile from the aunts' cottage, where there was no room for visitors. Hot-water bottles and eiderdowns barely kept out the cold, and they slept fitfully, disturbed by wind screaming over the marshland, flattening tall, dead bulrushes, whirling snow over the grey North Sea. Towards dawn, the wind dropped and morning brought bright, washed-out blue sky and lemon light on snow, freezing hard. A local landowner, his deep lake frozen, threw his grounds open for the village to skate. As the short afternoon began to fade into early winter darkness, and the vast bowl of the sky filled and grew ominous with the promise of further snow, skaters swooped and raced and cut figures of eight. Andrew and Margaret Carswell danced, muffled in bright, striped university scarves, their breath white on air, sharp as a knife, that flailed their lungs and brought crimson blood to their cheeks.

'Look,' they cried, laughing, 'Sadeee, look.'

Sadie looked, following their flashing figures with narrowed eyes, beating her small hands against the cold, as they had taught her. Unsteady on miniature skates, she wobbled along the edge of the ice and they shouted, 'Stay there, stay there.' A village woman caught at her arm and nodded back to her parents, over the ice. Sadie, pulled back, put her thumb in her mouth, found it covered in woolly glove, encrusted with snow.

'Mummy . . .'

'Mummy's coming off soon, it's getting dark,' said the woman. 'You just stay there for a minute, like a good girl.'

Sadie stood at the edge of the ice, safe and cold and tired.

'Mummy . . .' she called longingly.

'In a minute,' said the woman, wiping a small boy's nose, looking forward to tea and crumpets by a glowing coal fire. 'They'll come off in a minute, pet.'

Sadie watched through gathering gloom. Across the dull grey gleam of ice she saw her mother pull away from her father, skating in wider and wider circles, laughing and teasing, until thinner ice near the middle gave way with a sharp crack. Her father flew on a reflex towards the gap in the ice, shouting her name, flung himself headlong towards the momentary gleam of water. It swallowed him up. Sadie stood staring. Someone picked her up, carried her up the bank, hid her face from the scene on the lake. She didn't cry or scream. She sat, pinched and obedient, struck quite dumb. Women, clucking and whispering, shocked, took her back to Mary Llewellyn's house, chafing her frozen hands and toes.

'What shall I do?' whispered Mary, distraught.

'The aunts,' one woman said.

'I suppose so,' said Mary, holding the child in her lap with tears on her cheeks. 'I suppose so.'

The policeman came quickly, shaking fresh snow from his heavy coat, sorrowful, heavy with authority.

'There'll be questions,' he said, an impassive fishing man from Brancaster. 'But the little girl can go where you think best, for now. Until we find out about family.'

'There's only the aunts. I know for a fact.'

'Then you'd best let them take her, for now, anyway,' he said.

Before they brought the bodies out many hours later, Mary sent for Great-Aunt Queenie and Great-Aunt Victoria. They came, thin as whippets, leathery faces hardened by fierce salt winds, bundled in thick brown socks folded over wellington boots, men's grey greatcoats and knitted scarves. They looked at Sadie, at each other, all discussion over in a single glance.

'She'll come home with us, now.'

'Can you manage?' whispered the vicar's wife, lingering, trying to be helpful, deeply mistrustful of the old women, who were reputed, in whispers, to be witches. Her husband travelled his parish of squat grey stone churches in remote villages, taking Christian Communion once a month to places where older, darker faiths flourished, nourished by isolation.

'Yes,' said Queenie dismissively, and the vicar's wife withdrew, offended and defeated.

'We'll do,' the old women said, holding out their hands to the shocked, mute child, meaning, *we'll manage*. 'She's ours. Come, Sadie, love.'

They enfolded her, thought the vicar's wife, *removed* her, like animals will isolate wounded young.

'I hope they let her come back to us,' she said to her husband later, when the tragedy, for the rest of them, was over.

'They're a godless lot,' he said shortly.

'They've made her a ward of court and said she can live with the old aunts,' fretted his wife. 'What are we to do?'

'Nothing. Let the lawyers and welfare people sort it out, and leave them be.'

'You mustn't give up, dear,' said his wife, shocked.

He looked out of the window, over the dull grey sea obscured by rain.

'Sometimes you have to leave Him to look after His own,' he muttered. 'We can't be expected to understand or make sense of everything.'

'Losing both parents?' ventured his wife. 'How do you understand that?'

'Oh, I don't know, what can I do? Visit?' demanded the elderly man testily, his lined face reddened by cold and annoyance. 'And get thrown out on my ear? Why ask for trouble? They'd put the hex on me for interfering.'

'Oh, really,' said his wife, who was not a Norfolk woman and failed to take these matters with proper seriousness. Her husband knew better.

'I shall pray,' he added, as a pragmatic gesture, and stamped off to do something meaningful, like overstoking the Aga with coke that hissed and spluttered and steamed, wet from the constant downpour.

At first Sadie was passive. She looked around the great-aunts' isolated stone cottage without recognition.

'Where is Mummy?'

'Your mummy died under the ice,' they said. 'With your daddy. You will stay with us, now.'

'Why?'

'Your mummy died,' they said patiently, 'under the ice. Soon, she'll be in the graveyard and we will go to see her.'

'Why?'

'We can't tell you why, only that she is dead, and you will stay here.'

'Where is Daddy?'

'Your daddy died under the ice. Soon he'll be in the graveyard, with your mummy.'

'Why?'

'We can't tell you why. You will stay with us, now.'

'Why?' sobbed Sadie, dry-eyed.

'You will stay here because you are our own good girl now. You will stay here.'

The litany went on, with long silences in between. Rain and sleet flew slantwise across the marshes and dunes on bitter winds as winter gripped the land in an iron fist and would not let go. February passed.

'Where is Mummy?' she shrieked one night, half waking to the gale howling offshore, screaming over sodden dead grass in ditches, banging a shutter on windows set in thick old walls.

'Mummy is gone, my lamb,' crooned Queenie, cradling her thrashing limbs, holding her tightly. 'You are here, with us. You are safe with us.'

The first tears slid from her eyes, stinging her chapped cheeks.

'The shock is breaking,' whispered Victoria.

'Kettle,' ordered Queenie shortly.

The Calor Gas flame glowed blue, ghostly. Victoria threw herbs into boiling water and blew on the brew to cool it.

'Here,' said Queenie, putting the brew to the child's lips.

The steam made Sadie cough. Sharp and foul, it watered her eyes and stung her throat. She drank it, Great-Aunt Queenie forcing the sedative liquid between her lips.

'Nasty,' she howled.

'Horrible,' agreed Queenie, setting down the cup.

Victoria leaned over Queenie's shoulder and stroked the child's hair. They waited in the glow of the fire, until Sadie sank into Queenie's lap, relaxed. Drowsy, the child began to cry freely.

'Your mummy has gone, darling,' murmured Queenie. 'Cry, now, you cry. You cry for your mummy and daddy. That's it.'

The storm raged across the headland, throwing hailstones and watery snow against warm windows. Victoria lit an oil lamp.

'She'll sleep now,' said Victoria, taking the child from Queenie's aching arms, putting her into the makeshift bed they had made for her in their own room. They took it in turns, the rest of the long night, to crawl shivering to the foot of their beds, to check. On her mattress, cocooned in blankets and feather pillows, Sadie slept.

Queenie and Victoria had lived all their lives in the only cottage between the hamlet of Ditchwell and the salt marshes. A quarter of a mile from the nearest house, its humped roof was barely visible in summer from the top of the dyke, so surrounded was it by bushes and brambles. On still, hot August days they could hear the soft sough of the tide on the long, flat, deserted yellow beach, reached by a path across the high dyke between the road and the sea. It was not a place the tourists found. Behind the cottage the great-aunts grew the few vegetables that could survive the poor soil, the wind and the salt. Living close to inhospitable nature, changeable, fabulous, and dangerous, the old women became secretive, inscrutable, as tough and tenacious as the roots of the pines that grew along the edges of the dunes. Keeping themselves to themselves was a lifelong habit. With time, they welcomed Mary Llewellyn into the cottage. They agreed, as it were, to bequeath her to Sadie, along with the money in the bank account and the proceeds from the sale of her home in King's Lynn, when their time should come. Mary, a grey-haired spinster who looked older than her years, was a true countrywoman, teacher at the village school, tactful, patient and wise. Taking nothing for granted, she never intruded, always came if they asked. She loved Sadie, and because she did, she and the aunts became friends.

When she was five, Sadie learned to swim. Queenie and Victoria drew straws to decide who should teach her. Victoria waded grim-faced in the shallows beside her, heroic in ancient knitted bathing suit and rubber cap on which waved limp white and yellow plastic daisies, standing in the green water like some sinewy old Dane on the lookout for a passing longboat, until Sadie overcame her fear and floated free, kicking and thrashing into the small summer waves.

'I can swim,' she yelled, lurching into the frilly water's edge, finding her feet.

'You can swim,' applauded Victoria, looking longingly at her towel left on the sand. 'Let's go and tell Queenie, shall we?'

'Look,' yelled Sadie, throwing herself backwards into the water, showing off.

'It is worth it,' said Queenie sternly, when Victoria complained and shivered, blue from the shanks downwards, numb at the toes. 'She would have a fear of water, otherwise. You know perfectly well she mustn't have that.'

Martyred, Victoria warmed her old feet in mustard soaks and Sadie swam like a fish before the summer was out.

They taught her the names of birds and animals, wild flowers, herbs and grasses, and how to use them. Sadie, ten years old, a stocky, wiry-haired imp with strong brown limbs and great grey eyes, knew the seashore from Old Hunstanton to Brancaster like the back of her hand. One afternoon Queenie went down to the end of the dyke, across the stream that flowed between the ditches and the beach, and shaded her eyes. Near the water's edge, Sadie crouched under the hot midsummer sun, her blue cotton dress bleached by salt water.

'Look at it, poor thing,' she said, watching a gull whose broken wing trailed uselessly over the warm sand. 'It'll die.'

'If you can catch it, the bird people will take it in,' called Queenie.

Sadie held out her hand.

'Come,' she called, 'come here.'

It flapped desperately, leaving circling marks in the wet sand.

'Come,' whispered Sadie.

The gull stopped, panic fluffing its feathers, snapping its beak.

'Here.'

Sadie waited, crouched low. It limped towards her,

and she raised her hands, fingers spread wide, palms outwards.

'Poor thing,' she murmured, 'poor thing.'

The gull bent its head and walked under the small shadow cast by her outstretched hands.

'I'm hot,' said Sadie, surprised.

It lowered its beak to the sand and stood as if dying.

'My hands hurt,' said Sadie, flexing her fingers.

'Look,' said Queenie from the top of the beach.

The gull ran several yards down the beach, took off at speed and rose into the air, wheeling strongly away.

'It can fly,' cried Sadie. 'It doesn't need the RSPB.'

Queenie's voice was sharp.

'Your hands were hot?'

'They aren't now.'

'Just now?'

'Yes.'

'I came to call you in.'

Obediently, Sadie got up off the sand.

You have the gift, Queenie thought, staring at her great-niece with hooded eyes.

'It flew away,' cried Sadie, pleased.

'She has it,' Queenie told Victoria when Sadie had gone to bed. 'What shall we do?'

Victoria thought for a long time.

'Nothing. Let her go, and forget about it,' she said.

Queenie sighed.

'She's wild, a bit fey, and always on her own,' said Mary Llewellyn on parents' evening. 'It is not a good preparation for life.'

'Preparation for life,' snorted Queenie. 'What's that?'

Mary persisted.

'I've been wondering what we should do. She has to change school next year, you know, and living where you do is not going to make getting to King's Lynn easy. I wondered if you'd like us to help.'

'Help?' asked Queenie reluctantly.

'Yes.'

'You said wild. Wild and dreamy?'

'Otherworldly, and very little discipline,' said Mary firmly, feeling the restlessness of other parents waiting. 'You do know what I mean, I'm sure.'

'Ah,' sighed Victoria, at seventy-four five years younger than Queenie. 'I can remember being young and dreamy with very little discipline, can't you, darling?'

Mary's open face darkened in a frown and she said sharply, 'I'm quite certain you understand very well.'

'Our great-niece needs what?' demanded Queenie, bending her ear with her hand, to hear.

'Young company and a more normal life,' said Mary Llewellyn loudly, taking the bull by the horns.

'I told you so,' murmured Victoria.

'Company?' Queenie ignored the normal life.

'*Young* company,' persisted Mary.

The sisters sat in a formidable twosome in front of her desk, their weatherbeaten faces inscrutable.

'She has company,' said Queenie.

'Gannets and samphire,' said Mary scornfully, 'won't get her far.'

'Her mother and father were from round here,' they said in chorus.

Mary ploughed on, meeting the old women's knowing, devious gazes.

'Is that what you want for her? You know perfectly well what I mean. Herbalism and spells and potions. It won't do in the twentieth century. She's bright and capable and one day she'll have to earn a living. She has to live in the real world, get away.'

They rubbed old, aching fingers and looked sly.

'Her parents would have wanted her to have a career, go to university, like them,' cried Mary. 'You can't stop her doing that.'

'Those are things we don't know about,' creaked Queenie at last. 'Those are things we don't know how to do.'

'Then let me.'

'Take her away?'

'She's not yours to keep,' said Mary, knowing that they meant body, soul and spirit, and determined they should not possess her.

'She has the gift, you know. She's a beauty,' murmured Victoria wistfully.

'Animals are beautiful, and the samphire covers the mud in autumn and is beautiful,' answered Mary levelly, 'but it's not human beauty. Don't pretend you don't know what I'm talking about, because I've lived in these parts all my life, and I know what goes on.'

They stared at the floor, unmoved.

'Witchcraft,' hissed Mary under her breath, afraid of her own words. 'Send her away, before she gets trapped.'

They regarded her for a long moment, hostile. Then Queenie said, 'Where?'

'Boarding school. There's enough money and we could get help from the local authority, I should think.'

'We'll hearken to you,' said Queenie, heaving her old bones out of the low child's chair.

'My God, they came out of the Ark,' Mary thought, waving them courteously out of her classroom door, goose bumps on her skin. Round these parts, you never quite knew what might be lurking behind closed doors and closed faces. She turned to her patient queue.

The evening over, the spooks came back.

'We lose policemen round here, and they don't get found again,' she said aloud, putting the children's work away neatly. 'Don't meddle. Why are you meddling, Mary Llewellyn?'

She closed and locked her store cupboard and went to turn out the lights by the door.

'Listen to me,' she said irritably. 'There's no such thing as witches, and the bats we have in our lofts are just bats,' she snapped at the empty classroom. 'Those daft old biddies can pay for boarding school if they want to, they've got say-so over the money her parents left.'

She caught herself looking over her shoulder, walking

the half-mile home to her cottage facing the sea on the civilised side of the main road.

'You can go if you want to, but we'd rather you stayed,' creaked Queenie, holding Sadie between spread knees, her darned woollen skirt holding the child like a spider's web.

'You can go,' said Victoria bravely. 'Don't listen to her.'

'If you go, you will fail us,' said Queenie.

Ten-year-old Sadie raised dreamy grey eyes flecked with silver.

'I'd like to go to school, Great-Aunt Queenie.'

'You will not belong.'

'Not belong, Great-Aunt Queenie?'

Victoria said sharply, 'That's quite enough, Queenie. Stop it.'

'Very well, she shall go.'

'Without any nonsense,' snapped Victoria, narrowing her eyes angrily.

Queenie smiled and spread her knees wider, letting Sadie go, looking up innocently.

'And what nonsense would that be?' she asked.

'No nonsense at all,' repeated Victoria, scowling. 'I know you.'

Inscrutable, Queenie merely shook her head and observed that what would be would be, and that they would have to leave it at that.

Chapter Two

That autumn, in 1961, when Sadie was eleven, the great-aunts, Mary Llewellyn, the court and the Education and Welfare Departments between them contrived to send Sadie away to school.

'I don't want to go anywhere, I didn't mean it,' Sadie cried, frightened by whispered conferences held when they thought she wasn't taking any notice. Passionate by nature, she became unruly by upbringing, unused to discipline, wild in the way a small, half-tame animal is wild, used to kindness of an instinctual sort, bewildered by rules beyond the small, indulgent world of Mary Llewellyn's schoolroom. Once the idea of going away to school was in the air, she had more than once yelled in tantrums that she *wanted* to go to school, so there. Unmoved, the women sent her measurements off by post to some uniform shop, as the aunts would put it, and back came dark skirts, shirts, pullovers and ties, that bunched up and hung heavy around her small frame.

'I hate it,' sulked Sadie, pulling angrily at the cotton cuffs poking out from an oversized jumper, loose on her flat, narrow chest.

'Oh, my, there's knickers for everything,' said Victoria thoughtfully, impressed and puzzled, 'Doing sports, Sunday best, everyday, good gracious. Fancy. They won't keep you warm.' She held them up critically. The aunts had peculiar, shapeless, scarecrow garments that hung limp and dripping on the line during summer, stretched and sagging with water, wintering mysteriously out of sight.

'Long johns,' sniffed Mary. 'Really, you *cannot* send her to school with long johns.'

Victoria meekly folded a pile of elastic-legged knickers with pockets back into their cellophane wrappings and gave in.

'I don't want to go,' mumbled Sadie, biting her thumbnail to bits. It usually got their attention, but Mary just said, 'If you do that at school, they'll put something nasty-tasting on, to stop you,' and went on picking over the clothes spread all over the leaning old sofa.

'Look, here's your gymslip,' she cried. 'There should be a belt.' She rummaged in brown paper.

'It's by the sea, you'll feel at home,' Queenie told Sadie, determination that she *would* feel at home giving her the look, thought Mary, hiding a smile, of a tortoise faced with a juicy piece of lettuce.

'It's the best school we could afford,' murmured Victoria.

'I want to go to school in King's Lynn, like everyone else.' Sadie hung over the back of the sofa and scowled at the heaps of uniform.

'You aren't like everyone else. Everyone else has a mother and a father,' said Queenie ruthlessly.

'It's for the best, pet,' said Mary.

Sadie kicked idly at the sofa, looking through her lashes to see if they noticed.

'Stop that,' snapped Victoria.

'Getting her right away from here is what you want, isn't it? You want her away from our influence, don't you, away from our *little ways*?' demanded Queenie under her breath. 'Might as well call a spade a spade.'

'I didn't mean quite that,' Mary whispered back, uncomfortably aware that that was exactly what she had meant when she suggested Sadie should go away to school. Queenie glared at her, as shrewd and sharp as a knife.

'Huh. But since it's her money,' Queenie ploughed on, having made up her mind to go along with Mary, 'she might as well spend it.'

'Anyone would think,' hissed Mary Llewellyn, putting her mouth close to Queenie's ear, 'that you hadn't agreed in the first place. But you know very well that you did, so stop trying to make things difficult.'

'Who said it had to be easy? Anyway, we're buying her a future, aren't we?' snapped Queenie.

'She's buying herself a future,' answered Mary, goaded into pedantry.

'Hah,' snorted Queenie, unmoved.

Undercurrents of possessive love and mutual hostility eddied between them that late summer, until the first days of September when it was time for Sadie to go. She sulked and stormed by turns, but it was shadow-boxing. Ignoring their own squabbles, they closed ranks on her, determined she would go.

'It's for your own good,' they said, implacable.

She sat, the day before she was to leave, by the empty grate, hearing the chimes of the ice-cream van half a mile away across the ditches, stopped in the village street. In the tiny scullery, Victoria boiled pans of water over the Calor Gas, to wash her down so she'd be clean and tidy, ready for tomorrow. Sadie listened to the clang of the preserving pan, the biggest container they had, and the notes of 'Greensleeves' floated tinnily over the muddy ditches in the early afternoon quiet. By the time she'd run to the village, the van would be gone.

'You can stop pulling a long face,' said Victoria. 'There'll be plenty of ice cream where you're going. Tuck shop in the school, it says in that shiny thing, that brochure. They look after your money for you, and you get it handed out, Miss Llewellyn says. Ice cream and sweets.'

'*Really?*'

'Yes,' snapped Victoria, 'really.'

Sadie cheered up.

When the first day of term came, Mary tried to make up for sending Sadie away by taking her to school herself. Guiltily, she left her sitting on her trunk, small, frightened and pale-faced, thick curls cropped almost to her scalp beneath a panama hat. In uniform, all tucks and turned-back sleeves, bought to grow into, she looked a sad waif. Mary kissed her cheek, uncertain how to leave, but the school, used to such moments, chivvied her away with bright, cheery cries and see-you-soons, she'll-writes.

'She'll love it,' she lied, arriving back at the cottage, 'when she's settled in.'

'Humph,' snorted Queenie. 'Victoria's moping,' she added spitefully.

'I'm going to miss her,' snapped her sister. 'And so will you, only you are too wicked to say so.'

'Oh, Lord, don't squabble. We'll all miss her,' sighed Mary.

'You wanted to send her away, only you were too spineless, so I had to do it for you. So don't start complaining, Victoria,' said Queenie in a cold, level voice.

The sisters glared at each other with sunken, long-sighted eyes.

'Please don't start bickering,' sighed Mary.

Chapter Three

Boarding school was a terrible shock. Sadie missed the great-aunts sorely. She refused to conform, hid in corners, kept well away from confident girls with loud, carrying voices. High ceilings seemed to her to echo every unfamiliar sound. Bells, hundreds of hurrying feet, knives and forks and the scrape of plates in the cavernous dining room, opening and closing of so many doors, behind which mysterious things went on. She read the school rules, pinned up for perusal on her house notice board, and, standing apparently doing nothing, found herself chivvied and scolded for wasting her time.

'I'm reading what to do,' she said sullenly to the prefect.

'The rules are, you don't stand around reading rules when the dinner bell has gone.'

'But . . . how do I know?' cried Sadie. 'I don't know the rules unless I read them.'

'Scram,' ordered the prefect.

'It's not fair,' muttered Sadie.

Towards the end of her first term, Miss Harper, who taught biology, had a frog in a jar on her desk. It had some leaves and moss and a bit of water to sit in and was not intended for them.

'The frog is for the third year,' said Miss Harper, shooing girls back to their seats. 'We're doing its life cycle. From spawn, to tadpoles, to baby frog, to spawn . . . you all know it already. So go back to your desks.'

'That frog doesn't like being in a jam jar,' said Sadie from the front row of desks, 'It's unkind.'

'I don't think frogs have feelings,' said Miss Harper, 'so I don't suppose he thinks much one way or the other. But he'll go back in the pond when we've finished.'

'Look,' said Sadie, pointing.

The frog made a desultory leap at the side of the jar and plopped back into its puddle, discouraged.

'It wants to get out,' she insisted.

'That's enough, Sadie,' said Miss Harper. 'The frog will do nicely until after period six.'

'Won't,' hissed Sadie, and was quelled by a thunderous look from Miss Harper.

As soon as the teacher's back was turned, she puffed out her cheeks, crossed her eyes and stuck out her tongue. The girls sitting near her coughed with laughter and Miss Harper turned suspiciously.

'Frogs do have feelings,' said Sadie stubbornly.

'Oh, for goodness' sake,' snapped Miss Harper, and screeched the chalk horribly on the blackboard, in annoyance.

'Froggie,' they jeered.

Sadie ground her teeth with fury, knowing she'd asked for it.

'Froggie Carswell's got webbed feet.'

Half a dozen first years encircled her, laughing as she tipped the frog back into the pond at the far end of the school grounds.

'Was your mother a gypsy? 'Cos you talk like one.'

'I bet she was.'

'Froggie Carswell's a gypsy . . .'

'Did the Harpy say you could have her frog?' demanded the ringleader, a tall, puppy-fat girl who wore a brace on her teeth and whose father owned a chain of bookstores.

'She asked me to put it back,' said Sadie, bent double at the pond's edge so that they should not see her cry with rage.

'Ooooh, she *asked* me . . .'

'Gypsies eat frogs and hedgehogs, don't they? Yuck,' said the plump girl, pulling a face.

Sadie turned on them, ankle-deep in muddy brown water.

'I'm not a gypsy, and my dad was a lawyer, only he's dead. So shut up.'

'What are you standing in the pond for, then, getting soaked? Matron won't half shout.'

'She's crying,' said black-haired Maria Theresa Giangelli, from the same class as Sadie, sounding uneasy. 'Leave her alone.'

Sadie climbed out of the muddy water, dead leaves and bits of pondweed trailing round her ankle socks.

'Why are you crying, Froggie? Frogs don't cry, they've got cold blood,' jeered the plump girl. 'Everyone knows that.'

'You are being a pig,' said Maria Theresa, looking after Sadie running away, empty jam jar in one hand, up the long sloping lawn to the grey stone school at the top.

'Better than being a reptile,' retorted the fat girl.

Maria Theresa's sense of fair play was outraged.

'I wouldn't want to be a pig with fat porky chops,' she snapped. 'Like some.'

The plump child, who was Jewish, flushed and chewed her braced teeth.

'Froggie's got a friend,' they yelled after Maria Theresa as she headed up the slope after Sadie. She didn't care a fig for their teasing. She followed Sadie into the building and tried to find her. But Sadie vanished until the supper bell, by which time Maria Theresa had other things to do.

'Little Sadie Carswell isn't happy,' reported her housemistress to the headmistress. 'And she talks to herself.'

'A lot of gels do. Especially when they're new. Has she made friends?'

The housemistress looked dubious about the numbers who talked to themselves, but one did not openly disagree with the head.

'I don't think so,' she said. 'She's not a joiner-inner.'

'Work?' demanded the head.

'Good enough, on the whole.'

'Matron got any worries?'

'Matron says she's the healthiest child in the school, but doesn't know the meaning of order.'

The headmistress leaned her chin in her hands. 'She'll learn. We're here to teach her.'

'What is she doing at Easter?' asked the housemistress.

'Going home.'

'Those peculiar aunts?'

'They're the only home she has.'

'Poor child,' said the housemistress, meaning well.

'When those Labour people start trumpeting that we're elitist,' said the headmistress irritably, 'they could try asking why a lot of our gels are here. Oil parents, divorced parents, dreadful parents, dead parents, bored parents, feckless parents. I could tell them a thing or two. But do they want to know?' She fixed the housemistress with an eagle eye and dared her to argue. The housemistress, who had heard it all before, sighed patiently. 'Can you imagine what one of those state schools they make such a fuss about would offer the Sadie Carswells of this world?' finished the headmistress, not expecting an answer.

'I'm not absolutely clear what we are offering, except a very lonely and costly education. She's a fish out of water,' answered the housemistress bravely.

'Then I'm afraid she'll have to learn to swim,' answered the head briskly. 'We are the world Miss Carswell wishes to grow up in, and that's her family's view as well. She'll come out of the doldrums. She's simply unfortunate.'

'I do my best,' said the housemistress stiffly.

The headmistress nodded. 'To tell you the truth,' she said, 'I'm not sure that on a scale of misfortune, Miss Carswell is any worse off than the rest, and she's better off than some.'

'Orphaned,' began the housemistress indignantly, 'running wild like an animal. Aunts who are presumably gaga, stuck in the middle of nowhere, and then send her here? No worse off?'

The head, tired of the argument, fixed her with a cold and haughty glare.

'Contrary to some of our gels' families, they are obviously devoted, and,' added the headmistress heavily, 'they pay her fees on the dot.'

The housemistress got up to go.

'Oh, yes, oh, dear me, silly me to forget *fees*. On the dot, too. Absolutely.'

The head glared. The housemistress went to hurry out before she lost her very small advantage.

'Give her something to do,' said the head to her subordinate's retreating back. 'Put her in the hockey team or something, give her a challenge, involve her.'

'Teamwork,' said the housemistress over her shoulder, 'is not exactly Miss Carswell's forte.'

'I don't know,' mused the head. 'I've a feeling we have a crusader in that child. I gather she made a frightful fuss about a frog.'

'Joan of Arc wasn't much of a teamworker, either,' snapped the housemistress sarcastically. 'Crusaders seldom are. They're by nature chiefs, not Indians.'

'Then you'll have to soldier on as best you can,' said the head dismissively.

The housemistress didn't dare to slam the door.

Easter came and Sadie went home to Norfolk.

'I hate it. I'm not going back. I'll stay here, with you,' she yelled half-way through the holidays, helping them dig their patch in a bitter Easter wind, forking in manure, sucking blistered hands.

'You can't,' Queenie panted sternly, hacking with a trowel at half-frozen ground, like Boudicca wielding an axe, 'and you know it. You've got to go back.'

Bent and shrivelled, a sack tied round her waist to keep the soil off, wellingtons flapping on stringy sparrow legs, Queenie picked at the unfriendly soil and refused to argue. A wheelbarrow stood to one end of the vegetable patch, a robin on its handle watched with possessive, challenging eyes, quite unafraid. Victoria, bent double, old overcoat down to her ankles, chirruped at the bird and clucked her tongue. Sadie felt a heaviness in her chest, a great dragging doubt. She knew that no one else's family looked like that; other people's parents had smart clothes, smart cars and smart, loud voices. Thinking about it tormented her, dragged her in two, belonging to neither side fully any more.

'I hate it,' she shouted again, tears of rage in her eyes.

Victoria drew herself up, planted her spade in the mud.

'You hate what?' she demanded.

'School,' said Sadie in surprise.

'Is that all? Then stop it. Do you think you are the only child who has to bear what it doesn't like?'

Sadie stared defiantly, then lowered her eyes. 'I don't like it,' she repeated stubbornly, her child's cheeks flushed with cold wind and fury.

'Then you learn to like it. She is old, and tired,' Victoria pointed at Queenie, 'and so am I. Do you want us to worry and fret because we haven't done right by you? We won't be here one day, and then what would you do? You listen, now, and understand it's for your own good.'

'I don't want to worry you,' cried Sadie sullenly.

'Then do your duty,' snapped Victoria.

Sadie wiped her nose on the back of her hand.

'They call me Froggie,' she mumbled.

Queenie cackled, faded eyes fixed on the ground.

Victoria shuffled away towards the cottage.

'Never mind Froggie, girls are spiteful but it won't last. You do what she says, you hear?' hissed Queenie.

'You'd let me stay, I know you would, if you'd tell her to let you.'

'No,' snapped Queenie, 'and that's final.'

'I do love you, Great-Aunt Queenie,' whispered Sadie.

Queenie raised watery old eyes and gave a ghost of a smile.

'That's my girl,' she said.

Chapter Four

Maria Theresa Giangelli, who had followed Sadie into school after she'd put the frog in the pond, was in boarding school because her father and brothers were making a pile of money in hairdressing and restaurants. Giovanni Giangelli, her father, made the hairdressing salon fortune in Islington. Jove and Michelangelo, her elder brothers, were busy making the restaurant fortune in Soho. Maria Theresa, being the only girl, was endowed with the responsibility of climbing the social ladder and marrying well. Everyone in the Giangelli family, father, mother, daughter, sons, daughters-in-law, parents-in-law, right down to the babies and assorted first and second cousins, whether in London or Italy, was expected, in one way or another, to pull their weight.

Giovanni Giangelli came to London during the war. He fought reluctantly, misguidedly and briefly for Mussolini and fetched up in East London as a POW digging potatoes in Victoria Park. He loved England, English girls and chips. He saw the error of his political ways, was extremely helpful on one or two matters to his captors, married an English girl, Frances, the minute the war ended and was eventually allowed to stay. He taught her to cook pasta to perfection and criticised her chips. In post-war Islington, he set up a hairdressing and beauty parlour in the basement of a bombed-out building, bought cosmetics and perms on the black market, and opened his doors. He could barely keep up with demand.

In the early Sixties he did up new premises in Upper Street in stripped pine and Habitat blinds just as they were becoming fashionable, put blown-up posters of The

Shrimp on his walls, hired a receptionist with hair back-combed into a rock-solid beehive, a pert nose, perfect teeth in a wide, guttersnipe grin, and what came to be known as a boob tube. He put her in the window, her shapely backside to the punters, perched on a stool. The newly coined unisex side of the business shot through the tastefully cladded ceiling. Giangelli expanded, bought the premises next door and installed a beauty salon. It started out modestly, never looked back. He stopped being merely a crimper and began to market self-indulgence and *style*. Paunchy, raunchy, excitable, and reassuringly expensive, he brought chic to Islington around the time Islington tidied itself up, restored and gentrified its battered houses and brought chic to property prices. They both prospered and flourished.

Giovanni believed in money and God. He was a devout man. 'New money?' he would roar, enjoying himself. '*New* money? Money is money, old, new, money *buys*. God don't like scroungers,' he'd add, a belief nourished by his black-market days. 'You ask Nonna, hey?'

Nonna, his mother, lived in Rome, had been widowed forty years, and what Nonna didn't know about the Turf you could write on a postage stamp. She had taught her son the laws of probability and their application to money and horses before he could read or write.

Success still meant long hours and devotion to profit. Maria Theresa's bronze-haired mother, Frances, suspected devotion to the boob tube as well, though she never could prove it. To her own and everyone else's surprise, she was the one who left. She left Giovanni for an American toyshop tycoon after a series of spectacular screaming matches that had their neighbours cowering, wondering whether to call the police.

It happened because several times a year Marcus Hackett came to visit his British relatives. His grandmother had married a Canadian, who had moved to California after the war in search of the good life and the sun. Her daughter, Marcus' mother, had in her turn married a homesick Englishman in exile to IBM. Marcus, brought up a very

English American, to hum 'God Save the Queen' silently under his breath when his Junior High class took the oath each morning in front of the flag, was wholly confused, and fancied that by staying regularly in London and having a thoroughly British short back and sides in Giovanni's, he was celebrating his roots. Unmoved by the boob tube, he began gradually, despite recurrent jet lag, to notice the proprietor's wife's dewy skin and knowing grey eyes. He always booked in at lunchtime, because she would come in to take over reception for the lunch hour, make him a cup of tea, brush his hand with hers as she gave him the cup and saucer and smile a smile that stirred his heart, under the speculative stare of her husband, winding a perm in the next chair. It would all have stayed a harmless bit of fun if they hadn't bumped into each other one wet afternoon in Canonbury Square.

'You know each other?' he said foolishly, finding her drinking tea in his aunt's kitchen.

'My daughter Maria Theresa and your cousin's children go to school together,' said Frances.

'It's a small world.'

'Especially round here. I have to go.'

She pushed her cup and saucer on to the draining board, and looked out of the window over the green square.

'Bother, it's raining.'

'Stay till it stops,' offered Margaret, Marcus' aunt. 'There's no need to rush off just because he's come.'

'I'll lend you my umbrella,' said Marcus, thinking that getting it back would be an excuse to see her again.

'No, you'd never get it back,' said Frances, turning down temptation.

'Then I'll take you,' he said.

He walked her in the rain, the long way round, a way back to the salon that made no sense at all unless you just wanted to be with someone.

Maria Theresa told the story with relish. She and Sadie sat side by side in the sun on a wooden bench, on a

Sunday afternoon. The school was very quiet, no other girls in sight.

'The next thing I know, she's gone to America to live in Los Angeles,' she explained in a strong North London accent, waving her arms dramatically in the air, 'with the toyman.'

Sadie was impressed.

'My dad went mad and then he got all quiet. Then he shut me up in my room every evening, and said I had to study, so he could sneak a different girl into the house every night. Then my brothers came, and had a big punch-up with my dad, and he calmed down and got all angry and miserable and horrible for ages, and didn't go out and stopped shutting me up in my bedroom, and he got to know Rosalie, who was one of his hairdressers. She's quite old, and he married her, and now they're all right. They parked me here while they try to have *bambini*. No luck yet, she's a bit old,' her white teeth gleamed maliciously, 'though I wouldn't mind, really. I like babies.'

'What about your mother?' breathed Sadie.

'They share me,' pronounced Maria Theresa loftily.

'How?'

'They all had to go in a lawyer's office and not fight, which I think was not exactly easy-peasy, and they had to agree to share me between here, Los Angeles, where my mother lives, and Islington, where my father lives. And sometimes we go to Rome, where Nonna lives.' Maria Theresa stuck her *retroussée* nose in the air and sighed, a weary, woman-of-the-world sigh. 'You get used to it, you know, the packing and the hanging around at Heathrow. I still have to fly unaccompanied minor, and those people are so *boring* that meet you at airports.'

Sadie's eyes grew round as saucers.

'You've been to America?'

''Course. Lots of times. Four.'

'Are you a jet-setter?'

''Course.'

They sat in silence. Maria Theresa leaned her head on

the back of the bench and closed her eyes in the sunshine. At first crushed, Sadie began to fight back.

'My aunt's a witch,' she announced.

Maria Theresa's black eyes flashed amusement.

'Not a gypsy?' she said meanly.

They stared down the long grassy slope to the clifftop; beyond it the sea shone silver. Sadie dealt the same card again.

'She's a witch in Norfolk.'

'Do gypsies eat hedgehogs?' Maria Theresa had a persistent streak.

'How do I know?' snapped Sadie. 'Witches are nothing to do with gypsies.'

'Can she cast spells on a broomstick?' jeered Maria Theresa, taking the bait at last.

'She *sees right inside you*,' hissed Sadie.

'I've been in Concorde.' Maria Theresa played an ace.

'Great-Aunt Queenie can make animals and birds and people get better. They used to come up from the village and ask her for herbs. She knows all the herbs, and she makes potions. So does Great-Aunt Victoria, but I don't think she's as good as Great-Aunt Queenie.'

'Potions,' said Maria Theresa, trumped at last. 'What kind?'

'All sorts.'

Maria Theresa looked dubious.

'Getting-well ones, and putting-the-hex-on ones, though she says you mustn't talk about them, and love ones. She can do everything.'

'*Love potions?*' squawked Maria Theresa, about to lose the game.

'Love potions,' repeated Sadie smugly.

Maria Theresa wound a thick, glossy lock of jet-black hair round her finger and said, 'Wow.'

'I'm an orphan,' added Sadie, overplaying her hand, just to be on the safe side.

'*Really* an orphan?' demanded Maria Theresa.

'My parents drowned.'

'Oh.' Maria Theresa contemplated the awfulness of that,

and then a thought struck her. 'Why don't your witchy aunts come to visit, take you out for tea, then?'

Sadie thought of Great-Aunt Queenie in her sacking apron and wellington boots, getting off at the station, taking the bus, coming up the long drive to the school, hooted at and hustled by Landrovers and limousines, who would think her the . . . cleaner. Sadie shrugged unhappily.

Maria Theresa's eyes gleamed with shrewd sympathy. 'I know what you mean. When *they* were deciding all the things about getting divorced, they fought *disgustingly*. They were so embarrassing, I wanted to die. I used to dream that they died and had this beautiful funeral where everyone cried and said nice things, and I knew they weren't like that at all, but they were nailed up in their coffins, and behaved for once. Isn't that awful? Do you think I'm an awful person?'

'I don't think so,' said Sadie cautiously, to Maria Theresa's disappointment.

'Life is sad,' pronounced the precocious child.

'Some of it is,' Sadie agreed diplomatically.

'Let's be best friends,' suggested Maria Theresa graciously.

'If you like,' said Sadie.

'You can come home with me in the hols,' Maria Theresa ordered. 'Can't you? Would you be allowed?'

Sadie had a fleeting vision of Maria Theresa's couture luggage full of Biba and Quant, piled in Queenie's cottage among the boots, spades, reed matting and crocheted rugs on the old horsehair sofa.

'Come and stay at your house?' asked Sadie, who had never heard of such a thing.

''Course.'

'I don't think I'd be allowed to ask you,' said Sadie weakly.

'We're Italian,' shrugged Maria Theresa, as though that explained everything.

I bet you're allowed, thought Sadie. I bet you're allowed practically anything you want.

'I'd be scared to stay with witchy Aunt Thingy, anyway,' Maria Theresa added rudely, needing to win this round.

Sadie, guiltily, was hugely relieved.

Sadie was invited to Islington, and was allowed to go.

'What did you expect? It's what we sent her to that school for,' snapped Queenie when Victoria moped because Sadie went to Islington instead of coming home to Norfolk. 'And may I remind you that you were the one who insisted.'

Mary Llewellyn, now one of the sisters' few visitors, watched Victoria with anxiety.

'She's a bit wandery, isn't she?' she said carefully to Queenie, not wishing to alarm her. 'Do you think she's quite well?'

'She's sulking because Sadie's gone off with her grand friends,' said Queenie tartly. 'She's got only herself to blame.'

'I hope so,' said Mary. 'I hope that's all it is.'

The long summer holidays at the end of the year when Sadie and Maria Theresa became best friends wore on into a warm Indian summer September and the new term. They'd had the time of their lives in London. Introduced to the white-fronted four-storey Islington house, Sadie's big grey eyes popped out of her head.

'What a funny little thing,' cried Rosalie, the day after they came home for the summer. 'She's rather sweet. Where did you say she comes from?'

'Norfolk,' said Maria. At home they dropped the Theresa part of her name.

'I've never been to Norfolk,' said Rosalie, ending the subject.

'It's seaside,' said Maria.

'Nice. Go and find something to do,' said Rosalie.

She watched the two girls sitting kicking their feet in the garden on her canopied lounger.

'Funny how opposites attract,' she remarked to Giovanni.

'Are they opposites?'

'I wish we had a real sister for her.'

She reached to kiss him, but he laughed and pulled away.

'Not now, Rosalie,' he said. 'I get back to the shop.'

Rosalie tossed her head angrily and felt unlooked for stirrings of fellow feeling for the first Signora Giangelli.

'Gianni, you come home tonight, you hear?' she yelled, leaning over the banisters as he banged the front door. She shook her fist at the empty hallway, and felt foolish.

'Silly fool,' she said to the empty stairwell.

Down in the garden, through tall, open windows, her shrill voice reached the two girls. Maria Theresa rolled her eyes and shrugged her narrow shoulders eloquently.

'*Plus ça change . . .*' she whispered to Sadie, showing off.

'*Plus ça* what?' said Sadie. It was her introduction to family life, and she loved it.

Chapter Five

The Giangellis lived at a pace Sadie had never dreamed of. There were always things to do, and if there weren't, they quickly found something to fill the gap.

'I'm bored,' complained Maria, after only one week of holiday, waiting to go to Rome to visit Nonna.

'All right, let's go shopping,' said Rosalie, who never seemed impatient or bossy, more like an elder sister than a wicked stepmother. 'Let's go shopping for the beach.'

They took the tube to John Lewis, Marks & Spencer and Selfridges, cruising the crowds in Oxford Street, all barging along, heads down, with practised ferocity. Sadie was stunned by the shops and the speed and the jostling, bad-tempered shoppers. They bought swimsuits and beach towels, sunblock, hair conditioner and sandals.

'I got a yellow polka-dot bikini, it's itsy bitsy, teeny weeny,' sang Maria, dancing on long brown legs across Oxford Circus, heading for Carnaby Street.

'And we go topless,' she confided, skirting a street vendor. 'We get lovely brown boobs.'

Sadie, having as yet little in the way of any kind of boobs, blushed scarlet.

'Why do you have to take so *much* to the beach?' she cried, to cover the perplexing moment. 'When I go to the beach in Norfolk, I just go.'

'The sun and sea dry your hair and ruin your skin,' explained Maria, hefting parcels. 'Italian women age, and they don't look so good,' she added, wrinkling her nose, ridiculously worldly-wise.

Sadie helped to carry their heap of parcels, and was dazed.

'Next year,' cried Maria as they went past Liberty's, 'you can come with us to Italy and see Nonna. We'll go all round Rome, and do the sights.'

'Will we?' cried Sadie, dazzled.

The following week, the Giangellis flew to Italy and the Islington house was closed up.

For four weeks Sadie stayed at home, and saw the little stone cottage and the vegetable patch through tragic eyes, knowing now what a hovel it was.

'I wish I could make it more comfortable, more *easy*,' she cried remorsefully. 'I didn't know.'

'We've lost her,' said Queenie, when she had gone down to the beach for a swim in the cold sea. 'She's got all those tubes of stuff, and she wants us to move to the village.'

'What did you expect?' said Victoria acidly. 'She has to change to keep up with where we've sent her. What else could you expect her to do?'

'Has to, has to, what's has to?' growled Queenie, deliberately obtuse.

'Life and Fate,' said her sister. 'We've changed her life and her fate. No good grumbling she's different.'

'Humph,' grumbled Queenie, anyway.

'No bathroom, no shower, no kitchen. I'll talk to Miss Llewellyn – there must be a way to make it better,' cried Sadie.

Queenie slammed her wrinkled hand on the back of a lopsided old chair. 'You'll do no such thing,' she shouted. 'You won't interfere.'

The umbilical cord was severed, as they had planned, as Sadie got angry.

'You're *impossible*,' yelled Sadie.

Three years later, at school, one wet and windy day in the middle of the Spring term when they were about to take O levels, Sadie was summoned.

'What have you done?' demanded Maria Theresa.

'Nothing, I don't think.'

She waited outside the headmistress' door, searching her conscience for the few small crimes anyone could possibly know about.

'Come. Sit down, Sarah.'

Eyes lowered, she waited politely.

'I'm afraid I have some very bad news.'

Panic gripped Sadie.

'Miss Llewellyn telephoned,' said the head.

Sadie felt giddy.

'Your Great-Aunt Victoria passed away in her sleep, last night. No one had any idea, and no warning, except that she was very old, Sarah, and it was time for her to go.'

'Yes.'

'I'm so sorry to have to give you bad news.'

'It was time for her to go,' echoed Sadie dully.

Oh dear, what terrible timing this is, the exams just weeks away, thought the headmistress, keeping her feelings to herself.

Shocked, Sadie longed to be dismissed, to get away from those all-seeing eyes.

'I'm here if you would like to come and talk to me,' offered the head kindly. Sadie shuddered.

'I never knew anyone who died,' said Maria Theresa tactlessly just before bedtime. 'What will your other aunt do? Is she old, as well? D'you think she'll die too?'

'She isn't going to die,' shouted Sadie. Guiltily, Maria Theresa heard muffled sobs coming from underneath Sadie's blankets. They went on and on, and in the end she crept out of her bed, and knelt by Sadie's.

'I wish I could stop you crying,' she whispered.

Sobbing, Sadie moved over in the narrow bed and Maria Theresa climbed in. Children, thought the housemistress coming to wake the little dormitory in the morning and finding them fast asleep together, comfort children much better than grown-ups can do. She left them, and let them sleep in.

* * *

Not long after, less than a couple of months, Queenie was propped in bed, breathing shallowly.

'I had a feeling we wouldn't hold on to her for long after Victoria went,' whispered Mary Llewellyn, her arm round Sadie's shaking shoulders.

'I've neglected them and been awful. I should have been here, and come back all the holidays. I should have helped, and then she wouldn't be ill . . . and, and . . .'

'Now look here,' said Mary firmly. 'Don't you go upsetting that old lady. You've done just what she wanted, so don't go spoiling it by saying you're sorry.'

'Have I?' Sadie hiccuped in surprise.

'Yes, you have. You're happy, and that makes Queenie happy. That's what she wants more than anything.'

'I'm scared,' sobbed Sadie.

'Of course you are, but Queenie isn't afraid,' said Mary in a low voice. 'And we've got to look after her, now, and help her to go peacefully.'

Sadie slumped in her arms and howled.

She went to the funerals, one so very shortly after the other, and thc housemother sewed black bands on to her uniform sleeves. She had a letter to say that the cottage was hers, and that it was being closed up securely. Mary Llewellyn said she'd cleaned, scrubbed and cleared it, ready for boarding up.

Sadie cried afresh, crumpling the letter, splattered with tears.

'Now you're really an orphan, aren't you?' said Maria Theresa curiously. 'What does it feel like?'

'It doesn't feel like nothing,' yelled Sadie, incoherent.

'What will you do?' Maria Theresa pursued the matter determinedly.

Sadie uncrumpled her letter and smoothed it out.

'Spend the summer with Miss Llewellyn,' she said desolately.

'Dad and Rosalie said I was to tell you to come and stay with us, as long as you want, if you want.'

'Everyone dies in Norfolk,' Sadie said wretchedly.

'Then come and stay with us,' urged Maria Theresa.

'But you're going to America to stay with your mother.'

'Only for four weeks,' said Maria Theresa. 'That's not long. And it's all right. Dad says you're welcome, and would you like to work in the salon while I'm away, just helping out?'

Sadie smiled for the first time since Queenie's funeral.

A heavy, changeable summer brought frequent showers and fitful sun breaking occasionally from behind low, flat, cloudy skies. Giovanni taught Sadie to hand perm-papers, make customers' drinks, sweep up clippings and be useful. The boob tube showed her how to fill the appointment book, and one day when business was slack, they fixed hair attachments to Sadie's tight curls, and she had ringlets down her back in a shining cascade. Rosalie put black mascara on her lashes and lipstick on her mouth and said, 'You'll be a heart-stealer, won't she, Gianni?' Maria's brothers, much older, with wives, restaurants and *bambini* of their own, eyed her when they came round, and Gianni scowled.

'You got nothing to do?' he shouted, and Jove grinned and winked. Michelangelo winked back, dark eyes twinkling above a thick black beard.

'You not busy? I make you busy in a moment,' Giovanni yelled meaningfully, shaking his fist.

They sauntered away.

'And take the lipstick off,' he growled at Sadie.

They all went to see Maria off at Heathrow, and then Giovanni, Rosalie and Sadie went to welcome her home again. She galloped down the roped-off corridor for arrivals, pushing a trolley piled high with expensive baggage and things from the duty-free.

'She looks so *experienced*, doesn't she?' Sadie sighed enviously.

Then Maria saw them, shrieked, flew her trolley round the end of the barrier and flung her arms round Giovanni's neck.

'Not *too* experienced,' murmured Rosalie.

'I'm here, it's me,' she screeched, her arms still wrapped round Giovanni's neck. 'I've been to Disneyworld and Hollywood and New York because they had business things to do . . . I don't know how many planes I've been on, and I'm jet-lagged as hell,' she announced importantly.

Several people turned and smiled.

'Calm down,' cried Rosalie, pushing Maria Theresa's baggage out of other people's way.

'You're so brown,' said Sadie enviously. 'It's been rotten weather here.'

'It's funny to be back,' burbled Maria Theresa. She started pushing her trolley again and eyed one of the airport snack and sandwich bars. 'I'm thirsty.'

'Wait till we get home,' ordered Giovanni, who detested airports.

'Home, where is that? Oh yes, London,' shouted Maria Theresa, impossibly overexcited.

'Oh, Gawd,' mouthed Rosalie.

'Oh, for goodness' sake,' muttered Sadie.

'Love your hair,' trilled Maria Theresa in the back of the car, heading back down the A4 into London.

'Do you like it?' said Sadie.

'Yes.'

Creeping through central London's heavy traffic, Maria Theresa fidgeted.

'I've been compressed for hours and hours and hours, and it makes you thirsty. Can we stop and get a Coke?'

'I can't stop in this,' growled Giovanni, in second gear all down the Marylebone Road, bad-tempered.

'Daddeee,' whined Maria Theresa.

'Spoiled,' muttered Rosalie crossly. 'Frances gives in to her and she gets all her own way and we have to put up . . .'

Giovanni pulled the Jaguar over and pointed. 'Maria, there's a newsagent's over there, they'll sell Coke. Hop out, mind the traffic and be quick.'

Maria Theresa hopped out and stood waiting to dash. Traffic roared past, hooting angrily.

'Get a move on,' shouted Giovanni. 'I can't stop here long.'

The hairs on Sadie's skin prickled.

'No,' she screamed. 'It's the other way.'

'What?' asked Rosalie, turning round to look over the top of her seat.

'She's looking the wrong way,' shrieked Sadie.

Jet-lagged Maria Theresa looked left and the road was clear. She stepped out. A silver Mercedes with CD plates and a driver in black glasses screamed on its brakes and swerved, catching the back of the Jag, leaving tyre marks burned into the road. They spun to a stop. Around the tangled cars, traffic tried to pass, tried not to stop.

'Gianni? Maria?' croaked Rosalie, wiping blood from her face.

A woman came from the pavement and said, 'They've called an ambulance.'

'Where's Maria . . . ?'

Rosalie saw the woman's face.

'She's dead.'

The woman shook her head. Giovanni lay half-way through the shattered windscreen, his eyes closed, unmoving. Sadie lay across the back seat, shocked, unhurt.

The woman stared at Giovanni, and Rosalie saw his neck was at an impossible angle.

'Don't move in case you're hurt yourself,' said the woman faintly. 'They're coming.'

Rosalie reached out for Giovanni and howled. In the distance, sirens screamed.

Chapter Six

Widowhood, a suddenly and seriously disabled step-daughter and the informal inheritance of a waif adopted by Giovanni, unceremoniously bequeathed to her by his death, devastated Rosalie. Having been a plump, conventionally pretty thirty-six-year-old, full of life and laughter, in love with her husband, she became a neglected, frowsty woman, wall-eyed with crying. Nothing had prepared her for loss on such a scale, and she had nightmare fears that she would never cope. The Giangellis gathered round her, tried to help her through. They spent as much time as they could in the Islington house. Sometimes Rosalie was somewhat less than grateful..

'Dead people and accidents,' she cried tipsily one afternoon over a family meal which none of them ate, 'are so bloody *busy*. D'you know what I mean? Forms and undertakers and policemen and autopsies and wills and bills. I was never so busy in my life.'

Rosalie's mouth drooped with despair. Their faces crowded in on her, crammed around her dining table, gathered together, presenting a solid front to disaster. They picked at lumps of French bread and olives and salami, starters to a meal no one really wanted to eat. The heart gone out of them, they eyed Rosalie's desperation uneasily. She was a hairdresser who took care of her own hair, and she was proud of her appearance. But now her silver-bleached hair was black at the roots and stringy, dragged carelessly behind her ears. Her skin was pallid and puffy from too much crying, too much red wine, too little sleep. Photographs of women in the Blitz, thought Jove with sudden insight, had that raw, taut look about them. It was the look of exhaustion.

'What do we do,' Rosalie went on when no one spoke, swirling dark ruby wine in her glass, trying to focus, 'if Maria comes out of that spinal unit like a *cabbage*?'

They froze. Wine slid round and round in Rosalie's glass, the colour of blood, her fingers too taut, the stem of the glass about to snap. Then she put it down on the tablecloth and peered round at them, all peering back, anxiety written large on their faces.

'Do you know, you're all so bloody black,' she said owlishly. 'With all that black hair, black eyes, black expressions, black clothes, you should hang upside down in a cave and come out at night.'

'It's all right, Rosie,' said Jove. 'Take it easy.'

'It's all right, Rosie,' she mimicked. 'Like hell it's all right. Cabbage, so there. I've said it again.'

'Really,' muttered Jove's sharp-faced wife, Sissy, 'I wouldn't boast about it, if I were you.'

The other sister-in-law, Mags, sat next to Sadie at the end of the big oak dining table, her three-year-old son asleep in her ample lap, her big thighs supporting him cosily. She stroked his hair absently and said, 'Of course Maria won't be a cabbage. Cabbages is when your brain's gone. Her brain's all right, it's only her legs. She's Maria in a wheelchair, that's all. Don't you let her hear you saying cabbage.'

'She's practically as helpless as a baby,' snapped Rosalie. 'And since I'm the one who's going to have to look after her, I'll call a spade a spade, if you wouldn't mind.'

She drank the dregs in her glass and looked down the table for the bottle, picked it up and peered at it with disappointment.

'Empty. Open some more, Angelo.'

'We ought to ask Frances what she intends to do about Maria,' began Sissy, drawing an outraged glare from Rosalie.

'Oh, oh, here we go,' muttered Jove.

'Ah, shall we talk about dear Frances?' said Rosalie thinly.

Michelangelo pulled the cork from another bottle of Valpolicella.

'Let's hear what we ought to be asking Maria's sainted mother,' suggested Rosalie ominously. She folded her arms and sat back in her chair, inviting an argument.

'*Pas devant les enfants*,' murmured Mags, unheeded.

'It's no good getting all upset, Rosalie,' Sissy said calmly. 'She's Maria's mother and she's got a right to be asked about Maria.'

'Maria's mother,' screeched Rosalie, banging her glass on the table, spilling wine in a spreading stain on the white cloth, 'walked out.'

'Stop it,' said Mags.

'She came marching in here from Heathrow like she still owns the place, and all through the funeral it was do this and do that, and off she goes again. That woman,' Rosalie looked as though she might be grinding her teeth, 'is poison. She never says thank you, or would you like a hand, or Maria can come to America and *we'll* push her around in a chair for the rest of her life.'

'We'll all help look after Maria,' said Sissy compassionately, realising that the responsibility preyed dreadfully on Rosalie's mind, realising also that not all stepmothers would take it on at all, and they should be grateful for Rosalie's unthinking acceptance of it. 'We won't leave you to cope all by yourself.' She meant to be sisterly, merely succeeded in making Rosalie feel patronised.

'I wanted Gianni's baby,' Rosalie shouted, losing control. 'I never asked for Maria in a pushchair.'

She began to cry, raggedly, into their embarrassed silence.

Mags said awkwardly, 'It's just that this is Maria's home, and yours as well, so it seems . . .'

'Seems what?' shrieked Rosalie. 'Like, oh, good old Rose'll cope.'

'You don't have to . . .' began Mags, but the shouting woke the child on her lap. He began to wail and thrash his legs.

'One minute you're saying Maria's like your own child, and the next it's all this can't do, won't do,' cried Sissy crossly, out of patience. 'Just say what you mean, will you.'

'You always were a silly bitch,' said Rosalie thoughtfully.

They glared the length of the table and the family held its breath.

Jove's fist came crashing down, making glasses and dishes jump and clatter. The wailing child caught its breath with fright and began hiccuping.

'Enough,' roared Jove. 'Maria is going to come home and we're all going to look after her. You are going to stop yelling and shouting and fighting, and you,' he rounded on Rosalie, 'are not having any more of that.'

He snatched the Valpolicella and stood with it clutched to his chest.

'Your shirt,' said Sissy patiently, pointing.

Jove dabbed at the stain where it had spilled and put the bottle down again.

'Men,' snapped Sissy, giving him a tissue. 'It won't come out.'

'Salt,' said Sadie. 'Put salt on it.'

'And what are you going to do?' demanded Sissy, noticing her for the first time.

'Go back to school, I suppose,' said Sadie timidly.

'You could give Rosalie a hand in the holidays,' suggested Sissy brusquely.

'You can't expect her to do any such thing,' started Michelangelo.

'I can expect what I like,' snapped Sissy. 'Your father was good to her. You stay in the family, you take the rough with the smooth,' Sissy told Sadie bluntly.

'Stop it, Sissy, she's only a kid,' said Mags sharply. 'That's not fair.'

'Leave her alone,' cried Rosalie. 'It's her and me against you lot, isn't it, love? You and me and Maria. You'll give me a hand, won't you?'

Their black eyes boring a dozen holes in her head, they waited for her to say something.

'Yes,' said Sadie, sounding braver than she felt in the face of a monstrous demand.

'Huh,' said Sissy. 'Oh, will you look at her?'

Rosalie's head drooped slowly forward between her hands and came to rest on the tablecloth. Breathing heavily, she was fast asleep.

'It's harder for her,' remarked Sissy more kindly. 'She's lost her husband.'

'It's you who has a go at her,' cried Mags accusingly.

I miss him, too, thought Sadie, but Giovanni belonged to them, not her. She was filled with a dull, dragging guilt that he was dead, that Maria Theresa lay in a hospital bed. She was always so strong and well; other people died and she didn't even get a bump or a bruise.

'Don't take any notice of Sissy's tongue,' whispered Mags, leaning close to Sadie. 'Her heart's in the right place. If you can find it,' she added audibly, making sure Sissy heard her. Sissy scowled. Then, as though they'd got their anger and loss and misery out of their systems for the time being, the atmosphere lightened, life returned to normal.

'Go on, then,' said Mags, pushing her son off, shooing him to go play in the hall with the other children.

'Do you know, I'm starving,' announced Sissy, reaching for the cooled dishes on the table. 'Let's heat it all up and eat.'

Rosalie slept on, at the head of her table. They forgot their squabbles, enjoyed their meal.

They were feeling contentedly full, peeling fruit and picking at bits of cheese when the phone went, startling Rosalie awake. Confused, with an aching head, she heard

Michelangelo shouting down the line in fast, ululating Italian.

'Is that Nonna?' she asked, rubbing her eyes. 'How long was I asleep?'

'She was ringing to say she's coming. This time the aeroplanes are flying,' said Michelangelo, coming back to the dining room, the call over.

Giovanni's funeral arrangements had been punctuated by outraged international telephone calls. Nonna, grounded in Rome by striking ground crew, was unable to come. She wept and shrieked and begged by turns, but the planes sat on the tarmac of Leonardo da Vinci Airport, unmoved by any amount of pleading, and Giovanni was finally laid to rest without his mother.

'She's coming now, just like that?' said Sissy.

'Just like that. On her way. You know Nonna,' shrugged Michelangelo. 'Let's be grateful. She'll sort us out.'

'Hallelujah,' murmured Sissy.

'How long for?' asked Mags.

Jove rolled his eyes, sat down and said, 'Ascot, Sandown Park, Kempton Park, Grand National, the Derby . . .'

They smiled, then began to laugh.

'She'll be here *ages*,' said Mags with satisfaction.

'Pardon?' said Sadie.

'Gee-gees,' said Mags, amused. 'You just wait. She sits with her nose up against the TV screen, getting *that* excited, saying the rosary faster and faster, like the bloke doing the commentary. You know, they go faster and faster when the horses are nearly there, and Heaven help Our Lady if Nonna's nag doesn't win.'

'Nonna likes horse racing?' asked Sadie.

They all burst out laughing.

'And how. Nonna thinks Mother Mary is a gambling woman,' explained Jove, crossing himself automatically. 'She says any virgin faced with an angel telling her she's about to become the mother of God made a canny calculation of the odds, and had to have had the soul of a gambler to have gone along with it. A long shot, you see. I don't know about the Virgin, but Nonna was born with a gambling soul. She's always done it. Horses, cards, occasionally the dogs. She draws the line at slot machines, though. Won't touch 'em.'

'Good heavens,' exclaimed Sadie. 'Isn't that blasphemous?'

'Probably,' grinned Michelangelo. 'But Nonna has direct dispensation from the Lady herself, being two of a kind.' He winked cheerfully.

'Maria used to say we'd go to Rome to see her, but we never did,' said Sadie, noting that Nonna's coming even cheered up Rosalie. If Maria Theresa's gambling grandmother was coming, the Giangellis without Giovanni might not be so bad after all.

'Rosalie won't dare have a nervous breakdown now,' whispered Sissy into Sadie's ear. 'So you can cheer up.'

'I am cheered up,' said Sadie.

'Takes time, getting over everything,' said Sissy kindly. 'Don't look so worried. It's hit us all very hard.'

'For Maria it's for always,' mumbled Sadie back in Sissy's ear.

Sissy stared at her thoughtfully.

'I don't know about that,' she said. 'I think she'll be all right. Don't think you've got to have two broken legs to look her in the face, you know. You don't.'

Sadie's face flamed.

'No need at all. She got hurt, you didn't. No one's fault at all,' repeated Sissy shrewdly.

When they'd all gone, leaving Rosalie to sleep off an afternoon hangover, Sadie sat alone in her bedroom and cried for the first time since the accident. She felt heady and blotchy and hideous, but for a while, thinking about Nonna coming, and how it had cheered them all up, and about what Sissy had said, she felt a good deal better.

Chapter Seven

Isabella Maria Giangelli, whom everyone called Nonna, bowled off the plane at Heathrow at a fast waddle, leaving the air hostess on the door looking after her with a genuine smile. In her black lace-up shoes, she sped along the corridor to the carousel and stood foursquare, waiting for luggage, a short, squat little monolith, in black from head to foot, save for a thick mass of pure white hair pulled into a luxuriant bun on the nape of her stout little neck. Brown skin full of wrinkles softened shrewd, observant black eyes and a full, decided mouth. She pulled her cases off the carousel with a series of thuds, scattered bags, carriers, a half-drunk half-litre bottle of *acqua minerale* and several copies of *Sporting Life* around her and looked round surreptitiously for a likely victim to carry it all. A British bureaucrat on Brussels business in Rome and London collected his overnight case and noticed a short, fat, elderly Italian woman tussling with cases. He caught her eye.

'*Andiamo*,' Nonna muttered, pushing the largest case with her foot. She bent forwards, put one hand in the small of her back, and groaned, plucking at the handle ineffectually.

'Look, you all right?' he asked, hesitating, casting round for help.

'*Sì, grazie*.'

She puffed again.

'I'll get you a trolley.'

Nonna watched, her eyes liquid with admiration. He pulled a luggage trolley towards the carousel and piled on her bags.

'Someone meeting you?' he asked, putting his own case on top of hers, starting to push.

'*Sì.*' She nodded vigorously, straightened up like a ramrod, beamed and surged ahead like a tug in full throttle. Throwing up a slipstream among throngs of passengers heading for the exit, they steamed through the green channel at Customs and round a bend to where crowds waited for arrivals. Isabella stopped dead and her sweating businessman, to avoid running the trolley into her ankles, stopped with a backwards jolt and stubbed his own toe painfully.

'Ouf,' he gasped, clutching his Burton bag. 'Can you manage now? OK? You can manage?' he shouted, to be sure she understood. Nonna beamed and before she had a chance to answer, part of the crowd surged towards them and she disappeared under a scrum of hugging and kissing and jostling. Someone hugged him by mistake and a kiss landed on his cheek.

'Thank you for carrying all her bags,' someone yelled. Outraged, he fought them off. They all shouted at once, no one listening. Through a gap in the mêlée Isabella caught his eye, smiled like a cherub and said in perfect, charmingly accented English, 'I shall manage very well. Thank you.'

'I will never, ever again,' swore the businessman as he stood in a queue for a taxi, straightening his tie and cursing the ache in his toe, 'help dear little old foreign white-haired ladies.'

Behind him, the Giangelli family sobered up. Rosalie gazed around the vast concourse, plunged back into reality.

'The last time we were here we were meeting Maria,' she said, saying what nobody wanted to hear, tactless.

'Come on, let's get home,' said Jove.

Michelangelo nudged Mags towards the car park exit.

'I told you everyone coming was silly,' she complained. 'It was daft to bring two cars.'

'Rosalie and Sadie couldn't come by themselves,' said Jove. 'Too many bad memories.'

Nonna trotted through the swing doors to the car park and stood waiting.

'Not the Jaguar car any more,' she said softly.

'It was a write-off,' said Rosalie. 'And in any case, I never wanted to see it again.'

'But you drive,' Nonna pointed out. 'You do so well. When a horse throws you, you get back on, and it is the same with the car. Bravo.'

'We are not doing well. In fact, we are doing terribly,' answered Rosalie, suddenly sounding depressed.

'Yes, you are,' said Nonna decidedly.

'Maria, you see,' Rosalie told her, 'is never going to walk again. You will see how frightful it is.'

Jove put cases into one boot and Michelangelo piled the assortment of bags and hand luggage into the other.

'Which car are you going in?' Rosalie asked.

'With you,' Nonna looked round at who was going where. 'What is the matter with that little girl?'

Sadie sat in the back of Jove's Rover, shivering uncontrollably, her eyes brilliant with tears.

'That's Sadie, she was in the car when the accident happened.'

'I can't face going down that road again.' Her teeth chattered.

'I'll go a different route,' said Jove. 'Find a hanky, and don't panic.'

'She's Maria's friend. We've kind of adopted her,' said Rosalie, putting her head in the car and rummaging on the back ledge for tissues, handing them to Sadie. 'Here, dry your eyes. Nothing's going to happen.'

Nonna, climbing in beside Sadie, produced a large linen handkerchief smelling of eau-de-Cologne.

'Jove, drive home,' she ordered, giving Sadie the handkerchief. Rosalie climbed in the other side and they were off. Passing beyond the Heathrow boundary, Rosalie's nerve went.

'Oh, thank God,' she wailed suddenly, like a little child. 'Nonna, thank God you've come.'

'I haven't got another handkerchief,' said Nonna. 'If we're all going to cry, we share.'

'We?' sniffled Rosalie, giving up being grown-up and capable and nearly forty, bawling her eyes out on Nonna's comfortable black bosom. As they drove well clear of Heathrow she pulled herself together and sat up.

'We're all trying to be strong, and look at us, bawling like babies.'

Nonna met Jove's eyes in the rear-view mirror. Something gleamed suspiciously on his cheek. He looked shamefaced and shrugged.

'We all want someone else to be the strong one, if you know what I mean. We all try to cry on each other's shoulders. It has been a terrible time.'

'You make me the strong one, heh?'

He grinned guiltily, like a small boy.

'It was brave to come to the airport,' said Nonna, shaking Sadie gently. 'Never mind crying.'

'Spots and red blotches. You look awful, Rosalie,' sniffed Sadie, managing to stop.

'Carrier bags under the eyes,' said Rosalie.

'Headache,' said Sadie.

'Red nose,' said Rosalie.

'Sore throat. But I feel a bit better.'

Nonna took the tissue box and put it back on the ledge.

'We don't need them,' she said.

'We'll have tea when we get in,' said Rosalie. 'I made cakes and one of the girls in the salon brought one round. They're kind. And Sissy isn't here because she stayed behind to make sandwiches.'

'Do you fancy some music?' asked Jove.

They listened to the radio for the rest of the way back to Islington, dry-eyed. Nonna watched crowded pavements slide past as they got into the city, and her rosary beads slid one by one, secretly, through her fingers, as she prayed for strength for all of them, to face whatever was to come.

Chapter Eight

When the silver Mercedes threw Maria into the air, the fall broke her back. For seven months she stayed in the spinal injuries unit where she was taken after the accident. At first, she thought she'd get better. She couldn't and wouldn't believe anything else. And it was, at first, a possibility, because no one could tell how badly she was injured, or whether her injuries might heal themselves.

'You might mend, you know,' said her consultant encouragingly, in the first week or two, when she grumbled and complained and got depressed at having to lie so still. 'We won't know for six weeks or so how much permanent damage has been done, or indeed, if any,' he went on, raising grizzled grey eyebrows below a high, domed head that had lost a lot of its grey hair, his observant eyes full of kindness. 'You're in spinal shock, you see, as well as goodness knows how much other shock. It's a waiting game. It gets everyone down.'

'Some game,' muttered Maria angrily.

'We'll watch you like a hawk for movement. Anything at all. Any twitches and wriggling, and we can take it your spine is beginning to heal itself,' he pronounced cheerily, trying to give her courage.

'My toes wiggle,' she said, with instant certainty.

The doctor pulled back the thin sheet covering her naked body and looked at her toes.

'Go on, then. Wiggle away.'

Maria bent all the willpower she could summon into her feet and ordered her toes to move.

'I'm sorry,' he said sadly, letting the corner of the sheet drop. 'Not yet.'

'They moved,' yelled Maria furiously. 'I felt them.'

He shook his head.

'If I got up,' she persisted desperately, '*then* they might work.'

'You have splinters of bone embedded in your spinal cord,' he said patiently. 'If you start thrashing around you'll do more damage. Six weeks. Give things a chance to heal. And keep still.'

'They don't let me keep still,' she complained sullenly. 'There's all this turning over and flipping about and arranging me. I bet they wouldn't like being arranged like they were posing for a still life and not being able to move.'

'We are preventing pressure sores and contractures,' he said with immense patience. 'We've been over and over it.'

'They go over and over me,' snapped his patient. 'They keep pushing and pulling me. I'm public property. And I thought boarding school was bad. Huh.'

'You wouldn't want your legs and feet to curl up in claws, would you? We'll keep them straight and supple for you.'

Maria waved her fingers in front of her face and scowled, looking like a baby playing with its hands.

'We'll keep the rest of you in working order,' he said cheerfully, putting his hands in his pockets. 'It could be a lot worse. You're lucky, you know, a lesion at L3 means you'll be well able to stand and walk and lead a perfectly normal life.'

'Not real walking. A wheelchair isn't normal,' cried Maria frantically.

'You'll do some real walking and, sure, you'll have to use a wheelchair a lot of the time,' he said evenly. 'You are a normal, attractive, intelligent young woman. A wheelchair doesn't use you unless you let it.'

Maria, shocked, paralysed and as unmanageable as her own legs, fell from rage into depression and back to rage, and wasn't in the least convinced.

* * *

Everyone agreed that the best thing for Sadie to do after the tragedy was to go back to school and get on with everyday life. She went back obediently and tried to do as she was told, but she had terrible nightmares and migraines, and lost weight. The school staff, noting the change with concern, held a meeting to discuss what they should do.

'It's the shock, she'll get over it,' said Matron, who advocated carrying on as normal and letting Time heal everything.

'She doesn't concentrate,' said her housemistress worriedly. 'I'm not at all sure she should have come back to school. Who is responsible?'

'The court,' said the headmistress.

They talked it over, got nowhere, and agreed to consult the Welfare.

'Keep things as normal as possible,' said Jones-Carson, the childcare officer from Norfolk who had kept a distant eye on Sarah Carswell for years. Near retirement now, he had never done anything beyond the occasional check that she was where she should be, and the housemistress eyed him with intense suspicion. He was a shrivelled-looking man with a shrivelled-looking mouth and thick-lensed glasses that made his eyes bulge like a fish's. The housemistress, who thought that any sensible child would run away from him in fright, folded her arms in silent objection to his presence, and waited. They sat in conference in the headmistress' study. He tapped his briefcase with nicotine-stained fingers and delivered a surprisingly wise piece of advice, with which she entirely agreed.

'Perhaps it would be a good idea if Sarah went as often as it can be arranged to see Maria Giangelli.'

'*That*, at last, would be something normal,' remarked the housemistress under her breath. No one took any notice and no one had any better ideas, so at break-time they brought Sadie in and sat her on a wooden chair in the middle of them, and put it to her that she should go to visit Maria.

'She won't want to see me,' muttered Sarah Carswell, confronted by Jones-Carson's offer.

'Now look,' said the housemistress firmly, 'that's nonsense. Why ever wouldn't she want to see you? You're her best friend. Goodness, the two of you are like sisters.'

Because I'm alive and she's as good as dead, and her dad is dead, Sadie wanted to shout. Everyone is dead. All the time, in lessons and out, she suffered from a vague terror that if she started shouting, she wouldn't be able to stop, and everyone would stare at her with horrified, accusing faces. Sometimes at these moments she felt icy cold and her feet went numb. She caught the magnified eye of the Welfare man who looked like a herring. She hated him.

'I don't know,' she mumbled.

'The accident wasn't your fault, Sadie, none of it is anyone's fault. It's just something that happened and no one could help it,' he said, his crumpled little mouth opening and closing like perished rubber. She sat, tight-lipped, tightly controlled, taut with self-control.

'She doesn't want us to help,' muttered Matron.

'There are too many accidents,' Sadie heard herself say, the words coming out of her mouth of their own accord, as though a control button had suddenly switched itself off in her head. 'People I know have a lot of accidents, don't they? The ice broke.' She wished she could stop the words coming out, but she couldn't. 'That was two. Then I wasn't nice to Victoria, and that was three, and then Queenie, that was four, and Giovanni makes five, and Maria is six.'

'Those weren't all accidents,' cried the housemistress. 'Sarah, your aunts died of old age. It was natural and nothing to do with you or having accidents.'

'Who will be number seven?'

'Sarah,' said the headmistress warningly.

Jones-Carson drummed his fingers and pursed his lips meaningfully.

'Stop that *at once*,' ordered the housemistress. 'That's hysteria. There isn't going to be any number seven.'

The head took matters into her own hands.

'I think the best thing you can do is go and see Maria

Giangelli, stop imagining things are worse than they are, and get to grips with reality. Heaven knows, it's bad enough, but you're making it out to be worse.'

Sadie shook her head.

'She's dramatising,' remarked Matron, looking at Sadie critically. 'Aren't you, young lady?'

'She's not,' said the housemistress stoutly. 'She's got ideas in her head, and no wonder. I think she's very frightened.'

'We're a bit of a prima donna,' said Matron primly.

'That's decided, then,' said Jones-Carson, putting away the file he'd brought out of his briefcase. They hadn't needed it; the answer was plain. They decided to send Sadie to Islington for a week, assuming the Giangellis would welcome her.

'They'll get over it, people do,' said Matron, putting chairs back neatly against the wall.

The housemistress felt pleased that she'd never liked the woman in the first place.

Nonna took Sadie to see Maria. Rosalie had a dark-blue Capri which Nonna, her eyes just above the level of the steering wheel, drove with ferocious concentration, her face puckered with determination, muttering *a sinistra, a sinistra* all the way there.

'All the wrong way round,' she grumbled, smiling like a cherub as she cut other drivers up.

Sadie held her breath, felt sick and fought a pounding headache.

'Maria is a bad patient,' announced Nonna when they reached a straight stretch of road. Rain spattered the windscreen and the sound of the wipers going thump, thump, thump, thump seemed to go thump, thump, thump thump right inside Sadie's head.

'Is she?'

Sadie imagined Maria's long, lovely brown legs all pale and limp, like maggots, not working, and thought if it were her legs, she'd just want to die.

'She is angry,' Nonna went on, glaring in the mirror at

the driver of the car behind her, 'like Donald Campbell back there. They both are *frustrati*.'

Nonna trod on the accelerator and Donald Campbell, prepared to overtake, drew back, hooting in protest, as they came to a single white line in the middle of the road.

'Is Maria frustrated?' asked Sadie, who hadn't thought of it like that.

Ignoring the road, slicked wet by the brief downpour, Nonna turned sly black eyes on Sadie, took her hands off the steering wheel and waggled a finger.

'It is very, very good to be a bad patient.'

'Is it?' squeaked Sadie.

'When you are angry, you fight. You fight, you get better.' The car behind howled its horn as Rosalie's Capri danced across the middle of the road, free of all steering. Nonna pulled it sharply back into line, and turned to Sadie again. 'So. We help Maria be angry and fight.'

'Do we?' croaked Sadie, longing for her to slow down and let the man behind go past, because he kept hooting and driving too close and flashing his lights. 'That man wants to go past,' she suggested timidly.

Nonna waved dismissive hands in the air, leaving the steering wheel once more to its own devices. Sadie felt faint.

'And what about you?' demanded Nonna, gunning the car, leaving behind an outraged driver, cursing that he hadn't taken the Capri's number to report it.

'Pardon?' said Sadie weakly.

'Do you fight when life is bad, like Maria?' She leaned towards the windscreen and peered, muttering in Italian something about rain getting heavy again.

Sadie watched the wipers and wished Nonna would stop talking nonsense and concentrate on driving.

They slowed for a large junction. The driver behind shot past and pulled up for traffic lights, glaring through his passenger window at Nonna, his expression changing to amazement. A little old woman, not the leather-jacketed tearaway he'd expected. He grinned with embarrassment.

'*Buffone*,' Nonna mouthed, smiling sweetly through raindrops, revving the Capri.

'Oh,' moaned Sadie.

Nonna screeched away. 'You better be ready to fight with Maria, because Maria will fight with you,' she advised bluntly.

'I don't understand what you mean,' Sadie admitted bravely.

'*Bé*. Maria will get better, but she will not be able to walk. Then she will have a big, big fight, to prove she is as good as she was before, and as good as you.'

Sadie listened and watched the wipers going thump, thump, thump. Nonna's words began to make sense. Nonna gave her a sideways look and went on.

'She loves you like a sister.'

A scarlet blush ran up Sadie's cheeks into her hair, greyish in the light from the dashboard. Italians might talk so openly about being angry and loving people, but she wondered if Nonna knew that other people definitely didn't.

'And,' Nonna went on, 'she will not be sure you'll love her, without her legs. It might be hard for *Maria* to love herself without legs. One day she will, and then it will be all right.'

Nonna swung the steering wheel with a scream of tyres and the Capri skidded inside the hospital gates. It had rained very hard, here, and they heard trees dripping on the roof of the car.

'Are you *cattolica*?' demanded Nonna unexpectedly.

'No. I'm Church of England, and I have to go to assembly at school, but I don't go to church,' said Sadie, finding that confiding in Nonna was getting easier and easier.

'Ah, a pity. We Catholics are *so* good on guilt.'

Nonna parked neatly in the middle of two spaces and took the key from the ignition.

'I'm scared. I have nightmares,' Sadie's heart bumped in her chest at admitting it. 'I get panicky and then I get panicky about getting panicky, and I'm scared of cars,' she added. In for a penny, in for a pound. No one else talked like Maria's grandmother, and she didn't seem to mind if you said things that people at school would say were rude.

Nonna chuckled sympathetically.

'Maria and my driving make you feel bad, heh?'

'Very.'

Sadie felt light-headed at her own truthfulness.

Nonna's grin vanished as she pursued what was plain as a pikestaff; Sadie's grief.

'And my son dying,' she added gently.

'Yes,' whispered Sadie.

'So, we have let you down, heh?'

That was a shocking revelation, all back to front. *They* had let *her* down?

Nonna leaned over and took one of Sadie's cold, clammy hands in her own warm fingers, and rubbed it.

'You polite English people, you say *niente*. Stiff lips, eh? In Italy, we don't, how do you say, sweep under the carpet. We shout. Maria is Italian, she shouts.'

Nonna seemed to be telling her to shout. Shout what? Everyone said shouting was unladylike and shockingly bad manners. Sadie, bemused, opened the car door.

'Mind the puddles,' said Nonna.

Greetings and kissing over, Nonna wandered off down the Acute ward, papers folded back at the sports page under her arm, in search of a quiet corner in which to study form on the St Leger line-up. She fell by chance into intense conversation with a patient at the far end of the ward, thrown by a horse, breaking his neck. Deliberately, she left the girls together.

'Please, Maria,' begged Sadie, 'don't do that.'

Maria lay watching the rain on the windows, her eyes rolled up, refusing to speak. Then she began a steady dry sobbing. It was pouring again, rain sliding down panes of glass as constantly as the turning team's shoes marched up and down, up and down the long, shiny brown floor. Sadie gazed nervously up and down the row of beds, guiltily wishing Maria would stop. Beyond a glass partition at the far end of the ward were dozens of vases of flowers, crowded together. The claustrophobia of so many flowers crammed behind glass, the idea of all that scent, made Sadie's head ache harder than ever. She'd brought summer daisies and honeysuckle, thinking to please Maria with fresh summer blooms that would make her think of Rosalie's garden. No one had told her that there was no room for clutter of any kind in a spinal injuries ward.

'We take turns putting the vases at the front, so everyone gets a chance to look at their flowers,' explained the nurse, taking the bunch from her. 'They'd get in the way in here.'

They would, thought Sadie bleakly, waiting for Maria to calm down, watching the team who turned the patients going their rounds, ceaselessly. Every two hours, over and over, back, left side, right side, and back again, turning and turning, to prevent sores, the constant enemy, rotting holes in the flesh that could kill. Anything that got in the turning team's way was removed without ceremony. A nurse took the sheet from Maria's furious hands and clucked her tongue.

'Now then,' she said patiently, pulling the sheet into a creaseless shroud under and over Maria's body, 'no lumps and bumps. And you mustn't fidget like that. You know better.'

'Fidget,' screeched Maria, banging her head on the bed. 'I'm paralysed. How can a paraplegic person *fidget*?'

'Easily. The bottom half doesn't know what the top half's doing, and it's bad for both. Lie still or you'll do mischief. We'll have to put you straight again. Silly girl.'

'Uuuurgh,' snarled Maria, her back to Sadie, stuck that way since she'd been turned just before they arrived.

'I wish I hadn't come,' whispered Sadie miserably.

Maria rested her head exhaustedly on her freshly crumpled sheet.

'I can't move,' she said dully.

'You've just been thrashing around like anything,' Sadie pointed out.

'I can't move my legs,' snapped Maria.

'You can move quite a lot of things, much more than I thought you could, from what they say.'

'Huh.'

'Maria?'

After a long pause she just caught a grudging, 'What?'

'It's horrible at school without you.'

Maria's shoulders tightened.

Sadie flushed.

'I might as well be dead, anyway, why should I care?' mumbled Maria.

'That's horrible,' cried Sadie, outraged.

The shoulders twitched angrily.

The turning team passed by the end of the bed, with white, powdered hands, very short nails, strong, expert arms.

'You are being a pig,' hissed Sadie. 'How do you think it feels, with you in here, and not being able to do anything, and wishing and wishing that we could make it unhappen, or it be us instead of you, or, or . . .'

'That I was dead instead of a vegetable?'

'Shut up,' yelled Sadie, leaping from her chair. She marched to the far end of the ward, past the nurses' station, past rows of beds with occupants much stiller than Maria. She stood, leaning against the pale cream wall of the corridor, and trembled with misery indistinguishable from rage. Maria tortured them all with her implacable resentment, her furious self-pity, her needing to hurt. She tormented all of them. Sadie told Nonna what she had said, crying on the way home to Islington. Nonna told the others, who agreed it had gone on long enough. The Giangellis turned for help to Maria's doctor.

They perched in two rows in front of his desk, uneasy.

'She's impossible,' said Sissy, defining the problem and sitting in indignant silence for the rest of the interview.

'She's scared,' said Sadie. 'And I don't blame her.'

'She's sick,' said Mags primly, crossing stout legs. 'What do you expect?'

'Not so sick she can't spit and swear,' muttered Jove. 'I don't know what she learned at that school, but some of the language . . .'

'She's going on eighteen,' said the doctor, the consultant's second-in-command. 'She's a pretty young woman. Has she got a boyfriend?'

He looked, thought Sadie, like the photographs of her father; dark, with a creased, clever, kind face.

'We're not allowed to talk to boys, at school,' she told him, blushing.

'Her father was strict with her,' said Rosalie. 'She never had a boyfriend so far as I know.'

'Well, now. Maria can't feel her legs,' the doctor began to explain. 'Most young women in her situation start off thinking that if they haven't got any legs no one will love them or want to marry them. It's enough to make anyone angry and depressed and scared. On top of that, she's lost her father. It's perfectly normal that she'd react the way she does. Would you rather she turned into a nice quiet cabbage?'

He grinned expectantly. They sat in stunned silence, avoiding his eyes, ashamed that he'd used the very word they'd . . . He grinned inwardly. It usually hit the mark.

'But, you see,' he carried on, feeling their embarrassment, 'Maria can still do most things just as well as she could before. The few things she can't do we'll teach her to do differently. There's no need for all this worry.'

'You try making her believe any of that,' muttered Jove.

'I don't know what to do,' said Sadie, suddenly finding her tongue and speaking for all of them. 'I get really furious with her because she lies there being beastly to me, and all I want to do is help her, and she won't let me. Sometimes I feel like saying, oh, have it all your own way and goodbye. And then I feel awful.'

They let out a collective sigh and looked at the doctor hopefully.

'Bravo,' murmured Nonna, silently telling her beads, her lips barely moving, letting them all get on with it.

'That's just it,' said Rosalie.

'It is,' muttered Sissy acidly.

The doctor shrugged. 'Then do that. Yell back. Say what you feel.'

'It'd upset her,' said Mags, 'and she's upset enough.'

'You're all upset. Why are you here in my office? Because you're upset. Are you going to let Maria have a monopoly on upsetting people?'

'Well,' exclaimed Jove, '*that's* a new way of looking at it.'

'You think a paralysed person isn't a real person with manners any more? You're going to *patronise* her?' demanded the doctor, throwing out a challenge.

They shuffled guiltily.

'No,' said Michelangelo firmly. 'We're not.'

'Then go and put her in her place,' suggested the doctor cheerfully, 'if she needs it.'

'Strangle her,' murmured Rosalie, *sotto voce*.

'I wouldn't mind,' said Mags cheerfully. 'I bet we've all felt like it.'

They all laughed for the first time in weeks, and trooped off to visit Maria and put all that good advice into practice.

Chapter Nine

The first Christmas since the accident brought crisis for everyone, as Christmas often will. Sadie obediently practised the 'Hallelujah Chorus', crammed uncomfortably on to the stage in the school hall with fifty other girls, rehearsing for end-of-term Carols and Lessons, to which parents, along with the rest of the school, would come. She tried to sing, hardly sounding a note, after the rocking carol brought a painful lump to her throat. The thought of the carol service and no one of her own there in the audience made her heart ache. She missed the Giangellis painfully and was very unsure of what would happen to her next.

A Christmas tree twinkled in the school's great entrance hall, hung with glass baubles and glittering stars. Girls painted snowflakes on the windows of classrooms strung with paper chains, putting out red crêpe-paper post-boxes for the great Christmas card exchange. A crib beneath the tree had a tiny papier-mâché infant laid on hay, little model parents gazing down in china-painted adoration. Sadie loved to look at it. But while excited girls eddied around her, looking forward to going home, to holidays and gifts, she felt only loneliness, heavy like stone, smooth and polished from ceaseless, secret fingering.

Sadie was to go to Islington for Christmas, and that should have been exciting. Instead, she was frightened of what it would be like, of how she'd fit in. Because, on Christmas Eve, Maria was coming home, just for one day and one night, for Christmas. It was all anyone talked about, Maria's coming home. The Islington house was being turned upside down for her. Nothing was too much trouble, too much effort, to get things ready and comfortable and welcoming for Maria. The more demanding Maria was, the more she showed she needed them by being impossibly needy, noisy and impatient, the more they loved her. Sadie, quiet, obedient and asking nothing, knew Rosalie and Nonna forgot her, because she had two legs, and wasn't sick, and didn't shout and yell and order everyone to love her. She just wanted them to, and wished they did, but they seemed to notice no one but Maria. Mother Mary in the crib seemed to move as Sadie's eyes blurred with tears.

When they found her bed empty and not slept in on the bright December morning of the last day of term, the headmistress raised the alarm.

'Where would she have gone?' asked the dour policeman summoned from the nearby town.

'Islington. The Giangellis, but she isn't there. I have no idea where else she'd go,' answered the headmistress.

'I have,' said the housemistress who had followed Sadie all through her school years, and knew much more about her than anyone else.

'Well?' snapped the headmistress, mortified at possible scandal and its effect on fees.

'Try Ditchwell,' said the housemistress softly, hiding her contempt.

Ditchwell's village policeman and Mary Llewellyn found Sadie trying to prise off the boarding on the cottage in the salt marshes. Dead leaves and dry stumps of neglected fruit canes lay damp and rotting among tall weeds, leafless brambles and stiff, sharp grass that crept up from the sand dunes on to what had once been the aunts' vegetable patch. The still, cold air carried the sound of her hammering to their ears with perfect clarity, as they hurried across from the village.

'Thank God we've found you. Everyone's been looking all over for you,' said Mary, standing in the weedy path, handing Sadie a key. 'Here, I brought it when they said did I know where you might be. I thought if you were here, you'd want to go in. You don't have to take the place apart.'

'She can't . . .' began the policeman.

'For goodness' sake,' snapped Mary, who had known him when he was in short trousers. 'She can look.'

'You've caused a lot of worry, young lady,' said the policeman, saving face.

'I didn't mean to,' she said unhappily.

Sadie stood and stared at the ground, her shoulders slumped in a green school raincoat. Mary took the key back from her, and opened the front door, as she made no move to do it herself. Inside was dank and stale. What few bits of furniture were left were sheeted and the place smelled sourly of mice. It was dark, wintry grey light coming dully from the open door.

'I don't know why I've come here,' Sadie said apologetically.

'Is something wrong at school?' asked Mary, peering around in the gloom. The cottage was tidy. When she had cleared it, after the aunts died, Mary had been meticulous. Now it was in added gloom, as spiders had sheeted the deep-set windows with webs through which little light could pass.

'No. There's nothing wrong at school.'

'I think,' Mary told the policeman, 'that you could go away and come back to my cottage later on and we'll see what we're going to do. She isn't going to run away. Are you?'

'There isn't anywhere to run away to,' said Sadie, beginning to shiver.

'There's a warm kitchen and a cup of tea and me,' said Mary. 'How about starting with that?'

'I'll let them know she's here, seeing as she's with you, Miss Llewellyn, though by rights she should come down to the station,' said the policeman, and they listened to his footsteps, fading quickly on the soft earth of the track.

'What has happened?' asked Mary, when he'd gone.

Sadie sat down on the edge of the leaning old sofa and told her about Giovanni and Maria Theresa.

'This is dreadful,' said Mary. 'I wish I had known.'

'No one talks to me,' confessed Sadie. 'Sometimes I wish I was in a wheelchair, so they'd be sorry. Then I feel sorry, because that's a wicked thing to wish.'

She rubbed one of Queenie's crocheted blankets between her hands, longing painfully for the old days, to go back to childhood and the ancient aunts, to have everything changed, the painful times wiped out.

'You are so very young,' murmured Mary, seeing the loneliness in the face she could just make out in the half-light from the door. Gulls wheeled overhead, screaming, and a patch of dead bulrushes rattled in a sudden little gust of wind from the sea.

'I'm not that young,' said Sadie. 'I have to leave school and earn a living soon. I'm seventeen years old. But I don't know what to do.'

'What do you want to do?'

'I wish I could come back and stay here.'

Mary shook her head and looked round the damp old walls. 'They'll never let you do that. You're a ward of court until you're twenty-one. You can't come here and live on your own.'

'This is *mine*,' murmured Sadie, stroking the old horse-hair sofa.

Oh dear, I was always afraid of this, thought Mary, waiting.

'Why won't they let me stay here?'

'It would be hopelessly impractical and probably not good for you. You're too young and this place isn't liveable.'

'Nowhere feels liveable,' said Sadie.

'I'm not surprised you're unhappy, but running away here isn't the answer.'

'I thought you'd understand, but you don't.'

She got up and went to the door, leaning on the old door jamb, her shoulders hunched angrily, facing up the track towards the village. Relieved to be out of the old cottage,

Mary locked the door behind them and with Sadie dragging sullenly behind, they walked back across the dyke to the village.

After tea and cake and a warm, crackling fire that smelled of pine cones, the rest of the story came tumbling out. An indignant Mary Llewellyn rang Rosalie.

'They've found Sadie in Norfolk,' Rosalie said, her hand over the receiver. 'She ran away back to her aunts' cottage by the sea. This is that teacher she used to know, on the phone. She says she's got Sadie with her.'

'*Mamma mia*,' cried Nonna. She grabbed her rosary and started to protest in rapid Italian, her eyes closed.

Rosalie went on listening to Mary's slow Norfolk voice, her face a study in surprise and dismay.

'We've had the school ringing up every five minutes since last night,' she said. 'We never thought of her going back to Norfolk.'

'Someone hasn't been thinking enough,' answered Mary acidly. 'This child is eating her heart out for a bit of love, and none of us have noticed.'

Rosalie knew that it was kind of Miss Llewellyn to say *us* when she meant *you*.

'What should we do for the best, do you think?' asked Rosalie.

Nonna muttered and clacked her beads and shouted at whoever was at the other end of Rosalie's ear to send her home at once.

'My mother-in-law says she should come home,' relayed Rosalie down the receiver.

'I think the trouble is, if you don't mind my being blunt, that she doesn't know if it is home. If you see what I mean. And it isn't really fair, I know, because Sadie tells me your daughter is badly injured. It's only because you've been so kind to her that Sadie thinks of you as family. She could always come here to me, though, if things are quite impossible.'

'We . . .' began Rosalie, but Mary went on.

'I'm afraid Sadie rather presumes on you but she has no real right.'

'She says Sadie presumes,' Rosalie told Nonna, puzzled.

'What does she presume?' she asked, frowning at the telephone.

'We don't quite understand.'

Nonna snatched the receiver.

'*Pronto*,' she snapped.

'I beg your pardon,' said Mary.

'Never mind all those *poliziotti* and that school,' Nonna ordered. 'Tell that silly girl to come home.'

'She might not want to,' said Rosalie, thinking for the first time how things must look to someone who wasn't here all the time. A pile of handrails lay against the wall, waiting to be put in the shower room they'd had built for Maria, on the ground floor. The plasterer hadn't turned up and they weren't ready. A hospital bed stood in the dining room and the turkey lay half defrosted on the draining board, its giblets glued inside it by ice so Rosalie couldn't get it stuffed and in the oven. Eight Giangellis plus their assorted children were coming for Christmas dinner, to be with Maria. They'd eat squashed into the kitchen because the dining table was on its side on the upstairs landing, to be out of the wheelchair's way. A commode sat in the hall, waiting to be installed in the dining room, making everyone snigger and crack terrible jokes that Maria must never hear. Rosalie's life, like her house, was upside down and now Nonna was holding the telephone, eyebrows raised haughtily in the way she had when she didn't quite grasp what was being said. Rosalie sighed and felt martyred by forces beyond her control.

'The school and that wretched childcare man have been ringing up, wanting to know what on earth is going on,' Mary continued crossly. 'No one seems to have noticed she's still shocked after that terrible accident. I'm sorry to say so, because it must be dreadful for all your family, but I've got her sitting here and she has been crying her eyes out about it all, and I think you ought to know.'

'I notice,' said Nonna flatly, her English not quite so

good on the telephone. 'There is a lot of things to notice when you got a son dead, a granddaughter sick, a widow and a little girl 'oo is scared. I told her what I notice.'

Mary sighed.

'It sounds as though you'd like her back, in spite of everything,' she said.

'Tell her to come home *pronto*,' ordered Nonna.

'They want you to go back,' Mary said to Sadie, sitting by the fire. Outside it was dark with the dense, complete darkness of unlit countryside, and the cold sky twinkled brilliantly with stars, threatening a hard frost that night.

'*Sì*?' shouted Nonna down the phone.

'I'm sure she will. After Christmas,' said Mary. 'We'll ring you again.'

Sitting hugging her knees by the fire, Sadie felt safe. Mary held the receiver, raising her eyebrows to ask if that was all right, before she rang off. Mary Llewellyn looked so strong and kind and *safe*. Sadie nodded gratefully.

After all the excitement, Christmas Day was bright and cold and very quiet. Bells rang out across the flat countryside for morning service, and people walked briskly, bright-cheeked, their breath coming white. Sadie and Mary walked on the dunes after lunch, well wrapped up. They went right down to the edge of a flat grey sea, the tide far out down the vast, wet beach.

'I don't want to go back to school, I hate it,' said Sadie, wading in borrowed wellingtons into the shallow edge of the water.

'You should go back. You need to get qualifications. Why don't you go to university? Your mother did.'

'I'm not clever enough. I want to get a job.'

'Then staying here is a bad idea. There's no work round here. King's Lynn is full of people who have no jobs.'

They skirted round some rocks and small deep pools and walked on, two tiny figures between the vastness of beach and sky.

'I wished I was dead, at school,' said Sadie.

'You shouldn't think, or say, things like that,' answered Mary, shocked.

'Maria does. She says things like that all the time.'

'Just because Maria Giangelli behaves badly doesn't mean you should do it, too,' snapped Mary.

They came to more rocks, thickly covered with sharp, dark-blue mussel shells, and perched on the edge, their faces to the sea.

'Do *you* ever get lonely, Miss Llewellyn, all by yourself?'

'Good heavens, yes,' said Mary, surprised. 'But I'm mostly too busy to notice. Why do you ask?'

Sadie went bright pink.

'I wondered if I could stay and live with you?'

Mary looked at her sharply, then smiled and said more gently, 'There are a lot of reasons why that isn't a good idea, but you can come and stay as often as you want, as long as you want. But I think a better life for you is in London.'

'I suppose I'd better go back the day after tomorrow, then, hadn't I? Will that childcare man let me stay?'

'In Islington? I think so.'

'And get a job and not go back to school?'

'I suppose they can't force you,' admitted Mary reluctantly.

They got off their rock and turned back along the darkening beach.

'I'm glad I ran away. It's sorted things out.'

Mary eyed her dubiously.

'Don't make a habit of it. In future, ask, because you worried everyone to death.'

Sadie gave a sunny smile and with their backs to a freshening wind and the incoming tide, they walked over the great, flat beach towards the lights coming on all over the village.

Chapter Ten

When she got back from Norfolk, all the misunderstandings ironed out, plans laid for the future, Sadie found the house in Islington looking as though a bomb had hit it. A dismembered metal bed and its mattress, a mahogany commode and a pillowcase stuffed with linen waiting for the laundry cluttered the hall when she arrived four days after Maria went back to the spinal injuries unit. The tree's lights winking on and off in the lounge and cards cluttering every surface were all that remained of Christmas. Those, and the cold remains of turkey in the fridge, which Rosalie looked at gloomily and said did Sadie fancy it in tinned curry sauce because she hadn't got round to going shopping and it was all they had.

'You could mince it,' suggested Nonna.

'Can't be bothered,' answered Rosalie. 'How was Norfolk?'

'Norfolk was lovely,' said Sadie. 'I'd forgotten how lovely. I don't mind turkey curry.'

'I do. That curry stuff is horrible. I don't know why I suggested it. Anyway, I've aired your room,' said Rosalie. 'It's a pity you missed Maria.'

'She needed a lot of stuff, if the hall's anything to go by.'

'Stuff is going to be a way of life. Half of it went back with her, and those men still haven't put the rails in. We had to put her on and off the loo because there's nothing to hold on to. That commode was a waste of time. I spent ages getting hold of it and then she says she'd sooner die than sit on it. How about turkey omelette?'

'She's all right, then?' asked Sadie cautiously.

Nonna grabbed the dish of dismembered turkey from

Rosalie's indifferent hands and began picking meat off bones.

'She's bossy and impatient and we all ran round her like a stirred-up ants' nest. I'm shattered,' said Rosalie grimly.

'She came to Mass,' said Nonna happily. 'Get the eggs, Sadie, and there are mushrooms in the salad box.'

'Mind you,' admitted Rosalie, 'she's not as much hard work as I thought. But she *will* do everything for herself, and it takes such ages.'

'*Ma che ingrate che sei*!' muttered Nonna.

'It was you who was frightened she'd be a cabbage, and now she's not, you're complaining,' said Sadie. 'That's not fair.'

'Am I complaining?' sighed Rosalie. 'I don't mean to. I'm glad you're back, Sadie, though goodness knows what we're going to do. Between you and Maria, I'm going grey.'

'What you're going to do is beat eggs and slice mushrooms,' said Nonna firmly, handing Rosalie a whisk.

Sadie set three places at the old pine kitchen table. The smell of hot butter, garlic and tarragon filled the room and the pan sizzled as Nonna poured in a stream of beaten egg and began to stir with a wooden spatula. She added a handful of cut-up turkey and let it cook. Slicing brown bread, her mouth watering, Sadie watched her standing at the stove in a big red pinafore, black sleeves rolled up to her elbows, ebony beads hanging from her waist, gold links catching the light.

'It was nice to see Miss Llewellyn, but I am glad I've come back,' she said, chewing a bit of brown crust.

'I don't know what it was all about, and I'm not going to pry,' said Rosalie. 'Let's just get on with getting on.'

Nonna sliced omelette on to three warm plates. 'What are you going to do now?' she asked.

'Get a job.'

'What kind of job?' asked Rosalie. 'You could go into the salon. Do reception. We need good people,' she added hopefully.

'I was thinking more of doing social work,' said Sadie.

Rosalie pulled the cork from a bottle of wine and filled their glasses.

'All right. Let's drink to that,' she said. 'Here's to our girls, in the New Year, and here's hoping you're well and happy, perishing nuisances that you are.' She finished her toast with a grin.

Sadie found tears in her eyes.

'Eat,' ordered Nonna heartlessly. 'Don't waste good food, crying.'

Sadie did as she was told.

'Social work?' said Nonna, picking up the question after they had eaten, mopping egg from her plate with bread.

'Why do you want to do that? I should think it's hard work,' said Rosalie.

'It would be interesting. I'd like helping people, and you can do it without having to go to college or anything. They'll train you on the job.'

Rosalie refilled their glasses and said wouldn't it be all down-and-outs.

'It's not all down-and-outs,' said Sadie. 'It's people with problems. All kinds.'

'People with problems give me a headache. We've got enough of our own, I'd have thought,' remarked Rosalie.

'Maria is not a problem,' said Nonna firmly.

'I have to earn a living,' Sadie said. 'That's the way I'll try to do it.'

'I've gone back to the salon,' said Rosalie. 'Giovanni left a good bit, but not so as I can retire like Lady Muck.'

'Lady . . . ?' muttered Nonna, mystified.

'You should show us how to make our fortunes on the horses,' said Rosalie, laughing. 'Do you win much?'

Nonna wiggled her hand in a gesture that said, win some, lose some.

'We could make a syndicate.' suggested Sadie. 'Like they do on the pools.'

'Pools,' snorted Nonna contemptuously. 'Pools is no skill.'

'Social work it is, then,' sighed Sadie. 'Shame.'

'First, you do the dishes,' ordered Rosalie.

'Now I know I'm really home.' Sadie pushed back her chair.

'Maybe I teach you something,' said Nonna, as if making a concession.

'What?' asked Sadie, putting on an apron.

'We go racing when Maria comes home. A day out and I show you what to do.'

'Ascot, hats and Maria on wheels. She'll love it,' cried Rosalie. 'Can I come, for a giggle?'

Nonna pursed her mouth. Betting was no giggling matter.

'Well, pardon me for speaking,' said Rosalie, getting up to dry dishes.

Behind her back Nonna pulled a face and winked at Sadie.

'You, me and Maria,' she mouthed.

Sadie, grinning, put a soapy hand up to her face so that Rosalie couldn't see, and winked back.

Chapter Eleven

On a cold, sunny February day in 1969, Maria came home from hospital for good. Shortly before that, Sadie found herself a job as a social worker and started eagerly out on adult life, her enthusiasm undimmed by working in discouraging premises. In a particularly run-down part of the East End a single-storey concrete building with rusting black metal windows housed the Mental Welfare Department where Sadie was to work. It stood on a corner between two busy roads, anything green and growing ruthlessly suppressed by petrol fumes, and a large expanse of grey concreted car park surrounded by a chain-link fence. New members of staff were told, not entirely jokingly, that it kept the mental welfare officers in, but failed to keep the public out.

She had her interview for the job in January. There were a lot of questions, and then Duncan Armstrong, Chief Mental Welfare Officer, put his patched elbows on the table, leaned towards her and asked in a strong Glaswegian accent, 'Why do you want to do this kind of work?'

There were three of them on the other side of the table. Duncan, she had met before for an informal chat, and could barely understand him. He was near retirement, shabbily dressed, and enjoyed a biting sense of humour. Beside him sat a Medical Officer of Health who sported a nervous tic that made Sadie's cheek jump in sympathy, and on his other side was a very overweight red-haired woman in pale-blue crimplene, whose name and function Sadie failed to catch. She was too busy being nervous at the introductions stage.

'I like people,' she said, realising too late that it sounded naïve. 'I think I'd like helping them.'

'Why?' demanded the crimplene woman in a reedy voice that belied her size.

'Pardon?' said Sadie, at a loss as to what she meant.

'Why do you like people?' Duncan filled in helpfully.

'I don't know,' Sadie said, feeling she was digging a pit into which she was about to fall, and emerge jobless. 'I just do.'

Three pairs of eyes scrutinised her.

'Well, I think I do,' she said, making things worse.

'A lot of the people who come here are pretty unlikeable,' Duncan said casually. 'How will you deal with that?'

'Oh. Are they?' squeaked his victim, nonplussed.

'Our job is to do what we can for people who are often mad, bad, miserable, manipulative, shifty, demanding and ungrateful. They break appointments, tell lies, and rarely say thank you if we get things right. Can you cope with that?' he demanded.

'They can't all be horrid,' protested Sadie.

The crimplene woman snorted loudly, got out a handkerchief and blew her nose deafeningly. They waited until she'd finished.

'Not horrid, Miss Carswell, disturbed and difficult,' said the medical officer, glaring at Duncan. 'It isn't our job to be judgemental.'

'Sure it isn't,' he agreed affably. 'But I still would like to know how you'll deal with such people, Miss Carswell. If you think people are likeable, you might be in for a shock.'

Sadie gazed at the floor and considered.

'I've got a friend,' she began, 'a kind of adopted sister, who has been paralysed in a car crash. She had to stay in hospital for ages and ages and she was hateful about it. If I'd known her only in hospital, I wouldn't have liked her at all. But I knew she was only being horrible because of what had happened, and it was hard for her to cope. I should think that even nice people are all the things you just said, if they have enough bad luck.'

The medical officer beamed and capped his pen. Duncan guffawed and leaned his chair back so far Sadie thought he'd fall off it.

'Wet behind the ears but of the right stuff. Miss Carswell, we'll be happy to have you, if you'll have us,' he bellowed, and stood up to shake her by the hand with a paw like a vice. Sadie was massaging her fingers when the crimplene woman shook the copy of Sadie's application on the table in front of her.

'One more question,' she piped. 'What effect on you do you think it's had, losing your parents at such a young age, and really having to make your way alone?'

'What effect?' asked Sadie, surprised.

The woman nodded, as if expecting her to go on.

'I don't think it has. I don't really think about it.'

'Ah. You don't think about it?'

'No.'

They stared at her. The medical officer said, 'Would you like to wait outside, Miss Carswell, while we have a word?'

Sadie stood in a shabby corridor with windows and a bench down one side, watching a biting north wind blowing old newspapers beneath the wheels of passing buses. A tramp rooted in an overflowing bin fastened to a bus stop, a balaclava pulled over his face making him look not quite human.

'No,' said the crimplene woman, who was a psychiatrist pulled in for the interview because no one else was available. 'I think there could be an underlying disturbance that could make difficulties for her and for clients.'

Duncan drummed his fingers on the table impatiently. 'We have enough trouble attracting staff. We'll deal with problems in supervision and training,' he growled.

'I think she'll be very good,' put in the medical officer.

The crimplene woman frowned. 'I shall record my doubts but I won't veto the appointment. After all, I suppose there is no history, is there?'

'No history,' said Duncan.

She put her large, square-nailed fingers on the table and rose.

'Don't say I didn't warn you if she gets into trouble.'

Duncan gave an exaggerated sigh and she bridled angrily. They had disliked each other happily for years.

'I take it we've made a decision?' he said sarcastically.

'Call her in,' snapped the psychiatrist.

'You're hired, Miss Carswell,' bellowed Duncan down the corridor, deliberately annoying the woman behind him. 'Come on in.'

The wind moaned through the thin walls and as a lorry went by, they shook. Lights not on, the place was half dark.

'I'm hired?' Sadie said, coming forwards into the light from the interview room.

He looked over his shoulder and turned back, grinning.

'Don't let them bug you, it's all right,' he muttered, then opened the door wide and ushered her back in.

'Welcome aboard,' he said jovially. 'Eventually we'll have better premises, when someone decides to spend some money. We're waiting for Seebohm to reorganise us.'

Sadie wondered if Seebohm was an interior decorator or some kind of administrative clerk. She wanted to hug herself with excitement; these were things she'd be finding out.

Maria, preoccupied with being home again, had to work hard at daily life. She began to adjust, painfully. As things got easier, she had more time on her hands, was bored, became jealous of Sadie's work. It sounded important; Sadie had power, was sometimes called out at night to do mysterious, powerful things.

'How do you stand it?' Maria demanded one morning, having heard the telephone go in the night.

'Stand what?' said Sadie.

Maria wrinkled her nose.

'Batty people. Loony bins.'

'I love it.'

'I wouldn't like to get up at two in the morning

to take some nutcase to hospital. Why do you have to?'

Just give me the chance, is what you mean, thought Sadie.

'I have to sign the section,' she explained. 'A section is when you put someone in hospital and they won't go voluntarily.'

'That's stupid,' sniffed Maria derisively. 'No one wants to go to hospital. If they do, they must be mad.'

'The mad ones are the ones who don't want to go.'

'That's back to front,' announced Maria, frowning.

'If someone doesn't know what they're doing, or is senile, you have to tell them what to do,' argued Sadie. 'Don't you?' she insisted anxiously, when Maria just narrowed her eyes and looked thoughtful. 'You can't leave people to starve, or harm themselves.'

'I wanted to die when I knew my legs weren't going to work ever again.'

'There you are, then,' said Sadie, vindicated.

'No, I'm not. I knew exactly what I wanted. I just changed my mind, later. If I'd put a plastic bag over my head, it would have been just what I wanted, at the time.'

'You have to have the last word,' snapped Sadie.

Maria smiled angelically. Sadie sometimes wondered uneasily if things weren't all back to front, and that Maria might be right, knowing better than social work theorists what real choices the deprived and disadvantaged faced.

Chapter Twelve

Nonna showed no sign of going back to Italy. Rosalie went back to work in the salon. Sadie worked long hours, often coming home from meetings after supper. The Seebohm Report had changed everything.

'We've all had to give up being mental welfare officers, or childcare officers,' said Sadie, 'and be just social workers. We all do everything. It's exciting.'

'Exciting puts dark lines under your eyes,' remarked Rosalie. 'You look tired.'

'Duncan has resigned. Some people don't like change,' said Sadie.

'There's change and there's change,' Maria pointed out. 'Look at me.'

'I do,' said Sadie, 'and you look wonderful.'

'I do not,' snapped Maria.

'I've got reports to write,' said Sadie, refusing to argue.

'I'll do the dishes,' said Rosalie.

'*We'll* do the dishes,' retorted Nonna, giving Maria's chair a sharp tug. 'Madame can dry.'

Rosalie listened to them clattering in her kitchen. Maria and Nonna spent a lot of time on their own. It was high time, thought Rosalie, that Maria came out of purdah, got on with living, like everyone else, and found herself a job. Rosalie, fiercely lonely for Giovanni, sighed and went to help in the kitchen.

The following afternoon Maria lay on her side and angled a hand mirror so that she could get a good look at her bottom.

'Oh, for French knickers,' she sighed, examining her skin with minute care, as she had been taught to do every day in the spinal injuries unit. 'Silk ones. I'd give anything. Is that a bit red, do you think? Just there.'

Nonna, used to the daily ritual of Maria's skin care, bent creaky knees and looked closely at her granddaughter's unblemished derrière.

'No.'

'Thanks.'

Nonna handed her a pair of cotton briefs. 'Why shouldn't you wear French knickers?'

'Why should I?' snapped Maria, pushing her waist-length black hair out of her eyes. 'Who cares what kind of knickers I wear? No point tarting your bum up when you can't feel it and all you do is sit on it all day. All anyone's interested in is whether it's got patches turning into pressure sores. Charming. No one could care less whether it's pretty.'

Nonna looked critical.

'Well, they don't,' Maria said sulkily. 'Do they?'

'That young man who fell off his horse made big eyes in the hospital.'

'Dennis-who-fell-off-his-horse doesn't count,' Maria snapped.

Nonna stopped folding clothes, put the bundle in a drawer and folded her arms. Maria sat up, half dressed, and pushed her legs over the edge of the bed. Nonna's black eyes were hard as nails.

'What've I done now?' demanded Maria, seeing her expression.

'Why doesn't he count?'

Maria banged the side up on her wheelchair and refused to answer.

'Because he's in one of those,' shouted Nonna, waving her arms angrily. 'And so are you.'

'Thanks for reminding me,' snapped Maria.

Nonna pounced, shaking an enraged finger in front of Maria's nose.

'Don't you dare,' she roared. 'Don't you dare talk like that. If you look down on that young man because he is crippled, you look down on yourself.'

Maria thudded herself into her chair and grabbed Nonna's arm unsteadily.

'Don't you ever, *ever* use that word,' she hissed. 'I'm not a *cripple*.'

'Cripple-*talk*, Maria. *Non hai altro che autocommiserazione*, Maria.'

'I am not full of self-pity,' shrieked Maria.

'*Sì*.' Nonna's finger jabbed again.

'No.'

Nonna stepped back and planted her hands squarely on very square hips.

'*Va bene allora*,' she said softly. 'Giovanni left you some money, heh?'

'What's Dad got to do with it?' demanded Maria, rearranging herself angrily, finishing dressing.

'Because,' hissed Nonna, shaking her fist, 'now we go to 'Arrods and spend some.'

Maria stared at her little tub-shaped grandmother.

'Whatever on?' she demanded rudely. 'A dozen black Italian grandmother outfits? Harrods say they sell everything but I doubt there's much call for them.'

Nonna threw Maria's shoes into her lap, whirled the chair round and headed for the front door.

'Hey,' yelled Maria. 'I'm not ready.'

'I am,' bellowed Nonna, racing the chair down the newly built ramp and pulling up with a jolt by Rosalie's Capri. 'Get in.'

'*What for?*' howled Maria, landing in a heap on the back seat.

Nonna, lifting her legs in after her, yelled, 'Knickers.'

A passer-by looked round, startled.

Maria lay still and thought about it, and a grin spread over her face. Nonna, banging the folded wheelchair into the boot, heard her giggle.

'A dozen French silk knickers,' said Nonna bossily, putting the key in the ignition.

'You can't park near Harrods. It'll be an awful palaver with the chair,' gasped Maria, struggling upright.

'I park near 'Arrods.' Nonna drew away from the kerb with a squeal.

'Oh, God, let anyone try to stop you. Nonna, will you please go slower, you're scaring me stiff.'

Nonna parked just on the corner of Hans Crescent and the Brompton Road. A traffic warden moved from her surveillance post just by a Harrod's entrance. Nonna hopped out, opened the boot and pulled out Maria's chair.

'They can get past,' she said haughtily, looking up and down the overcrowded street. A chauffeur-driven limousine veered past and blocked the road completely, disgorging Arabs into Harrods.

The warden opened her mouth to protest.

'If you dare, you write your ticket,' said the small round woman in black. 'Get out, Maria.'

'It's triple lines on a corner. You can't possibly,' protested the warden reasonably.

'If you have no heart, may God forgive you.' Nonna propped Maria in the chair and clutched her cardigan just over her left breast.

'*Uffa*.'

'You all right?' asked the warden.

Nonna gazed at her reproachfully and considered her to be justly employed, in shape closely resembling a parking meter; all long thin legs in monstrous lace-ups and great pigeon chest.

'*Mi fa male qui*.' She beat gently on her breast. 'But the child . . . Our Lady will bless your *gentilezza* to the child,' she shook her head mournfully and her voice hardened, 'but I think She will not forgive your *multa per sosta vietata*.'

Maria fussed with her cushions, hiding her scarlet face. 'Parking ticket. Italian,' she muttered hysterically, seeing the warden's baffled face.

'*Ebbene, andiamo*,' said Nonna breezily.

'Let's go.' Maria struggled to keep her face straight.

'Poor child, so little time,' mouthed Nonna, rolling her eyes tragically at the warden, charging with Maria's chair at a goods entrance. Open-mouthed, the woman watched them manoeuvre and disappear into the store. While they shopped, she stood guard over the Capri, in case anyone tried to give them a ticket.

Maria's lap was piled high with boxes and parcels.

'Twelve knickers, three lace bras, heels and a parrot,' crowed Nonna with satisfaction, hurtling out of the goods entrance.

The traffic warden stared at the tall cage balanced on the arm of Maria's chair and asked, did it talk.

'It's rude,' cried Maria, 'aren't you?'

She shook the parrot gently in its cage and it hopped angrily along its perch and screeched.

'It is an Irish parrot,' said Nonna, leaning on the Capri and admiring the bird.

'How do you know?' asked the warden seriously. 'I never knew they had parrots in Ireland.'

A Harrods doorman wandered up and stood with his hands behind his back, watching the stream of taxis edging round the Capri.

'In zoos,' he said, worldly-wise.

'Ah,' said the warden, enlightened.

Maria poked her finger through the cage and the bird snapped at it viciously.

'He's got a vile temper. That's why your owner called you bad names and sold you, isn't it, Polly?'

'You can't call a he *Polly*,' remarked the doorman. 'What bad names?'

Maria went bright red.

'Fooka,' said Nonna impassively.

'Fooka the Irish parrot,' choked Maria, hysterical again. 'He opened his beak in the pet department and squawked and the saleswoman nearly died. He was dancing up and down screeching, with this drop-dead look in his eye, and suddenly he shouts this word. They said he thinks it's his name because he's so revolting his owner called him it all the time. But he's sweet, aren't you, Fooka?'

The parrot snapped his beak loudly and glared.

The warden looked disapproving and wandered off, peering hopefully at meters. Nonna went round and opened the boot.

'I got some lovely high heels,' said Maria, planting Fooka's cage on the pavement.

The middle-aged doorman looked down at Maria's feet.

'High heels? Irish parrots, certainly, but if you don't mind my asking – heels?'

'Why not?'

He raised his eyebrows.

'You don't have to go dancing to like heels.'

'Absolutely not,' he said earnestly.

'That bird can go in the back,' muttered Nonna to herself, opening doors. 'Rosalie gets psittacosis. Big trouble, that bird.'

'I wedge them behind the footrests and they stop my legs jumping. Practical and pretty.' She pulled loose trousers up a pair of very slim ankles.

'Oh, yes,' he said solemnly, 'very, very pretty.'

Maria beamed and handed him her parcels while she pulled herself into the car.

'Good luck to you both,' he said, handing her Fooka and shutting her door. The parrot screamed and subsided sulkily into a corner of his cage, closing his eyes, dismissing them all. Nonna watched the doorman's back convulse in laughter as she started the engine.

'He fancied me,' said Maria.

'*Basta, basta*. Cripples I don't hear about no more. *Progresso*, eh?' muttered Nonna happily.

Fooka gave a last, outraged shriek, snapped his beak, then huddled in sullen silence for the rest of the journey home.

Chapter Thirteen

A year passed. Maria learned shorthand and typing from a correspondence course and sometimes helped out in the salon, doing reception work. Nonna went twice to Italy for brief spells, and came back. Sadie worked harder than ever and the Giangellis settled once again into the kind of routine that they had thought was gone forever. They needed, thought Nonna, a bit of excitement.

'I have tickets,' announced Nonna one Saturday, pulling an envelope out of one of her many capacious black pockets.

'What tickets?' asked Sadie, busy ironing. 'Parking, by any chance?'

'You should be a policewoman, heh, you so law-abiding,' Nonna tucked in her round chin and looked mischievous, opening her envelope.

Sadie shook out a miniskirt, slid it over the end of the ironing board and said the uniform did nothing for your legs.

'Huh,' snorted Nonna, eyeing the short skirt.

Maria, trying to learn to knit, ignored references to legs, and concentrated on knit one, purl one, slip one, as she sat by the window, her profile outlined against the afternoon light filtering through Rosalie's nets. She planted her needles in her lap with exasperation and complained, 'It's no good, the stitches keep dropping themselves. What tickets?'

'Royal Ascot,' said Nonna triumphantly. 'We go to the races for Maria's birthday.' She flourished her envelope and began to hum 'Happy Birthday to You'.

'Don't you have to be posh to go to Royal Ascot?'

asked Sadie, holding up her steaming iron to see the water level.

'Huh, I bought them at Christmas. You get in quick, anyone can go.'

'Hats,' cried Maria, abandoning her knitting. 'Ascot is hats. We'll wear posh hats.'

'I haven't got a hat. They don't suit me. I look like a gnome,' grumbled Sadie, filling her iron.

'Not so much a gnome, more a wet blanket.'

'Some of us have to work for a living,' snapped Sadie, stung. 'We can't all swan around when we feel like it.'

Maria pulled a mocking face and Sadie shook her iron angrily, steam hissing from its vents.

'Well,' she added, a bit shamefaced, 'if you had a job, you wouldn't be able to, either.'

'I'll get a job,' said Maria airily.

'You ought to do what that Disablement man told you.'

Maria turned away from the window, wheeled round smartly and looked Sadie squarely in the face.

'Don't *ever* social work *me*,' she said evenly.

'I'm not.'

'Then don't.'

'She is only twenty,' said Nonna, to keep the peace.

'I'm only twenty and a half,' Sadie said. 'But I had to get on with it. Just because she's in a wheelchair doesn't mean she can't work.'

The atmosphere crackled.

'Is not so easy for Maria,' said Nonna softly, forbidding further talk.

'But that's why . . .'

'*No.*'

Sadie flushed, rejected.

'We'll go shopping,' cried Maria, perking up.

'You take it all for granted,' Sadie protested.

'You can take things for granted, too, if you want,' Maria pointed out. 'Whatever you choose.'

'We buy a dress. A dress for a princess,' said Nonna, determined to pour oil on troubled waters. 'What's that place has long dresses?'

'*Princess*,' muttered Sadie furiously.

'Laura Ashley,' said Maria, ignoring her.

'Milkmaids,' snarled Sadie. 'Laura Ashley is milkmaids, not little Italian princesses.'

She scowled, pulling the plug out of the socket, winding the flex round the iron in the way that always made Rosalie unwind it again.

'Boring royal families. Vote for Wedgwood Benn and abolish the lot,' she snapped, and banged the ironing board shut.

Nonna glanced at her knowingly, her eyes half-shut.

'A long dress will catch in the wheels,' said Maria diplomatically.

'You won't buy a ballgown,' said Nonna, picking up the knitting.

'And I don't know that I'll get time off work on a Friday,' sighed Sadie, abandoning her bad temper, looking dreamy. 'Ascot,' she went on. 'D'you think the Queen will be there?'

'You just said abolish the lot,' Nonna pointed out.

'I didn't mean it.'

'I know,' cried Maria, inspired, 'what about a trouser suit?'

'Trousers for women? Not at Ascot. They don't let you in,' said Nonna.

'Trouser suits are fashionable. They'll have to let me in. I'll wear a hat as big as a wheel, with ribbons and roses.'

Sadie began to giggle.

'I know you. You'll sit there, a princess in a wheelchair, and defy them to turn you away at the gates, and if they do, they'll put it in the papers, and you'll get into Ascot, wear trousers and be *famous*. You'll have everything.'

In Sadie's eyes, Maria seemed to shimmer in the bright light from the window. Rosalie's Casa Pupo floor lamp stretched its long metal neck gracefully over her chintz settee, pushed back against the wall. House-proud Rosalie had pushed everything against the wall. Two armchairs made tide marks on the wallpaper. Widened doorways had been plastered and their jambs refitted but, after a year, still waited to be painted. Rosalie ran round clearing clutter every time they put down a book or coffee mug, so that Maria's wheelchair passed easily in and out, up and down ramps to kitchen and shower room.

Fooka hung in his great gilded cage from a big hook in the ceiling, to keep him safe from the cat. He liked to swing from side to side, casting shadows on the white walls, running up and down until there was birdseed all over the carpet, making Rosalie shout. Fooka would cackle and bang his beak on his bars, sneering. When he really got on her nerves, Sadie imagined letting him out. When she confessed to it, Rosalie said he was tame now, and it would be cruel to let him go, because the other birds would kill him. Anyway, she said, she was rather fond of him, and never mind his atrocious manners.

'Stupid overgrown budgerigar,' muttered Sadie, just to tease him. 'Gaudy crow.'

Fooka eyed her suspiciously, his head cocked on one side.

'I hope you come. You ask them to let you go. You take your, what do you call it?' said Nonna.

'Time off in lieu.'

Time off for all the extra hours she worked in a dingy office, trying to ease so many problems, the neediness of too many people, most of them much, much older than her. She knew they looked at her with calculating doubt.

'Sun and champagne and my birthday party. You can tell me how to win lots of money.' Maria held her face up to Nonna, inviting a kiss. Fooka let out a great screech and sidled to one end of his perch, his head swivelling agitatedly from one to the other. Maria laughed.

'Fooka's jealous. Kiss, kiss, kiss,' she teased.

'Bugger my bunions,' snapped Fooka in his nastiest voice and retreated to the far end of his perch, fluffing his bright green back in a huff.

'*Well*,' said Maria equably, 'that's a new one. All for a kiss. My word.'

'Bigger my . . . *what*?' demanded Nonna.

Sadie choked.

'Can he come to the races?' asked Maria innocently. Nonna opened her mouth indignantly, realised she was being teased, snapped it closed and got hiccups. She held her breath. Fooka watched with narrowed eyes. No amount of telling him to shut up and covering him with his cloth would stop him hiccuping and holding his breath derisively, off and on, for the rest of the afternoon.

'He learns new tricks. We'd better watch what we say,' said Sadie.

They laid the table for supper, Rosalie home, grumbling that her ankles puffed and ached after a hectic Saturday in the salon, Maria wheeling round the table, setting out serving spoons. Sadie put napkins in wooden rings by each place.

'I'll get a job,' said Maria, remembering their earlier words. 'You're right. Just don't be so bossy and stop looking like that.'

'Like what?'

'A social worker,' said Maria, laughing, finding her funny. 'Cheer up.'

'What do social workers look like, then?' Sadie resignedly took the bait.

'Grim to the hilt with good intentions. Frightfully bowed down and earnest.' Maria's eyes twinkled. 'A joke.'

Sadie failed to appreciate it.

'I was cheered up until you said that,' she snapped.

After supper, they watched television. Rosalie picked up Maria's knitting, did a few rows to see her on her way. Fooka preened quietly, sitting up at attention to hiccup in between pecking furiously at the underside of his wings. He peered anxiously at Nonna, waiting for a reaction. Sadie lay back in her armchair and watched him, imagined letting him out, an exotic stranger to be killed, as Rosalie said, by lesser fry with dull brown British feathers. She supposed it wasn't too surprising.

Think how the dingy lesser fry must feel, confronted by his gorgeous foreign plumage. Sometimes, studying what she saw as her plain face in the mirror, in contrast to Maria's dark and foreign beauty, she felt like lesser fry herself.

Chapter Fourteen

On the glorious June day following Ted Heath's victory in the 1970 general election, Nonna gunned the Capri down the lanes towards Ascot racecourse, coming north. She'd got lost, and they were heading for Guildford when Sadie, studying the map with a puzzled frown, persuaded her to turn around and go back. Hedges of bright blue rhododendrons flashed past, dappled with sunshine. On the front seat lay Maria's cartwheel hat and a pair of three-inch high heels which didn't really go with her yellow trouser suit. But would she listen? Nonna, taking a rare look in her mirror, caught sight of Sadie, carefully made-up to look pale and interesting, gazing out of the window. Nonna thought it made girls look anaemic and limp. She hoped Princess Anne would be there. She never looked anaemic or limp; she looked sharp and lean and rode like an angel. Nonna trod the accelerator in a fit of excitement. In the back of the car the girls clutched their seat and groaned.

'Princess Anne,' Nonna murmured dreamily.

They laughed. There had been a ruckus over their criticism of one of the Princess's hats.

'She looks like a liquorice allsort,' Maria had said critically, while watching a television report on Ascot earlier in the week.

Nonna put her head on one side, scratched her chin and considered. The nine o'clock news showed the princess in an open carriage, sporting a wide-brimmed striped bowler hat. It sat uncompromisingly on her head, and did not improve her.

'*Sì, ĕ vero,*' she agreed reluctantly.

'She looks frightfully horsy,' remarked Sadie.

Nonna sucked her teeth in disapproval.

'Why are the French and Italians so fascinated by the royal family?' demanded Sadie.

'She is *un' amazzone*,' snapped Nonna haughtily.

Sadie, deflated, wondered what Amazons had to do with it.

'*Sìsìsì*,' mimicked Fooka, pecking languidly at his bars. He had taken to imitating Nonna. She glared, making him cackle with laughter. Rosalie kept saying it was a pantomime and when would they all grow up?

'That'll be the day,' Sadie said, sneezing.

Fooka turned his back, fluffed his brilliant feathers and sulked pointedly. He knew she didn't like him. He made her sneeze and itch. Getting ready for Ascot, she found red blotches on her arms.

'I'm getting more and more allergic to that parrot,' she said, showing them to Nonna and Maria.

'Could be anything,' said Maria.

'Liquorice allsort,' muttered Nonna, unforgiving.

Sadie went back upstairs, scratching. Her white mini-dress and white boots did nothing for her blotches. She got calamine from the bathroom cabinet and dabbed it on, threw wet cotton wool at her waste basket, and missed. She sighed.

'How do you deal with a delinquent parrot?' she asked the empty bedroom. In the silence that followed, she got up and put the wad of cotton wool in the bin, where it belonged.

'You want to go out for a little walk, Maria, before we go in the car?' Nonna asked, downstairs. 'After you go to the toilet.'

'You want to go round to the betting shop?' answered Maria kindly.

Nonna shrugged, grinned and said no, not at all.

'Is done already. Cawston's Pride romped Queen Mary Stakes. His great-granddam was called Salmonella but it don't seem to have done him no harm. Flight Dancer was left standing and I win good money. And 'Umble

Duty won, bless her grey legs. So I, what do you call it?'

She snapped her fingers, thinking.

'Ploughed the profits back in?'

'*Sì.*'

'Ante-post betting,' said Maria, who had been learning a thing or two. 'Betting well ahead, you get better odds than leaving it to the last minute.'

Nonna said only *really* good odds if you did it weeks before.

'Why not just bet at the race, today?'

'I bet off-course on Connaught. Very good odds, if he runs. *Ma*, off-course, there is tax, so . . .' she explained, waving her hands and shrugging.

'Form, odds, handicaps, tax and tote,' sighed Maria. 'However do you choose who's going to win?'

'Form. And we bet on the tote,' said Nonna firmly. 'Odds are better but is not so interesting. Maybe some bookies give tote odds. And maybe they don't.'

'Why isn't it so interesting?'

'You don't know how much you going to get if you win.'

'OK, anything you say. We'll bet on the tote,' agreed Maria.

They sat in the back of Rosalie's car, their laps filled with *Sporting Life*, *Racing Post*, sharing a *Timeform*, picking winners and spending big fantasy money. After Sadie spotted they were going to Guildford, they did a U-turn and then had to concentrate on looking for signs to Ascot.

The heath was a glittering mass of cars in the sun. As they pulled into their parking slot, bumping over grass, the white and grey terraces of the Royal Enclosure and Tattersalls rose behind them. Maria craned to look.

'Oh, my God. Look at them all,' cried Sadie.

'I am,' said Maria. 'It's much bigger than I thought.'

'Not there. There.'

Sadie pointed through the windscreen. Nonna opened her door and climbed out. Through the sound of cars parking, shouts of car-park attendants, muted barking from the grandstand tannoy in the distance, the entire Giangelli family yelled Happy Birthday, Maria. On the grass stood a table covered in white linen, piled with plates and glasses. Four silver candlesticks held pale-gold candles, burning with invisible flames in the sun. Nearby, his backside sticking out of the end of a white caterer's van, Jove supervised the food, brought fast and fresh, in urns and dishes, glass and fine china, up main roads from his restaurant kitchen, complete with a grinning waiter.

'Wow,' yelled Maria, trapped in the car until Nonna and Rosalie brought her chair to the door. 'Oh, wow. Sadie, look at that.'

'No one told me, either,' said Sadie, astonished.

Sissy's little boy pushed a grubby, lumpy envelope into Maria's lap.

'He's been waiting all week to give you that,' said Sissy, coming over.

Maria held the long string of pasta beads in the palm of her hand and said, 'You made it for me?'

'He did,' said Sissy.

'Put it on, then,' she ordered, bending her head so that he could reach.

'Fab,' she said, arranging the pasta-shell necklace on the front of her trouser-suit jacket. 'I shall outshine the Queen. How's that?'

'Lovely,' said Sissy.

'I won't take them off until I get home.'

'All you need now is a tiara. Shall we get out?' said Sadie.

They picnicked uproariously. The children drank weak, watered wine and got sleepy. All over the Heath, racegoers picnicked from open car boots full of hampers and cool bags of chilled champagne. Mags brought birthday cake, lit candles. Michelangelo led 'Happy Birthday' with a roar that would have done credit to Caruso. The whole field joined in.

Maria was flushed with embarrassment and sips of champagne.

'I'm a bit woozy,' she cried.

'We're going in the Silver Ring, where the kids can watch the horses and run around safely and sit on the grass with an ice cream,' said Sissy, folding the tablecloth neatly and stowing it in a hamper.

'Tattersalls. Princess Anne, 'ere we are,' said Nonna hopefully.

Maria's wide-brimmed straw hat, threaded with roses, honeysuckle and creamy lace, cast her face into shadow. Sadie's boater was trimmed with deep-crimson ribbon, the colour of blood on her white dress.

'Very nice,' said Jove, admiring her trim, muscular legs in knee-length white boots. There was a lot of leg between the top of the boots and her very short skirt.

'My *hat*, if you don't mind.'

Reluctantly Jove raised his eyes appraisingly.

'Very, very nice.'

'What about me?' cried Maria.

He considered her.

'Drop-dead gorgeous,' he pronounced.

In the hot sun, Sadie's arms itched. She longed for ice and calamine, cold water after wine. Her head buzzed sleepily, felt heavy and languid. Crowds banged car boots shut, drifted in swelling numbers across the grass to the tunnel leading to the Tattersalls entrance.

'Time to go,' cried Nonna.

Sadie cradled her hat, listened to Maria chatter. Nonna's hat was a shiny straw chimneypot with one black ribbon. Sadie pushed Maria over the grass after the chimneypot, thinking, nice and drop-dead gorgeous. Thinking about it did nothing to take away the sting. She sighed. Maria was drop-dead gorgeous and she was plain. Jove came up behind her, to carry Maria down and up the steps.

'Sorry,' he said out of the side of his mouth. 'You look lovely. Really you do.'

Sadie tried to laugh. He put an affectionate arm round her shoulders.

'Remember that day you wore bright-red lipstick, and we stared at you, and Dad kicked us out of the salon and said to leave you alone?'

Maria's chair went bumpety-bump over the grass.

'I remember.'

'We thought you were drop-dead gorgeous then. Dad would have killed us if we'd said so. His little girl.'

'I was Giovanni's little girl?'

Jove, suddenly serious, said softly, 'Oh, yes. Didn't you realise?'

'I don't think I did.'

Sadie stopped pushing for a moment and put her boater jauntily back on her head. Then she gripped the back of the chair firmly, grinned at Nonna and tried out a bit of Italian.

'*Andiamocene.*'

'*Tally ho*,' cried Maria.

'Is hunting, *tally ho*. This is racing,' said Nonna.

Then they were at the mouth of the tunnel, and it was Jove's turn. He carried her down the steps, up the other side, and into Tattersall's turnstiles.

Chapter Fifteen

Nonna fought her way through dense crowds, arrived where she was aiming at, Sadie and Maria in tow, sighed gustily, unconsciously rubbed her beads in reverent delight, and surveyed the Ascot paddock. Marvellously English, its rich green grass was shaded by one great tree that sighed in a small breeze that took the edge off the heat. Crowds struggled to and fro, stood packed at the fence, the lucky few perched on rows of stools, sprouting like mushrooms at one end of the paddock. Behind them were bleached wooden seats in a couple of tiers. Women in high heels climbed and balanced, looking over a sea of heads. The first horse not yet out, the grass empty, they leaned on the fence, studying race-cards. It was curiously peaceful in the presence of so many people. The wind in the leaves sighed over the voices of the crowd, lowered out of respect for horses nearby.

'Is special, heh?' breathed Nonna.

Sadie nodded, surprised. She had not expected to feel moved, and she did. It was a very special place.

Ascot was not all magic, but it was all crowds. They'd fought their way through picnic areas just inside the entrance, negotiated rows of trestles packed with people, through a concrete concourse, all bars and beer and betting windows. At round tables crowds drank, studying sporting papers, queued to bet, voices roaring, magnified and echoing between harsh grey concrete walls, a frantic place.

A grassy strip between grandstand and racecourse was crammed three deep with long rows of bookmakers.

'There's dozens of them,' cried Maria, surprised.

Signs in many colours displayed bookies' names, repeated on rows and rows of leather holdalls, gaping, waiting for money.

'There are women bookmakers,' whispered Sadie to Nonna. 'I thought it would be only men.'

'Why are you whispering?' asked Nonna, amused.

'They might hear me.'

Nonna snorted merrily. 'So?'

Rebuffed, Sadie watched bookmakers chalk odds, scanning the grandstand with intently narrowed eyes.

'He's signing, like a deaf person,' she said.

Jim Fish of Luton, on a royal-blue stand, balanced on a small stack of wooden boxes, twiddled his nose, thumbed his ears, drew high-speed circles on the crown of his head. Just as suddenly he dropped back into casual chat with a punter, leaning down to listen. He nodded and money changed hands, into the holdall. Sid Hooper next door had a dark-red stand, clashing with Bob Puttard of Yeovil's bright orange. David Philips of Torquay stood next, in sobersides black.

'What is he doing?'

Sadie watched Mr Fish tap both elbows vigorously as though trying to keep warm, staring intently at the grandstand.

'Do you know what he's saying?' asked Maria.

Nonna shook her head.

'Looks like manic semaphore,' observed Sadie.

'He's laying off bets,' Nonna said.

'I thought the whole point was to lay them on,' Sadie was baffled.

'Odds change,' said Nonna.

'Oh,' said Maria vaguely.

'Most people,' explained Nonna, leaning on Maria's chair, 'bet round the corner, off-course. In the shop. Odds change. One lot in the shop, when you bet, new odds when the race starts.'

'That makes sense,' said Sadie, trying to follow the unfamiliar ideas.

'Betting shop bookies settle bets on the starting prices. Starting prices are the odds offered at the time the race starts. They are decided here at the racecourse, not in the shop. Some bookmakers give you tote odds, but most of them pay out on the starting price.'

'Oh,' said Sadie, not seeing at all.

'*Ebbè*, most of the time punters don't go to the races. They stay at home and bet off-course at the bookie round the corner. *Sì?*'

'Like you.'

'*Ebbè*. Off-course bookies try to influence the starting price here, because that is the price they pay out on. They don't like to pay out more than they have to.'

'They wouldn't.'

'If there's a lot of bets in the betting shops, the betting shop bookies try to make good starting odds, heh?'

Sadie was surprised Nonna's English was up to such complexities.

'They send messages, to try to fix the odds so everyone's happy,' said Nonna. 'Off-course bookies send messages to on-course bookies. They want to bring the odds down and bring the starting prices down. They have to tell each other to lay off big bets here.'

Maria, tired of technicalities, cried, 'Let's be frivolous and squander our money. I'm betting on favourites. Favourites only, for me.'

They all lost the first race.

Wandering away, Sadie shuffled through the throngs again, and was lucky. Someone got off one of the benches by the paddock as she came up. She sat down and looked around. Men in black and grey tails ambled to and fro, exquisite women on their arms. Upper-crust accents cut the air with drawling, neighing vowels and little shrieks of well-bred top-drawer excitement. Money, thought Sadie. Not just money, *wealth*. Her thoughts drifted perversely to work, to Mrs Lucy Lightfoot and her six children, another on the way, whose husband beat her up. Sadie pleaded with her, took her to look at one of the new women's refuges.

'Tell 'er to fuck off,' remarked Mrs Lightfoot, when confronted by the story of Erin Pizzey, ''cos I ain't goin' in no refuge with this lot.'

Her children milled, in dirt and undress. She glued a fresh fag on her lip and stared dismissively at her social worker with hostile eyes, one of which was black.

'You could at least tell the doctor how you got those teeth-marks and broken ribs last month,' urged Sadie.

'And you could mind your own business and bugger off,' Lucy suggested sourly.

Sadie sighed. The battered and the deprived were seldom in the least bit grateful. She came back to the present with a jolt as a phalanx of jockeys marched by, astonishingly small, in cheerful colours, stars and stripes. She watched them talking to trainers and owners on the green, green grass under rustling leaves. Champagne and Berry Bar, said a sign beyond. Surely all this great crowd couldn't be wealthy. The Giangellis weren't, and they were here at Ascot. But they weren't poor, either. She studied little groups of racegoers standing near by and couldn't decide which were more elegantly beautiful, the people or the horses.

The second race was starting. They parked Maria at the edge of the track, muscling people aside to get her chair in, so that she could see. Then they left her and pushed their way up jam-packed stands. The tannoy barked into life, waiting for the off.

'Use these.'

Nonna had binoculars. Sadie focused and saw the yellow gates come into view, the horses milling about. They disappeared into the starting gates. The tannoy shouted, 'Under starter's orders.' Then it yelled, 'They're off.'

Cheering came on a rolling wave from the right and broke around them. Riders shot past on their way to the finishing post. The crowd went quiet. The tannoy announced the winner to another great cheer; winning bets were confirmed, losers littered the stands with torn, discarded tickets.

'Better luck next time,' said Sadie, letting her ticket drop. 'Maria's lost, as well.'

'I won,' said Nonna smugly, and went to get her winnings.

They went to find Maria.

'I'd love a cup of tea,' murmured Sadie. 'It can't be all booze.'

Nonna hitched herself on to one of the metal toadstools at the paddock's edge and said no, no tea.

'Toilets?' muttered Sadie resignedly.

'Toilets,' said Nonna under her breath. 'Probably impossible, and anyway, she doesn't want pulling and pushing about in her lovely clothes. You have tea, if you want. Don't tell Maria.'

Sadie opened her raceform card, and tried not to feel resentful that Maria's bladder should stop her having a cup of tea. She resigned herself; it just would. She stood on one foot, easing aching toes in new shoes, as the next horses left the paddock for the track.

They lingered. The paddock was quiet in between races, and they had almost agreed to miss the race, in order to keep places by the paddock fence, when Sadie said, pulling Maria's chair around, 'What's the matter? What's that noise?'

Maria slapped at her arm, shook her head, knocking her hat crooked, twisting in her chair.

'There's a bee,' she cried. 'In my hair.'

'What?' cried Nonna, looking up. A great cloud of bees, swarming and wheeling, headed straight for them. Everyone ran.

'Oh, God,' howled Maria, fumbling at the wheels of her chair. She couldn't see for the oncoming swarm, a great buzzing cloud that gathered itself and dived with determined precision into the shady recess of the underside of the stationary chair. Clinging to the rug they'd brought to put on the grass, thrown over the back of the chair, the bees swarmed happily into a busy brown clump. Maria sat frozen, her mouth half-open, trying to scream. A squeak of pure terror came out.

'They won't sting,' called a voice urgently. 'Don't panic.'

Well away from the agitated bees, a small crowd who had been on their way to the stands hung back and watched a young man cross the grass.

'They won't sting you,' he said, seeing her horror. 'It isn't nice to have them all round you like that, but they won't sting.'

A lot of bees still whirled excitedly in the air. Brushing them away gently, he squatted down by her chair.

'Someone has gone to get a box to put them in,' he said. 'A few minutes. You won't get stung.'

Maria's face trembled.

'When they swarm,' he said, taking her hand, trying to reassure her, smiling, 'they're so full of honey, the silly creatures can't bend their tails to sting. They stuff themselves, to last the day, while they swarm. They can't hurt you.'

'Get me away,' screeched Maria, finding her voice.

'Hold tight.'

He picked her out of her chair and took her away from the bees, put her down on the grass, her back to the bleached seats, all empty of people. Away in the distance, the tannoy barked the off.

'Are you her sister?' he asked Sadie, crouching down, fanning Maria with her enormous hat, scattering roses on the grass.

'Sort of. Thank you for helping.'

Maria had her eyes closed, half in tears.

'She'll be all right in a minute,' he said.

'You know about bees?' asked Sadie.

Course officials came with a cardboard box, stood looking uncertainly at the back of Maria's chair.

'My father used to keep them, down in Sussex.'

'I think they want you to tell them what to do.'

A course official held out the box. Their saviour took it, held it under the swarm, shook the rug smartly. The bees fell into the box in their clump.

'Put them somewhere cool and they'll quieten down,' he said, handing them over.

'Are you all right now?' He came back.

Nonna sat on the grass, looking upset, holding her beads in one hand. 'She couldn't get out,' she said, sounding shocked.

'Some tea,' he suggested.

'I couldn't get out,' echoed Maria, realising he was handsome.

'Ugh. A *huge* swarm,' muttered Nonna, shuddering. 'No tea. Thank you.'

'That's not a big swarm,' he said. 'That's a cast.'

Maria looked up at him, outlined against bright blue sky. He towered over her in grey tails, his shadow short on the grass behind him.

'What?' she said faintly.

He thought that if they continued to chat calmly, she'd feel better.

'The hive breeds several queens. They have to leave, and they take half the hive with them. If a whole hive swarms you're talking about two or three feet of solid bee hanging from something or other. They'll stop to rest anywhere, and they liked the look of underneath your chair.'

'Resting?' she said indignantly, retrieving her wits.

'They don't go far when they leave the hive. They stop and wait for the scout bees to look for a new home. They'll rest anywhere. It depends on the weather. If it's rainy they might stay several days, until the scouts come back, and then you'll find the beginnings of a honeycomb on the branch, or wheel hub, or whatever. On a day like today, they might stay half an hour and move on. You find them in all sorts of places, down chimneys, underneath cars. They like a home with a small entrance best, like a woodpecker hole or a hole in a roof. They spotted your chair and saw a good squat. When they do that, they're in before you can blink.'

'*Un' ape*,' muttered Nonna, recovering.

'That little cast won't last long,' he went on, sadly.

'Why not?' Sadie was interested. They all sat together on the grass, like old friends.

'There aren't enough of them. That's only half the hive. They need thirty pounds of honey to last them through the winter. By the time they've bred a few babies and sorted themselves out, they've no bee-power left for honey. They'll starve.'

'That's *terribly* sad,' said Sadie.

'They need looking after. Put in a hive with another cast, they'll settle down and be fine.'

Sadie was thinking how bees starving because they wanted a home of their own was extraordinarily poignant and was a reflection on the cruel ineptitude of some of nature's more short-sighted arrangements when a roaring came from the stands, overlaid by shouts from the tannoy as a race was run.

'I think we go 'ome,' said Nonna.

'Could I take your telephone number?' asked Maria's rescuer. 'I'd like to know you're all right.'

He was maybe nearer thirty than twenty, now they'd gathered themselves enough to take notice. Tall, slim, with wavy, light-brown hair, he had a long, mild-looking face, protuberant, intelligent brown eyes and a pair of jug ears to rival Prince Charles'. With a light, clipped voice, he spoke with that friendly self-confidence that sometimes comes from having had an easy life, and in Philip Howard's case did not.

'Oh, yes,' breathed Maria, coming to life.

'Oh, yes,' mimicked Sadie, behind her back, trying not to giggle. 'We *have* made a quick recovery.'

Nonna looked very sharp, and frowned. Sadie subsided.

He held out his hand to Maria. 'Philip Howard,' he said, formally.

'Maria Giangelli,' said Maria breathlessly, all eyes.

'Oh, *really*,' muttered Sadie, 'bring on the violins.'

He was looking at her, too, as if waiting. She held out her hand to his.

'Sarah Carswell.' She rummaged in her bag and noted their telephone number down on a leaf torn out of her diary.

'I'll give you a ring.'

'Yes,' sighed Maria. 'Please.'

They watched him disappear towards the stands.

'Before you say a word,' hissed Sadie, to squash her, 'someone's got to get you back in your chair, and Sir Galahad never thought to offer.'

'We'll manage,' sighed Maria, staring at the spot where he'd vanished from sight.

'Oh, my God,' mouthed Sadie.

Nonna laughed beneath her chimneypot hat.

'We 'eave her in,' she said, bringing the chair.

''eave 'o, then,' said Sadie, and together they helped Maria in.

'That's the second time I nearly died,' announced Maria dramatically in the back of the car.

'You didn't nearly die,' snapped Sadie, fed up with histrionics, 'you nearly got stung.'

'I wonder if it'll be third time lucky,' shouted Maria, overexcited, dramatic as ever.

Oh, really, thought Sadie, sighing and scratching her arms without noticing. After an afternoon out of doors, the blotches had almost faded and her skin was pink from sun. It had been lovely until the bees arrived. She caught Nonna's eye in the mirror again. It winked understandingly. Sadie tried to ignore Maria's burblings.

'Ears,' she said meanly, when it got too much. 'I bet they called him Big Ears at school. They used to call me Froggie, remember?' she added wistfully.

'What ears?' demanded Maria. 'Whose ears?'

'True love is blind as a bat, they say. If that's true, this is definitely true love,' said Sadie, leaning back and closing her eyes. Maria chattered on, found no response and fell quiet. They both half dozed. Nonna drove with ferocious concentration, so they made much of the journey home from Royal Ascot, in convoy with the others, with barely a word between them that wasn't about Philip Howard.

Chapter Sixteen

'It's the bee man, for you,' called Sadie, holding her hand over the mouthpiece of the telephone on the Saturday, a week after the Ascot fiasco.

'Ask him to wait a minute,' hissed Maria, undoing the brakes of her chair hurriedly.

'She's just coming,' said Sadie.

She closed the door to the hall, could hear Maria's voice but not what she was saying. Fooka dozed and she itched. She was certain it was his fault. Maria sounded excited, through the closed door.

'Is he nice?' asked Rosalie, sitting at the kitchen table making a shopping list.

'Of course he's nice,' snapped Sadie.

Rosalie looked up from her list in surprise.

'Well,' said Sadie crossly, 'knowing Maria, who else but a knight in shining armour would turn up in her hour of need?'

'Isn't there anyone nice at your office?' said Rosalie, trying to side-step whatever it was that made Sadie so prickly.

'My office is full of people. I wouldn't say they're all nice. You get some odd people being social workers.'

They heard Maria laugh, a light, delighted laugh that brought Fooka to life. He hiccuped and held his breath half-heartedly, noticed Nonna wasn't there and dozed off again.

'I'm allergic to that parrot,' said Sadie.

'I'm allergic to perming chemicals. You just have to get on with it.'

'Perm chemical when you're a hairdresser is one thing, a bird is another,' said Sadie, trying to be reasonable.

'He's Maria's pet,' answered Rosalie, as if it should be obvious.

'Maria's the pet round here,' retorted Sadie.

'He's got my hat, and he says can he come and give it back?' burbled Maria, throwing open the door. 'I said he could.'

'When?' demanded Rosalie.

'This afternoon.'

'*Now*?' cried Rosalie. 'Then you'd better start tidying up, *pronto*.'

Open-mouthed, they watched Maria disappear into her room and heard drawers banging open and shut feverishly.

'I meant, tidy up in *here*,' cried Rosalie. There was no answer. Rosalie sighed. 'Oh, Lord, now she'll spend hours changing her mind what to wear.'

'Sir Galahad has come with a vengeance,' yawned Sadie, half-heartedly starting to fold newspapers and plump cushions. 'We had a full orchestra playing at Ascot, when they met, and choirs singing. Oh, dear, you should have been there.'

Rosalie shot her an old-fashioned look and wondered in the back of her mind how they were going to handle Maria in a wheelchair, in love. The words of the doctor in the spinal injuries unit came back, and she eyed the empty doorway thoughtfully. Sadie followed her train of thought and rolled her eyes comically.

'Heaven help us?' she suggested.

Rosalie pulled a face, and, caught in a moment of complete understanding, Sadie pulled one back.

Nonna was a worse curtain-twitcher than Maria, thought Sadie, amused. They'd lurked all afternoon, watching the pavement for Philip to arrive. Hearing a car pull up in mid-afternoon, Nonna was there in a flash, looking out of the window, clutching her rosary in disbelief. Outside was a vision of heaven, a dreamboat – dreamwheels, to be exact – parking its long, elegant bottle-green snout beside Rosalie's wrought-iron railings.

'*Mamma mia*, a *Morgan*,' she yelped. 'Maria, quick.'

'They must have put him down for it when he was born,' remarked Rosalie, looking over her shoulder at the car and the man at its wheel. 'You have to wait about seven years before you get one of those things. He doesn't look old enough. Is that him?'

From Maria's suffused face, she saw that it was.

'Let him let me drive it,' Nonna implored under her breath, nearly breaking her beads in agitation. '*Che lo volesse il cielo*. I go slow, I swear I go slow. Maria, you don't let him go again. You ask, can your grandmother have a *leetle* go in his magnificent automobile.'

'I can't ask him anything,' cried Maria, 'and don't you, either, or you'll embarrass me to death.'

'No one goes slow in that, anyway,' Rosalie pointed out. 'What would be the point?'

'Not over one hundred, I *swear*,' gabbled Nonna.

'Kilometres?' murmured Rosalie.

'*Ma che sciocca che sei*,' snapped Nonna. 'Miles.'

Crowded round the window, they ducked guiltily as Philip Howard heaved long green corduroy legs over the low driver's door, stood up, ran long fingers through hair tousled by wind, and reached into the ledge at the back for Maria's hat. He stood, looking at the house, talking to the man in the passenger seat, turning the hat idly in his hands.

'Sir Galahad looks a bit like a hare, all ears and big brown eyes,' remarked Rosalie critically.

Maria shot her a hurt look.

'Who's that with him?' breathed Rosalie, misting up the window so that no one could see properly.

'He wasn't at Ascot,' said Maria, craning round the curtain to see an ape of a man get out of the Morgan and join Philip on the steps. She peered, intrigued, from her point of disadvantage, too low down in her chair. Lanky Sir Galahad, his green metal steed parked behind him, rang at the door.

While Rosalie made tea, they sat on her chintz sofas

and talked about bees and Ascot. When they ran out of reminiscences, there was an awkward pause.

He has got adorable ears, like Prince Charles, thought Maria, trying not to stare at Philip, fussing her chair self-consciously. Nonna pretended to go to help Rosalie, and sneaked upstairs instead to gaze out of a window at the Morgan, hands clasped in supplication, praying from the bottom of her heart. '*Please*, I don't usually nag, but just this once . . .'

Downstairs, Sadie sat next to Dougal Monroe. Philip hoped they didn't mind Dougal coming with him, he said, but they'd come from seeing a business acquaintance together . . .

'Not at all. I'm pleased to meet you,' chirped Maria, looking at Philip, meaning she was pleased to meet Dougal, her social aplomb in tatters. Dougal grinned knowingly. He was, thought Sadie, amazed, like an amiable Godzilla. She studied him furtively, as he made polite, lilting conversation with Maria. Well over six feet, a bulky Welshman scarred and broken-nosed from rugger, he was a mountainous presence in Rosalie's tidy sitting room, cup and saucer balanced in one huge paw. A scar on his cheek puckered heavily shaved blue-shadowed skin very slightly, a second caught his lip, turned up a full and sensual mouth, leaving him permanently quizzical beneath thick, spiky black hair. Rugger muscles now running a little to seed gave him a softness, a bumbling air and a premature whisky paunch that belied an acute, ruthless business brain. Dougal Monroe, Cambridge graduate, fostered his clumsiness and made it an asset, fostered it to the point where business competitors who knew no better thought him a joker. They seldom laughed twice. Just now, he laughed too loudly at something Maria said, then cleared his throat, embarrassed. Sadie, unable to drag her eyes away, and unable to think of a word to say, discovered, as Rosalie poured tea, what sexual magnetism was, tingled all over and was scared stiff. Dougal's presence hit her with all the subtlety of a sledgehammer. She willed her legs to stop quivering and prayed he wouldn't notice. An adorable sign, thought Dougal, picking up signals with the ease of a bat in the path of a moth, of how delightfully young and ignorant she was. Sweet. They sat in taut and different silences, averted from each other.

It was Fooka who broke the ice and threw them all together. One of Rosalie's best teacups rattled in its saucer as Philip Howard sneezed uncontrollably and tried not to spill his drink.

'He doesn't like birds,' explained Dougal, grinning. 'Not the feathered sort.'

Philip scowled, sneezed and wished he'd shut up. Sadie warmed to anyone afflicted by Fooka.

'They make him sneeze,' Dougal went on, stating the obvious in an accent straight from the valleys, undiminished by Cambridge.

'That parrot makes me itch,' said Sadie, her words coming out in a squeak of tension, finding something to say to him at last. 'Join the club.'

Dougal turned and looked at her with interest. 'You can get nasty things from parrots,' he said cheerfully. 'Not that they bother me.'

Fooka scuttled across his perch and looked down at the visitors with a malevolent yellow eye. Sadie could have sworn he understood.

'I'm terribly sorry,' gasped Philip, buried in a handkerchief.

Maria's hat lay on the floor by her chair, trimmed with dead roses and dead honeysuckle.

'You can't go on like that,' said Rosalie. She fetched a pair of stepladders and went to take Fooka down from his hook in the ceiling.

'He's used to air-conditioning. Very rarefied, our Phil. A bit of suffering won't do any harm,' sang Dougal.

'I thought they only had that air-conditioning in America,' remarked Rosalie from the top of the ladder. 'You have to be rich.'

'Not people. It's our computers need air-conditioning.'

'Computers? Have you got computers?'

Dougal laughed and said Philip was *something* in computers.

'What sort of something?' asked Sadie.

'Got my own company,' said Philip, between sneezes. 'Tailor-made systems for industry.'

Rosalie and Nonna stared, deeply impressed.

'I work for him, for my sins,' Dougal went on. 'Known him all my misspent life, haven't I? He'll go on sneezing for ages, even if you take the parrot out. Why don't we go out instead? Then Philip'll stop hooting and you won't have to go to all that bother.'

Rosalie rested Fooka on the top of the ladder and said, what did they want to do? Fooka lunged for her fingers and banged his beak furiously on his bars as she snatched them away.

'Nice bird, isn't he?' said Dougal. 'Does he always go for you?'

'Only when someone upsets him,' said Maria sweetly.

'Make your minds up,' pleaded Rosalie, sitting down on the top rung of the ladder, balancing Fooka's cage on her knees. He ranted up and down his perch, frustrated at not drawing blood.

Ignoring them, Philip leaned close to Maria with his handkerchief pressed to his nose.

'I brought the hat as an excuse. I wanted to see you again,' he muttered. 'Can I take you out, so I can stop making an absolute ass of myself?'

Maria beamed.

Philip sneezed.

Sadie scratched.

Fooka flounced and screeched hoarsely.

'I'll wring your dratted neck in a minute, you're nothing but trouble,' threatened Rosalie, wobbling on the ladder. 'Sadie's right, Maria, we should get rid of this creature. He's horrible.'

'He is,' agreed Maria, unruffled. 'They said so in Harrods. They thought no one would ever want him and that's why we bought him. He was cheap, poor thing. He needs a lot of love. He's deprived.'

'Love,' snorted Rosalie. 'He's simply vile. That's all there is to it.'

Philip sneezed.

Nonna longed for them to go somewhere, to give *her* an excuse to go outside and look closely at the Morgan when they got into it.

'Let's go to Epping,' said Philip, getting a grip on himself. 'Would you like to go to Epping?'

'Let's go to Epping,' cried Maria, starry-eyed.

'Epping,' murmured Nonna encouragingly, sidling towards the door.

She watched the Morgan edge away from the pavement and turn out of the square towards Upper Street. With its top already furled back, they'd lifted Maria into the front seat beside Philip, crammed Dougal and Sadie into the back in shared discomfort.

'There's no room for her chair,' Rosalie pointed out.

'There's no room for anything,' said Nonna wistfully. 'Unless you're driving.'

She walked round the car, admiring it with an expression she usually only wore when looking at a particularly fine horse.

Maria, her face almost hidden by the Ascot hat, stripped of its withered flowers and tied under her chin with a scarf, was radiant.

'I'll either stay in the car, or they'll have to carry me. I'm not heavy. They can park me on the grass somewhere.'

Rosalie fetched the rug the bees had clung to, to sit on.

'You know,' she said when they'd gone, 'I sometimes wonder if she even notices her legs.'

'She notices,' said Nonna. 'She won't let it matter. Except for bees.'

'That Philip might not let it matter, either, by the looks of things,' said Rosalie. 'He asked her if she *wanted* to go to Epping, not if she *could* go to Epping.'

'He did,' agreed Nonna.

'That's nice.'

'It's not nice, it's natural.'

'Maria doesn't expect things just to happen like that. Not any more.'

'Sadie, I worry about. Maria, never.'

Rosalie cleared the steps away.

'Whatever makes you say that?' she asked, coming back.

'She is – how do you say – insecure.' She looked very thoughtful and Rosalie waited. 'Bit like Fooka, our little Sadie. Like Maria would say, deprived and inclined to bite.'

'*Bite*?'

But Nonna refused to be drawn further, reflecting that Philip Howard, who had an eye for racing-green Morgans and his own tailoring company, and knew about bees, could perhaps be expected to have good taste in other directions as well. The odds were against a healthy young man falling in love with a girl with no use in her legs. But Nonna knew about long odds, and that sometimes the outsider romped home. If Maria played her cards right, thought Nonna gleefully, she might yet get a go in that car.

'*E possibile*,' she muttered, clicking her beads ecstatically.

Philip Howard, sitting on the rug in Epping Forest, watching dappled sunlight play through leafy branches on to Maria's glossy hair, was in a euphoric mood, and might have agreed. Sadie sat with her back against a fallen tree and told Dougal Monroe all about Mrs Lightfoot, and the dire frustration of having clients who asked for help and wouldn't take it. She scratched absently at her Fooka-induced bumps.

'You ought to put something on that,' he said, sitting astride the tree trunk, displaying thighs on a similar scale to the tree.

'I'm like Philip, allergic. It's not bad enough to get rid of him, or take pills. It's just really annoying.'

She held out her bare arms, shivering in anticipation that he would touch them. He simply sat on the tree.

'And ugly,' she added.

'Oh, I don't know,' he said, sliding along the tree trunk and looking closely at her outstretched arm as if he hadn't seen one before. 'I wouldn't say that. Definitely not ugly. Rather elegant, in fact. Why don't you get a place of your own? Tell the parrot to get stuffed.'

'I couldn't do that.'

'Why not?'

'Money, I suppose,' she said vaguely. 'And I promised to help look after Maria.'

'Money can always be fixed. And she doesn't look to me like she needs much looking after.'

Maria's voice was full of laughter, and Philip said something that made her break into giggles. They lay on their elbows under the trees, the smell of last year's leaf mould and pine cones rising sharp and strong from the ground.

'I suppose you're right. I've been taking things for granted. She relies on Nonna quite a bit, but that's mainly because Nonna's there all the time. Maria can do shorthand and typing and talks about being a secretary, but it's hard to find somewhere a wheelchair can get into. She doesn't really do anything, but she's always busy. I don't know how she does it.'

'Steps and doors, office loos,' he said. 'Tricky.'

'We all thought she'd need us, but she's fine. She certainly doesn't need me to look after her.'

'Think about it. Never too soon to get into property,' he suggested.

'A place of my own? I never thought I could.'

Dougal slid down the tree trunk and sat, leaning beside her, his arm carelessly against her own. Suddenly it was difficult to breathe.

'I'll buy you a housewarming present,' he confided, leaning close. 'What would you like?'

'A stuffed parrot?' she quavered, unnerved.

Maria looked over. 'What about parrots? What are you plotting, Sadie?'

'A bit of long-overdue taxidermy.'

'I like women with a sense of humour,' said Dougal. He touched her arm appreciatively, leaving a burning sensation on her skin that had nothing to do with Fooka.

Chapter Seventeen

Maria, in love, was insufferable and daily reminded Sadie of the burning fingerprints Dougal had left on her arm. Mistrustful and wary, half wanting to see him constantly, half wanting never to see him again, at work she volunteered to do more than her fair share of emergency call, to be out of the way of Maria's mooning and Philip's frequent visits.

One damp Sunday afternoon brought an attempted suicide. She stood on the banks of the canal that ran through Victoria Park, down to the River Lee, feeling mud and cold seep through her inadequate fashion boots, contemplating the ridiculous and the autumn landscape. The ridiculous was a ginger youth floundering in armpit-high water, trying to drown. The landscape was derelict factory lots and, further down, weedy grassland dotted with abandoned cars, casually strewn rubbish stretching away on the far side of the water. Somewhere an Alsatian barked frenziedly on the end of a chain, defending some rundown, filthy-windowed building full of rusting metal and rolls of wire. On dank, rank air, the smell of wet clay and rotting weeds was strong as acid in the nostrils. Sadie watched an empty Coca Cola can drift by, marooned on a little sodden island of half-eaten sausage and chips, discarded by someone fishing earlier.

'He's got weights round his neck,' whispered the would-be suicide's mother. A hunched little woman in duck-egg-blue market-stall crimplene, she spoke without moving, through a lipless mouth, in rapid, reluctant bursts.

'I can't see anything in all that thrashing around in the water. What sort of weights?' asked Sadie patiently.

'Grandfather clocks and a chain round 'is waist. It's under the water. You can't see, but I'm telling yer.'

'Silly sod,' remarked an ambulance man. 'It barely covers 'is ankles. Fancied a paddle, did 'e?'

'It's what the weights are for, to keep 'im under,' breathed the mother, face stiff as a ventriloquist's. 'Only it ain't deep enough.'

The ambulanceman looked long-suffering.

'Someone'll 'ave to go in and pull him out. Darren,' screeched his mother, coming to life, 'they're comin' in to pull you out, you stupid bugger.'

Her son thrashed half-heartedly in the water and began struggling ineffectually towards the other side of the canal.

''E never could do nuffink properly,' said his mother bitterly.

'Why did he do it at all?' asked Sadie sadly, wishing the doctor would hurry up out of some Sunday-roast-and-red-wine stupor, turn up, and put this poor soul somewhere less haunted, somewhere dry.

The little woman shook her head.

'Has he done anything like this before?'

You're so crossly matter-of-fact, he must have, thought Sadie, hugging her arms to herself, longing to be home again in the safe, sane world of Rosalie's kitchen.

'They told 'im to,' admitted the small woman reluctantly, watching out of the corner of her eye at her son floundering in the greasy black water, as if looking sideways-on was safer.

Alarm bells rang. Those were strange words. They? Who are *they*? Oh, oh, Sadie sensed real trouble.

'Who told him?' she asked gently. 'Did they tell him to go for you with a carving knife?'

The woman regarded the long gash in her hand with dreadful detached curiosity, ignoring the question. The wound was bandaged, but had become a bloody mess in the struggle to try to make her stay in the ambulance. She'd climbed out, though, standing vacantly at the water's edge, staring at her son waving his arms as if posing for some dreadful holiday snap.

Sadie turned back to Darren.

'OK, that's enough. If you won't come out, we'll have to get you out, and we'll all get soaked and fed up. Why not do it the easy way?'

He was about nineteen, wide-eyed with fright, the bushy ginger hair, as tightly curled as Sadie's own, dark and wet. He was trying to grow a beard. She wondered what having enough future to plan a beard said about a suicide attempt.

'You've certainly got attention, if that is what you want,' she called, as police arrived with the doctor, running along the towpath, ready to scare him out of any remaining wits. 'I only hope it's the sort you want, because I don't think it is, somehow.'

They squatted down in a row, tried to coax him out, to be gentle and not to scare him any more.

'It won't do no good, 'e's daft,' said his mother, her arms folded over her sparrow chest, watching dispassionately.

'Where's his father?' asked Sadie.

The woman looked at her contemptuously.

'No dad?'

'Just like 'is dad, that one, no bloody use. I ain't seen 'im in fifteen years.'

Darren's arms flailed weakly, his eyes rolled up in his head, and he slid, gurgling gently, beneath the water.

'Get in there,' shouted a paramedic.

The water was cold and horrible. It hid things. Sadie hated to imagine what. In East End waters you could find anything; bodies, old prams, broken glass, a Tesco trolley. You name it. She shuddered.

'Quick,' cried the doctor.

The paramedic, made of stern stuff, jumped in. Darren's mother removed herself to the shelter of the ambulance doors as they rolled him on to the towpath and tried to wake him up.

'He ain't drowned, 'e's drugged,' she said offhandedly.

'You need stitches and a tetanus injection and a lie-down,' shouted Sadie, exasperated. 'Go and sit in the ambulance.'

The woman turned watery eyes on her and sniffed disdainfully.

'Let them bring him up to the ambulance,' repeated Sadie softly, trying not to frighten her, weighed down by the infinite sadness of it, 'and we'll get someone to see to both of you at the hospital.'

Darren's mother scuttled round the doors towards the towpath.

'They said 'e'd have to go in. 'E always gets upset and does summat stupid.' She contemplated her soggy bandages. 'We do try,' she added, 'but do 'e listen? They won't let 'im. We all 'ate Claybury.'

Sadie rounded on her, alert.

'I thought you said he hadn't done anything like this before, and now it turns out he's been in Claybury.'

'He ain't never done *this* before. That's what I thought you meant.' She thrust her bloody hand in Sadie's face.

'Why were you quarrelling?' demanded Sadie, recoiling.

'Quarrelling?' she hissed scornfully. 'Why would me an' 'im quarrel? It's them what quarrel.'

They climbed into the back of the ambulance and waited for the attendants to settle Darren, the whites of his eyes showing, on to a stretcher.

'They told 'im to.'

Sadie had a sinking feeling again. Too many people were arguing. One plus one was making a lot more than two.

'Who,' she said carefully, pronouncing the words clearly, 'told Darren to do what?'

''Is voices.'

'His voices. His voices told him to cut you, and jump in the canal.'

'Don't you let on I said.'

Sadie caught the derisive eye of the man opposite, tucking a scarlet blanket around the dripping Darren. They lurched off across the grass to the nearest park gate. Strollers in coats and mufflers stared after them.

'I take it you hear voices, too?' she said wearily.

Darren's mother looked away shiftily.

'You've both been in Claybury, haven't you?' Sadie said,

putting two and two together resignedly, coming up with the correct answer.

'Per'aps.'

They jolted over grass and picked up speed.

'And 'is brother,' she added for good measure, making a clean breast.

Sadie watched the doctor give Darren an injection. 'Darren's brother hears voices, too?'

The woman nursed her blood-soaked bandages, and stared at her with empty eyes.

'Do you know what he's taken?' the doctor asked, not hoping for a sensible answer.

'The lot, probably,' said the little woman matter-of-factly. ''E generally does.'

'The lot of what?'

'What the doctor give 'im.'

'What did the doctor give him?'

'Same as these.'

She fumbled with her good hand in a cracked plastic handbag and held out several brown medicine bottles.

'These are yours,' said the doctor, reading the labels.

The little woman dripped blood into the plastic bag, looking for another bottle.

'These are what they give you for schizophrenia,' said Sadie, reading the labels in the doctor's hand.

'Words,' mumbled the woman. 'Don't mean nothing. 'E's always been a homebody.'

The ambulance turned out of the park into the road and picked up speed, racing for the London Hospital not far away. Sadie sat with the bottles in her hand, unbearably depressed. A sad homebody in a tower block, entombed in crumbling grey East End concrete and inside the nightmare world of his own head. And inside the nightmare world of his mother, thought Sadie. Like double-yolked eggs in one shell. Triple if there was another one, too. Claustrophobia tightened her ribs and her arms itched.

'You'll have to go back in for treatment, when they've pumped him out,' she said.

Darren's mother lowered her worn face into the bloody

and comfortless folds of her plastic handbag and began to cry.

'I suppose I'll have to spend the rest of the afternoon getting you booked back into Claybury,' Sadie added, putting a warm arm around her client's birdlike frame. 'You can't go on with your voices fighting each other, putting him in the canal, bossing you senseless and all carved up in the muddle. We'll get that hand stitched and then try and sort out the mess.'

'Together . . . you leave me an' 'im together?'

The plea came, muffled wetly, out of the plastic bag. Darren grunted, eyelids fluttering.

'My God, mothers and sons.' Sadie felt like sharing their despair herself.

She rang Claybury and spoke to the male nurse on the Acute ward.

'Amelia and Darren Barnard,' she said. 'Old friends of yours, I think?'

He knew them well.

'So do you,' he said, with a grin in his voice. 'Have a look tomorrow and you'll find a nice fat file in someone's caseload. You watch the old girl, she generally comes in with a fight.'

'He's been pumped out, and she's had stitches. Neither of them needs to stay in here, so it's over to you.'

Mrs Barnard sat on a trolley in Casualty, clutched her bag and refused to budge, like a wounded old crow, all skinny limbs and snapping beak.

'She looked so downtrodden when I first saw her,' sighed Sadie.

'You ain't takin' me without 'im,' screeched Mrs Barnard, when they tried to persuade her to go of her own accord. 'I ain't goin' nowhere.'

'You're both going. The minute the papers are signed,' said Sadie grimly. 'Someone's got to look after you.'

'Back again like a bad penny?' grinned the charge nurse. 'Messing up people's Sundays. Dear, oh dear.'

'Don't blame us,' snapped Mrs Barnard, marching straight down the ward to her place in the dormitory.

He laughed, turned to Sadie.

'How many of us are there, this time?' he asked sardonically.

'At least four. Probably more. When their voices get on each other's nerves, there's hell to pay and they go jumping in canals.'

'Shocking,' said the charge nurse.

'I don't know how we cope. How do *you* stand it?' she asked, trying to joke, bone-weary.

The big black man grinned, his teeth white.

'You see the funny side or you end up in the funny farm yourself,' he said.

'A sense of humour? Is that the secret?'

She tried to rub away a growing headache. A sense of humour didn't sound enough to deal with lifelong, nightmare pain.

She crept in at half past eleven, expecting everyone to have gone to bed, opened the kitchen door carefully, so as not to disturb Maria, and found Nonna in Rosalie's old wooden rocking chair.

'Bad, heh?' she said, seeing Sadie's drawn face.

'It just took a long time.' Sadie threw her coat over the back of a chair and sat down at the table. 'I'm shattered.'

'You had anything to eat?'

'I'm too tired. Did Dougal ring?'

Dougal rang quite often. Nonna wasn't sure that she approved.

'He rang.'

'Any message?'

'You ask Maria. She took it.'

'I'll go to bed.'

Nonna shook her head and made to get up.

'You eat. Is no good not eating. You get ill.'

Nonna heated a tin of soup and made toast, while Sadie tried to take the charge nurse's advice and tell the story humorously.

'Do people get better?' asked Nonna. 'In that place?'

'They'll be put back in a chemical truss.'

The charge nurse was wrong. It wasn't funny.

'You can't change life,' said Nonna.

'I can't change anything. That makes it worse.'

'*Sì.*'

'I am going to buy a car, I decided on my way home,' said Sadie, forcing herself to cheer up. 'It would all be easier with a car. I can get a cheap loan from the department.'

'Everything could be easier,' said Nonna. 'Fooka and Maria. All of us.'

Sadie looked up in astonishment.

'Giovanni wanted to adopt you,' Nonna told her abruptly. 'He talked to Michelangelo and Jove. Before he died. He was going to ask you. Him and Rosalie. You should know.'

'I didn't.'

'Are you unhappy here?'

Sadie sat very still and then said abruptly, 'You know what gets to me? Maria and Rosalie are so optimistic. They are so *happy* all the time, I could scream.'

'You need not be jealous,' said Nonna evenly.

'I'm not.'

'You are jealous. Worse than sisters. You ever think Maria is jealous of you?'

'No.'

Nonna pursed her lips and stared Sadie down, bringing a scarlet flush to her cheeks.

'Get a place of your own, no Fooka, no Maria. No nonsense.'

'What would Rosalie say?'

'Rosalie would be pleased,' said Nonna firmly. 'You got any money?'

'Probably not enough.'

'Go and see. You find a little flat, you got two homes. One here. One there. Is much better. Shot of that parrot.'

'I thought you liked Fooka.'

Nonna's expression gave nothing away.

'I'll think about it. Thank you.'

She felt tired to death and excited. Darren in the canal went round and round her head until she forced him out by thinking about what Nonna had said. She imagined a place of her own and dreamed of it in the short night left, until the alarm shrilled, waking her to a new day. Exhausted, she rubbed her eyes, faintly recalling something good. Then she remembered what it was, and sprang out of bed.

Chapter Eighteen

At work, Sadie shared a cramped, crowded office with five smokers. It had stained, flaking pale-green walls. In moments of reverie she wondered if ICI made special town-hall paint to fill orders in quadruplicate for over-diluted, insipid pastels. On six battered desks, telephones rang constantly. The air reeked of menthol cigarettes and a faint sour tang from milk gone off on a table in a corner, where cheap powdered coffee and an electric kettle provided creature comforts. Sitting finishing the paperwork on the Barnards, Sadie ran her fingers over her forehead, trying to smooth frown-lines.

'There's a woman in reception wants to know about bereavement counselling for her mum. I said someone might be able to tell her about *Cruse*,' said a secretary, poking her head round the door. The girl nearest the door got up and went out.

A very fat woman in the corner began to giggle.

'What?' said Sadie.

'Cruises. My daughter's boyfriend works on a cruise liner. He's a steward. The ship's doctor was a woman, and one night she got called to a passenger who had a wedding ring on his willie.'

'Whatever for?' said the secretary, staying to listen.

'Doing something interesting that made him get all excited. He was in a terrible state. A bottleneck, if you get my meaning.'

The secretary snickered.

'Well, there was a scene when the female doctor turned up. He wasn't having a strange woman looking at it, so they got my daughter's boyfriend to put a white coat on.

The doctor sneaked up on a chair and peeped over the top of the cubicle curtains, and mimed at him what to do. He liked it so much, the boyfriend practically had to fight him off for the rest of the cruise.'

The girl who had gone to see to the bereavement client came back to find them all laughing.

'That woman's mum doesn't need counselling, she needs a trip to the psychogeriatric unit,' she said. 'She's been peeing in the fireplace and won't let anyone in. She's got the door on the chain and if anyone tries to get in, she says fifth columnists look just the same as you or me and they're out to get her. Anyone fancy the job?'

No one did.

'It's unusual to *pee* in the fireplace,' remarked Sadie. 'Do you think that daughter is telling the truth?'

'How should I know? Someone'll have to go and look.'

'Pooh,' said the very fat woman.

'It must be awful to be old,' said Sadie. 'And who'd be a social worker, anyway?'

Beside her desk, up close to the ceiling, Dolly Fiske's backside stuck out of the racking full of files that covered the walls on two sides of the room.

'Overworked, underpaid and never a good word,' Dolly said mournfully, muffled by dust and stack upon stack of beige card-covers. 'Never mind the odd thank you. Hah.' She scrabbled in the racking, dropped several files on to the floor, and emerged triumphant. 'Here you go. It's here in our splendid filing system. Jolly good.'

She began to climb down, changed her mind and stayed at the top, starting to search afresh. Watching her short legs in lemon-coloured tights finding toeholds on the racking, Sadie sighed. Misfortune was mostly boring. Every now and again it was violent, colourful, exciting. People did unspeakable things like cooking their babies in frying pans or battering their families to death. But mostly it was dull, the interesting cases usually someone else's. She looked at the files piled on desks, in drawers, on long racks of shelves, bulging from briefcases split at the seams.

'We're as batty as our clients, to work here,' she

said cheerfully, going down a short corridor to slap the Barnards' thick folder on her supervisor's desk. He could check what she'd done. Going back, she found the lemon-yellow legs still hanging out of the top of the racking, right over her desk. Dolly Fiske's backside wavered, squeaks of effort and frustration came from the back of the racking.

'Dolly, you've been rooting around up there for *ages*,' said Sadie. 'What *are* you doing?'

'There's another file. I've got one, and I'm blowed if I can put my hand on the other. Wait a minute. Catch.'

Sadie caught it. Dolly wore extremely short skirts, coloured tights and wonderful hand-knitted jumpers. Dolly knitted like others painted, big, bold, colourful works of art, sunflowers, poppies, psychedelic patterns, traditional Aran and once, after a visit to an art gallery, a Gauguin-like nude. She had a forty-inch chest well suited to the display of her work. From the racking, her bleached-white head craned over and demanded a leg down.

'We ought to get danger money. I bet they're breaking the Shops and Offices whatsit rules, making us climb up there,' she puffed.

Clutching a discoloured, dusty folder, Dolly perched her pear-shaped bottom on Sadie's desk and riffled the pages.

'This old girl just died and the hospital want to know if we've got an address for the daughter. Sounds like she hopped it when mum went potty. This goes back ages. We fitted her with bath aids in nineteen sixty-five. Dumpty, dumpty dum . . . Went senile,' she muttered, flicking over pages, 'in-patient, out-patient, in-patient . . . no, not here. I'll ring them.'

She shook a menthol cigarette out of a squashed packet and offered one to Sadie, who shook her head.

'Lucky thing, not to smoke.'

'I don't like the smell,' said Sadie.

Dolly groaned, her cornflower-blue eyes bloodshot. 'God, I've got a hangover.' She held the cigarette critically and glared at it. 'Heavy going last night. I gave old Ali Baba the push.'

Sadie giggled, embarrassed. 'You shouldn't call him that. It's terribly rude.'

'It is,' agreed Dolly, unperturbed, 'but what can I do? Haven't a clue what his real name is. Totally unpronounceable. He didn't mind my calling him Ali Baba. It was our little pet name. Anyway, it doesn't matter now.'

'You'll meet your match one day,' Sadie warned darkly, 'and then you'll know what it's like.'

'You can't teach me anything about what it's like,' drawled Dolly, puffing furiously. 'Not after finding my old man in bed with his best friend and me coming home early and catching them at it, because I was pregnant, and all he can do is cry, and say he still fancies me because he's bi.'

Dolly's plump, shapely shoulders quivered with laughter. They'd all heard the story a dozen times, and tales of what happened later, and about her cynicism when it came to men. She introduced Ali Baba to her close friends, but put on a fine display of indifference. Sadie liked the small, gentle Turkish psychiatrist, whom Dolly met while rescuing a ninety-year-old from his naked perch on some prefab steps under the gas holders in Stepney. Neighbours called the police, who called Dolly, who called Ali Baba. Ali Baba had spoken with immense courtesy to his demented patient, who understood not a word. Dolly, touched, fell in love. At first, he was distant, confused her with his foreign manners, spoke garbled English and made her cry a lot. The tables were turned when he fell in love with her. When they fell in love with her it was always the beginning of the end.

Dolly coughed with watering eyes and felt in her pocket to see if there was a paracetamol or two left. She came up empty-handed and lit another fag instead, her rosebud mouth puckered around it with distaste.

'I hear you got lucky with old Mother Barnard. Bet that made your weekend. Listen to the zoo,' she added more cheerfully.

In one of their interview rooms there was a ruckus; shouting and a baby crying.

'Monday. Let me guess,' said Sadie, holding up a biro-stained finger as if to see which way the wind was blowing. 'The Rowntrees have squandered their giros on fags and beer and now they're raising merry hell because they've got nothing to buy the baby food with.'

'Bingo,' cried Dolly, picking cobweb off her rucked-up orange jumper, which made an eye-watering contrast to the lemon legs. 'When will the dear things ever learn?'

'If they could learn things, they probably wouldn't be here,' said Sadie.

'Don't be daft. Those perishin' Rowntrees are cunning as monkeys. They learn, all right. All their sweet, bug-eyed little kids are professional whingers by the age of two.'

'You should have seen Mrs Barnard on Sunday. It's people like that who give me the creeps.'

'Families are dead sinister places, didn't you know?'

'My parents are dead.'

'I sometimes wish my parents were. Two sandwiches short of a picnic. They drove my sister mad. I got out and she got stuck.'

'I didn't know you had a sister.'

'Mum ought to leave, but she won't. He doesn't hit her, or anything.'

'What does he do?'

'Spins webs of lies and half-truths. He traps her and isolates her. You can starve to death inside a marriage,' Dolly said grimly. 'Dad's mad. You should see what goes on, but it's a big secret. Chinese water torture. Drip, drip, drip and no bruises.'

'It sounds awful,' said Sadie, embarrassed at Dolly's sudden revelations. Private things were best kept private.

'If you could kill someone with silence, she'd be dead,' Dolly went on. 'She tries to talk to him. You should see it. He stands in a corner with his arms over his head, like one of those old men you get wandering up and down the corridors in Claybury. He drives her crazy, so she's screaming, then he walks out, goes for a stroll, and when he comes back it's all over.'

'Lots of people are quiet,' suggested Sadie hesitantly.

'That kind of quiet is solitary confinement.'

Sadie looked doubtful.

'I've seen him look at Mum and say, ah, all these years married, and still to get pleasure from it . . .'

'But that's nice.'

'You'd reckon. Mum had been at the sherry, and spent lunch telling him how she's always wanted to leave him, and she's dead miserable, and feels she's dead already, and only stays because she's got no money and is scared to go.'

'Oh,' said Sadie.

'They don't live on the same *planet*,' Dolly went on bitterly. 'He teases and baits until she's screaming at him, but he just goes on and on frustrating her, until you want to kill him. Then she takes her handbag and they go upstairs, and you know exactly what they're doing.'

Sadie fidgeted uneasily, wishing Dolly would stop.

'It's sick. Then he puts her back in the broom cupboard until he fancies it again, and all's right with the world.'

'Broom . . . ?' Sadie asked, baffled.

'The way he ignores her, she might as well live in a coffin and only come out at night.'

'*Dolly*.'

'He'd have made a good Nazi,' observed Dolly philosophically, squashing out the end of her cigarette in the lid of a Nescafé jar.

'Are you sure it's as bad as that?'

Sadie regretted her words. A dull, wretched flush crept up Dolly's fat cheeks. Her very white, even teeth showed in a grimace.

'It isn't the sort of thing *anyone* makes up,' she said bitterly.

'I just thought you could usually *see* when people are barmy,' said Sadie apologetically.

'You don't have to be gibbering and picking your nose with your eyes crossed to be batty. You just have to fantasise the real world away and keep your wife in an emotional broom cupboard.' She tucked a stiff, dry strand of over-bleached hair behind her ear and fingered it. 'Look at this mess. What do you put on split ends? I'd like a perm, but the hairdresser said he wouldn't touch it, or it'd all fall out.'

'Try henna. That wax stuff.'

'Henna, you reckon? OK. Can't make it worse. Anyway, being crazy runs in families, but it's nothing to do with genes,' remarked Dolly offhandedly. 'You won't find me getting married again, ending up like them.'

'You never know. You might meet someone really lovely,' Sadie urged, the image of Dougal bringing her out in goose bumps. 'They're not all like that. You've been unlucky.'

'I jolly well do know, and pigs might fly. But thanks for listening,' said Dolly.

They went out for lunch together.

'Ali Baba cried,' said Dolly, looking into the counter in the Wimpy Bar for inspiration. She loved her food. 'What do you fancy? Burger?'

'Just coffee.'

'We went to the curry shop and breathed vindaloo all over each other, and got tight as ticks,' she said, paying for apple pie and a doughnut and a plastic mug of coffee, 'and then it was all, come on back to my place, I love you, I love you, I love you. I looked at his sweet, earnest little brown face and I thought, Oh, my God, I can't bear it.' She quivered with laughter. 'I think he wants to marry me.'

'You *think*? Don't you know?'

'How would I? I can't understand a word he says. But you should have seen the body language, darling.'

She laughed and winked.

'You are *horrible*,' cried Sadie, scandalised.

'He had tears in his eyes,' Dolly went on, unperturbed, 'but that might have been the chicken phal and lager. I got the distinct impression at one point, though, they might have been tears of passion.'

Sadie was curious. 'How do his patients cope? His English can't be as bad as you make out. You're exaggerating.'

Dolly looked reflectively at the formica table and stirred the sugar bowl with the end of her spoon, making swirling patterns.

'I'm not exaggerating. I don't suppose they make head nor tail of him, any more than me.'

Sadie began to hum, half laughing . . .

'Peter Sellers to my Sophia Loren, over the poppadoms and pickles? Hah, no way,' snorted Dolly, biting into a doughnut. Blood-red jelly squirted all over her fingers.

Sadie felt pedestrian and boring compared to Dolly, who didn't seem to care about anything.

'You say some shocking things,' she muttered.

'*People* are shocking,' answered Dolly sweetly, licking off the jam.

'You make the NHS sound like the Tower of Babel,' protested Sadie.

'It is, in some departments. Anyway, it's over. I told him to sling 'is 'ook. I'm fed up with Turkish delight.'

'You say *awful* things.'

'And you're so *young*,' snapped Dolly.

'Stop it. I can't fall out with you until you finish my sweater,' cried Sadie. Dolly was knitting a knee-length Aran jumper, if Sadie paid for the wool.

'I only fall out with men,' said Dolly sarcastically. After lunch she took a great pile of files from her desk, lit a menthol fag, visibly girded her bright-yellow loins for hard work and went off to make house calls. She wasn't seen again in the office that day.

Sadie had interviews booked and stayed in the office. By mid-afternoon she'd seen half a dozen people.

'Phone,' called someone, putting her head briefly round the interview-room door. 'Oh, you're busy. Shall I ask them to call back?'

The clock over the door said just past four. The smell of coffee floated in from the open door, making her mouth water. The depressed, pregnant punk teenager with Sadie twitched her mohican hair and scowled at the interruption. The coffee failed to drown out richly mingled odours of sweat, leather and some very strong, musky scent. The phone call offered escape.

'I'll take it. Tell you what, I'll ring the hostel now,' she said, turning back to the punk, 'and see if they can book you in well before the baby.'

Closing the door on the girl, she went down the corridor to her desk and picked up the receiver. The dialling tone hummed.

'Bother,' she snapped. It rang again while she was looking up the number of a hostel for unmarried mothers.

She heard pips and then Rosalie's voice.

'Sadie?'

'I think we got cut off.'

'I ran out of money. Got change in the canteen.'

'*Canteen?*'

'I'm in the unit with Maria,' yelled Rosalie against a burst of background noise. She sounded a bit strangled.

'Why?'

Rosalie breathed down the receiver.

'Rosalie?'

'You're going to laugh,' Rosalie said defensively, 'and it isn't funny.'

'*What* isn't funny? You aren't making sense.'

'She was cleaning Fooka's cage and let him out.'

'Who was?'

Maria, of course.

'He bit her,' Rosalie cried, hurrying the silly story along. 'He landed on her shoulder and she thought he was going to murmur sweet nothings, like he likes to, and he did. Only he got carried away and chewed her ear. She couldn't get him off, and she fell, trying to fight him off. She's in X-ray now, and they think she's broken an ankle. She should care; she can't feel a thing, and she's sitting there feeling a complete ass. You try telling a radiographer your parrot gave you lovebites. I can tell you, they've all been in hysterics.'

Lovebites from a parrot. Rosalie was right; it wasn't funny. It was hilarious.

'I bet you're laughing,' said Rosalie.

'I am not laughing,' choked Sadie.

'Yes, you are. Anyway, they've got her in here, to sort out her leg, and keep her under observation, in case she gets an infection, or sittawhatsit, that you catch from parrots. And lying still, like this, she could get sores. It's a nursing job. She can't come home, so it'll be a while . . .' Her voice tailed off, sounding suddenly depressed. The pips went and Rosalie fed in her last coin.

'What do you want me to do?'

'Nonna's here, with me. She's in a state because she thinks she should have been helping Maria with that wretched bird.'

Sadie shook her head speechlessly.

'Are you going home at five?'

'More like seven.'

'We'll stop on here.' Sadie heard an unspoken something in Rosalie's voice and waited.

'Sadie? Would you do something?'

'Probably.'

'We couldn't get hold of that dratted bird. I ran round with the mop, to try to get him to come down, but he was sitting jeering on the curtain rail when the ambulance came. Can you catch him and put him back, before he gets out. I wouldn't mind feeding that little feathered Hitler to the cat, but I don't want Maria worrying.'

'What if he bites *me*?'

'Put a bag over his head, or something. Look, the money's about to go.'

Sadie stood staring disbelievingly down the phone as Rosalie rang off. *Put a bag over his head*, indeed. Resigned, she dialled the unmarried mothers and booked an interview for her client.

Leaving with directions to visit the hostel, the punk

shrugged and spat in the gutter. Bleedin' social workers were all so fuckin' uptight. After she'd been to make her phone calls, that Miss Carswell looked fit to be tied. The punk grinned happily and sauntered on.

Chapter Nineteen

Evidently Nonna had been making cakes when Fooka sank his beak into Maria's ear. Sadie found the mixture still in its bowl on the kitchen table. Its pale, curdled surface was pocked with a neat grey medallion of bird dropping. She stared at it with loathing. There was no sound but a dripping tap and the faint tock-tocking of Rosalie's Swiss wall clock in the hall. Every half an hour a wooden cuckoo bounced out and squawked, making the unwary jump out of their skins. It had been cuckooing eight o'clock when she came in the front door.

'Where the hell are you?' she said, biting her lip. Fooka had the run of the house now he was out, because they'd left doors open, and he could be anywhere. The cats hadn't got him, because if they had there would have been feathers and carnage all over the place. She glanced in all the downstairs rooms. No carnage. 'Pity,' she muttered, cursing their lethargic old cat, for whom Fooka would have been more than a match. It could have brought in neighbourhood reinforcements from back gardens crawling with ginger toms. Surely cats could organise a tasty treat like Fooka. They hadn't seen their chance, and the cat flap in the kitchen back door was innocently closed. Damn. The Swiss clock tock, tock, tock-tocked. It was getting on for half past, already dark. She saw herself reflected in the kitchen window, ghostly, and jumped, heart pounding, as a voice came from the ceiling.

'Kiss, kiss,' suggested Fooka from the top rail of the old-fashioned donkey on which Rosalie aired their washing.

'You'll give me heart failure,' she shouted, scared.

He scuttled across sheets neatly hung out to dry and peered down at her curiously.

'I'll murder you,' she threatened, furious.

She fetched his cage from the sitting-room floor, where it lay upturned, water and birdseed all over the place, and put it on the kitchen table with its door wide open.

'Come on, Fooka, get back in.'

The parrot hopped and turned his back derisively.

'Fooka,' yelled Sadie, 'get in.'

Even handling the cage brought her out in itchy bumps.

'Get *in*,' she shouted.

He began cleaning his feathers, standing on one leg.

Sadie scrabbled in the dresser, found half a bag of birdseed and scattered it over the floor of the cage. She looked to see if he was interested. Fooka snapped his beak and disappeared among the washing again.

'Oh, for God's sake,' shrieked Sadie, 'get back in there, before you do any more harm.'

She unwound the rope that raised and lowered the donkey and began to let him down. Fooka scuttled to the end of the rail nearest to her and leaned forwards as if about to take off, gathering himself together with a purposeful air.

'Don't you *dare*,' screamed Sadie.

He poked his head out as far as it would go and screeched. It was his daring her, not the other way round. Scenes from Hitchcock's *The Birds* flashed through her mind. She started to sweat. Fooka very slowly drew back and sat upright on the donkey, level with Sadie's eyes.

'No you don't,' she said, backing away.

He followed her along the rail, glaring. She felt behind her on the front of the cooker for tea towels, anything to flap at him with if he went for her.

'Seed, Fooka,' she wheedled.

'Kiss, kiss,' he said quietly.

'Stuff kiss, kiss. Birdseed, you stupid budgie. In your cage.'

He disliked her tone and began to sidle rapidly sideways, screeching.

'Oh, *God*,' yelped Sadie, nearly in tears, and threw the drying-up towel at him.

Fooka raced down the sheets and into a row of lacy bras Maria had bought in Harrods the day she bought him. Toes caught, he skidded, slipped and fell, entangled in a bra, squawking and flapping among the sheets, unable to take off.

'Got you,' she cried, and pounced.

Fooka, bundled in a sheet, played dead.

'No you don't,' she said grimly. 'Thank your lucky stars that I'm too scared to wring your lousy neck because it'd upset Maria. God knows why. Keeping you is absolutely perverted.' She fed him, wrapped like a mummy, into his cage, stuffing the single sheet in. It didn't leave much room to move.

'Get out of that,' she snapped, fastening the cage door.

A dry hiccup came sadly from the bundle and a good bit later Fooka emerged, looking depressed.

'Serves you right,' said Sadie, glaring.

Fooka began to preen his rumpled feathers, pointedly ignoring her.

She stood, arms akimbo, trying not to scratch the inflamed skin where she had touched him and the sheeting.

'We can't go on, you know,' she said, half believing he was listening intelligently. 'Maria will be away for ages and Nonna will be back to spending all her time in the hospital. Rosalie needs to go to work. She worries enough about Maria without me as well. And I know what's going to happen. Now they'll be out *all* the time, and busy, and it'll be, oh, Sadie, be a dear and clean Fooka out, and you should be all right if you wear gloves. Well, I'm not all right. I itch just looking at you and I can't stand any more of it. Anyway, I *hate* you.'

Fooka hiccuped at her enraged tone and cracked his beak gloomily.

'Growing-up time,' she told him furiously.

A yellow eye stared back.

'Time to move out.'

She made a mug of coffee and sat at the kitchen table. The empty house and dejected parrot were sad, oppressed her. She longed not to be there when they came home from the hospital. It would be Maria, Maria, Maria . . . And, have you caught that bird?

'Where shall I go, though?'

Fooka picked at his sheet, his birdseed hidden underneath. She gazed into her coffee and tried to shake off a feeling of gloom. Cheer up, it may never happen, she told herself. It didn't cheer her up. Perhaps that was the trouble. She didn't make things happen, just drifted along. Maybe Fooka was a kind of message to take her life into her own hands. She went into the hall and picked up the phone.

Dougal Monroe lived in one of a maze of small roads sandwiched between Golders Hill Park and Hampstead Heath. He had bought his house when he first came to London. Four storeys of red brick, it was long and thin and had windows to match, which faced south at the front, making its rooms light and airy. In poor condition, lived in for fifty years by a woman who did not maintain it well, it was an executor's sale, and going cheap. Long before it became fashionable, Dougal renovated its former Victorian glory, painted all the walls white and lived in untidy comfort and increasing affluence. He let the basement as a flat, which more than took care of the mortgage. While Fooka sulked in Rosalie's kitchen, Dougal was listening to Beethoven. He turned the hi-fi down and answered his ringing telephone. He listened to Sadie with a half-smile on his battered face, conducting the London Symphony Orchestra with one hand.

'I need to move out, and I need somewhere to stay,' she said, at the end of a long, improbable and garbled story.

'Come over here?' he suggested, stopping conducting.

She hesitated.

'I can hear that creature chuckling to itself,' she said nervously. 'It's evil. I don't like being alone with it.'

'I'm offering asylum,' said Dougal lightly.

Asylum wasn't all Dougal was offering. The times they'd been out together, he'd made it perfectly plain what he was offering. The cuckoo flew out and strained on its spring.

'Cuckoo, cuckoo, cuckoo . . .'

Dougal laughed and at the full, throaty sound all the fine dark little hairs on her arms stood up.

'Out of the frying pan, into the fire,' she cried, dodging the cuckoo's manic jerkings.

He chuckled. 'The only feathers around here are in the duvet.'

Hah, duvets, she thought, seeing his untidy house in her mind's eye. Dougal shopped at Heal's in Tottenham Court Road, had duvets, designer furniture and a colour television. Other people had blankets, three-piece suites and black and white telly. Dougal kept inviting her to share his duvet and when she wouldn't, Dolly called her a prude.

'I'm boring, old for my age, serious and a prude,' she agreed, unable to make up her mind, to take the plunge into Dougal's bed and Dougal.

'For goodness' sake, lighten up a bit,' Dolly had said.

Dougal said he loved her. He said he fancied her like mad. Sadie, half-sick with excitement and doubt, thought about white weddings, honeymoons, Dougal's crooked, sensual mouth, and wondered if life could ever be the same once you'd shared a duvet. Shared a duvet. It wasn't the same as falling in love, and she was scared it might just be falling. But she longed to lighten up.

'This is infatuation,' she warned, when the cuckoo had pinged back behind its little wooden doors. Cold logic must surely put him off.

'Not for me,' he coaxed down the telephone, as if to a child. 'I tell you what, I'll come over and get you right away.'

He heard her uncertainty in her silence, over the line.

'Look, there's a spare room,' he said offhandedly. 'I'm not Bluebeard and I don't seduce young women against their will. You are welcome to stay here if you want to.'

'Come and get me,' she said in a small voice. 'Please, Dougal.'

'Be over in half an hour.'

She heard delight in his voice.

'No.'

'I can't do it in much less. Hampstead to Islington.'

'No, I mean, I'll leave now, in a minute. Otherwise they might be back and I'll have to explain, and I can't.'

'I don't suppose you'd have to explain as much as you think,' Dougal said calmly. 'I think they'd understand very well, if you'd give them the chance.'

Fooka scuffled angrily, his cage full of sheet.

'I'll meet you,' she cried, starting to gabble. 'Rosalie's keys to the salon are here. I'll wait in there. You know where it is.'

'As you like,' he said cheerfully. 'It's only a bird, you know, and two very nice people. You do get worked up.'

'The salon. It doesn't matter if you don't understand.' She put the phone down, gripped with irrational terror that Fooka might get out, Rosalie and Nonna materialise through the front door, hurt and tired and worried about Maria, so she couldn't go . . . Bundling clothes into a case, she left a note on the table that she'd gone to stay with a friend, hoped they wouldn't mind, sorry about Maria, Fooka was in a sheet in his cage and be careful because he was furious and she'd ring in the morning. Grabbing the salon keys, she brought herself up short. Rosalie would have to wait to be let in in the morning, standing on the pavement. That was hardly fair. Then Fooka hiccuped, a sound that seemed so full of menace the hair rose on her neck. She ran, slammed all the doors, shutting him in the kitchen, turned off all the lights. Leaving him in darkness, she fled.

Chapter Twenty

Philip Howard and Dougal Monroe appeared to have nothing in common, but had for years been the closest of friends. Ever since they could remember, they had looked after each other. Prep school misery, for Dougal paid for by scholarship money, forged common ground, strengthened by public school quarantine, also on scholarship money, from everyday life. For a while, they were half in love, read D. H. Lawrence and *The Seven Pillars Of Wisdom* together, grew out of it and matured into brotherly affection rooming together at Cambridge.

After Cambridge, they went separate ways. Dougal went to business school, became an accountant and worked in a bank. Philip idled for some months, making his mind up, happened by chance into computers and saw his road ahead. He worked for IBM for eight years, resisted the corporate pressure to become a company man, broke away and set up on his own, taking a few key people with him. Still in close touch, he persuaded Dougal to come in as financial director. They specialised in industrial systems and prospered.

They worked well together. Dougal, Welsh, restless, larger than life, was a miner's son blessed with cunning intelligence. He was tall, which puzzled his parents, who were short. His character, forged from generations of men who worked down the pits, had iron determination and an aptitude for rugby football that took him a very long way when it came to surviving at school. Used to fighting his way against odds, self-sufficient, he could be cold, calculating and mean in the boardroom, immensely affable in private. He was not a risk-taker, unlike Philip, born, as

Dougal said sourly, with a silver spoon in his mouth, so he could afford it. Philip would laugh, insulting him by calling him a Welsh Tory. It was true.

Dougal loved money and money men, wore suits that bagged at the knees and the bottom, and big woolly sweaters, and was very wary of women. Easily bored, he had a magnificent baritone, and sang his heart out in the bath and in a Hampstead amateur choir. He had no time for Dylan Thomas, with one exception, which was Richard Burton reading *Under Milk Wood*. That was because he adored Richard Burton. He didn't care when Philip said he was a philistine. He never went home, embittering his mother who, after all the sacrifices made on his behalf, tried too late to live her own life, her bitterness betrayed by pursed and puckered lips into which scarlet lipstick bled.

Philip was a complete contrast. He was old money, good suits and corduroy at weekends. He, too, lived in Hampstead. His grandfather had been Lord Someone-or-Other, whose youngest son, Philip's father, was a GP. He died going to help victims of a foggy pile-up on the newly opened M1, when Philip was sixteen. The fog was patchy. A youth of nineteen, ignoring all warnings, was driving the last of the cars to run into each other, taking Philip's father with him into bloody oblivion. He had been picking his way between smashed vehicles, the first on the scene.

Anne, his mother, picked up the pieces of her shattered life and went back to work full time, leaving Philip at boarding school. An architect, she built extraordinary homes for ordinary people; homes for women, with kitchens that worked for the baked beans and fish fingers cook, had enough cupboards out of reach of small children and never looked out over brick-wall vistas. Anne Howard's designs were hailed as classics, always in demand, betraying real liking for the people who lived in them. Warm and amusing, elegant and down to earth, an enigma, she was a classic herself, a very English beauty, long-necked as a swan, long-legged, long-nosed, long-haired. A well-bred, successful woman, she enjoyed the common touch, adored beautiful things, had an imaginative eye for the pedestrian, loathed *kitsch*. Philip's father was the love of her life. She never wholly got over his death and never married again, though she was asked often enough. When Philip used part of his father's legacy to buy the Morgan his father had ordered for himself six years earlier, she stroked its long green snout, smiled, made him a present of a pair of leather driving gloves and said not a word about danger. She never drove it herself.

Philip's and Dougal's differences resulted in frequent creative, profitable sparking of tempers. They had a rare gift for reaching agreement without having to see eye to eye.

'When I need a yes-man, I'll sack you,' Philip would bellow, Dougal's inaudible answer two fingers waved from his end of the modest executive corridor. They had the top two floors of a Sixties office block off the Finchley Road. Unglamorous grey paintwork and white walls surrounded grey computers the size of filing cabinets humming quietly in dimly lit, air-conditioned rooms, grey utility cord carpet silenced the feet of people used to working behind blinds, away from sunlight, at flickering terminals. Philip and Dougal had unshaded windows and no terminals. Neither could actually use a computer, nor were they good at selling them. What they were brilliant at selling were ideas and answers to other people's problems, worked out by people who *could* use their humming computers. They planned and managed an expanding staff, took over a third floor when it became vacant, spent their time tirelessly searching for people to hire who could do what they wanted, and had a great deal of success.

The summer they met Maria and Sadie at Ascot they had taken a box, invited their clients to come and drink a tin bathful of ice-cold champagne and ogle beautiful women. Occasionally they watched the horses, too. It was a way of drumming up goodwill and business, and went on expenses. Business, said Dougal, needed drumming. Times did look gloomy. Government and unions all set to lock horns had him worried. Nearly nine months after the Ascot trip he was even more worried.

'The economy's sliding into recession, Ted Heath is hell-bent on joining the EEC, which is lunacy, and Phil is serious about Maria,' he groaned. Normally a most tolerant chap about other people's politics and taste in women, he clutched his brow and despaired.

'Is it because she's in a wheelchair?' Sadie had asked suspiciously, when he looked gloomy about life in general, and Phil in particular.

'Nope. I like Maria.'

'What's the matter, then?'

He'd been sitting in his comfortable, untidy clutter of books and records, with his feet up, absently fingering the puckered scar.

'Dunno. Things seem to be sliding. It's bad times.'

'I don't think you're telling the truth,' she said. 'I think you mind a lot about the wheelchair.'

He glowered. Glowering did not improve him, rather made the two of them look like Beauty and the Beast. It was *sort* of *partly* the wheelchair, he admitted to himself grouchily. It was bad *image*. Image was important when you ran a thriving company that you didn't want to see go down the drain. Phil was threatening to damage their corporate image. Dougal felt indignant, and the strains of Mahler coming from the music centre were not calming. He whipped the record off and sat back in angry silence. Brotherly love went only so far. Self-interest went the rest of the way, and he felt his was being threatened.

'My goodness, you look hideously grumpy,' remarked Sadie, unruffled.

'Thank you, Little Red Riding Hood,' snapped her wolf, offended. 'You certainly have a way of going straight to a chap's heart.'

She gave a sunny smile and went back to her book. He felt depressed. She didn't understand, and he'd never bothered with un-understanding women before. It bothered him how much he bothered with this one. It was becoming a habit and made him deeply uneasy about his own intentions. His intentions about Sadie were good, and he wasn't used to it. He felt happier with bad intentions;

love 'em and leave 'em. He drummed his fingers silently on the armchair. One way and another, Dougal could see trouble ahead.

Denying how prejudiced he felt about Maria being disabled, led Dougal to believe that everyone else felt the same way as he did. He dreaded raised eyebrows and barbed comments among their clients if Philip married Maria. God knew what their competitors would make of it – spread the word that it was something only a chap with serious personal problems would do. They'd destroy Phil's credibility, call him a wimp. Dougal, liking firm, muscled legs, himself, visualised the wedding night and shuddered. He found it difficult to stop thinking about it, alternately fascinated and ashamed of his thoughts.

'I've got money in it,' he yelled, exasperated, slamming a rock-like fist into the arm of the chair.

'Your piggy bank?' asked Sadie, not taking her eyes from her page. 'You sound like you want to break something.'

'The company.'

'One day you'll float it, and then you'll be rich,' she remarked, not really interested. Why wasn't she interested? Usually women were very interested in his money. Dougal, panicky, was more and more sure that Philip's marriage would lead to his being mocked as a wimp, would lose their clients' confidence, lose business and run them both into ruin.

'I'm going to talk to him, spell it out if I have to.'

Sadie put her book down.

'You keep interrupting. It's drizzly but it's not cold. Shall we go for a walk?'

They marched round the heath in sou'westers and yellow raincoats, her head barely reaching his shoulder. Dougal, with Sadie's hand tucked into his pocket for warmth, held on to her and cheered up.

He carried out his threat and Philip turned out to be deaf as a post. In Cambridge they'd had unspoken agreements never to share women and never to interfere in each other's affairs. Those agreements stood firm until Dougal, obsessed with profits and protecting a valuable workforce painstakingly put together, assumed privilege and stepped over the line. Dougal's good intentions nearly broke up a lifelong friendship. One afternoon Philip complained about seeing Maria. Dougal grabbed his chance.

'It'll always be like this, you know.' He grabbed the bull by the horns, blundered straight in, head down, as if into the thick of a rugger scrum. 'You'll turn into a nursemaid,' he bellowed, his singsong voice carrying the length of the executive corridor. 'It'll be bad for you and bad for her.'

'What are you talking about?' demanded Phil.

'*Marriage*,' yelped Dougal, getting it out at last.

Maria in hospital, ankle broken and a pressure sore on one heel, nursed with immense care, still took a long time to recover from Fooka's lovebite. Philip, complaining about the time and driving it took to see her, about the frustration, gave Dougal the opening he wanted. It was a mistake.

'I don't think so,' Philip said mildly, his round, protuberant brown hare's eyes serious, 'and in any case, she's coming home soon.'

He signed letters piled before him. April winds gusted beyond their office window, bending tall thin saplings, freshly planted inside wire tubes, protection against vandals. The council was trying to smarten the paved square outside their building. It had rained earlier, the wind drying wet pavements beneath the feet of rush-hour crowds. On the far side of the square a pub was crammed and noisy, its sign squeaking in the wind.

'Fancy a pint?' asked Philip, tapping his letters into a neat pile.

'I'm serious about this Maria business,' said Dougal.

'So am I.'

'Don't you *worry*?'

'What do you think I should worry about?' asked Phil, in a deceptively friendly kind of way. Dougal, too het-up to see warning signs, blundered on.

'Sidelong glances and people wondering if there's something wrong with *you*. Your marrying Maria will be

God's gift to our competitors. I can hear the gossip now.'

Philip leaned back in his chair and looked down his long nose at his best friend with a wondering expression.

'Why don't we call in the receivers right now, and not bother waiting?' Dougal was almost wringing his hands.

'Go on,' Philip said encouragingly.

An alarm bell rang faintly in the back of Dougal's head, sending urgent warnings that meek and mild responses to insults were not quite right. He ignored it, scowled, looking more like the Beast than ever. 'Someone has to say it,' he muttered uncertainly.

'What exactly does someone have to say?' asked Philip coolly. He ran his fingers through his shock of hair and asked with dangerous concern, 'Maria, or Maria's wheelchair, Dougal. Which bothers you most, old chap?'

Dougal's chair legs hit the floor with a thud and he leaned across the desk anxiously.

'Now, look, it's not me . . . it's the others. I have to raise money and it's a confidence game. You'll be sending me to the bank with one arm tied behind my back if you make a cock-up of your private life. They'll be laughing behind our backs. Bang goes confidence. What am I supposed to do then?'

The mild hare's eyes and jug-eared face in front of him went steely and lost all resemblance to any kind of rabbit. Dougal recoiled. Looking at Philip in this mood was like looking at the nose cone of an armed warhead, all pointed, and straight at *him*.

'Can't be much of a man if I can't do better than a disabled girl. Must be short on something? That what's bothering you?'

'I wouldn't have put it quite like that, myself,' Dougal growled, beginning to see the disaster he was in.

'Let's hear how you *would* put it, old son.'

Dougal's considerable bulk fidgeted.

'Ah,' he began, casting around the office walls for inspiration as to how to climb out of the hole he had just dug for himself and fallen into with a resounding crash.

'Go on.' Philip very carefully moved a row of pens one by one two inches to the right of where they had been.

Dougal, learning wisdom too late in the day, fingered his scar and kept his mouth shut.

Philip got lazily to his feet and reached a long arm across the desk. Dougal's dark silk tie tightened round his throat as Philip gripped it. 'I may have to look for another financial director. Understand?'

'No need to lose your rag,' Dougal spluttered, going purple.

'Out,' snarled Philip, giving the tie a last, vicious wrench.

Dougal choked, got up as casually as he could, and got out.

Standing loosening his collar, breathing again, he looked out of his own office window, at yet more rain falling in gusting, swirling drizzle. He was taking Sadie to look at a flat, a place of her own. 'Women need their independence,' he argued at first, using feminist logic to discourage her from getting possessive, wanting to cling. She showed no sign of doing either, and he panicked when he started noticing estate agents' bumpf in the post.

'What is this?' he demanded.

'I'm looking for a place of my own. Like you said.'

Bewildered, hurt and angry, he left the pile of printed details on the kitchen table.

'You don't have to go, you know,' he said grumpily, pretending to be insulted.

'Yes I do. We always said I'd find somewhere of my own. It could take a while, though, if you don't mind.'

Mind. Standing there, alone in his office, Dougal, chastened by Philip's rage and the threat to his job, tried to grapple with the fact that he didn't just not want her to go. He wanted her to stay.

Philip kicked him while he was down, he thought angrily. There had been no need to repeat it.

'You meddle, and you'll clear your desk,' he'd said,

standing just beyond the doorway, briefcase in hand, on his way out.

Dougal's expression would have done credit to some medieval gargoyle carver, working in finest Welsh granite.

'I'm going to ask her to marry me,' Philip went on, ignoring the freezing atmosphere. 'I'm telling you, although it's none of your business, because you might like to think over whether you can go on working for me.'

'I've no intention of resigning,' Dougal said, rigid with rage.

'Good. See you tomorrow.'

Philip, his blood brother, his *alter ego*, went down to get the Morgan from its parking space, to roar off down to Maria. To his extreme mortification, Dougal felt stinging tears in his eyes, tears of bitter jealousy. Philip was Maria's. Things would never be the same between them, once Phil married. Pauline, his secretary, went by, pulling on her coat. He turned away abruptly and made out he was absorbed in the view from the window, hiding his stricken face. Then he went and closed his door and sat down heavily at his desk, to lick his wound in secret.

'Oh, *fuck*,' he cried, realising that the truth was, he was lonely and jealous and sad. The good old days were gone and he did not know what would take their place.

The racing-green Morgan stood in the hospital car park until late that evening. Maria and Philip played backgammon on a board on the side of Maria's bed. When she saw him come in at half past six or so, Nonna found she urgently had to go home.

'We play poker,' she confided, 'but she's no good. She don't care. She has to *want* to win. You try.'

'I'm surprised you can concentrate on poker here. Where on earth do you find the energy?'

'Rosalie comes some days. We don't come together no more. We share.'

'Does Sadie come much?'

Nonna's expression went bland. They walked together to the Way Out sign in the corridor.

'It won't last, it never does, with him,' said Philip. 'You don't have to worry. Even if it does,' he went on, contradicting himself, 'he's not a bad chap. He's got a heart of gold, tucked well away, but you find it once you get to know him.'

Nonna looked doubtful, then shrugged a very Italian shrug, as if to say she had an open mind, but . . .

'That bird is a monster. I don't blame her, running away, but we *mind*. Is she 'appy?'

'I don't think she's staying with him. They are looking for a place for her, to buy. Dougal knows about mortgages and things. He'll get her fixed up.'

'*Va bene*,' observed Nonna politely, not understanding such arrangements. They seemed cold-blooded.

He waved to her as she turned, toddling down the corridor, three Sainsbury's carrier bags of Maria's washing clutched to her chest. It was time to lay his cards openly on the table.

'Your grandmother says you should be practising poker,' he said, going back to Maria's bed.

'I hate poker. I'm bored. I was waiting for you to come.'

'I got caught, discussing something with Dougal.'

'What?'

'Nothing important. A personal matter.'

She wondered if the personal matter was her. If it were, she knew very well what Dougal thought; it was easy to read his face.

'Get the backgammon out, then,' she said, for something to do.

They set up the board and tried to play, but the visit dragged. They were anxious and awkward. Before they knew it, it was time to go. Philip was curt, frustrated that he was playing straight into Dougal's accusation of wimp. Half-way down the ward, he turned on his heel, marched purposefully back.

'Maria,' he began forcefully.

'Visiting's over,' urged a nurse pleasantly.

'Maria. I wanted to ask you . . .'

The nurse stood her ground, waiting. Philip cursed inwardly. Maria looked all eyes, in the shadow of the light over her bed.

'He's going,' she told the nurse. 'I was going to give him this.' She held out a paper bag.

'Night, night,' said the nurse meaningfully.

Maria called after him softly. He turned again.

'Only read it if you really, *really* want to,' she said.

Sitting in the Morgan he switched on the dashboard lights, opened his present. It was a pamphlet about living with disability. He sat for a long time, reading, rain falling again on the soft top of the car. It was the answer to the question he'd been too cowardly to ask, an invitation, a brave commitment.

'She loves me,' he roared at the car park, thumping the steering wheel, startling an elderly consultant getting into his Bentley. Pulling out of the hospital gates, he turned the radio up to a deafening pitch. It was playing *The Marriage of Figaro*. Philip sang Mozart in an out-of-tune baritone all the way across west London, to Hampstead and home. They were playing it just for him.

Chapter Twenty-One

Dougal and Sadie did not find flat-hunting a lot of fun.

'They are all horrible,' she complained, tramping cold wet streets at the end of a wretched January.

They looked and looked, and got nowhere. Estate agents looked down their noses, said it was a bad time of year. Come back in the spring.

'I suppose I'll have to wait. I get a rise later on. I can hardly afford one room, never mind a flat.'

'You don't want to rent,' said Dougal, hoping to discourage her from going. While Sadie scanned the *Evening Standard*'s To Let columns, Dougal eyed her toothbrush next to his in the bathroom, and was pleased she hadn't found somewhere.

'No one buys at this time of year. Leave it.'

'We understood I'd get my own place.'

'Why? I like having you here.'

She had her elbows on the work surface in the kitchen, the paper covered in red circles and ticks and scribbles. Probables, possibles and no-goods.

'They're too expensive, too far from work or I hate the sound of them. Listen to this. Non-smoking girl, own room, garden flat – that means basement and damp – share amenities. Animal-lover only. I bet that means five poodles and another damn parrot. Catch me with another animal-lover.'

He slid his arms around her.

'Stay here.'

Sadie kissed his cheek and picked up her red biro.

'It's work, as well. When I get called out it's not funny

to have to drive half-way across London at three in the morning.'

'Change your job?'

'Dolly's offered to put me up.'

'That woman is an interfering nuisance,' shouted Dougal.

Sadie turned on her stool, gave him a long, withering look.

'All right,' he muttered, shamefaced. Jealousy, he thought uncomfortably, was becoming a habit, new to him, and it wasn't one he liked.

Dolly had looked beady when Sadie admitted running to Dougal the night Fooka got out. She'd treated Sadie to a very old-fashioned stare.

'Is he all right?'

Sadie flushed. 'I don't know what you mean.'

'Yes you do,' snapped Dolly.

Bright-red, soft-eyed with memory, Sadie admitted to sharing more than Dougal's duvet.

'Did the earth move?' demanded Dolly nosily.

Sadie flushed deeper than ever and Dolly grinned wickedly.

'Are you going to marry him?' she asked, nosier than ever.

'Dougal isn't the marrying kind.'

'Hah, they all say that.'

'Don't try and make me feel tacky,' cried Sadie indignantly. 'Living together without getting married is what I wanted.'

'Sure,' said Dolly sadly, not believing a word of it.

'And I thought you weren't romantic,' Sadie cried, incredulous. 'Talk about double standards.'

'It's different at your age. You're young.'

'So I've got bags of time,' snapped Sadie.

'Something'll turn up,' she told Dougal, looking at property for sale in *The Times*. She was swathed in one of Dolly's jumpers, an intricate pattern of creams and browns in fisherman's wool, big and bulky, almost to her knees, over tight jeans. Her thick, almost African-like curls haloed her head like a black dandelion clock. She looked as delicate as a flower in the heavy jumper, bent over her paper. Dougal had never wanted to protect anyone before and he fought back grimly against wanting to protect *her*. He poured himself a Scotch and his stomach rumbled. 'Fancy going out to eat?'

'No, thanks. I got some eggs. You can make us an omelette.'

Dougal stared in astonishment over the rim of his glass. Usually women wanted to please him, to stay, were eager to go out and be pampered. Until he'd had enough, and cooled. Then they threw tantrums and burst into tears and called him a bastard. She just told him to do his own cooking. He felt at a loss.

'Go on, I'm starving,' she said, moving so that he could get to the cooking cupboards, get out the frying pan. He finished his whisky and poured another, sulking hopefully. She took no notice at all. He got an egg out of the door of the fridge. It slipped through his big clumsy fingers, smashed to the floor.

'I'm no good at this,' he complained, waiting for her to get annoyed and take over.

'Eggs are easiest to mop up with kitchen paper,' she said, not looking round.

Dougal wiped up his deliberate mess furiously, and got out the rest of the eggs and the pan.

The following day it snowed, blanketing the heath and a million back gardens with sparkling white, turning the rest of London into greasy, half-frozen pavements, roads lined with dirty wet slush. A gritter spread sand and salt in erratic little heaps down Fitzjohn's Avenue. Sadie followed a line of cars down in early-morning darkness, all trying to get past the gritter. They crawled, nose to tail, brake lights winking on and off, on and off, exhausts belching grey and steamy. Sadie turned on the radio for the seven o'clock news and tried to warm her hands. Through Gospel Oak and straight down the Holloway Road was her usual route but Dougal, his car in for service, wanted dropping off near the Finchley Road. *He* didn't have this absurd drive every day. He could have walked, anyway, if he wasn't so lazy. Letting him out at the bottom of the avenue, Sadie wiped misting-up windows, faced the long stop-start drive across central London and resigned herself to being late.

She sat and hooted beneath their office window. Dolly ambled out, wrapped and shaped like a Christmas cracker in holly-berry red, her woollen coat down to plump ankles swathed in mahogany suede knee-length boots with heels.

'My God, are we going on a call looking like that? You look like a French madame. Where's the poodle?' Sadie leaned across to open her door, feeling put-down and dowdy in her warm grey coat and black court shoes.

'So long as one of us looks respectable,' answered Dolly, climbing in with much huffing and puffing. 'And you look respectable enough for two.'

'I don't know how you get away with it,' grumbled Sadie, pulling out into traffic. 'And will you put those revolting things away.'

Dolly obligingly squashed the pack of menthols back into her bag and sat watching fresh snow drift down in minute flakes. The heater circulated oily air and exhaust fumes and the traffic crawled.

'Another day, another dollar,' muttered Dolly, burrowing into her wraps, longing for a fag. She caught Sadie's sidelong glance and didn't dare.

They had a joint visit to make, one that could turn out very tricky. Parking outside the Mother's Hospital in Hackney, Sadie clipped closed the windows of the little *deux chevaux* and pulled a briefcase off the back seat. Dolly bounced deliberately in her bucket seat, swaying the small car from side to side.

'It's like riding on a cow,' she said. 'Why didn't you get a proper car?'

'Proper cars mean proper money,' snapped Sadie, getting out.

'I suppose,' agreed Dolly, struggling to get upright on to the pavement. Sadie gave her a hand and pulled.

'Just don't mention diets,' warned Dolly, straightening herself.

'Me?'

'Let's get this one over with,' said Dolly.

Her boots clackety-clacked on paving stones as she walked into the hospital grounds.

'I've got a bit of money left from my parents, but I wanted to spend it on property, not depreciating assets like cars,' said Sadie, locking her car and catching up.

'That man is teaching you a thing or two. Depreciating assets, eh?'

'That man is back-pedalling like mad. Where are we going?'

'Postnatal. Over there. How, back-pedalling?'

'First he played it dead cool. Practically ships that pass in the night, with the emphasis on the night. Not a permanent berth for my toothbrush. Now it's he's never felt this way about anyone before, and is this love?'

'Is it?'

They walked, heads down against driving wet snow, along covered concrete paths linking rows of single-storey brick maternity wards, hurrying to get into the warm.

'I don't know. I like him a lot and he's fun. I don't know if that's love.'

'If you don't know, then it's not.'

'Hm. This place is like a chicken farm,' remarked Sadie.

'Plenty of hatching,' retorted Dolly.

Sadie clutched her briefcase in both arms, rested her chin on the top, pushed through a swing door backwards. Throat-catching hospital smells and a mouthwatering lingering of that morning's fried bacon met them, and the bawling of a dozen babies.

'I don't know how anyone stands it,' muttered Dolly.

They pushed through more green-painted doors into the

ward where Cherie Sangster had given birth to twins and was flatly refusing to take them home. They had come because the hospital wanted them to persuade someone, somewhere, to sort out the mess.

They were met by the registrar, a short, slender Indian with a waist-length plait of black hair straight down the middle seam of her white coat. It made her look like a little girl, until they looked into her face and saw a tired and angry woman. Born in Brick Lane to parents who spoke no English, she had fought like an alley-cat to get where she was, had marked traces of a Cockney accent, was used to being called a dirty Paki and was completely without illusions.

'Home is the top floor but one of a tower block where if the lift isn't out of order, which mostly it is, you cross your fingers and hope that this is your lucky day and that any rapists and muggers waiting to get in pick someone's else's ride to share. You fancy having two babies up there?' she demanded, getting down to business.

'No,' said Dolly truthfully.

The small brown woman eyed Dolly's flamboyant outfit appreciatively and snapped, 'Then you can't blame her, can you?'

'We haven't come to blame anyone,' Sadie pointed out. 'We've come to try to find a way out, and to let you have your bed back.'

Dolly, Sadie and the registrar clustered together and gazed up the ward. Their problem was leaning on the end of her bed, chewing gum. Her mouth went round and round and round.

'That is Mrs Sangster,' said the doctor.

'Mrs?' demanded Dolly disbelievingly.

'Courtesy title.'

Cherie Sangster had tied up her thin yellow hair into a bristly little ponytail on top of her head, pulled her candlewick dressing gown tight as a corset, shoved painted toes into pom-pom slippers. Without make-up, shadow-eyed with exhaustion, still with childlike, perfect skin, she'd made an effort to look her best. Sadie's heart sank. Cherie Sangster looked barely fifteen.

'She is seventeen,' said the registrar.

Dolly pulled her lower lip thoughtfully and shuddered. 'Those blocks sway in high winds. You can actually feel it. I'd be terrified. I *am* bloody terrified every time I go up one,' she corrected herself.

The doctor looked from one to the other, her hands in her big white pockets, waiting for them to do something useful.

'Shall we go in the office and not stand here staring at the poor little soul?' suggested Dolly.

The registrar led the way.

'The trouble is,' said Sadie, 'she lives with Mum and Mum's boyfriend. If she takes the babies home, it's technically overcrowding, and the mother says she'll get into trouble with the housing department. What Mrs Sangster elder really means is, she doesn't want them back.'

'She wants to jump the housing list and get a house,' said the doctor. 'She says so. She doesn't care and nor do I. Can you get her one?'

Sadie shook her head doubtfully.

'Mum's got a two-bedroom skytop job. They'll go mad all stuck up there together with two screaming babies and nowhere to go except straight off the balcony forty, fifty floors up, or whatever.'

Dolly folded her arms and returned the doctor's glare without flinching.

'Where's the father?' asked Sadie.

'Father is probably the mother's boyfriend. No one's owning up. She has to go somewhere. She can't stay here,' said the doctor flatly.

'She'll be back next year, you know,' warned Dolly. 'The boyfriend won't stop wanting his oats. We'll have this all over again.'

The doctor looked grimmer and angrier than ever.

'This is a housing department problem,' said Sadie.

'Good. So long as she can stop being our problem,' said the doctor.

A cleaning woman shoved a bucket along the floor with a grey mop, humming 'Onward Christian Soldiers' in a loud, passionate hum, her face beaming. She seemed to be the only cheerful woman in the ward. It was, Sadie reminded herself, suppressing a grin, a Salvation Army hospital.

'How about sending her home, and telling her we'll sort it out from there?' she suggested, watching the bucket disappear beyond their doorway.

Dolly looked at them both pityingly. Cherie chewed frantically, able to see their heads through the office's big windows, sensing a plot.

'Once she's home,' explained Dolly heavily, easing from foot to foot, her boots killing her, feet swelling in the overheated office, 'who is going to take a blind bit of notice? So long as she's here, and making a nuisance of herself to *doctors*, she's got more clout than the poor little sod's ever had in her life or ever will have again. She's not so stupid.'

The registrar sighed and began to climb down.

'You know that. I know that. It doesn't solve it, and I've got the powers-that-be breathing down my neck, wanting the bed. Especially, we need the cots.'

Sadie couldn't help imagining two tiny babies screaming all night in a swaying tower block while Mum's boyfriend came out on the prowl. It made her feel sick.

'OK.' Dolly made up her mind.

'Yes?' demanded the registrar.

'The housing department are going to have to listen to this one,' Dolly said gleefully, enjoying the prospect of twisting their arms. 'I'll have a word with the girl.'

'Good luck,' murmured the registrar, a ghost of a smile on her face. Dolly was back in a flash.

'A word is all you get, as well, the four-letter sort,' she reported. 'She isn't exactly friendly, is she?'

'I ain't takin' 'em home,' yelled Cherie, barricaded behind her bed, shoving gum into her cheek, like an angry hamster, 'so you needn't fuckin' stand there fuckin' tellin' me what to do, 'cause I ain't fuckin' takin' 'em nowhere.'

'Eloquence. You see?' murmured Dolly.

'I'll suffocate 'em if you make me take 'em back there,' she threatened. The ward sat transfixed, mothers clutching babes to their breasts, newborn ears covered. Cherie's babies, side by side in transparent cribs, woke with a start and began to scream. Desperation, thought Sadie, a sound that made her deeply uneasy.

'You see,' said the doctor sadly.

'She'll do it, too,' said Dolly. 'I'd take that threat very seriously, if I were you.'

'All right,' said Sadie, putting Cherie's file back in her briefcase. 'I'll get my supervisor to take it up with Housing. Get someone with clout to deal with it.'

'And tell her to shut up, or they'll take the babies away. One more threat like that, and she's in all sorts of trouble,' said Dolly.

'*We'll* take the babies away,' muttered Sadie, 'is what you mean.'

'Place of safety,' said Dolly.

'Safe? They would be *safe*?' said the doctor incredulously.

'Physically safe. From any other point of view those kids are lost already. You are right. We have to do what we can,' said Dolly, sorry for the Indian woman's well-controlled anger.

'They might drop the bomb tomorrow,' said Sadie. 'Safety is an illusion. Do you belong to CND?'

The Indian doctor's face brightened but Dolly plunged ahead.

'For heaven's sake, don't bring that up here,' she snapped. 'That's a stupid argument.'

'Just *do* something,' begged the doctor.

Dolly went into her estate-agent act.

'Would madam,' she demanded of the doctor, waving a finger in Cherie's direction, 'prefer something *bijou* in Dagenham with a nice view over Ford's, do you think, or a first-floor balcony job over towards the park on Kingshold? All mod cons, mostly cons but Mods are coming back. Regular entertainment of a Saturday night, when they get together for a bundle with a load of blacks, punks and drunks. Underground garaging for your stripped car, colourful graffiti and Kray twin clone security. Price, modest. Rent rebate because you're below the breadline, service charges by extortion only. Which would madam prefer?' Dolly displayed nicotine-stained teeth in an evil, sarcastic grin.

'A home of your own,' reflected the doctor from Brick Lane, sadly.

Sadie remembered the bees. Dolly grinned and began to march towards the exit.

'Oi. You fuckin' goin'? You ain't done nothing,' yelled Cherie.

Dolly advanced like the Light Brigade up the ward, fed up, about to speak her mind. At the sight of Cherie's babies, a mass of waving arms and legs, the indignation went out of her, leaving an aching pity.

'We'll do our best,' she promised.

Outside, flakes of snow still drifted from a dirty sky.

'We could do a place of safety order,' said Dolly brusquely.

'They are five days old,' cried Sadie. 'We can't take five-day-old infants away.'

'Did you see the mother?' demanded Dolly.

They came to the car and Sadie fumbled for her keys.

'Wouldn't it be better,' Dolly went on remorselessly, 'than your pram taking a jump over the balcony wall all by itself, or your pillow accidentally dumping itself on your face and smothering you.'

'She wouldn't.'

Sadie unlocked the car, threw her briefcase into the back, caught sight of Dolly's expression.

'Would she?'

'She would,' said Dolly cheerfully, climbing into the car, 'so they'll never risk not giving her what she wants. Put the heater on.'

'Babies,' said Sadie, starting the cold engine, 'are the ultimate weapon.'

'They'd *fry* the directors if Cherie Sangster did something awful to those babies because she hadn't got a place to live. Not to mention that you and me would be out of a job.'

They contemplated that in silence. Chugging down Mare Street, Sadie began to laugh.

'She's doing better than me. I'm supposed to be the one with the power, telling her what she can and can't do, but it's me looking all over for a place, while she sits there winding us all up.'

'Take a lesson in manipulation,' said Dolly.

'Better at it than we are, aren't they, clients? Manipulation, I mean.'

'Absolutely out of our class,' agreed Dolly, easing her feet out of her boots with a gusty sigh of pleasure.

Later that day, Housing agreed to make special provision. Sadie rang the hospital.

'Of course,' said the doctor acidly.

'We do our best,' said Sadie.

'We all do,' said the registrar coolly.

'I'm looking for a place of my own, myself. It isn't easy,' said Sadie defensively.

'It isn't,' said the doctor, slightly less hostile.

'Perhaps I should have twins,' joked Sadie.

'I've got a flat over the far side of the park. New conversions in Victorian houses. They aren't all gone.'

She gave Sadie an estate agent's number.

'If I get somewhere, how can I thank you?'

'Keep an eye on those babies. That girl is highly unstable.' The woman abruptly rang off.

'I'll take it,' said Sadie.

The estate agent, a scrawny woman in Harris tweed and with a plum in her mouth, could have stepped straight out of *The Lady*.

'This one has a garden,' she pointed out. Sliding patio doors led to a paved area, half covered in snow. Sadie slid them a little open, their breath steaming on bitter air.

'Barbecues,' she cried. 'We could have barbecues, and it's lovely and secluded for sunbathing.'

The estate agent smiled toothily. It was handy when clients had plenty of imagination.

'Cocktails on summer evenings,' she whinnied.

'*House and Garden* patio landscaping,' cried Sadie.

'You'd have room for a very small conservatory,' neighed the tweedy agent, all in the spirit of the thing.

Oh, the nostalgic memories. Sadie felt quite overcome, remembered tweedy teachers, tweedy mothers, daughters in jodhpurs in Landrovers, all with identikit teeth. There were more orthodontists, these days.

'She was a bit spiffing,' Sadie told Dolly afterwards. 'Boarding school was *full* of people like her.'

'*Spiffing*. Oh, *really*,' said Dolly.

Sadie kept her promise, putting Cherie Sangster's twins on the newly formed at-risk register.

'They're all yours,' said her supervisor. 'Visit and make sure you see the babies. Don't get put off by excuses.'

'I'm buying a garden flat,' she told him. 'The other end of Victoria Park. They've done some very nice conversions.'

'On your own?'

'Just me.'

'Put locks on your doors and windows. Be careful.'

'I don't want to live in Fort Knox.'

'Make it safe,' he said.

She asked Dolly what she thought.

Patio doors? Dolly's advice was to get a large dog. A German shepherd. The East End, she said, loved German shepherds.

'There isn't room to swing a cat,' protested Sadie.

'Get the police to tell you how to make it safe.'

'You're scaring me.'

'Good. Put locks on,' snapped Dolly. 'Don't be an ass and tempt burglars.'

'She's right,' said Dougal, depressed that Sadie was

really going. He kept thinking about asking her to marry him, but he wasn't sure she'd say yes. He couldn't face her turning him down, so he ruminated miserably and said nothing.

Five months later, she stood in the middle of her own sitting room, patio doors open to a June afternoon. She'd taken all their advice and had rung the police station and asked them to send someone over to advise her how to make the place safe.

The crime prevention officer stood in the middle of the barely furnished room; two yellow Habitat beanbags on grey fitted carpet, white-painted walls, a Swiss cheeseplant to one side of the patio doors. It was fresh and clean and pretty. Its owner was fresh and pretty, too.

'Nice. You've made it very pretty. Don't want break-ins spoiling it,' he said appreciatively, with a pronounced Norfolk accent.

He was a dead ringer for Eric Clapton, thought Sadie, lined, a bit haunted-looking, with introspective brown eyes and soft brown hair. He was taller than Eric, she guessed, but had that same suffering face that could melt any woman's heart.

'You're from Norfolk?' she asked.

'Norwich. You know Norfolk?'

'King's Lynn. I lived on the coast until I went to boarding school.'

'I stayed in Norwich until I got promoted down here, for my sins. Know your neighbours, do you?' he asked.

'No.'

'Best way is to look after each other. Keep your eyes open.' He began testing windows, looking at doors.

'I'll have to make friends,' joked Sadie.

He glanced at her. His grin lit up his face, made him younger.

'I guarantee you'll do that,' he said.

He took out samples and a catalogue of bolts, deadlocks and window catches, showed her which would be best.

'You could put bars on the windows, set them in concrete,' he said, running his hand down a long Victorian window. 'Though it's a shame, they have lovely proportions and it's nice to look out without seeing bars. You can paint them white, then they blend in better.'

'I don't want to make it a prison.'

He smiled, a slow, half-amused smile.

'I'm John Campling from Norwich. Would you fancy a drink in your local, Miss Carswell from the coast?'

Dougal expected her back. Dougal had been helpful over the flat, anxious to please. Caught on the horns of a dreadful dilemma, whether to fight her and alienate her over her going away, or whether to propose and get himself turned down, Dougal was tense, unhappy, difficult and becoming awfully trying.

'Sarah Carswell. I'd love to,' she said.

His handshake was warm and confident.

'I'll pick you up at half past seven.'

They crossed the park to the Three Roses, where they drank real ale and ate crisps. He told her about policing in Hackney. She told him about Cherie and how the police had left the ambulancemen to get wet when it came to rescuing Darren Barnard. He laughed. He knew the hamlet of Ditchwell, could envisage where the cottage would be. He knew the hidden path across the dyke to the deserted, glorious beach where Victoria had taught her to swim. He knew how to cook samphire and he knew the names of the marsh plants that Queenie had taught her. He also knew about the kind of work she did, about taking people to Claybury, about sections, about going to court. They had an extraordinary amount in common. Afterwards Sadie, shocked by his stories of crime and violence in the area where she now lived, did as he suggested. She put locks on everything, barred herself in. She felt safe, filled with delight at having a place of her own, delighted when he rang up to ask her out again.

* * *

Dougal came over with a housewarming present. He propped something heavy and large and oblong against the wall, stripped off a lot of brown cardboard wrapping.

'It's gorgeous,' cried Sadie.

He looked pleased.

They hung the ornate old Victorian mirror opposite the patio doors. It reflected the beginnings of a garden, made the room look large and light.

'I thought it would go well in a Victorian house,' said Dougal, looking for more than just thanks.

'It's absolutely right. You couldn't have given me anything nicer. Thank you, Dougal.'

It wasn't nearly enough. She didn't invite him to stay the night. Going home in the car, he wondered if this was the end.

Rosalie and Nonna brought Maria, newly out of hospital, pale from being too long indoors. The atmosphere was strained. They all wanted to mend bridges, unsure how to set about it.

'You just ran off,' said Maria. 'You upset them dreadfully. You should have heard the way they worried. It wasn't fair.'

'It was like a nightmare. You wake up and can't quite recapture what was so awful. It just was. I'm sorry I upset everyone. I didn't mean to, and it hasn't exactly led to a disaster, has it?'

Nonna shook her head. She approved with all her heart of what Sadie had just done.

'Bygones are bygones,' said Maria.

Nonna and Rosalie went out through the patio doors to stand looking at turned earth that would become a garden.

'Are you still seeing Dougal?' asked Maria.

'Not a lot, no.'

'Phil said he's playing it close to his chest and not saying much, and goes around looking terribly wounded.'

'I'm sorry Dougal's wounded. It won't last.'

'Sadie?' Maria sounded suddenly urgent. 'Philip asked

me to marry him while I was in hospital. I said I would.'

'You are sunny out here, you face south,' said Nonna, coming indoors.

'I just heard Maria's news.'

Her head whirled. Maria married to Philip, who was Dougal's best friend, meant Dougal and Philip and Maria . . . and she on the outside. Unless she went back to Dougal, this could split them apart.

'Next Easter they get married.' Rosalie beamed.

Maria wheeled her chair around, went out by the patio doors. Sadie's flat suited a wheelchair. Ground floor, no steps, open-plan, patio doors. If she married Philip, would she still come . . . ?

After they left, Sadie threw herself on to a yellow beanbag and got a headache trying to think all the possible consequences through.

'Dougal?' she said one evening, coming in late to hear the phone ringing.

'What have I done?' he demanded. 'You treat me as though I'm some sort of weed. I love you and I miss you.'

She was tired. It had been a long, hard, day. She held the phone just away from her ear, listening to him ranting on.

'You haven't done anything. You've been as kind as anything, and I sit here and look at my beautiful mirror, and it makes me so happy. Couldn't we be friends?'

'No,' he shouted, 'we can't. I'm a lot more than friends. Sadie?' She heard him suck in his breath, but before he could shout, 'Will you marry me?' she cut him short.

'Dougal, ring me tomorrow, OK?'

She put down the phone and for the first time since she'd moved away, he didn't ring back on the spot.

Chapter Twenty-Two

John Campling gave her a housewarming present, too. It was he who came and fitted all her locks.

'Making you safe,' he said, screwing bolts into the floor, to anchor her patio doors.

'Making me a prisoner,' she joked the following Saturday, watching him set wrought-iron bars over her windows.

'We'll paint them white, and you'll hardly notice. They aren't unattractive.'

'I'll try not to notice them,' said Sadie.

July passed into a dull August. It rained a lot.

'Don't you go away?' she asked him, as they sat in the crowded garden of Jack Straw's Castle one Saturday lunchtime. He'd driven her over for a long walk on the Heath. Recent light rain brought out the scent of a thousand roses and they spread their jackets over wet wooden benches, to sit down.

'I can't afford a holiday,' she went on, 'but I imagined you'd go to a hot beach somewhere.'

He fiddled with his beer, looked vague.

'No,' he said, 'I don't go away.'

'Not at all?'

'The occasional week. Nothing much.'

'I'd love to see the sea again,' she said wistfully. 'I get fed up with London. We lived so close to the beach, in Norfolk, I'd lie in bed, listen to the waves at night. They send you to sleep. Sometimes I dream about it.'

'Let's do it, then,' he said abruptly.

'What?'

'Go to the sea. You and me. A couple of days.'

He stared into his beer, frowning, not looking at all like a man suggesting a romantic escape. She had a strange sense that he was arguing something fiercely with himself. She didn't need to argue. She knew just what she wanted. She wanted him.

'I've got three days coming, in lieu,' she suggested diffidently. He was still frowning. 'I could take them next week.'

'I'll have to wangle mine,' he said. 'I can't say right now. I'll have to ring you. Where would you like to go?'

It was so natural, it was as if it had always been meant.

'We could go to my cottage. The one by the beach. It's damp and unused, and there's no furniture. It's a hovel. But if you didn't mind roughing it . . .' She was intensely excited. 'I could ring Mary Llewellyn, who looks after it, ask her to open it up and give it an air.'

His brown eyes dropped, he looked old and haggard and lined. Sadie, frightened, wondered if she'd caused some awful, inadvertent offence. When he looked up again, the pain in his face had faded. He had made up his mind.

'Ring Mary Llewellyn. I'll see what I can do about leave,' he said.

They drove up in his car, racing very fast, unafraid of being booked, up the M11, skirted Newmarket, crossing to Mildenhall and the gigantic airbase at Lakenheath, where fighter planes like angry hornets roared in low over high, forbidding perimeter fences. At Castle Acre they turned towards King's Lynn, and three quarters of an hour later nosed down the almost impassable track to the cottage, smelling the sea. The sun came out.

'So this is it,' he said, turning off the engine.

'It's tiny.' She was afraid he'd be disappointed.

'It's magic.'

He got out of the car, stretched stiffly and peered inside the open front door.

'Your friend has been.' He pointed.

Sadie came over and looked.

'She's left us a primus, and coffee and milk and tea. Isn't that kind?' she said. She went to get their bags, and sleeping bags, out of the boot.

'There used to be some old mouldy furniture. Someone's taken it all away.' The cottage was quite, quite bare, the windows dusty.

'Mouldered away,' he said, bringing in a case. 'You can smell it.'

'I warned you.' She felt sad. There was nothing left at all of the aunts. Just bare walls and a stone floor.

'Suits me. Listen, you can hear the sea, like you said.'

'Just over the dyke.'

'We'll go swimming.'

The sleeping bags lay unrolled at their feet, and if they were to swim, they'd need to undress.

'I . . .' began Sadie.

The cottage was dim, sunlight lay beyond the open door, waves stroked and sucked sand, whispering.

'That's what I could hear, as a child. My aunts slept in a great big bed, with me on the floor at the end.'

She was gabbling, acutely aware of him, nervous.

'Sarah,' said John Campling. 'Don't be frightened. I love you.'

She wasn't afraid after that, and for a long time they might have been alone in the world.

They had three days. On their way home, they stopped in King's Lynn, strolled hand in hand by the river, walked round the market.

'Let's go to Sainsbury's,' she said, 'to save going when I get back. I need food for tonight.'

They stood in a checkout queue while the girl changed her till roll and got into a muddle.

'I don't mind,' whispered Sadie, 'it gives us an excuse to linger. Put off getting home. I shall love even Sainsbury's if you're in the queue with me.'

His face tightened.

'I can't stand in Sainsbury's queues with you, Sarah.'

'Well, all right. If you hate shopping that much, I'll do it for two.'

The queue shuffled forwards. A supervisor fixed the till roll. The girl began shoving goods down the belt with a bored expression. John Campling said in an agonised undertone, 'Do you think we can ever be just friends again?'

Astounded, she leaned on her near-empty trolley, looking up.

'Why?' she asked, confused.

The girl on the till, her eyes as blank as marbles, watched the customer fill in a cheque. John turned his back to the till, put his lips to Sadie's ear.

'I love you.'

'I love you,' she whispered back.

'Remember I love you.'

'You look like you just saw a ghost,' she whispered. 'What's the matter.'

'I have a wife,' he said.

'Shall we wait a bit longer?' demanded the cashier sarcastically, her empty belt rolling and rolling, waiting for them to put their groceries on it, as if it were any ordinary day, any ordinary moment. Sadie pushed her trolley to one side, left it standing with the evening's small necessities.

'Some people,' sniffed the cashier. 'Next.'

'Why?' Sadie's teeth chattered and she didn't care if he could hear them. Around them, the car park filled up for late-night shopping; children, up too late, grizzled, sat in trolley seats and sucked their fingers.

'*Why?*' she cried.

'She's been ill for a long time. Multiple sclerosis. It kills everything. Except my responsibility.'

She watched women wheeling shopping, piling it in cars, as if nothing was amiss . . .

'I believed you,' she said dully.

'You're the first woman I've loved since my wife,' he said. 'I thought maybe I could go through with it. I can't.'

'With what? Lying?'

It began to rain again, a fine mist, lacing their hair with pearly droplets.

'I can't leave her. What I mean is, I don't want to leave her. I wish I did. It would be easier.'

'You love her,' said Sadie flatly.

'I can't leave her.'

'It's the same thing. It just comes out in different ways.'

He looked at her, unsurprised by her words.

'The trouble is,' he said, 'I could only love the sort of person who would understand.'

'Will you drive me home,' she said, very cold and shivery, 'and when we get there, I want you to go away, and not come back. Ever. I couldn't bear it.'

She dozed fitfully on the way, awoke in tears.

He leaned over, took her hand.

'No,' she said, pulling free.

His face blurred with misery.

'If you ever want me, I'm there.'

'I'll always want you, and you won't be there,' she answered.

The outskirts of London crawled past. Her sunburned shoulders chafed, her stomach felt as though she had swallowed stones. Her head ached wretchedly.

He carried her case in. Her flat was cool and very quiet. The cheeseplant needed watering. She undid the bolts he'd put in, drew the glass doors open, let fresh air in.

'Do you want a cup of tea, before you go?'

'No. I love you. I haven't lied.'

'You never said her name.'

'Jane.'

'Go home to Jane,' she said.

When he had gone, she sat listening to the traffic, a hum from the other side of the park. The bars on her windows cast evening shadows, then it was quite dark. She locked and bolted every lock and bolt, then went to bed and cried all night, inside the prison he had made.

Chapter Twenty-Three

Surrounded by John Campling's locks and bolts and bars on the doors and windows of her flat, Sadie felt more and more imprisoned. Outwardly imprisoned by security, inwardly imprisoned by bitter betrayal and grief, she realised that John had made himself her gaoler. She asked herself a thousand times, why? Try as she might, she could not believe that he had meant to hurt her. The more she went feverishly over and over the three days, the more she believed he really loved her, was as much a prisoner as she was. His prison was Jane's illness and that he loved and could not leave her. Sadie felt she might go crazy, trying to understand how real love and conscience could cause such pain, and after a while, she stopped trying to understand anything, concentrated on surviving it instead.

Brokenhearted, she tried to pick herself up and carry on as though life still had meaning. She felt as if in three days she had had everything, lost everything, and at moments she was giddy with despair, alternately hating and envying Jane Campling, imagining what she might look like, imagining all sorts of things. Her imaginings went round and round in obsessive, guilty circles, always coming back to the same shameful place; Jane, like Maria, disabled, in a wheelchair. There was no place for envy. It wasn't decent. But she burned with it, anyway, couldn't sleep, became thin and wretched. Just as she thought perhaps this shameful thing would never ease, it did.

She was on the mend, as if convalescing after a wasting illness, when Maria married Philip Howard the following Easter. In mid-February Nonna helped Rosalie send out invitations to the wedding. Sadie turned her own silver-engraved card over and over, propped it on top of the television, against a wooden lamp, wished it were an invitation to a wedding of her own and had a good cry. She was unmistakably getting better, because after the good cry she felt angry, managed to cheer up, and dismissed John and Jane Campling from her mind. That evening, a raw and foggy evening with London smelling like old flannels, Maria rang up. Could she and Nonna come over? They wanted, she said, sounding excited, to ask if Sadie would do a great big favour. Sadie said tomorrow, a Saturday, would be fine, closed her curtains against the dark and murk outside and for the first time in a long while, rummaged in her kitchen cupboards, finding nothing but some out-of-date packet soups, a nibbled packet of cornflakes and some mouse droppings. Mice came in from the park when it got cold, getting into her basement, garden flat with no trouble at all. Wondering whether warfarin or a kitten was the answer, she put on coat and scarf and gloves, went down to the fish and chip shop, ate a hearty supper, and decided on a kitten. It would kill the mice and be company as well.

In the morning, the fog had lifted and a brisk wind blew. Crocus leaves and buds scattered the grass in the park and a robin hopped bossily on her little patio when Sadie threw out crumbs. She realised that she'd slept well and deeply, felt almost happy. She cleaned her flat, went shopping in Sainsbury's and hardly thought about the Camplings at all. When Nonna and Maria came in the mid-afternoon, she brought coffee and biscuits and wondered what they wanted.

'I'm too old to be a bridesmaid,' she said, pouring the coffee, 'if that's what you want.'

'Not a bridesmaid. More special,' said Maria.

'Matron of honour? You have to be married to be a matron of honour.'

'No, I want,' cried Maria, her eyes shining, 'to walk to the altar. From the church porch. Will you walk with me?'

'Can you?' asked Sadie, astonished. 'How?'

'She can,' said Nonna. 'She can walk with callipers. She does it at home, she can do it in the church.'

'I can, if I'm not scared. If I get scared, I seize up and can't move anything at all. I could do it with sticks and you and Michelangelo on either side, so I know I won't fall.'

Sadie imagined wedding dresses and polished church floors and callipers and sticks and too many people in a narrow space, and Maria read her expression. Doubt. Nonna clamped her mouth into a straight line and sent such a scowl in Sadie's direction that it took her breath away.

'I'll stand on my own two feet to be married,' Maria said defensively, 'so don't look at me like that. I want to start as I mean to go on. You've got to help me. Sadie?'

'Of course I will,' said Sadie hastily, quelled by Nonna's ferocious glare. 'Do I have to wear a frilly dress?'

'Not a frilly dress. We've only chosen the colour. We thought a tailored dress or a little suit. Frills would get in the way,' cried Maria anxiously.

'Pale green,' murmured Nonna.

'You see, it's all planned, as usual,' Sadie said, resigned, half-amused by their innocent bullying.

'Rosalie's doing the planning,' remarked Nonna, 'as the bride's mother.'

'Stepmother,' said Maria.

Nonna shrugged, consigning Frances to where she belonged. Nowhere. Sadie fetched their coats from where they lay on her bed.

'Here, we're due for power cuts in a minute. They gave us the rota of cuts on the radio. The heating and lights will go in a minute. It'll be freezing, so put these on.'

'We had two hours in the dark yesterday. We played cards by candlelight and froze,' said Maria.

Sadie lit a candle and put it beside the wedding invitation. As the hands on her kitchen clock reached four, it was already dark outside, and on the hour exactly the power switched off. Rolling cuts forced by the miners' strike reached Hackney again. Nonna grumbled and mumbled in angry Italian. They sat in candlelight and overcoats, their good mood depressed. The small flat quickly cooled and became chill. Nonna fussed.

'We should have remembered blankets,' she said. 'We should have brought a hot-water bottle. Her legs need to be warm.'

Sadie knew Maria's circulation was poor. Cold was dangerous. She fetched blankets from her bedroom and tucked them round the wheelchair.

'Put the gas on,' ordered Nonna.

They parked Maria in the kitchen doorway and lit all the gas jets on the cooker.

'Bills,' muttered Sadie. 'What makes the miners think we can afford this nonsense?'

'How's work?' asked Maria from inside her igloo of blankets.

'Frantic,' Sadie said shortly. 'All this doesn't exactly help.'

'It must be dreadful if you're old, or you've got a baby. What happened to that girl with twins, who wouldn't go home?'

'Cherie? They gave her a maisonette. She ended up with the pick of three, would you believe. Two in Dagenham and one in Kingshold. Silly girl chose Kingshold, worse luck. If she'd gone to Dagenham, someone from an area office over there would have looked after her. As it is, I drew the short straw.'

'How often do you have to go and see her?'

'Every couple of weeks. Her mum's there most of the time. They sit with the babies rolling around on the floor, smoking and eating chips all day. They seem perfectly happy.'

'Perhaps they are,' said Maria.

'They feed those babies tea mixed up with dried babyfood in their bottles. You've never seen anything so revolting. Green sludge. They're fat like Michelin babies, but you'd rather stick your head in a wasps' nest than say anything she thinks is critical. The other day I asked how she managed with the cuts and she looked at me as though I'd just crawled out from under a stone.'

'They're driving Rosalie batty,' said Maria, pulling her coat around her. 'At the salon they keep having to send people home sopping wet. The driers turn off. She said she did a perm the other day and she had to stick the woman's head in a basin of cold water. Said she squawked like anything, but if she hadn't washed the perm lotion off, she'd have had a bald, berserk client.'

'I wish I had straight hair.'

Sadie pulled a long strand of ebony-coloured curl out straight and let it go. It sprang back like a corkscrew.

'Rosalie would do hair attachments for you, like Dad did,' suggested Maria. 'You could have them for my wedding.'

Blackness pressed at the windows, not a streetlamp for miles, east London all blacked out. Burglars would have a field day, thought Sadie uneasily, remembering some of John Campling's stories, glad Nonna and Maria were there. The candle seemed to burn brighter, throwing deep, wavery shadows, making darker corners.

'I suppose,' she said, out of the blue, 'Dougal will be there.'

Maria pulled her blankets tighter around her and said, 'Philip's asked him to be best man. There's nothing I can do.'

'I thought he would. I don't mind,' Sadie said airily.

'Dougal might mind your being there.'

'He might. I can't help it. If you want me to walk you up the aisle and Philip wants him as best man, we'll have to put up with each other.'

'Dougal said you'd found someone else, but you haven't, have you?'

'There was someone I went out with a few times. No one special.'

Sadie put her hands deep in her overcoat pocket and was glad the darkness hid her from Nonna's piercing eyes. She couldn't stand the silence that followed her lie.

'He was married. I found that out and didn't see him any more.'

'A pig,' cried Maria.

'Not at all. There was just no future.' Before she could stop herself, she added, 'His wife is in a wheelchair.'

Maria's black eyes glinted in the blue glow of the gas jets burning on the top of the cooker. The candle guttered as Nonna's breath hissed.

'I think about things like that,' said Maria. 'Don't think I don't.'

The three women sat in the cold and the dark and the eerie light from the gas, pondering the frightening meaning in what Sadie had said.

'Dolly always laughs and says, tell men to take a running jump,' said Sadie, trying to redeem things, and failing.

'That's what you did to poor Dougal. You weren't nice at all,' said Maria, getting her own back.

'I didn't. I just didn't want to live with him. It was he who said it had to be all or nothing.'

'You hurt him.'

'Well, I'm sorry,' yelled Sadie, losing her temper. 'I'm sorry if poor Dougal, who is used to getting his own way and having just what he wants, had the bad luck to *feel* something for a change, when I didn't feel the same. We're not all like you and Philip.'

'Uh, huh,' coughed Nonna warningly.

'Mr and Mrs Perfect,' snapped Sadie furiously.

'Really,' Maria sighed.

Patronised, Sadie drew away, her face set hard. The gas jets hissed.

'The lights come back soon,' suggested Nonna hopefully.

'There's a heater in the car. Let's go home,' said Maria.

'I don't drive,' said Nonna firmly. 'No lights, no traffic lights. Plenty accidents. We wait.'

They had thawed and were chatting again when the lights came on.

On their way out, Nonna said, 'Rosalie said, come to lunch tomorrow, if that Scargill lets us cook it.'

'Sorry I said what I did, it came out the wrong way,' mumbled Sadie.

To her astonishment, the old woman poked her in the ribs with a stubby, mittened finger.

'Maria will walk to her wedding to show *you*.'

'Me? Show me what?'

'I'm ready,' shouted Maria, waiting for Nonna in the car.

'She will show *you* she's as good as you. Real woman, not doll in a chair.'

'*Me?*'

'We coming,' yelled Nonna, and lowered her voice. 'English saying, six of one, 'alf-dozen of the other. Granddaughters, heh? You think about that.'

Sadie flushed with pleasure and embarrassment. Nonna had never called her her granddaughter before. She waved and closed the door as they drew away, went shivering into the brightly lit sitting room and felt the warming radiator. Granddaughter, eh. As she thought about it, the candle sank in a pool of wax and went out.

Rosalie put her knitting in her lap, looked at Nonna sucking her teeth and frowning, and said, 'All right, what is it? Are the girls fighting again?'

'Maria never forgets she is in a wheelchair. She knows it every minute of every day, and she won't let it stop her doing *anything*. Sadie doesn't notice the wheelchair any more and behaves as though Maria is the same as a girl not in a wheelchair. She don't know how much Maria cares.'

Rosalie nodded vaguely. 'They can both be selfish,' she said.

'They can,' said Nonna shortly, as the lights went out.

'Not again,' cried Rosalie, 'I thought we'd had them for today. I could strangle that Scargill.'

'Scargill,' muttered Fooka.

'And you, if you start screeching, I'll strangle you instead,' snapped Rosalie. 'Go to bed.'

Fumbling in the dark, she threw Fooka's cover over his cage.

'Look at us,' she said. 'Them and their cuts and their three-day week. Drat the lot of them.'

She banged Fooka's cage, making sure the door was shut, for good measure.

'Scargill's a *berk*, heh?' said Nonna.

Rosalie grinned, fumbled for the door. Nonna followed her up the stairs, Maria already in bed.

'Your English isn't half getting better,' she said to Nonna as they reached the landing.

Nonna beamed.

'*Berk*,' she repeated loudly, with enjoyment.

'*Berk*,' said Fooka with relish, from under his cover. He adored Nonna and Nonna's words.

Nonna chuckled and felt her way to bed.

Chapter Twenty-Four

Wintry weather and power cuts meant Cherie Sangster mostly stayed indoors. For weeks, her head felt funny, as if it was coming adrift from the rest of her body. She kept blinking rapidly, trying to see clearly. Things were just out of focus. She kept thinking she could see things out of the corner of her eye, just out of reach, like someone creeping up on her, ready to pounce. She was nervy, irritable and tense. Something strange was going on. She went down to the doctors and had a long wait.

'Nuffink,' she said, when her GP asked her what she could do.

'Why have you come to see me, then?'

Cherie batted her head with her hand and said it felt funny.

'Funny, how? Headache?' the GP asked patiently.

'Just tired, I suppose.' Cherie wished she hadn't come, but had listened to common sense that said it was no good trying to explain anything to *them*. 'You should try being banged up with two kids all day. Your head would go funny, too,' she said rudely.

'I have been. I know what you mean,' said her GP. 'You look tired and run down, and if you ate a bit more, I'm sure you'd feel better.'

'Can I have something for me nerves?' Cherie sat stubbornly in front of her, waiting. She wouldn't leave without a prescription and if she did, she'd write off the surgery altogether and not come back. They needed her to feel she could come back, against that day when she might need help. And she was definitely tense and nervy and depressed and stressed.

'All right,' her GP said, writing the prescription for valium, 'come and see me again in a couple of weeks.'

Cherie snatched the prescription and fled.

At home, she shook all the blue valium pills from the little brown bottle into her hand and wondered if they'd stop the buzzing in her head. She put them back in the bottle. Something had to stop. Cherie nudged a bottle closer to a baby, where it could roll over on its back and suck, lying on the floor. It dropped the bottle and shrieked. She jammed the soft, old teat into its mouth and it chewed furiously with inflamed, teething gums.

'It won't be you,' Cherie snapped at Johnny, 'will it, you won't stop your yellin' and gobblin' and smellin', will you?'

Johnny's pale eau-de-nil eyes watched her warily. She went out to make Jason his bottle as well. They never let up, except when she put them down to sleep at night.

Give her some peace otherwise? Cherie grinned derisively, spooning dried food into an unwashed jug. Not a chance.

Next time she went down to the doctors, it was for the babies. They screamed blue murder in the waiting room, until one of the partners came out and said he couldn't hear himself speak, and would she keep the babies quiet. Other patients scuffled and glared and tried to read the ageing magazines piled on the table. A telephone rang insistently on the desk and a cold draught swept everyone's ankles each time anyone went in or out of the fingermarked glass door to the street.

'It ain't easy and I'm doing my best,' snapped Cherie, looking daggers, muttering something much ruder under her breath. Her mother, Beryl, lit a fag, caught the receptionist's finger pointing angrily, pretended she hadn't seen the 'no smoking' sign. She pinched the fag out, put it pointedly back in the packet, mumbling. Lipreading, the receptionist's mouth twitched with outrage. Then, when they finally got in, the doctor made it clear they had partly wasted their time.

'They were premature,' she explained. 'We don't give premature babies the combined jab. Didn't your Health Visitor tell you?'

'She don't come round much. They was only a *bit* premature,' said Cherie, determined her waiting wouldn't be in vain, ready to argue the toss.

Beryl started to pull clothes off the baby on her lap. 'I'd have thought they'd need their jabs more,' she insisted.

'It's a contraindication,' said the overworked GP. Beryl paused in her undressing, baffled. 'I mean, I'd advise you not to let them have the whooping-cough jab. They had slight breathing problems over their first day or two and for babies like that, it's not a good idea to give them whooping-cough jabs. You can't have the combined one, you see. If you make another appointment, we can get separate jabs, without the whooping-cough bit.'

'No one said they had breathing problems at the 'ospital,' said Cherie. 'Why not?'

'I think you were a bit upset at the time,' said the doctor blandly. 'I don't suppose they wanted to worry you, when there wasn't any need. They were fine. And they look fine, now.'

Mother and daughter sat in the cramped consulting room, clutching the babies; two round, peach-coloured faces working at dummies, identical eau-de-nil eyes staring at the doctor staring at them. She sniffed and carefully kept a neutral face. The babies needed changing.

'No jabs today?'

The GP shook her head. 'We have to get the medicine in. Tell the receptionist to give you an appointment next week.'

'All right,' said Cherie, compromising. 'I'll take something for the nappy rash.'

'Frequent washing and lots of fresh air is best,' began the doctor, moving with relief on to uncontentious ground. 'Leave their nappies off as much as you can. Keep them dry.'

Her patient looked scornful.

'They'll pee on the carpet. You know what boys do. They spray. Dirty little buggers.'

'Some of that pink cream,' demanded her mother firmly.

The GP sighed. The prescription deal. Obediently she wrote one out.

'What about vitamins?' she asked, signing the form. 'Do you get them from the clinic?'

'Abidec from the 'ealth visitor,' said Cherie triumphantly, chalking one up to herself. The doctor had expected her to say 'No.'

'Fluoride?'

Cherie sniffed.

'Do you give them Abidec regularly?'

That blank expression, thought the doctor, meant she didn't and there was no use telling her to. The discussion was over.

'My daughter's tired to death,' said Beryl, jamming a dummy back in a baby's mouth. The baby fought to spit it out again, but she held it in grimly.

''er hair's all falling out, as well,' Beryl went on, challenging the GP to do anything about it.

Cherie, thought her doctor, who had children of her own, looked like a child from a concentration camp, anorexic and sunken-eyed; legs like sticks. It was pointless to argue. The money went on tea and fags and baby-food. At least they looked nourished and plump. As for hair falling out, hydrogen peroxide did the rest. 'Do you eat and sleep at *all*?'

Cherie hoisted her baby on to her shoulder, grabbed the prescription for nappy cream, and stalked out.

'What does she fuckin' know?' she complained, stuffing the twins into a double pram with torn hoods, that the clinic had found for her. With proper hoods, she would've been really proud of it.

'You could 'ave told her what it's like,' said Beryl, 'when they play up all the time. She might have given you somethin' to make em' sleep.'

Cherie turned bleak and angry eyes on her mother, her gaunt, child's face framed by limp peroxide hair, her mouth bitter. She'd been pretty and rosy-cheeked once, with the soft slight curves of near-womanhood.

'Leave it out, Mum.'

'You watch it,' warned Beryl. 'They could take 'em away. You got that social worker coming round, and you'd better mind out or she'll take 'em away.'

'I shouldn't care.' Cherie looked down at the thrashing mass of limbs in the pram, wet nappies, wet red mouths, ready to scream. She sucked the dummies to clean them and shoved them in the mouths like corks. She started to push furiously.

'She might have given you something,' argued her mother, lagging behind. 'That stuff in a bottle. What's it called?'

Cherie turned, leaning on the pram handle, waiting. 'Phenergan. You can buy it, an' I tried it, an' it don't make no difference. If you cut down on the fags, you wouldn't be so bad yourself.'

Beryl, grey faced, caught her breath, lungs waterlogged with emphysema. The twins spat out their dummies with enjoyment, and shrieked. Cherie, just eighteen, spidery limbed with starvation, bent double behind the heavy pram, began to push her graceless burden home. Traffic roared, a line of lorries revving at the crossroads, edging forwards, not giving way. Traffic lights killed by power cuts left a free for all. Power cuts had killed Beryl's lift and Cherie's cooker. Killed the heating. Dog eat dog. Cherie soldiered on.

They had shopping to do on the way. PG Tips and Tesco's blended whisky. Staff of life, loaded under the babies' lumpy mattress, well out of sight of the woman who patrolled Tesco's, pushing a trolley with a bag of potatoes, a box of cornflakes, a sliced loaf and cartons of washing powder. Nothing that went off. Round and round she went, in a headscarf, like the Queen. Cherie found her funny.

'Silly bitch,' she jeered. 'Security's tattooed on 'er fore'ead.'

'It's the Clark's shoes,' said Beryl, grinning, slipping tea bags into the pram. 'And no yoghurts.'

Cherie parked the pram in front of her little maisonette and put on the brake.

'Hullo, Cherie,' said Sadie, making her jump.

Shamelessly fishing whisky from underneath her sons, Cherie tucked the bottle under one arm and hauled a baby out by its armpits.

'I suppose you want to see 'em,' she remarked, 'so this is very convenient. 'Ere they are. We just been down the doctors. She'll tell you. All right?'

The baby in the pram stopped writhing and stared at Sadie with interest.

'Are they ill?'

'I took 'em for their jabs,' said Cherie virtuously, 'but she wouldn't do them.'

'Why not?'

'Said they shouldn't 'ave 'em.'

'Are you all right?'

'Me arm's droppin' off,' snapped Cherie, hitching the baby up.

'She's not all right. She's tired to death,' puffed Beryl, coming up behind.

A cat sat washing itself in Cherie's tiny, weedy front patch and all her curtains were tightly shut, her windows blank. Up and down grey concrete walls, on the sides of tower blocks, on the fronts of Cherie's four-storey block of maisonettes, graffiti spat anger, misspelled. A group of black youths kicked a football up and down, while a woman yelled from a balcony, couldn't they be quiet. A radio played heavy metal somewhere and a dog wandered, scratching, and sniffing round dead-looking trees, its ears up, wary of cats and large feet kicking the football, ready, it knew from experience, at a moment's provocation to kick *it*.

'Do you mind if I come in?' asked Sadie.

''Course I bloody mind,' snarled Cherie, 'but since when did that make any fuckin' difference?'

'It's too cold to stand outside.'

Cherie banged open her front door, dumped the baby on the floor and dragged the pram and its howling occupant indoors, where it took up what little space there was.

'There,' she snapped, putting her whisky on the draining board in a tiny kitchenette. 'What d'you want now?'

Beryl took nappies off the back of the kitchen chairs and said she'd see to the babies. Cherie sat down and began to read the label on the whisky bottle.

'Shoulda drowned 'em in a bucket at birth,' she remarked, just to provoke the welfare woman.

The kitchen smelled of cigarettes, wet washing and staleness. Weak, wintry grey daylight filtered gloomily from behind closed blinds. The top of the cooker was piled with half-used boxes of Farex, dried carrot and tomato dinner, rusks and a small tank in which bottles soaked, teats upended, floating on top of Milton.

'Are you getting your stuff from the clinic all right? Do you sterilise everything?'

Cherie glanced at the tank automatically, and Sadie thought, that's its usual place. She must never use the cooker.

'Want a cup of tea?'

'Please,' said Sadie bravely, bracing herself for lukewarm tea with condensed milk, in a mug that could have walked off on its own. Cherie plugged the kettle in, dropped tea bags into mugs, leaned on the edge of the sink, waiting for the kettle. 'Watched kettles never boil,' she remarked, less hostile.

Sadie wanted to ask her when she'd last eaten, but it would make Cherie go straight back inside her shell and not come out again. 'Why wouldn't the doctor do their jabs?' she asked instead.

'They were premature. She said they can't have whooping cough, so we got to go back.'

'I didn't know you didn't give premature babies the whooping-cough jab.'

'Fancy you not knowing something,' said Cherie sourly. 'What's wrong with this thing?'

She took the lid off the kettle, put her finger in the water, looked up at the bulb in the ceiling. It had been so dim, they'd barely noticed.

'Power's off again.'

Beryl arrived in the doorway. 'They're done.'

Rhythmic howls came from behind her.

'They're hungry,' said their grandmother, putting disposable nappies into a bin. Cherie bent over the kettle, rubbing her forehead, trying to massage away the pain behind her eyes.

'They'll have to eat it cold, then.'

She straightened up, took a box of baby food from the pile on the cooker, dumped the contents into a mug with cold water. She pulled a face.

'Jesus. 'Ere, see if they'll eat it,' she ordered, holding out the mug and a teaspoon to her mother.

'Mum's goin' back,' she told Sadie, as Beryl propped the babies up in the pram, side by side, spooning baby food as fast as she could into identical cuckoo-like mouths.

'Your mother's going home? Will you manage on your own?'

'She's 'ad enough.' Cherie gave a mirthless laugh. 'Can't blame 'er, can you? She says she can't leave Ron to 'imself any longer. But really, she's 'ad enough.'

'Couldn't Ron come here and lend a hand?'

The look in Cherie's eyes told Sadie who the babies' father was. It was a taboo subject.

'Doesn't your mother *mind*?' asked Sadie bravely.

Cherie, trying to make baby milk with stone-cold water, turned her back contemptuously and didn't answer.

'You better keep an eye on 'er,' said Beryl in an undertone. She sat wreathed in smoke. In the other room, Cherie fed Jason and Johnny cold milk. They gulped it down.

'Shan't bother boiling water in future,' she remarked. 'Buggers couldn't care less, could they?'

'Don't you think she'll manage?' hissed Sadie, out of Cherie's earshot.

Managing, she reminded herself, meant different things to different people, and she must not be judgemental. First

Commandment of social work: though shalt not judge. Beryl snorted and had an appalling fit of coughing.

'Yes,' she said sarcastically, 'I expect she'll manage.'

'I'll come regularly,' promised Sadie.

Beryl stared at her incredulously.

'Well, now, that'll make all the difference,' she jeered, and wheezed painfully into another fit of coughing. 'You do that.' She ground out her cigarette in the top of a Nescafe jar and lit a fresh one.

'Is Ron their father?' demanded Sadie.

'So I got to get back, you see,' Beryl insisted, blowing out a long stream of smoke, as though Sadie hadn't spoken. Brick walls, she thought, bewildered.

Cherie came back with two empty bottles. 'You still 'ere?' she said rudely, throwing the bottles in the sink.

'I'm just going,' answered Sadie, pulling her coat round her.

'Good riddance.'

Cherie watched her walk away, peering round the edge of the blind.

'She ain't so bad,' said Beryl. 'You don't 'ave to get on the wrong side of everyone.'

The twins lolled in their pram, dozing, their bellies full. Cherie picked the whisky bottle out of the sink and unscrewed the top.

'Fuck the lot of you,' she said wearily.

The following morning Sadie had a supervision session. Going through a pile of cases, they came to Cherie.

'Ah. How is it going?' asked her supervisor.

'It's a waste of time,' said Sadie. 'Why am I visiting? All we're doing is waiting for the axe to fall. Something awful is going to happen to those babies. I know it is.'

'So far, she's given us no excuse to ask for a place of safety order. She doesn't abuse them. She's there all the time, as she should be. The GP has seen them within the last few days, and they're in good shape. What can we do?'

'She treats them like animals and Cherie herself looks like death.'

'Ah. *Quality* of mothering is what you're talking about.'

'Yes,' snapped Sadie.

He shook his head. 'Uh, huh. Not our job to judge unless she's harming them.'

'It has to be life and death before we do anything?'

'You're over involved,' he said.

Her jaw dropped. 'I care.'

'You're putting your own values on to Cherie and finding her short. You shouldn't do that.'

'I want to do something to help those babies,' she said bleakly.

'Cherie hasn't broken the law,' he said blandly. 'We can only monitor the situation.'

She tried one last time. 'I have a feeling by the time we've finished *monitoring*, those babies will be *dead*.'

'You seem very anxious about your work.' He leaned forward with professional concern. 'Shall we increase your supervision?' he offered.

Pompous, lying *ass*, she thought, stifling the words before they could get out and get her into trouble. Over-emotional and over-involved, he wrote in her records. He increased her hours of supervision.

Chapter Twenty-Five

Dougal and Philip, having spent a miserable week making people redundant in their offices, sat drinking Chablis in a trattoria on Belsize Park, drowning their sorrows. Beyond the steamed-up restaurant window, trees heavy with buds dripped steadily under a ceaseless downpour. The weather matched their mood nicely. The tables were covered with pink gingham cloths and candles in Chianti bottles, and the restaurant was crowded with gilded Hampstead youth and lunchtime businessmen in Burton suits. It was much more cheerful inside than out, but it wasn't enough to raise their spirits much.

'Here's to the three-day week and redundancies,' said Dougal gloomily, raising his glass with a scowl. 'What a bastard.'

'I hate sacking people,' said Philip. 'I *liked* every single person I sacked this week.'

'It's business,' said Dougal with his mouth full, chewing a breadstick without enjoyment. He put the broken breadstick back in the pot on the table. 'Why do Italians like eating crusts?'

Philip took no notice. He watched a very young waitress clearing tables. She had a mole on the outer edge of one eye. It made her look lopsided and rather glamorous.

'Maria and I had a bit of a row. She blames me.'

'My word,' said Dougal sarcastically. 'A *row*. Are the lovebirds pecking each other, then? Dear oh dear. Blames you for what?'

'Sacking people. She gets worked up about people being unemployed and thinks I'm some kind of monster.'

'You'll have to explain the facts of life to her. Wage-bills and productivity.'

'She thinks if I wasn't selling computer systems, all those nice people running card indexes and writing things down on bits of paper would keep their jobs. She doesn't understand the computer revolution,' said Philip wryly.

Dougal grinned maliciously and opened his mouth to crow again about lovebirds, when the waitress came for their orders. They both wanted spaghetti. Philip pulled a bundle of paper out of his pocket.

'One large bungalow,' he pronounced, spreading estate agents' blurb on the table. 'We'll convert the roof into an office, for me, and do our living all on one floor. Perfect for Maria.'

'Where is this?' asked Dougal, turning the papers over, looking for an address.

'Barnsbury.'

'You're going to swap Hampstead for *Barnsbury*?'

'So that Maria can be near her family.'

'You'll be surrounded by in-laws,' remarked Dougal. The thought seemed to amuse him and he sat studying the Chablis label with his mouth twitching. Then inspiration struck him. 'Why don't you get your mother to do an interior for you? Disabled design. I bet there's a huge market for that and no one exploiting it.'

'Why didn't I think of that?' Philip turned his mild, protuberant eyes on Dougal and sounded almost angry. When Philip was annoyed the tips of his ears went red.

'Because I'm the ideas man,' said Dougal cheerfully.

The waitress with the mole by her eye put plates of spaghetti in front of them, handing them knives and forks wrapped in red paper napkins. She had very long, dark lashes and pale-grey eyes in an oval face, lifted from ordinary prettiness to striking by the blemish. It would once have been called a beauty spot, and it was easy to see why. Dougal stared at it, fascinated, then slid his eyes openly over the rest of her. She grinned boldly, pushed the spaghetti in front of him and wiggled her hips teasingly as she walked away. Dougal's hungry expression reminded Philip of something.

'Sadie is going to be Maria's helper at the wedding. You and she not speaking, or what? It won't be awkward, will it?'

'I'm sure we'll manage to be civil to each other,' said Dougal, leaning back in his chair, trying to catch the girl's eye again, for more wine and another chance to tease.

'Any chance you might get together again?'

'Ask Sadie,' Dougal snapped, knocking the empty wine bottle flying, windmilling his long arms to indicate to the girl that he wanted another. Philip, controlled and dapper, watched Dougal's performance resignedly. He could be worse and often was.

'You and Sadie are both so bloody stubborn, you suit each other down to the ground. Why don't you get together again? It'd make everyone happy.'

Dougal dabbed at a little shower of bolognese sauce on his dark suit and said expansively that he was getting it together nicely with a blonde he'd met at a dinner party, thank you very much. The girl banged a fresh bottle of Chablis on the table and flounced off.

'Is it something we did?' asked Philip, looking after her indignant back.

Dougal grinned. 'I goosed her.'

Philip knew him too well. This was the old, insecure Dougal with a large mouth, a chip on his shoulder and size twelve feet he kept tripping over. While he'd been with Sadie, he'd softened, relaxed, been much more together. Philip watched the performance with the waitress and sighed. By the end of their meal, she was thoroughly offended. To Philip it looked more as if Dougal were desperately unhappy. Blondes and dinner parties? Dougal having a good time? He didn't believe a word of it. Dougal, so far as Philip could see, was still in love with Sadie.

Chapter Twenty-Six

A week or so after Philip and Dougal had lunch in the trattoria the sun broke through after ten dull days of rain, shone into Rosalie's sitting room and brightened Fooka's feathers. Enjoying its warmth, he craned over the very end of his perch, watching the drama below. He loved raised voices and this morning there had been plenty, the two voices he loved best raised against each other, driving him into a state of feather-ruffling, perch-dancing excitement. He squawked and banged his beak on his bars. The figure hanging in a funny disjointed position jerked into life.

'*Walk*,' yelled Maria.

For weeks, she'd gritted her teeth and told her body to do as it was told, and *walk*. It fought back. It dragged and lagged and twisted. It spasmed and twitched. It hurt where she could feel it, refused to cooperate where she couldn't. It humiliated, infuriated and frustrated her into hysterics. Nonna brought a cold wet flannel and mopped her granddaughter's face. Maria balanced unsteadily on crutches and let fly, spoiling for a fight – about anything that came to hand. She didn't care.

'I suppose you'll go back to Rome after I've gone,' she shrieked. 'I suppose you'll go and leave me. Why should you care? I don't care.'

'Maria,' said Nonna, her voice steely.

'I am trying,' shouted Maria. 'Don't think I'm not. Perhaps it doesn't look as though I'm trying, but let me tell you, I am, I am, I *am*.'

'You think we can't *see* that?'

'Yes. No. No one can see what it's like,' she panted, wobbling, wrong-footed even worse by her own outburst.

'*Maria*,' said Nonna reproachfully.

Maria sniffled. She had tried to make conversation while she and Nonna daily struggled up and down the room, practising walking. She ground her teeth and tried to be brave, but pain was nothing compared to frustration. *That* was what drove her into hysterics . . . that and Nonna going away. The thought brought fresh tears.

'I want my legs back,' she howled, crying, unable to reach a handkerchief from her crutches. Nonna tried reason and wiped her nose for her with a clean tissue, like a baby.

'I am here a long time. I am sometimes 'omesick. I miss my apartment, and Rome.' She held out the cold flannel, a peace offering. 'And when you are married, you don't want an old grandmother poking her nose.'

'That's what *you* want. *I* want legs,' yelled Maria, pushing the flannel away childishly. 'I don't want wet cloths. I want *legs*. And I don't want you to go, and I want *legs*,' she ended breathlessly. She teetered on one useless foot and banged a crutch hard on her leg. Furious, Nonna grabbed her.

'You want your wedding day in the unit, all sores? Listen to me, Maria,' she roared.

Nonna *never* shouted.

'*Stop* this. *Basta. Ti dico basta*! It is enough, Maria.'

Maria, hung, crucified on crutches, and sobbed. Fooka scuttled up and down, agitated. He liked shouting, not crying. He peered down, frustrated.

'I can't walk up the aisle,' wept Maria.

'*Sì*,' said Nonna, meaning, yes, you jolly well can.

'I *can't*,' her granddaughter wailed.

'*Sì*, you can walk,' said Nonna.

'Help me, then,' howled Maria, a little girl. 'I'm stuck,' she went on in mounting fury. 'I can't move. I can't sit down, I can't go forwards, I can't go back, I'm *stuck*.'

She swayed, padded callipers biting at trousers, up to her thighs, crutches creaking. Nonna planted herself foursquare, patrician nose to patrician nose, hands on hips, solid as a tug. They suddenly looked very alike.

'*Shut up*,' yelled Nonna. '*Chiudi il becco*!'

Maria hiccuped in astonishment. Fooka, beside himself, heard his favourite sound and hiccuped back.

'*And you*,' yelled Nonna, shaking her fist.

Maria shifted her crutches and balanced, tear-streaked face calmer.

'That's better. Now then,' said her grandmother.

'What?'

Nonna backed off and rummaged in a sideboard drawer, pulled out a booklet.

'Oh, don't start . . .'

'*Listen*.'

'I'm tired,' wailed Maria, and had such a look from Nonna that she quailed. 'I know what that booklet says,' she said sulkily.

Nonna found her place, began to read it aloud, anyway.

'If a lesion is below L3, a patient should be able to walk quite a lot in everyday life and may eventually be able to rise unaided and walk as much as several hundred yards. A low-level lesion may leave the patient able to climb steps.'

Maria hung her head.

'Where is your lesion?'

'L3.'

Several hundred yards.

''Ow long is the aisle, Maria?'

'Don't go on and on.'

'You don't sulk, then.'

'I'm not sulking.'

'*Allora, va bene*.'

Nonna snapped the booklet shut. She'd won.

'All right.'

Maria gave in, heaved her crutches straight, took a deep breath, and began to walk.

'Left, right, left . . .' said Nonna, walking beside her. Up and down, up and down,

'You've given up masses of things for me. I'm sorry I said what I did. But I wish you didn't have to go.'

Nonna smelled sweet and safe and familiar; of eau-de-Cologne, freshly ironed cotton, and somehow of love. Maria wanted to cry again.

'Left . . . left,' went Nonna remorselessly.

'You hardly ever watch the racing,' Maria went on sadly, 'and you haven't been round the corner to the betting shop in ages. Hardly since we went to Ascot. And you get really tired when I'm grotty. I notice, you know. I'm not all self.'

'*Bene*,' answered her grandmother briskly. 'One more time round, then. One more.'

Exhausted, Maria leaned on her sticks.

'You can look after yourself now,' said Nonna briskly. 'And your 'usband. You'll be busy.'

Maria crumpled. 'If you really want to know, I'm scared stiff.'

'You should be. Marriage . . .' Nonna brought the wheelchair over. Her knees cracked as she knelt to loosen Maria's callipers. '. . . is hard work. For you, maybe harder.'

'If I tell Philip that, he says there isn't anything we can't do, if we want to. No such word as can't. I get no sympathy, I can tell you.'

'Sympathy,' snorted Nonna. ''Oo said *can't*, and walked ten times round the room, heh?'

Maria eased herself into her chair. 'Me.'

'Then why you want sympathy? What for?'

Maria looked at the untidy litter of crutches, callipers, padding and wet flannels, depressed by the unending clutter of disability.

'Maria Theresa Giangelli,' hissed Nonna, leaning on the arms of the wheelchair, eyeball to eyeball, 'You *walk* to be married, in that beautiful dress.'

The dress was carefully designed to look good in and out of the chair, full and ruched and wide-skirted, smothered in silk roses. The dress would dwarf the chair, not the other way around.

'I will,' said Maria.

'*Bambina mia*, you better had,' said Nonna.

Chapter Twenty-Seven

Standing in a front pew in church, on Maria's wedding day, Nonna looked at her granddaughter's veiled dark head, upright and steady at her new husband's morning-suited shoulder, and offered up an impassioned *grazie* to Her Lady. That day, Maria walked tall. All the anguish of the past weeks was worthwhile; the wedding photos showed a radiant girl. Rosalie was fond of remarking that no one looking at the pictures would ever guess at the padding and callipers Maria wore underneath that fabulous gown.

'Unless you were there,' answered Sadie, giggling.

Things hadn't gone entirely to their original plan.

Sadie's instructions had been to hand Maria her crutches, when she arrived at the church, for the walk down the aisle, and to follow closely, in case anything went wrong and Maria stumbled. She was to have the folded wheelchair ready, as well, just in case. They'd practised and practised, and everyone knew Maria could do it. On crutches.

On the day itself, Sadie waited in the church porch, trying to ignore the presence of Dougal. She was in a pale-green silk suit, with short skirt and high heels. It made her look like a bud, thought Dougal, pretending he didn't see her, a fragrant, long-stemmed bud. He fiddled with the carnation in his buttonhole, suddenly depressed, feeling the hired morning suit tight across his broad shoulders, grey like his mood. He waited with Philip, the ring in his breast pocket, everything under control. Unseen in the porch, Sadie watched his sturdy figure turn slightly and say something in an undertone to Philip, who stood very upright and willowy in darker grey, his round eyes blinking nervously, more like an anxious, gentle hare than ever. Sadie watched Dougal as furtively as he watched her, neither willing to climb down and be the first one to speak. In rehearsals they had been stiff and correct with each other to start with, she in a tracksuit, he in slacks and desert boots, Maria in her chair, and then up on her crutches, wore a net curtain on her head to get into the spirit of the thing. Getting into the spirit of it had ended in clowning and farce, had them all weak with laughter, faces aching, collapsed on the altar steps, predicting dire disasters on the day. Sadie remembered then everything she so liked about him, but the memory of John Campling was strong and sweet and sad, so that when Dougal diffidently asked her, in his deep Welsh voice, to come for a drink one evening, she shook her head and turned away.

Now, on a mild and cloudy afternoon, the moment had come. The atmosphere was electric, the church packed, waiting for the bride, everyone whispering, scuffling, craning their necks hopefully, for the first glimpse of Maria. People were saying she planned to walk . . . there was murmured speculation. There was a lot of speculation . . . Dougal felt Sadie's gaze on the back of his head and carefully didn't look round. She looked away at the sound of a car drawing up, the scrunch of wheels on gravel, right up to the church door. Maria and Michelangelo, who was to give her away, had arrived. The church almost stilled, half held its breath. No one heard the muted argument going on in the porch.

'You need them,' Sadie whispered furiously, just outside the church door. 'You *have* to.'

'No.'

Maria pushed the crutches back at Sadie and tucked her hand under her brother's steady arm.

'You'll fall *over*,' hissed Sadie.

'I won't fall over.'

'Tell her,' pleaded Sadie, looking at Michelangelo.

Hidden by the cream crinoline looped heavily with roses,

heavy callipers bit her legs. To swing her feet forward, Maria had to balance on each leg in turn. It would be agonisingly slow, and without sticks, she would topple.

'But . . .'

'No,' thundered Maria in a whisper.

'You *can't*,' hissed Sadie. 'You'll spoil . . . you'll fall over.'

'Shut up, she won't fall over. It's a surprise,' whispered Michelangelo. 'We've practised. She can do it if we hold her hands.'

Sadie stood, awkwardly holding out a pair of crutches, uncertain, unhappy.

'If you fall over, don't you *dare* blame me,' she hissed.

'Walk my other side,' whispered Maria, beginning to giggle at Sadie's dire expression, 'and don't let me start laughing or I'll wobble.'

'Oh, my God,' muttered Sadie, putting the sticks down, foreseeing disaster.

Michelangelo, bushy-bearded, solid as a rock, covered his sister's hand with his and gave a broad smile of encouragement.

Sadie, wiry hair already escaping its pins underneath the same pretty straw hat she'd worn at Ascot, all dark green ribbons and pale-green formal suit, gave in, dumped the sticks on a bench in the porch and said, 'It's your wedding. You do what you like. Here, wait a moment, you'll catch.'

She knelt behind Maria, straightened her trailing veil over the crinoline, and the hoops of roses, their hidden purpose to keep the silk from tangling with the callipers.

'You're ready,' she whispered.

Michelangelo stuck out a foot, waited for Maria to balance herself, and gave marching orders.

'Left leg first.'

Sadie skipped into line.

'Go,' Michelangelo ordered.

The organist, poised, saw them coming, held one high, long note, and slid gracefully into the 'Wedding March'.

Philip glanced at Dougal, who raised his eyebrows sardonically and mouthed, 'Not too late to run.'

Philip frowned. A muted babble broke out, above the music. He'd planned not to turn and look, not to make her self-conscious. The muted babble became a loud, excited babble. He turned to find Maria just behind him, walking on Michelangelo's arm, holding Sadie by the hand. His jaw dropped.

'Look, no hands,' Maria whispered, under the sound of the music.

His long face, impossibly like a startled hare suddenly alert in the middle of a field, comical with astonishment, made her start to shake with laughter. But she steadied herself, took her hand from her brother's arm, let go of Sadie. Philip did not move one inch towards her, would not diminish her. Maria walked three steps she would remember all her life, alone, then reached out.

Everyone was there, of course. Of the bride's family, only Frances was missing. There had been what Jove described as an *atmosphere* when someone suggested that the bride's mother should come to stay. Rosalie, tight-lipped and outraged, called a family conference. They said it had to be Maria who decided. Maria consulted Nonna. Compromise. They sent an ordinary invitation to Frances, pointedly leaving her to make her own arrangements. Frances, reading the negatives correctly, sent a delivery of a canteen of Heal's Finnish cutlery instead.

'Nice,' commented Rosalie, mollified.

'Very,' agreed Maria, and they left it at that.

Rosalie cried, as was proper. Giovanni's many friends and old clients came, bringing back the memories. Her own widowed mother, five feet tall and five feet round, sat beside her in the front pew like a pale-blue blancmange, aquiver with sympathy. Handing paper tissues to her widowed daughter, she enjoyed herself immensely.

Anne Howard, slim, still young, dark hair hardly touched by grey, sensed her son's shoulders stiffen as he promised to love and cherish Maria. She silently promised to love and to cherish Philip's wife, herself. If his father had only lived to see . . . Anne blew her nose discreetly and daydreamed while the service drew to its close. We have a formidable alliance here, she thought, coming back to the present. They will be splendid together.

Dougal, getting ready to hand over the ring, caught Sadie's eye. He lifted an eyebrow and she looked away. He cleared his throat and she looked back involuntarily. He grinned and gave a slow wink. Sadie stared at the top of Maria's veil, glassy-eyed. Dougal sighed dramatically, his hands behind his back, clasping two beige gloves, looking sidelong at her. Dougal, we've hurt each other enough, please give up, thought Sadie. Philip held out his hand.

'Uh,' said Dougal, his mind still on Sadie and how all that hair escaping in falling curls made her look as if she had just got out of bed . . .

'Ring,' hissed Philip.

The back of Dougal's neck went scarlet as he opened empty hands. He cast about on the floor with his eyes.

'Must have dropped it,' he mumbled.

'I didn't hear anything fall,' whispered Maria.

Sadie reached out and picked Maria's wedding ring off the thumb of one of Dougal's beige gloves, and handed it wordlessly to him. After that, he minded his step, carried out his duties impeccably and sang hymns in a glorious voice, rich and full and beautiful. Sadie sighed, wished things were different, imagined herself at the altar with him, and thought it was a shame it wouldn't happen.

Nonna, totally at home and at ease in church, behaved less well than Dougal. She beamed and chuckled audibly, nodding her head in answer to the priest's questions, repeating the vows to herself, not entirely under her breath, and, thought the officiating priest, watching her out of the corner of his eye, enjoyed the ceremony as uninhibitedly as the Good Lord would wish. Would that more people did so, he thought, waiting for Maria to finish her vows. Nonna was squashed into one end of the pew, on Rosalie's mother's other side. The price of one hundred rosaries promised to Her Lady if Maria did it, was perhaps a trifle mean. She doubled it on impulse. Two hundred rosaries for watching Maria win. Worth every minute of them, it had been better than winning the Derby. She fingered her beads happily. Behind her, Mags and Sissy and all their brood, along with cousins from England, half-cousins from Italy, relatives from everywhere and every degree of blood connection, friends, neighbours and Maria's consultant from the unit, watched with proud and speculative eyes as she married Philip that cloudy Easter Saturday.

The congregation poured out of the church to stand in a sluggish breeze, sunshine breaking through the clouds. Maria, pale and exhausted, leaned on Philip until Anne Howard brought her wheelchair. They milled around, posing for photographs. The photographer cajoled and choreographed groups, dancing around like a game-show host, calling to people to come on down, lining them up, bossing and joking and capering, demanding kisses and hand-holding from bride and groom.

'How about best man and best woman?' suggested Dougal, in Sadie's ear.

She tried to smile without encouraging him.

'Come on,' whispered Dougal. 'It's Maria's wedding day. Cheer up.'

'I am perfectly cheered up, thank you,' she snapped.

Afterwards, everyone was delighted with the photographs.

Guests began to leave, fetching cars parked in sidestreets to drive to the reception. Sadie beckoned the hired car to come as close as it could, to pick Maria and Philip up and take them through crowded London streets to Jove's restaurant in Soho. Confetti showered. Maria threw her bouquet to Sadie, who caught it, went pink and avoided Dougal's ironic eye.

* * *

It was a splendid wedding breakfast. Dougal read messages of goodwill and congratulations, made a short, amusing speech. Then voices called for Philip to stand up.

'Speech,' they cried, banging on tables. 'Speech, speech.'

Philip put down his glass and rose. Maria looked up at him. They had planned this moment, and what he would say, together. It was suddenly so quiet you could have heard a pin drop.

'I know what you're all thinking,' began Philip affably, leaning on the table, relaxed.

The atmosphere, instantly electric, betrayed itself in embarrassed scuffling and clearing of throats.

'You are wondering what it is like to be a paraplegic, and to be married to a paraplegic. You are *curious* about what our future and our marriage will be like. You are wondering whether we have a real marriage, a real future. Perhaps you're even feeling sorry for us. Or for me,' he added calmly, catching Nonna's encouraging eye. Dougal, crumbling half a bread roll in his fingers, gulped, hiding his astonishment. Philip looked down and grinned until Dougal reached for a bottle of wine and poured himself a glass. It overflowed. Philip went on grinning, then mercifully went back to his speech. Dougal, mortified, dabbed at the puddle of wine and wished himself a million miles away. Philip had his vengeance for Dougal's earlier interfering. Anne Howard folded her arms and gazed at her son steadily, silently supporting him.

'Well, we decided to say something about that, to put your minds at rest,' Philip continued cheerfully, 'didn't we, darling?' Maria smiled.

Nonna snatched her beads from her pocket. Make it three hundred rosaries that he doesn't say anything awful, and start quick.

Guests sat, some with their mouths open, others looking earnestly into the tablecloth, embarrassed, caught out by their secret speculations.

'My wife . . .' began Philip again.

Maria glowed at the word *wife*.

'. . . isn't going to sit at home, twiddling her thumbs, waiting for the world to come to her and make things happen. Maria is a woman to make her own destiny, and she lives her life to the full. You saw her today, walking. Maria meets life head-on, enjoys a challenge. She'll have no help in the house, no one running around after her. Maria will run our home – which Anne is going to adapt beautifully for her – herself.'

Anne Howard nodded slowly.

'And *I*,' said Philip clearly, 'have no intention of being any kind of nursemaid. I am Maria's *husband*.'

There was an outbreak of embarrassed consternation. Nonna stopped telling her beads, riveted. Maria flushed crimson.

'Maria is as able-bodied, in most respects, as you and me. She needs very little help, and mostly then it's practical things like the odd ramp, so that she can get around easily. Simple matters that we can see to, so that my wife can run her home and look after our children herself, like any other woman.'

At the word *children* there was an intake of breath around the tables, and people avoided other people's eyes. Philip, seeing it all, grinned.

'It just all means,' Philip went on, 'a bit more *planning*. Maria being paraplegic means we have to plan ahead a bit more than we might otherwise do. But that doesn't mean we can't be spontaneous. Anyway, we love making plans. We share our dreams and get to know each other better by making plans, and it's exciting. Maria is going to have driving lessons as soon as we are back from honeymoon. Michelangelo and Jove have given her an adapted car as her wedding present. So far as I know, there will be *nothing* my wife cannot do.'

'*Bravo*,' cheered Nonna, unashamed of the tears on her wrinkled cheeks.

Rosalie's mother sat with her mouth open, nonplussed. These weren't things to be *said*. Nonna nudged her sharply with her foot so that Rosalie's mother snapped her mouth closed and sat, pursed up like a button.

'If there are things,' Philip continued blandly, 'we can't do the conventional way, we'll do them differently.'

He stood up very straight, took Maria's hand in his.

'But we'll do them. We'll do anything and everything, and we'll enjoy it. My wife will make my life *more* exciting, *more* imaginative, *more* fulfilled. I shall do everything I can to deserve her. Thank you.'

A storm of clapping and cheering had drowned his last words. Remembering, weeks later, reliving it all with the photographs on her lap, Rosalie put the heavy albums down. The house felt strange. The honeymoon over, Maria and Philip were in Philip's Hampstead house while Anne worked on the bungalow. Rosalie and Nonna rattled round Rosalie's four storeys like peas in a pod. With Maria's clutter gone, the rooms were too tidy, too empty. The house felt hollow. Even Fooka's hook in the ceiling was empty, his taunts removed to Hampstead where he hung in a corner of a less-used room, reluctantly taken on board by Philip, who still occasionally sneezed. And Nonna had her ticket home to Rome, her room already half filled with half-packed suitcases, all the untidy preparations for leaving. Rosalie tapped the albums thoughtfully, a little frightened. For the first time since Giovanni died, she was going to be all on her own.

After Nonna left, to tearful goodbyes, Maria rang every evening, trying to paper over the great hole in Rosalie's life, but it wasn't the same. They would gossip half-heartedly, trying to be bright and positive. It was easy for Maria, radiantly happy, with everything to look forward to. Anne Howard had begun on the conversion, and Maria spent much time going over plans, choosing fabrics and colour schemes, overseeing work. She was busy. Rosalie was busy, too, working in the salon, running the place. It made her tired, kept her occupied, didn't fill the emptiness at home. Sometimes Rosalie didn't want to turn the key in her door, to walk through into silence. She often rang Sadie, but she, too, was busy, often not there.

'Sadie has had dinner a couple of times with Dougal, but it seems to be leading nowhere,' Maria told her one evening. 'Dougal's miserable all over again. It's a shame.'

'I wish I had a handsome, well-off man like Dougal asking me out,' answered Rosalie, depressed.

'You never know,' said Maria, 'you're young yet.'

'I'm not,' snapped Rosalie, soon to be on the wrong side of forty. Remarks about age didn't help.

Alone in the big house, she gathered together the heap of albums, to put them away.

'And what about me? Now what? Perms, tints and scrunch-dry finish. Is that it?'

Rosalie stacked the albums on a bookshelf and stood back. Outside was a warm evening. People lingered in the square, sat outside pubs on the pavement, strolled in parks, windowshopped, caught buses, hurried, worried, fought, made up, made love. Love. Rosalie thought her grieving for Giovanni long over, but in her empty house, her sense of loss was as fierce as ever.

'There must be more than this. Life's not over,' she said aloud.

But there was no one there to answer.

Chapter Twenty-Eight

It was a short, uncertain summer with day after day of warm, heavy rain. Often it was dull all day, dark early in the evening. Philip complained about the cricket, Wimbledon's first days were washed out, and then overnight, as English weather will, the rain turned into a heatwave, bringing sunburn, lethargy and more complaints. Maria and Anne Howard spent the unpredictable summer in the Barnsbury bungalow, pulling down walls, re-siting doorways, planning a wheelchair kitchen. They hardly noticed, and cared less about, the weather, except when rain held up the workmen, and for that reason were pleased when the heatwave struck London. It dried heavy clay soil, brought the bricklayers out in shorts and red, burned torsos, cheered everyone up.

Over in Hackney, Cherie Sangster's maisonette was stifling, her housekeeping sliding deeper into chaos and indifference as she drifted through long, hot days. The children, small bodies reddened by sun, whined and grizzled and clung around her knees. Every time she stood up and went anywhere, they came following after, crying to be held. If she held them, they wriggled crossly, cried to be put down. Cherie, exhausted, sat much of the day in a big old chair, with them piled in her lap like unhappy puppies. Some afternoons they played outside by themselves, pottering on short fat legs, grubbed fitfully with old spades, fingered, and sometimes ate, dusty grey soil, full of builders' sand and broken bits of cement. She sat just inside, in the shade, in cut-off jeans and T-shirt nicked in Tesco's, watching with lazy eyes, and chewing gum, her mouth going round and round and round. Jason or Johnny, she was often not sure which little boy was which, pulled himself up by her legs and clung to her, coughing.

'Stop it, will you,' she said, hauling him listlessly on to her lap.

The health visitor left expectorant linctus which did no good, because it tasted of disgusting chemical raspberry and they spat it out. She put it in their bottles and they sat there holding them, looking at her in disbelief, wouldn't swallow a drop, just screamed. They coughed and coughed. A cold gone to their chests, Beryl said, knowing a lot about chests. Cherie lit a fag and pushed her son, whichever one he was, off her knee. 'Go and play,' she ordered. The toy library lent the health visitor two tricycles on her behalf, red and blue plastic, small, safe for little ones to ride. Johnny and Jason squabbled constantly over them, always wanting the bike the other had, having tantrums. They only wanted each other's toys, and as soon as they got them, the fighting started all over again. It wore her out.

'My place is a pigsty,' she told her mother defiantly, meeting her down the market.

'Oh, yes,' said her mother, not listening. 'Me chest's bin bad.' It meant she wasn't going to help clean up. She wasn't going to help with money, either. Cherie owed rent for months back.

'They won't evict you because of the children, but you ought to *try* at least,' said the health visitor, trying to give elementary lessons on budgeting. Cherie didn't believe her. Who could budget on a giro? They'd evict her, and when they did, it'd be bed and breakfast or the kids in care. The prospect preyed on her mind.

'Screw 'em,' she concluded, sitting in her airless kitchen, lighting a fag from the butt of the last one, depressed. 'First sign of madness,' she remarked. She talked to herself a lot. There wasn't anyone else. She hadn't kept the payments up, so the rental shop had taken the telly back. Since then, she entertained herself. The boys didn't talk, just made their little noises. Sometimes they gave her the creeps because they were like two little pale pigs talking. Grunt-grunt, grunt-grunt. They knew what they meant.

'And you are pigs,' she said wearily, hauling the decrepit pram back and forth to Tesco's. 'Always eatin' and screamin' for more.'

Cherie hated all that eating, it upset her. And it cost more than her giro just to feed them, never mind the rent and the bills, even with the regular Tesco subsidy, and one or two others on the side.

She complained to the health visitor about all the eating.

'They're toddlers. Of course they have appetites. What else do you expect?'

'Not a lot,' snapped Cherie. She blew smoke over her visitor's head. They'd been through it all a dozen times. It bored her. The Carswell woman was worse, a whole different ballgame. She was harder, sharper altogether, knew what was what. The health visitor was a kind, well-meaning fool but Sarah Carswell made Cherie nervous. She poked around, undressed the boys and gave them the once-over.

'Looking fer bruises, then?' snarled Cherie, nearly in tears. 'If there's anythin' there, they did it theirselves. Always fightin' and fallin' off of those bikes. They ain't old enough.'

'I'm sorry if it offends you, but I have to look,' said Sadie calmly. 'You don't have to worry so long as they haven't got any.'

Cherie hated her. One hot afternoon in July, she went upstairs without a by-your-leave, and looked in the bedrooms. Cherie stood, furious, arms akimbo, at the bottom of the stairs, waiting to let fly, tell her where to go. The words strangled in her throat as she watched Sadie come down and stack the draining board.

'Getting on for a dozen,' Sadie observed dispassionately, clinking Tesco's whisky bottles, 'underneath your bed. Where on earth do you get the money?'

'So?' snarled Cherie, on the defensive, wishing she'd stuck to her good intentions about clearing up. Flies danced in the small, greasy room, blinds tightly closed over never-opened windows.

'How much of this stuff do you drink?' asked Sadie, detaching Jason or Johnny from her ankle being tugged for her attention. She picked the small boy up and held him on her hip, eyeing his mother dubiously.

'They bin there months,' said Cherie sullenly. 'I ain't cleared under there for months. I ain't got time.'

'You've got children to look after, Cherie. You're by yourself here. If you're drunk, they're at risk.'

Cherie made a monumental effort. She didn't scream, lash out, hit her, do any of the things she felt like doing, which would play straight into Sarah Carswell's hands. Instead, she lit another fag, kept her cool, acted contrite, stood like a child herself, tugging at her brittle hair with thin, nervous fingers.

'I don't get drunk. I 'ave a drink after a bad day an' if I can't sleep. Those bottles go back ages. I ain't very tidy and that ain't no crime.'

Sadie folded her arms challengingly, eyebrows raised in disbelief. Cherie opened her mouth.

'Can't smell nuffink, can you? Five o'clock and sun over the yard-arm an' I pass the breathaliser. Satisfied?'

Not exactly a Colgate addict, either, thought Sadie, backing away. No ring of confidence there.

'Where d'you get the money from?' she persisted unwisely, putting the child down again.

Cherie laughed in her face.

She never smelled of whisky, was never drunk when Sadie called round without warning, tried to catch her. Cherie always had a fag in her mouth and a cup of weak tea in the pot, and was always bored. The boys were dirty, not uncared for. Cherie seemed to love her children. The two women played cat and mouse. Sadie wrote every visit up with care, mistrusted Cherie absolutely, and waited with foreboding.

* * *

When the heatwave was at its hottest, Jason sat on the floor, blue, fighting for breath.

'That's a really nasty cough,' said Cherie vacantly. 'You'd best go down the doctor with that.'

She said it every day, thinking, it's hot, I'll take 'em tomorrow, meaning to. She didn't take them at all and that evening, Jason coughed until his chest was concave, then breathed in with a long crow. Johnny, mirror image of his small brother, coughed and coughed until he sicked his supper up. They sat side by side, breathing hard, delicate faces greenish, great aquamarine eyes filled with tears.

'You done that deliberately,' screeched Cherie, scraping it up with old newspaper, crying herself.

The children watched, unmoved, used to her screeching. It was August. Holiday time, everyone gone away, Beryl in hospital with the emphysema.

'They give 'er oxygen,' Cherie told them when she'd put the paper in the overflowing bin. 'You bloody look like you could use some. Give me a break and shut up.'

Johnny held out his arms. Cherie shifted her fag to the corner of her mouth and lifted him up, puffing smoke in his eyes.

'Sorry, pet.' She waved the smoke away. 'What's matter with you an' 'im? You get rid of that cold, and you be a good boy.'

She rocked the child quietly until he dozed. Jason lay on his stomach on the floor, sucking his fingers, also quiet for once. Cherie lit another fag with one hand and contemplated her little family. Outside the curtained windows, the sun glared, making her rooms hot. Stuffy, unbreathable air made her head ache. She seldom sat outside during the day, keeping away from neighbours' prying. More often, she sat just inside, watching Jason and Johnny, nappies off, bottoms scraped by paving stones and sharp sand. They coughed and coughed, though the heat made them drowsy, made them sleep. They coughed in their sleep, but at least they slept. Then Cherie felt better.

* * *

The cat-and-mouse game with her social worker continued as the days dragged by. Cherie had an advantage, a secret weapon Sadie didn't guess at; she practised ferocious self-discipline.

'She thinks I don't know she's tryin' to catch me out,' she remarked to the twins. It was early evening. Full of food and watered condensed milk with a dash of whisky, which they loved, Jason and Johnny lay in their cots.

'Come on then, sunshine,' said Cherie, leaning over them. They held out tiny sunbrowned arms obediently. Cherie tied four birdlike wrists to the bars with strips of sheeting. She did it with care. She tied them in with love, because Beryl said it stopped them climbing out, getting into mischief. Cherie had been tied herself, by Beryl, and never gave it a second thought. She tested the ties gently. They held. They would keep the boys safe while she had a little drink, and everything would be, as it was every night, all right. Social workers never called outside office hours unless you asked them, or there was an emergency. Cherie didn't have emergencies. She was very, very careful about that.

She took tea and a fresh whisky bottle out on to the weedy flagstones at the back, out into the sluggish air. The paving stones were hot and comfortless, so she fetched an old pillow and blanket, lay down on her side, poured half tea, half whisky into a cup. After the first couple of cups, the pressure in her head eased. She shook a chalky-blue valium into her hand, broke it carefully in half.

'Hmmm, hmmm,' she hummed tunelessly to herself. On the other side of her wall, several black kids roller-skated, one of them with a ghetto blaster under his arm. He twiddled the controls and instead of reggae, the 'Moonlight Sonata' filled the square at maximum volume. Surprised, people came and looked, opening windows wider. Turning her heavy bones to bathe in brassy evening sun, Cherie relaxed and closed her eyes, and listened to the thud and whisper of skates, the long, liquid piano notes, as amazing and as unlikely as a nightingale in Berkeley Square at midday. She smiled drowsily. Leaning up on her elbow, she sipped the last of her cup of whisky, and tipped it in the direction of the skaters on the other side of her wall.

'That is nice,' she mumbled. ''Appy Birthday to me.'

She was nineteen years old today.

Later, the piano long gone, shouts and whistles sounding nearby, then further away, a television from an open window squawking the ten o'clock news, she woke up briefly, had some more whisky, dozed, then drank a bit more. Dusk fell, deepened into the half-dark London night. Lights strung the concrete stairwells and corridors of the estate, blinked on up the high-rise blocks. Windows were pulled to. Around midnight she felt so good she broke her one absolute rule. Too sleepy to move, the freshening night air delicious on her skin, she took her third complete blue valium, washed down with her Tesco's birthday present of blended whisky, without going indoors to bed, without checking the boys. In the cool of the night, covered by the blanket and a light dew near dawn, Cherie slept a wonderful sleep, like the dead.

The refuse lorry woke her, emptying bins round the corner, banging and shouting and clattering. Flies rose angrily from broken bin-bags. The smell of rotting rubbish pierced the sweet early-morning air, killing the scent of yesterday's mown grass from the estate's inner square. Cherie dragged herself indoors, cursing. London began to stew, crowds pouring in and out of tube stations. Another day, another dollar. Another day, already warm and getting warmer; the kids were quiet. Cherie went upstairs.

She had not heard them coughing and coughing and coughing . . . until they were sick and unable to turn over, their arms tied down. She stared into the cots at small spreadeagled bodies. After a long time, she went back downstairs, swallowed the rest of the valium, a full pack of paracetamol, and as much as she could manage of a bottle of whisky before she fell down on the kitchen floor.

* * *

Four days later a neighbour reported an awful smell.

'God knows how she got it down her,' muttered John Campling, detective inspector in charge of investigating the horror.

He and Sadie met in the ghastly kitchen. Senior social workers and police officers jostled each other. John and Sadie, agonisingly aware of each other, were able to say nothing. He could make no move to comfort her.

That evening Sadie only answered the phone when it rang so long that she half guessed it was him.

'Come out and have a drink,' he said. 'We have to talk. We can't go on pretending we don't know each other.'

They drove into the Essex countryside, away from everything and everyone, found a village pub. They sat outside in deep shade, under an apple tree full of small green fruit, untouched glasses before them.

'She was so anorexic, she looked like a child. She *was* a child,' said Sadie wretchedly. 'She was terribly depressed, but in that kind of passive way that is impossible to help.'

'What will you do?' he asked.

There would be inquests and enquiries. The press had had a field day.

'I cry a lot,' she said abruptly. 'And I'm scared I'll lose my job and not get another one. Apart from that, I don't know. I daren't think.'

'How can two children have whooping cough, and nobody know?' he asked.

'It's hard to diagnose. And there's such a fine line between awful living standards and real neglect. Cherie went over it, but I couldn't see when or how. She was clever.'

'I suppose they'll try to hold you responsible.'

'The press will. They'll want someone to carry the can.'

'Is there anything I can do?'

Their hands touched as she reached for her glass. There were too many things that could not be said.

'We'll have to liaise, I suppose. It'll drag on and on. I'm sorry.'

He said reluctantly, 'Jane is home from hospital. She's in remission.'

'Good,' said Sadie dully. She drew a deep breath and tried to smile. 'That didn't come out the way I meant. I'm glad she's better.'

'Yes,' he said.

'I wouldn't love you if you were the kind of man who would leave his sick wife. The very thing that breaks my heart is the reason that I love you. It's the kind of people we are and it just can't be helped.'

She had not meant to tell him she loved him, but nothing seemed to matter any more. They sat side by side on an old wooden bench, under the little green apples. A bumble bee lurched through a thicket of hollyhocks, covered in pollen.

'Did you know,' she said, as he didn't answer, trying to cheer them both up, 'that a bumble bee is aerodynamically impossible? It shouldn't be able to fly.'

'That's how it is for me, too,' he said at last, ignoring the bee. 'And I want you to know, I love you, very much.'

'I know. Like the bee, and Cherie and everything else, it's impossible, though,' she said, tears in her eyes, 'isn't it?'

'I'm afraid it is, my love,' he said.

Chapter Twenty-Nine

John and Sadie had underestimated how bad the publicity would be. She had expected the press at the office, at the court, but she had not expected them to follow her home. Some did, looking for character assassination, baying for blood and headlines. Sadie, shocked and frightened, bolted herself in. She drew all her curtains, living in twilight, horribly aware of the irony, the fact that she was doing just what Cherie had.

When she ran the gauntlet of neighbours and reporters, and went to work, her supervisors and seniors questioned her closely, seeking to justify, defend and distance themselves, cautious, evasive. Then they came down overwhelmingly on her side. She had done all she could. No professional negligence.

'Tell that to the ghouls on the newspapers,' she said.

They wanted someone to blame, someone to crucify. She was cleared at work, but the papers didn't forgive.

'Nine-day wonder,' said Dolly, coming round to comfort and support, throwing down crumpled newspapers, into the sea of newsprint on Sadie's floor. 'They'll be slandering some other poor sod next week. They have to invent news if they can't find it, take no notice of them.'

'I have to take notice. They are *howling* for me to be sacked.'

'Of course they are,' said Dolly acidly. 'What else do you expect?'

'The truth.'

'You'll get that in the enquiry. You've written up everything you did. You recorded your disagreement over a place of safety order when your supervisor wouldn't give the go-ahead. It's all there. Just let it come out, and you'll be OK.'

'A safe place is what I need right now,' said Sadie miserably.

'Better pickings for the papers will come along than you,' snapped Dolly. 'Let's not exaggerate. It's not the first time a client's fucked up, and it won't be the last. It wasn't your fault and all you have to do is sit it out.'

'It was my fault.'

Dolly rolled her eyes in exasperation. 'Come *on*.'

'She was only a kid. I let her convince me she was coping, when I knew she wasn't. She *couldn't* have been coping, but I wanted to believe her.'

'Don't go saying that to the enquiry,' yelped Dolly.

'It wasn't Cherie I couldn't face, it was my own job, and the lies that go with it. I didn't have the guts to do what was right, and take those kids into care. So,' she went on in the face of Dolly's mounting outrage, 'I put it down in writing and kept immaculate records. Two children are dead.'

'Don't try and play God,' Dolly told her coldly. 'It's not in the job description.'

'Go to hell,' said Sadie tearfully. 'Those kids are *dead*.'

Dolly refused to go anywhere, handed her the tissues, determined to stick by her through thick and thin.

Guilt, Sadie discovered, grows on you and is a fast worker. Consumed by it, she stopped seeing people, was terrified they held her secretly responsible for three children's deaths, Cherie being hardly adult in the circumstances. Rosalie rang and tried to talk her out of it. Maria and Philip drove over in the Morgan, banging on Sadie's door, calling her name. She wouldn't answer. Dolly had to go in to work, saying she'd be back. When she came, the door was firmly closed on her, too, reducing Dolly to speechless indignation.

Letters from the director said she would be required to

attend meetings, write reports, submit to more questioning. She read them again and again, terrified, couldn't finish all the answers she began. She ran out of food, began to sleep in the day, sitting up all night with every light blazing, mortally afraid of the dark, and of sleep, because of the dreams. Rosalie wanted to send for the police, but Philip said, wait. In Italy, after distraught phone calls from Rosalie, Nonna stamped furiously into early Mass each morning, tried to talk some reason, woman to Woman. It seemed the heavenly lines were down.

The papers lost interest, the reporters went away. Arrangements for an enquiry into the affair, and into departmental procedures, plodded on. The whole business came off the boil, and Sadie should have been back at work. She wasn't. Philip said everyone was losing patience, wanted to go in and drag her out, make her see some sense. He and Dougal were in the cubbyhole they called the kitchen, making coffee in the filter machine, something they did not often do for themselves. It was Dougal's secretary Pauline's job, but she had called in sick with a cold. Philip didn't grind the beans finely enough and the coffee was weak and tasteless. Dougal swallowed it, listened to Philip's worrying, got frantically worried himself, told the girl in reception to take his calls, and left.

'Well, we've got a spare key, but I'm not sure I should give it to you. You could be anyone, couldn't you? You could be a serial killer, couldn't you?' chattered the retired teacher who lived in the flat above Sadie's. She had a silly, vapid face, and giggled at her own joke. Swathed in a baby-pink fluffy tracksuit, smelling of Johnson's powder, she made big eyes at the tall and handsome Welshman standing in the corridor and wondered fleetingly whether to invite him in. She batted her eyelids as a preliminary gesture. A sixty-year-old, going on six, is all I need, thought Dougal. Frustrated, he stifled an urge to push her out of the way and grab the key from wherever it was hidden. He counted silently to five and concentrated on being grateful that after enquiring at several flats, there was at least a key in one of them.

'This is an emergency,' he said with as much Welsh charm and friendliness as he could manage. 'I'm an old friend.'

The woman dithered.

'Oh, for God's sake,' he roared, 'you've read the papers. She needs help, or she'll end up in the same boat as that girl who died. You haven't smelled any nasty smells in the last day or two, have you?'

The powder showed pinkly on her face as her colour drained. She backed down her little hall and came back with a Yale key.

'She's got deadlocks all over the place,' she quavered, warning him. 'Don't blame me if it's bad down there – it's not my business to look after . . .'

Dougal snatched the key.

He wrenched the key round. It turned in the lock, but the door didn't budge. Deadlocked.

'Sadie, open the bloody door,' Dougal bellowed.

The pink fluffy tracksuit sidled downstairs and stood on the doorstep above Sadie's basement entrance, her mouth open.

'Sarah,' he roared.

A downstairs curtain in the house opposite twitched.

'Carswell, you open this door, or I'll fucking force it. I mean it. You've got one minute.'

He began to count. A woman came out of the house opposite and called, 'What are you doing?'

Dougal carried on counting. Inside Sadie's flat he could hear nothing move.

'Right,' he shouted for all the world to hear. 'Crowbar time. In the car.'

He was two steps up her area steps when a key scraped and the front door opened a crack. Dougal was inside in a flash. Sadie stood in a dressing gown, white-faced, great black rings under her eyes.

Dougal contemplated the spectre wordlessly.

'You look like a panda,' he said at last. 'What the devil do you think you're doing?'

'What do you want?' she whispered.

He put his hands in his pockets and sucked his lower lip as if in thought.

'I want you,' he told her. 'I want you, and you sure as hell need me, if present performance is anything to go by.'

'I'm busy,' she answered. 'Go away.'

He walked into the disordered flat. She had been pasting newspaper cuttings into a scrapbook. Scissors and paper-glue lay on the floor.

'Is this being busy?'

'Dougal, go away,' she begged.

Taking no notice, he squatted down and looked at them. Smudged pictures of the Sangster twins aged six months. One of Cherie aged fourteen, at a friend's wedding, her hair permed, barely recognisable. The papers had printed every photograph they could lay their hands on, together with columns of vitriolic print about social workers. These were carefully pasted into the scrapbook. Waiting to be pasted was a small, separate pile. He began to turn them over.

'Not those,' cried Sadie, snatching.

'Who are they?'

He held the small sheaf of cuttings out of her reach. A bright-faced girl and a dark, curly-haired young man. She in a university gown; a graduation ceremony. The same couple, girl in wedding gown, he in dark suit, carnation in his buttonhole.

'Who are these people?'

Her eyes looked glassy.

'My parents. It was in the Norfolk papers.'

'You were putting cuttings of your *parents* into a scrap-book with the *Sangsters*?'

'With photos of my aunts. And Giovanni was in the paper, as well, when he died. So I put them all in. I thought all the people who died would like to be together.'

Dougal felt sick.

'You're getting out of here, and you're coming back with

me, and we're going to find someone to talk this thing through with you.'

'I'm not dressed,' she said.

He had a feeling that any minute she'd regress completely and start sucking her thumb.

'Get dressed,' he barked.

He frightened her and she stood uncertainly.

'Are you angry with me, too?' she whispered.

It was more than his patience could take. 'I've had enough of this,' he roared, picked her up, marched past the gaping neighbours, dumped her in his car.

'We'll go back for your things another time.'

'I've got everything I need.'

'You haven't got anything.' He looked over his shoulder into the back seat, holding the key in the ignition. She still clutched the cuttings to her chest.

Dougal drove grimly.

'Where are we going?' said a small voice in the back.

'Home. Where there might be a bit of sanity,' he remarked, 'though looking at you, I wouldn't be certain.'

She smoothed the cuttings of her parents ceaselessly, making them smudged, unreadable.

'I'm going to die,' whispered Sadie.

'You're damn well not,' snapped Dougal, speeding through north London.

'Oh,' she said, sounding as though she was crying.

'You are just very, very shocked,' he said firmly, but after that he couldn't get another sensible word out of her.

Chapter Thirty

Everyone agreed that it was shock, and that shock took some getting over, and everyone accused everyone else of not having realised what it had been like for Sadie, and of not having been sensitive enough. Dolly said none of that, spent hours talking to her and eventually persuaded Sadie to get her GP to refer her to a good therapist. Life returned almost to normal, except that Sadie lived with Dougal and didn't go back to her flat.

As 1973 limped in political and financial disorder into 1974, Dougal speculated angrily that the Common Market, Arthur Scargill and the IRA were in cahoots to bring the great British public, and Dougal Monroe in particular, to their knees. He got very worked up about the economy, although when he calmed down and talked more quietly, he admitted that computers were a rare growth area, and he and Philip were riding a buoyant wave of success.

'Then what are you getting so upset about?' Sadie demanded, a sure sign that she was getting stronger.

'And,' he went on, disregarding the question, 'we'd be a lot better off if you stopped paying for petrol to go all that way to work, sold your flat and moved in here properly. A mortgage on an empty flat is daft.'

They trod what had become a well-worn track.

'The economy is a mess because of the electrical workers and the railways as well. It can't be an international conspiracy against anyone, because that lot are incapable of cooperating even with themselves for more than five minutes,' said Sadie. 'And I don't want to give my flat up, and my tenant pays the mortgage.

We've been through it all before, Dougal. Let's leave it, now.'

She lay on her side, tracing the pattern on the duvet cover on his bed with one finger, remembering a time when she would have got up and marched off to her own place. She had been brave and a fool. Wiser and utterly vulnerable, Sadie stayed and was glad to be protected.

'You belong here,' he said, sitting down on the side of his bed, stroking her unruly hair.

'I don't feel I belong anywhere at the moment.'

'I didn't say you feel it, just that as far as I'm concerned, you *do*.'

Sadie glanced up in surprise.

'There you are,' he cried. 'You underestimate me. I understand you better than you do. I bet they need social workers in Hampstead. Why don't you get a job around here?'

She tried to make a joke of it. 'I'm in disgrace, in a neurosis and in therapy. And unqualified. Getting another job is not exactly going to be a piece of cake, I don't think.'

He decided not to pursue the disgrace bit; she had been cleared by the enquiry.

'If you need qualifications, why not go and get them?'

'I'm sorry you worry about me,' she said evasively. 'You don't have to.'

Dougal liked worrying about her. It was the first time in his life he had cared enough to worry about anyone except himself, and he was thoroughly enjoying it.

The GP had suggested Eva, a therapist, a dark-haired, cool-eyed woman, alert and calm. She had listened to Sadie's distraught account of the Sangsters' deaths, which somehow ended up as an account, for the very first time, of what little she knew about her parents' deaths. They met three times a week. Eva was clever at listening.

'You sound pleased and a little triumphant that Dougal says he has to worry about you. You smiled, but you also clenched your fists, when you were telling me what he said. Do you like him to worry?'

'No.'

'I have a feeling that it may matter a lot to you that he worries, and that perhaps you'll make sure he does.'

'No. And I couldn't control him like that.'

Eva laughed and said not to underestimate herself. Sadie flushed and wanted to know what she meant.

'Controlling people is something we all try to do, up to a point. The more we feel hurt and powerless, the more we try to control.'

'That's not me,' said Sadie. 'Even when it's life and death, I can't get a bit of control together. Look what happens when I'm in control,' she added for good measure.

'Jason and Johnny died because of Cherie's problems.'

'It was my job to be in control if she wasn't. And I wasn't. That's why she died. I should have coped. Had more guts and a grasp on what was going on.'

Eva decided to say what she was thinking.

'You think people die if you are not in control?' she asked gently. 'If you are out of control, what happens?'

Sadie's eyes filled with angry tears.

'I never said that,' she cried. 'That's you putting words in my mouth.'

Silently, Eva handed her a box of tissues.

'It's OK to cry,' she said.

'I don't want to cry,' snarled Sadie, taking a wad of tissues, 'and it's stupid, because I don't know what I'm crying about.'

'Cherie abandoned her children.'

'I'm not crying about that,' howled Sadie.

'What, then?'

'They all abandoned *me*.'

Head in her arms, she didn't see Eva's nod of agreement.

'Poor baby,' she said sadly, stroking Sadie's head.

Sadie cried and cried and cried.

'You know what I think?' said Dougal, finding her red-eyed and weepy one day shortly afterwards, wanting to comfort her. She didn't want to be comforted. Crying made her feel better, stronger, and Eva said that when it was done, she'd leave the past where it belonged. Behind. Dougal put his arms round her and lifted her on to his lap like a child.

'Now then,' he began, 'what I think is . . .'

'You're going to tell me whether I want to know or not,' she said ungraciously.

'I think that Eva upsets you.'

'I go and see Eva because I'm upset. Not the other way round. Perhaps you ought to see her, too. Then you'd understand.'

'Not on your nelly. What I was going to say was, we ought to get married. I've been thinking about it for ages. Will you?'

'I don't know,' was all she could think of to say.

'Thanks a million,' muttered Dougal. 'In the face of such enthusiasm, I won't mention it again.'

Sadie blew her nose. 'That sounded awful.'

'It did.'

'I meant, let's go on the way we are. It's worked out really well.'

'You can't have children, just living together. It isn't fair on them.'

'*Children*,' she squawked.

'I'd like lots of children,' he said. 'With you.'

She leaned her head against his shoulder and closed her eyes. She felt very safe.

'I've a feeling I might not be very good at it. Wifing and mothering, I mean. I might be a disappointment.'

Dougal held her very close and said, 'I'll take the risk.'

She still had her eyes closed. A blackbird was singing loudly just outside the window, singing and singing. Whenever Sadie thought back over Dougal's proposal, that was really all she could remember. A bird singing its heart out by the window ledge.

'How about popping in at the registry office?' he asked. 'No fuss. Tell everyone afterwards?'

'Do we love each other enough to get married?' she

asked, opening one eye and squinting at him. 'Do we *like* each other enough to always be friends?'

She pulled back to see his face, slipped to the floor.

'Yes,' he said, getting out of his chair. The blackbird trilled like an opera singer, long arias, a hoarse would-be nightingale. He slid his arms around her again. 'Friend and lover,' he said. 'For life. It's a promise.'

They stood like dancers, his arm around her waist, she leaning back to look into his face, caught in that moment as if moving to some frozen musical beat. Frozen dancers. Her parents dancing, dancing over the ice, dancing to death. She burst into racking sobs. Astonished, Dougal pulled her close.

'Now what have I said?' he demanded, half laughing, half annoyed.

'I'll marry you,' she sobbed.

'Well, at least that's that fixed,' he said with satisfaction, 'but you don't *look* as though you're awfully keen. Do women always cry when they say yes?'

She couldn't bear to be alone any longer, and he was there, so safe and strong and he truly *wanted* her.

'I'm sure,' she said, wiping her wet face. 'Yes, Dougal.'

He whirled her round for sheer delight, whooping. Outside, alarmed, the blackbird flew away.

Chapter Thirty-One

In early spring, Anne Howard finished the conversion for Philip and Maria and gave it to them as a wedding present. She had extended and levelled the ground floor of the bungalow, so that all their living accommodation was easy for Maria to move around. The roomy loft space was converted into a study for Philip, reached by a narrow flight of stairs. Maria had never been up there. Philip offered to carry her up, to show her the bright, sunny room above, with new, deep dormer windows, but she looked up the steep little staircase and was frightened he'd drop her. It became a joke that Philip would have somewhere to hide, a place of his own. He took to calling it the den, as Americans do. Once they'd moved in, it didn't take long for them to get used to the idea that he had a place that was his own, where Maria did not go; the arrangement gave a feeling of independence, which they liked.

Once they were settled, they planned a housewarming party. Maria rang to invite Sadie and Dougal.

'You'll get caterers,' Sadie said, wondering if she ought to offer to help, not really having the time.

'Why?' Maria wanted to know. 'I'll do it myself.'

'For all those people? How many?'

'About eighty,' Maria said casually. 'I love cooking, and here, I can manage easily. I'm slow, but there's nothing I can't do.'

The elder Mrs Howard had designed a peach of a kitchen. As well as listening to what her daughter-in-law wanted, she borrowed a wheelchair, lived a disabled life for a week, making notes about everything from door-widths to sink-heights to flush edges so that nothing could catch on Maria's legs or chair. Lined with oak units in farmhouse style, the kitchen was warm and welcoming, the hub of the house. Quarry tiles and a gas Aga added luxury. Michelangelo and Jove made presents of professional standard cooking pots and tall jars for spaghetti. It was a dream of a kitchen, and, with cooking, as it were, in the family blood, Maria and her kitchen made eating a treat. Sadie, inclined to snatch snacks and eat out of packets until Dougal protested or they went out for a meal, liked to sit and watch Maria cook, but wasn't a lot of help. Still, eighty was a lot of people. She felt obliged to offer.

'Can I come over and help? Or bring something on the day?'

'You can come over and keep me company. You haven't in ages.'

'I'm not brilliant at company, recently. Dougal says I'm self-absorbed since Cherie, and I think he's right. It's taking a lot of getting over.'

'I talk enough for two,' said Maria cheerfully, which was true.

Sadie looked in the diary she kept next to the phone, and smiled.

'Come and be self-absorbed here. I've things to tell you,' invited Maria, sounding mysterious.

'I've got things to tell *you*,' answered Sadie, closing the diary. 'I'll give you a ring nearer the time and we'll fix something up. When did you say your party is?'

'Last Saturday this month.'

There was a strange silence on the line.

'Are you laughing, or what?' demanded Maria.

'No,' said Sadie, still sounding odd. 'I think there's a clash with something else, but I'll sort something out.'

It was marked in the diary. It was what she'd been looking at. The last Saturday in March was the day she and Dougal were to be married.

Their wedding day, and the day of Maria's party, dawned dull and overcast, raw and damp. It was a bad time of year for getting married, if you wanted wedding dresses and good photographs. They didn't.

'Just as well we're not dressing up. You'd have to hide it all under an overcoat,' remarked Dougal. They got up early, walked for half an hour on the heath, and found early primroses on a sheltered bank. Dougal picked half a dozen and gave them, mock solemn, to Sadie.

'I should have orange blossom,' she said. 'You don't have wild flowers for weddings. These have no smell.'

'I quite like wild things,' said Dougal, tucking them into her buttonhole.

'Is that why you like me? Because I can be a bit wild?'

'I was thinking more that you had tamed me. But you can certainly be different.'

Different. She marched beside him, half running to keep up with his long stride, keeping warm and thinking back to the days with Victoria and Queenie and old Mary Llewellyn, who was still in the village, still sent Christmas cards every year. They'd been different. It took a long time after one stopped being a child, to realise that one's own family were not quite like other people's. The great-aunts and Rosalie. Chalk and cheese. She was lucky. She'd had both, and it made her strong. She thought, too, on this wedding morning, of John Campling. The heartache hardly hurt at all, now. Hand in hand, she and Dougal hurried across the heath.

The registry office was busy with end-of-financial-year weddings. Dougal and Sadie waited in a draughty hall, huddled in their overcoats. The party before them emerged in a tense little procession. The skinny little bride shivered in a cream cotton Laura Ashley dress with short sleeves, goose bumps on her arms. Blue-lipped and wide-eyed, she didn't look old enough to be married. Family fidgeted and wandered around her, uncertain what to do next. The bride looked as though she might cry and a woman who looked like the Michelin man tucked a coat round her narrow shoulders and pushed her none too gently up the corridor to the steps, to have her photograph taken with the mooning, hunted-looking youth she had just married. A woman came out of the registrar's room to invite the next wedding party in, looked round, over Sadie's and Dougal's heads. Her gaze finally came to rest on them, both looking up at her expectantly.

'Are we waiting for you?' she asked, sounding harassed.

'I think we're waiting for you,' said Dougal pedantically.

'No wedding party?' she asked doubtfully.

'Just us,' said Dougal.

'You need witnesses,' she said crossly.

'Anyone'll do. The office cleaner?' joked Dougal.

Sadie saw her face close like a clam with disapproval, evidently feeling they weren't serious enough. Dougal grinned engagingly, winding her up with enjoyment. She was not unlike the estate agent who had sold Sadie her flat. They were a type. They all stood in the corridor, looking vaguely about for witnesses.

'We have a lot of people booked, so you'll have to decide,' she said.

A short man, a good match for the Michelin woman, was evidently the very young bride's father. He stood watching a youth with a shaved head take photographs. Sadie wondered how two such hugely fat parents could make such a pathetic, skinny child. Dougal caught his eye deliberately. The fat chap rolled his eyes comically, trying to disassociate himself from his family's antics for the camera.

'We need a witness,' said Dougal. 'Won't take a few minutes.'

'You getting married?'

In overcoats and scarves, they didn't look wedding material.

'Right now,' said Dougal.

The woman hovered in the doorway, her eye on the time. They had an exceptionally heavy schedule that morning. Michelin man saw a chance to get away from his newly acquired in-laws, back into the warmth of the registry office. He dived gleefully back into the registrar's room, together with another witness whom Dougal had grabbed from the corridor. While Dougal and Sadie got married, Michelin man's family hunted hysterically round town hall corridors, wanting him in the photographs. He was nowhere to be found.

'Try the nearest pub,' lamented his wife bitterly. 'On his only daughter's wedding day. Wait till I catch that toad.'

The toad signed his name happily with an illegible flourish in the register, for both Mr and Mrs Monroe.

'All the best,' he said, winking. 'Which is more than I can say for my lot. She's four months gone, and he's a prize wally. Never mind. It's an excuse for some serious beer.'

He patted his paunch cheerfully.

'If you wouldn't mind, we have others waiting,' said the registrar severely.

'Conveyor-belt weddings,' remarked their witness, sidling out of the door. 'Ooops, here we go. She's spotted me.'

Sadie and Dougal winced. Screeching and yelling came from the wedding party on the front steps, died away as they departed. The next party rushed in, slamming the registrar's door, leaving them in an empty hall.

'Where's a taxi?' said Dougal, going to stand on the steps, wet confetti blowing around his ankles, waving his arms.

'Where are we going?'

A cab did a U-turn and stopped at the kerb.

'Lunch at the Ritz,' said Dougal, opening the door, ushering her in. 'Where else does one take one's wife on her wedding day?'

They stopped and started in heavy traffic. Dougal slid his arm along the seat and said, 'Do you love me, Mrs Monroe?'

'Of course I love you. Dougal, let's try and make this work, let's *really* try.'

'Of course it'll work.'

The cabbie grinned. Dougal leaned forwards and slid the partition shut.

'Bet he hears all kinds of pillow talk,' whispered Sadie, embarrassed.

'How's this for pillow talk?'

In his mirror, the cabbie watched them kiss. Oh dear, oh dear, he thought, cloud nine today, down to earth with a bump in six months. The eternal triumph of hope over experience. Then he tactfully ignored them for the rest of the journey and when he dropped them off outside the Ritz he drew away, grinning, pocketing a quite enormous tip.

Champagne at lunchtime went straight to Sadie's head, dulling her so that she longed to go to sleep. The wedding ring on her finger felt strange and heavy. She tried hard to wake up, be bright and chatty, but her eyelids drooped as they made small talk over a prolonged lunch. It was delicious and made her sleepier than ever.

'Let's sit downstairs and watch the world go by,' suggested Dougal. She woke up a bit as he took her to the hall and ordered coffee. The pianist tinkled. Gilded plaster cherubs held garlands of flowers around the tall walls, chandeliers gleamed on glossy, well-coiffed heads of women whose high heels sank unsteadily into thick carpet. Dougal sat watching the crowd coming and going, enjoying himself, holding Sadie's hand with its shiny new ring. The beginnings of a headache stabbed behind her eyes and, all unbidden, the memory of Maria's radiant face, as she reached for Philip's hand at the altar. Sadie fiddled with her coffee cup and stared morosely at the pianist. This wasn't how it should be. Everything had changed, and nothing, and all the way home in a cab, she was oppressed by a feeling that, despite every good intention, their getting married was in some indefinable way quite, quite wrong.

The phone was ringing when they got home. It was Dolly, the only person who knew what they'd done. Sadie had wanted to invite her, as witness, but they'd agreed to be married on their own, and Dougal had persuaded her to stick to it.

'Congratulations,' shouted Dolly down the phone.

'Don't shout, Dolly. We went to the Ritz and had a lot of champagne and my head aches.'

'You *cannot* have a headache on your wedding night,' shrieked Dolly, shocked. 'Best thing is hair of the dog. Go down the off-licence, buy a load more champagne, go to bed, have some fun and get plastered. Aunty Dolly's advice for free.'

'We've got to go to Maria's party.'

'You're joking.' Dolly sounded horrified. 'Pleasing Maria is not something you have to do on your wedding day.'

'Maria doesn't know it's my wedding day,' Sadie pointed out, wondering why she got into this dilemma in the first place.

'Plan A is better,' said Dolly sharply. 'I'd stick to it, if I were you.'

'There's nothing really planned about any of this,' said Sadie, resigned. 'I shall take two aspirins and lie down.'

'Oh, *really*,' yelled Dolly. 'You're supposed to be *happy*.'

'I am. I'm happy and I'll be happier still if I can lie down and go to sleep.'

'That's not what I mean by happy,' snapped Dolly, giving up.

'Nor me,' said Dougal, listening to Dolly's shrill voice squeaking down the receiver, just catching what she said.

'He didn't carry me over the threshold,' Sadie added, to stop Dolly going on. 'What kind of a wedding do you call that?'

'This kind.' Dougal reached round, took the receiver away from her and put it down, and carried her upstairs to bed, instead.

It was impossible to miss Maria's first party. They got up with an effort and arrived late. The Howards' house was brightly lit from end to end. The curtains were not drawn against the wintry night and they could see milling crowds holding glasses, chatting, laughing, enjoying themselves.

'How am I going to tell them?' cried Sadie, locking Dougal's car. Coming over, still languorous from love-making, her champagne-head cleared, she'd begun to think, and it struck her for the first time that Maria and Rosalie and Nonna and Jove and Michelangelo and all the rest, who put such store by family and by doing things together, might find it hard to understand what she had done, might really *mind* what she had done, without inviting them. They went inside.

'You're late,' Maria called at the top of her voice, from where she held court in her fabulous kitchen.

'We couldn't get here earlier,' cried Sadie. 'How's it going?'

'Everyone's having a good time, I think.'

Maria surveyed her crowded house proudly, with a good hostess' watchful eye. Everyone looked as though they were having a splendid time.

'Judging by appearances,' observed Anne Howard, 'my plumber especially is enjoying himself.' Dressed in dark-blue silk, she leaned on the Aga with a glass of red wine in her hand, sounding amused. They all turned to look at Figgin the plumber, who caught them watching him, peered round the top of Rosalie's head, and grinned disarmingly. He was one of the Howard firm and had worked on Anne's projects for two or three years.

Anne had literally tripped over him. The short, acne-scarred figure slightly the wrong side of forty, with shaven head and orange habit, had skipped up and down Oxford Street along with a little crocodile of similar figures, for what seemed like eternity. Its feet ached, its belly rumbled and it was fed up with being stared at, pointed at and laughed at. Figgin had been warned of all these things when he asked to join them, but he had had no idea just how terrible reality could be. Cold rain trickled down his bald head, traffic fumes brought on his asthma and the bloke carrying the *Eat Nuts, Eschew Meat and Sin, The End Of The World Is Here* placard had given his shoulder a nasty sidelong blow in passing when the crowd jostled them against each other. The *End Of The World* bloke deserved whatever was coming, Figgin thought grimly, trying to dance in a straight line in the jingling circus act he'd joined in some forgotten moment of madness. As he skipped up and down the gutter, his bare foot caught a greasy beefburger paper and skidded. He came down in an orange, briefly indecent heap, and a hurrying woman almost fell over him. Instead of kicking him, which he half expected, she stood rubbing her stubbed foot. The little monk had extraordinary electric-blue eyes, rivetingly bright, almost giving off shocks. Anne had never seen eyes like them. As the crowds opened and closed around them, they somehow began to talk. Figgin poured out his misery. The rest of the gang jingled off into the distance, up towards Tottenham Court Road, never even looking over their shoulders to check he was still there. They went to Garfunkels and she fed him the kind of food he'd dreamed of for the past three months and had been forbidden.

'What are you going to do?' she asked, as he came to the end of his story and the end of his first course, watching him resist an urge to lick his plate. The acne scars were not so noticeable now he had colour in his cheeks, and those amazing electric, cobalt-blue eyes glittered beneath invisible lashes and brows. When his hair grew back, Anne guessed it would be nondescript mouse, and probably not a great deal of it. His unremarkable features, a knobbly nose, bony jaw and utterly ordinary mouth all served to emphasise those marvellous eyes. From what she had seen as he lay on the pavement in his ungainly heap, he was narrow and knobbly and bony all over. He reminded her of pictures of Mahatma Gandhi, and she felt amused by the ridiculousness of the comparison.

'I don't want to give up being a Buddhist, but I can't take any more hopping and jingling,' answered Figgin, unhappily aware that that was a very negative reply to a very nice woman who was going to pay for his meal.

'What do you like doing?' she asked.

'Praying,' said Figgin without a trace of a smile, because

it was true and did not make him embarrassed. 'And making things, and water and nice shapes and women and being useful. I love water, the sea, rivers, I love its *liquidness* and the colours in it,' he explained earnestly.

She'd raised an eyebrow.

'I said I *like* doing something useful, not that I *am* doing something useful,' he said placidly. 'And there haven't been any women since I joined that lot. Forbidden. Monks, you see. Ha ha.'

'Ever been in a real monastery?'

'That's over the top,' he said decidedly.

'Any qualifications?'

'Seven O levels,' he said to her great surprise. 'I wasn't always a drop-out, but once you drop out, it gets hard to drop in again, 'specially when you get that bit older.'

'Family?'

'Chelmsford,' he said, surprising her again. 'I go and see 'em sometimes. They think I'm not a lot of good, and they're probably right. My dad's a retired teacher and he's dead embarrassed if I turn up. Can't blame him.'

He gazed longingly at the sweet trolley, parked at the far side of the restaurant. She sipped her cooling coffee and recapped, seeing in the odd little man, despite his bizarre appearance, a lot of things she instinctively liked. 'Water, being useful, lovely shapes and praying. We'll ignore the women. Would you like to come and work for me?'

'What?' said Figgin, forgetting his manners.

'I'm an architect.'

Figgin gaped, and said humbly that he had never thought of being an architect. Seven O levels were only seven O levels and didn't go far.

'A plumber,' she said. 'What you have told me suggests you'd make an excellent plumber. We could send you to be trained, and then you could earn a good living working for me, and since no one would interfere with you if you did your work well, you could pray all you liked, while you work. Plumbing is a fairly quiet kind of job.'

'Pray as you earn,' said Figgin, ecstatic. 'You're on.'

* * *

Anne's impulse proved spot-on. Figgin turned out to be bright, loyal, hard-working and honest, and the best plumber she'd ever come across. He led a rather sober bachelor life in a Hackney house not very far from Dolly's. But where Dolly had rocking chairs, cosy wood fires and a basket of knitting by a Victorian brass fender, he had white walls, stripped wood, prayer mats, kelims and gleaming white radiators that kept the house like an oven. Dolly's house smelled of baking and logs, Figgin's of joss sticks, incense, burning essential oils, curry and paint. Figgin was an instinctive minimalist, Dolly an impressionist. She practised complicated and beautiful knitting patterns, Figgin practised transcendental meditation. Having been a drifter most of his life, having his own house brought out a pernickety, houseproud side to Figgin, and his place was always immaculate. Dolly, in a different style, loved her small house, too. They both adored food, especially red-hot curries, and when eventually they met, they got on like lifelong old friends.

He liked to describe himself as a man of his times. Once he was working full time and earning, he went for his holidays to Rikikesh in India in the wake of the Beatles, to sparkling crystal waters where the young River Ganges enters the plains for the first time, two hundred miles from its source. He went to sit at the feet of Maharishi Mahesh Yogi, the Beatles' guru, to learn transcendental secrets. He had everything he wanted, was becoming an artist, a sculptor, a symphonist in tubing, welding and watertight joins. Figgin was a truly happy man.

The paragon of the copper pipe had been welded to Rosalie almost since the start of the party.

'He's a real sweetie,' someone said.

'He ought to be married,' said Maria.

'He's barmy. Who'd put up with him?' grinned her guest. 'It's off to the old ashram every time he can save up the fare. He'll be lucky to find one who'll put up with him, and India's not everyone's cup of tea, is it?'

'Mother Teresa. I think she's amazing,' murmured Maria.

'No Mother Teresa where he goes,' said the guest, who obviously knew about it. 'You trip over holy men every which way. Ringo Starr called it Butlins in the East. That Maharishi has made an absolute packet.'

'What about poverty and chastity and the rest?' asked Maria, intrigued.

'Hah,' her guest snorted, 'what are they? He was charging American neophytes three thousand dollars a term to cavort around his camp in Indian feathers. Whoooooo,' he yodelled, pulling a mock bow and arrow.

Beyond the kitchen door, in the hall, Rosalie and Figgin, both exactly five foot five, shuffled and hopped to the Beach Boys, eyes closed, in a world of their own.

'If you want to know about cavorting, look at my stepmother,' giggled Maria.

'Figgin'll have her in a sari, she'd better watch it. He's having his ashes put in the Ganges, you know, when he dies. He's *quite* potty,' warned her friend, helping himself to a glass of red wine and wandering off.

Maria found it hugely funny. 'Figgsy in a dhoti? Short hairy legs and little white tum?'

Anne unwound herself from the Aga and refilled her glass and said what Figgin wore in his own time was up to him, but on site he wore immaculate overalls. They painted a picture, then, of plump Rosalie gone native like him, growing out her carefully ash-blonded hair, wound like a top into nylon silk saris and filigree ear-rings, murmuring mantras.

Maria and Anne were enjoying their joke no end, watching the real Rosalie, in a clinging red knitted dress, clutched to Figgin's breast, still swaying to music in the darkened room across the hall, when Maria felt a touch, looked up, and found Sadie's hand on her shoulder.

'This is a marvellous party,' said Sadie. 'We've come to find some food. Good heavens, you've been busy. Get a plate, Dougal.'

They joined the constant crowd helping themselves at the buffet. Maria caught Dougal's eye and thought he looked odd, a bit kind of *shifty*. There *was* something odd, but she couldn't have said what. Sadie, spooning dressing over salad, lifted her hand and the light caught her wedding ring. That was what was different.

'Sadie,' shrieked Maria, 'whatever have you done?'

A short time later the kitchen had cleared, the atmosphere freezing out any guest unwisely veering in that direction for food or drink.

'Ooops, beg your pardon,' muttered a business colleague of Philip and Dougal's, meeting a fishy stare from Rosalie when he came through the door in search of more wine. Jove handed it to him and the guest retreated hastily. His hosts were suddenly not at all a festive sight.

Maria was in tears, Philip coldly angry with them for upsetting her. Rosalie held Figgin's arm and kept saying, 'How could you? *How could you?*'

Anyone would think, thought Sadie furiously, that they had committed some awful crime.

'We just wanted our wedding to ourselves,' she repeated. No one seemed to take any notice of what she said. Dougal just stood, being no help at all.

'Let's not fight,' said Anne.

'Who is going to tell Nonna?' cried Rosalie, wringing her hands.

'Any more beer?' a voice said from the door.

As one, they turned and glared.

'Sorry,' said the guest, vanishing smartly.

'You are ruining my party,' hissed Maria. 'Can't you go and argue somewhere else?'

'Who is arguing?' demanded Dougal, coming to life. 'We came to bring you a housewarming present, to tell you we'd got married, and to have a nice evening. We could have stayed at home and had our honeymoon instead, only we didn't want to miss your party. I'm beginning to wish we had.'

'Why aren't you on honeymoon?' demanded Rosalie, implying, can't you do *anything* right?

'We're both too busy at work, and Dougal didn't think the end of the financial year was a tactful time to ask Philip for two weeks off. *Some* people do think,' cried Sadie.

'It really isn't your business,' said Dougal.

'It always was until now,' muttered Philip, genuinely upset.

Maria tried to pull things together, wheeled herself to the door, determinedly hospitable.

'Come on, let's get a glass of wine, and toast your wedding.' She manoeuvred her way slowly through throngs of people.

'I knew this was going to end in tears,' mumbled Sadie unhappily.

'Let's go,' muttered Dougal.

'I should have realised they'd react like this.'

'We should have listened to Dolly,' said Dougal regretfully. 'I knew Plan A was best.'

'*And* you've stolen our thunder,' Maria said, handing a glass of wine to Sadie.

'The house is lovely.'

'Not the house. I'm going to have a baby. Phil wants to make an announcement and I think your news has made ours a bit flat. He's put out, but he'll come round.'

'Oh,' said Sadie.

'No bad feelings, anyway.'

'Bad feelings,' squeaked Sadie, astounded. 'Who started it?'

'You did.'

Sadie's jaw dropped in amazement. All around them Philip and Maria's friends danced and drank and laughed, having a good time, only one or two aware of the little drama. Dougal wandered away, chatted. He knew most of them. Sadie was the odd one out. Her life and Dougal's, she realised for the first time, crossed only at small, isolated points. The others had most of their lives in common. On her wedding day, which should have been perfect, she had ended up feeling isolated from everyone she loved.

She left Maria smiling brightly, being a perfect hostess, and found Dougal.

'Let's go,' she said in his ear.

He put an arm around her shoulders.

'They'll come round. Give them time.'

'Please, can we go, right now,' she pleaded.

With hindsight, she realised that their sudden departure sealed the rift.

'To listen to them, you'd think we'd done something criminal,' Sadie told Dolly, smarting after Maria refused to talk to her on the phone. 'They've completely over-reacted.'

'I went home at the weekend,' snapped Dolly. 'Quite frankly, you're better off out of it.'

'Out of what?'

'Family,' said Dolly in disgust. 'My father drank half a pint of whisky, hit my mother, and blamed me for being there, putting him under stress. Forget it.'

'Family is what I always wanted,' sighed Sadie wistfully, 'and now look what I've gone and done. I didn't mean it.'

'Life's a pig. We always want what we ain't got, and the grass is always greener,' said Dolly unsympathetically. 'You just shrug and get on with it.'

Sadie pulled a face, gave a great shrug and resolved to try harder to see the funny side of things. It was far from easy, but she would persevere because Dolly was right; life was a pig and laughing at it was the best thing to do.

Chapter Thirty-Two

Sadie and Dougal sometimes wondered if they were workaholics. They led hectic lives. Mornings especially were always a rush, the two of them trying to get off in time to miss the worst of the morning traffic. Not that Dougal had far to go; it was Sadie who did the travelling.

'Well, Rosalie was wrong about one thing,' she announced, quickly scanning a long, scrawled letter written on airmail paper. She swallowed hot coffee, put her mug in the sink and the letter back in its envelope.

Dougal, going through his diary with a frown said absently, 'What?'

'Nonna does understand about the registry office and she says, take no notice, they're Catholic and pig-headed. She says if we get around to a honeymoon, she has lots of room, and why don't we go to Rome. Isn't that kind?'

'Very kind.'

He closed his diary with a snap and picked up his briefcase.

'Dougal?' said Sadie.

'It's time you were gone,' he answered, glancing at the clock on the oven. Sadie's kitchen was white and bright and tidy and rather little used. A digital clock glowed green on the fitted cooker. She had a collection of cacti on the windowsill above the taps, and sometimes she stared at them, and at the grassy, easycare garden beyond, and wondered what the significance of keeping very prickly desert plants was. Probably none. She followed Dougal out to the garage.

'Does Philip ever say how Maria is?'

'Maria's fine.'

The trees dripped after rain overnight and the sky was a clear, bright white, the air cold and fresh.

'Are they all still angry?'

'I don't think he ever was particularly angry,' said Dougal, who did not find civil war in the Giangelli family particularly interesting. He got into his car to back it out, opened his window. 'It's up to you to get things straight with Maria. You're as silly as each other.'

Watching his car pull away, she sighed. The civil war *did* matter. It cast a long shadow, and became a hook on which to hang a variety of grievances. When she and Dougal had a disagreement over anything, it was liable to turn to the family rift and they'd accuse each other. He called her emotional, over-involved, irrational. She called him an ostrich with a very long neck, deep in the sand. So long as nothing got in the way of Dougal's work, so far as Dougal was concerned, there wasn't a problem. He and Philip were as close as ever. Dougal described himself as a patient and reasonable optimist. Sadie said he was blinkered. It all got no one anywhere. Most of the time, they got on well, but it rankled that he would do nothing to bridge the gulf between herself and Maria, although because he saw the Howards constantly, he was the one with the opportunities.

'Men,' she snapped after the departing car, exasperated. 'I have every sympathy with political lesbians and hermits.'

They sounded simpler than being a wife, anyway.

'Oh, heck,' cried Dolly, on the way out of the office as Sadie arrived late, and fighting a load of files trying to avalanche out of her arms.

'You look grim,' remarked Sadie, seeing black circles around Dolly's drooping eyes. She did, she looked dreadful, her peroxide hair scraped back from a very pale and drawn face, her usual flamboyance woefully missing. Sadie giggled.

'You have non-matching shoes on,' she pointed out. 'Haven't you noticed? You're lopsided.'

Dolly stared down at her feet. 'No. Damn.'

'Are you ill?' teased Sadie. A hungover Dolly begged to be teased.

'Hangover,' snapped Dolly. 'As if you didn't know.'

'Solitary drinking again? You should give it up, you know.'

Dolly put the files down on the corner of Sadie's desk and tried to stack them into some kind of controllable order.

'I'm going to be late. Case conference. Listen, solitary *nothing*. I've met *him*.'

'Who?'

'Tall, with muscles, curly hair. Dreamboat,' breathed Dolly, closing her eyes. 'I've waited all this time, and there he was . . .'

'Good grief,' said Sadie, impressed. 'Whoever he is, he's hit you with a wallop. Do I know him?'

'No,' said Dolly sharply, eyes snapping open. 'You don't.' She swept files into her arms again. 'Got to go.'

'You're *jealous* of a bloke you've hardly met? I don't believe this.'

'We've met all right,' Dolly sighed. 'We met all evening and all night and all this morning until we had to get up and go to work. We *talked*.'

'All night?' Sadie began to laugh.

Talking to men wasn't Dolly's strong point. Their few words in common and his admiration for her knitting were the main reasons for Ali Baba's lasting so long.

'What did you talk all night about?' enquired Sadie sarcastically.

'Not your business,' snapped Dolly, kicking the office door open and doing a smart sideways exit with the bulging files.

'She's in love,' remarked their fat colleague, from her corner desk. She was shrinking, thought Sadie, looking over. She went to Weight Watchers and it worked. 'She's been on about him non-stop since she got in. You're lucky. You've missed the worst.'

Sadie opened a window to let in a breath of spring air.

Daffodils waved on the traffic island at the end of the road, blooming bravely in lead, fumes and dust.

'Did she say who he is?' she asked, turning back to the room.

A door opened and typewriters clacked busily. Two small children fought over a packet of chocolate buttons, just outside the interview room.

'A fireman.'

'Where did she meet a fireman?'

'Computer dating, I should think, like the rest.'

Sadie's jaw dropped.

'*Computer dating?*'

'Have I put my foot in it?' asked the Weight Watcher, unconcerned.

'I thought she had this amazing social life. One bloke after another . . . no regrets,' cried Sadie incredulously.

'She does,' said the Weight Watcher. 'It's all the men she meets off the computer. Perhaps she didn't say, because she thinks you're a bit strait-laced, dear. Prim.'

'*Prim!* Did she meet Ali Baba off a computer?' demanded Sadie disbelievingly. 'I thought they met rescuing some old bloke under the gas holders. Romance on call and all that.'

'That was afterwards. They did some calls together, but the computer introduced them. We helped Dolly fill in her form. She described herself as very attractive, her favourite colour red and said she wanted to meet tall, dark, handsome men.'

'She got Ali Baba,' shrieked Sadie, delighted.

Weight Watcher shrugged. 'That's computers for you. Stupid things. It dished out a few other marvels as well. One of them was an apprentice fire-eater in a travelling circus who never stayed anywhere long enough to make stable relationships, and he was twenty-three and lonely. The daft machine introduced him to Dolly. I think it got its wires tangled. Talk about fire-eating, he didn't know he'd been born until he met her.'

'Good grief,' cried Sadie.

It was mind-boggling stuff. She began to laugh. She

went back to her work, got the giggles, then the chuckles, then full-blown hysteria. Dolly, computer dating. She tried to sober up but filling out expenses forms wasn't enough of a distraction. She looked up her current supervision orders, found a couple of visits were due. Still grinning from ear to ear, she went out to chase up and persecute a couple of young delinquents instead.

Dougal very often worked late. Sadie was watching television alone when Dolly rang that evening.

'Come over,' she urged. 'I'm lonely. Jump in your car and let Dougal find his dinner in the dog.'

'I haven't got a dog.'

'You know what I mean. It's only eight o'clock.'

'Where's Superman?' teased Sadie.

'Night shift,' said Dolly mournfully.

'How did you meet?' asked Sadie slyly, to try her out.

'We bumped into each other in the pub.'

'Pull the other one.'

'We did.'

'Jen Jackson said you met computer dating. You never told me.'

'Why should I tell you everything?' said Dolly haughtily. 'I did not meet him computer dating. Most of them are wallies. I was in my local ordering a medium white wine, and he was ordering bitter, and we bumped elbows. Are you coming over?'

'Dougal's out with Phil.'

'If you ask me, he's a crack in the domestic mortar, our Phil,' said Dolly, getting her own back.

'What's that supposed to mean?'

'Dougal dances too much to his tune. And to Maria. Very funny set-up if you ask me, like a *ménage à trois*, with you on the side.'

Outraged, Sadie slammed the phone down.

It rang immediately.

'Sorry, *really* sorry. I'm tight,' came Dolly's voice. 'Didn't mean it. Been gobsmacked by Gosling. And medium dry Spanish.'

'You've had a hangover all day,' snapped Sadie. 'How can you?'

'Hair of the dog,' agreed Dolly.

'You're crazy,' yelled Sadie. 'What you say is crazy. I don't want to come over, thank you, and I don't want to meet your new elbow.'

'Elbow?' Dolly sounded mystified.

'Go away, Dolly, and let me be here when my loving husband gets home and wants a wife waiting for him. Keep your nasty innuendoes and *ménages* to yourself.'

'My word, you're touchy.'

Sadie cut her off, furious, and Dolly didn't ring back again.

Dougal came in late, smelling of whisky.

'We popped in for a couple,' he said, seeing thunder in his wife's face. He looked particularly boyish and rumpled, as though someone had been running their fingers through his thick, spiky hair. 'Celebration, sweetheart,' he urged, his lilt very pronounced after the whisky. 'We got a contract through we've been bidding for. *Major* contract. It'll pay our way for quite a while. Is there anything to eat?'

'Was Maria at this celebration?'

'No.'

'So she's been sitting at home waiting, like me.'

Dougal pulled his tie off, poured himself another Scotch from a tray on the dining table, threw himself into an armchair, looked into his glass.

'Working all hours to pay the bills,' he said, sounding deliberately martyred, 'and not so much as a well done. It's a hell of a market out there. We've sweated blood.'

'I work, too.'

'You don't have to. I'm starving,' he added hopefully.

'Dougal, are you *sure* Maria wasn't with you this evening?'

He looked at her, and she noticed at last that he was dead tired, his eyes bloodshot.

'What's put this bee in your bonnet? Maria is pregnant and paralysed. She has to be incredibly careful. The last place for her is in a pub. She goes to bed early and I understand she worries about skin breaks, pressure sores, Caesarean operations and whether all the nurses will be on strike when her time comes. To anyone except Phil, it is fantastically boring. Why do you want to know?'

She lowered her head, so that he wouldn't read naked jealousy on her face.

'You know all that? You stay close to them no matter what, but I get pushed out. I can't understand how it's all happened, Dougal. You and Maria and Phil are practically a *ménage à trois*, with me looking on.'

She heard herself repeat Dolly's ugly words. He rolled his tie into a ball.

'I haven't the faintest idea what you mean.'

She tried not to panic, hearing boredom in his voice. He got another Scotch, turned on the television, fell asleep in his chair.

He'd warned her. He always got bored. She locked up, turned off the television and most of the lights and went back to wake him.

'Let's go to bed.'

She cajoled and coaxed him out of the armchair. He put his arm round her shoulders and squeezed.

'You get some funny ideas. Try not to attack me when I've made a deal and had a few drinks. Bad timing.'

'I didn't mean to attack you.'

'I love you,' he said, rolling over, sliding straight into sleep.

'Me too.'

She slipped her arms around his back.

'Maybe I should stop working, be here more for you.'

''S nice idea,' he grunted.

'We could start a family.'

But he was fast asleep. A baby. She thought about that, lying wakeful until the early hours. A baby would make them or break them, she was sure of it, deep in her heart, though she could not have explained why. The question was, which?

'That's a fool's argument,' she imagined Dolly would say. Dolly was very often right, but . . . how could anyone ever know what having a child was like, until you did it? And then, it was too late. Baffled, she found not even the beginnings of answers to all the questions, and listening to Dougal's heavy breathing next to her, finally she, too, slept.

Chapter Thirty-Three

'I was a bear,' said Dougal next morning. 'But we got this *fantastic* contract, and all you could do was gripe.'

'I mind your having secrets.'

'I do not have secrets,' said Dougal, bewildered.

'There are things you keep me right out of.'

'Men do,' he said, as if it were self-evident. 'Especially men who were at school together like me and Phil.'

'If we had a son, would you send him away to school?'

'Probably,' he said lightly.

'I'm serious.'

'My love,' he said tiredly, 'you are *always* serious.'

'I'm not,' she protested.

But he was right, she was and didn't like it.

'Are you serious about making babies?' he asked casually.

She was taken aback. 'I've been thinking about it. What about you?'

'I'm a bit more enthusiastic than that.'

'Are you?'

Dougal looked at her, amazed. 'An excuse to own a cricket bat and play trains. What are we waiting for?'

'You never sounded as though you wanted a child. It's all work, work, work.'

'I thought we'd have children, one day,' he said. 'I took it for granted.'

'We don't talk enough, do we?' she said hesitantly. 'Sometimes I feel as though I'm trying to put a jigsaw together and none of it fits.'

'You could be more laid back,' he suggested, trying to stay cheerful. 'I like the idea of a little bright-eyed son to play rugger with. I'll take him to games.' He sounded slightly wistful. 'My dad used to take me to games, until I went away to school. We didn't do much together after that.'

'I didn't know.'

'You don't know me half as well as you think,' he said, more than half serious.

'Do you think we'd make good parents, Dougal?' she asked shyly. 'I spent most of last night wondering.'

He laughed. 'There's only one way to find out, isn't there?'

'It's me who does most of that kind of finding out,' she said quietly. 'Maybe that's why I'm scared.'

'Are you scared?' he asked, surprised.

'Yes,' she said, 'I am.'

Chapter Thirty-Four

The office was empty except for them, and unusually quiet. No phones had rung in the past hour, and they'd sat at their respective desks until Dolly couldn't bear the atmosphere any longer, and said she was sorry if she'd caused offence.

'I'm in love,' she explained plaintively, only half tongue in cheek, wanting to make up. 'People in love are crazy and need a lot of understanding from their friends.'

'You carry on the way you are, and you won't have any friends,' retorted Sadie. 'Especially at your age. You're not exactly a teenager.'

'The oldest one in the business,' sighed Dolly. 'Thirty-seven going on thirteen and still having fun. Go on, I'm doing my best to apologise.'

'*Fun*,' snapped Sadie, remembering poor Ali Baba.

Dolly's rouged and powdered plump cheeks curved in a grin. She was trying a new rinse on her over-treated hair and it was an unusual shade of pale pink, like very diluted Ribena. Quite striking, really, thought Sadie, trying not to smile, thinking that Dolly should look common with all the bleach and make-up and amazing clothes, but succeeded in looking interesting instead. Perhaps it was the blackberry-coloured sweater that rescued her from vulgarity right now; it matched her hair.

'I have fun,' said Dolly. 'More than you, Miss Prim.'

Sadie thought about Dougal's deal and whisky celebration and admitted to herself that, as usual, Dolly had it in a nutshell. She'd say outrageous things that no one else would dare, and hit the nail exactly on the head. However often she put her flamboyant foot in it, it was impossible to stay annoyed with her for long.

'I tell you what,' Sadie offered, 'I'll let you help me clean my flat. My tenant's moving out and it needs a going-over before the new one moves in next week.'

'That's a treat?' demanded Dolly sarcastically. 'OK, I'll help.'

They stood in Sadie's deserted flat and surveyed the mess. The cheeseplant had grown and seemed to be preparing for a final push through the ceiling, but most other things had suffered neglect.

'Not the world's most wonderful housekeeper, was she?' said Sadie, fingering thick grease on her cooker.

'Why bother with all this? Why don't you sell?' asked Dolly, rolling up her sleeves and putting on a pair of yellow rubber gloves. She set out the contents of a carrier bag on the work surface. Brillo pads, Vim, bleach . . . they'd raided the cleaning department in Tesco's, had seen Cherie's floorwalker pass by with her sparsely filled trolley, all unaware, not being streetwise like Cherie.

'I like having my own place, even if I don't live in it. And it's going up steadily. When I do sell, I'll make a lovely big profit.'

Dolly knotted an apron round her portly stomach and started filling the sink with hot water.

'You've got your own house,' remarked Sadie, throwing in a load of dirty grill pans and oven trays. 'I bet you wouldn't give that up, for anyone.'

Dolly scrubbed like mad and suddenly had very little to say.

His name, Sadie discovered, while both their heads were in the wardrobes, brushing out fluff, was Swan. Derek Swan. Known by some crooked logic as Gosling.

'He's a fireman.'

'Jen Jackson mentioned computers. Perhaps she was getting muddled with computer dating,' suggested Sadie innocently.

'It's the last time I tell her anything,' snapped Dolly, putting a dead moth into the dustpan with distaste. 'Jen Jackson's mouth has a life of its own.'

'Does he go up long ladders and hose burning buildings?'

'And rescues kittens from up trees,' said Dolly cheerfully. 'He can rescue me any time. He's got the most gorgeous hands, all big and strong, but gentle, for carrying things carefully with.'

Dougal had large hands, clumsy and these days a little plump, a gold signet ring on one finger. Philip's hands were long and bony, like daddy-long-legs. Sadie was contemplating her own hands, realising she'd never really looked at hands before, when Dolly took her head out of the cupboards and said, 'That's that done. Did your lodger have a cat?'

'She did.'

Dolly picked hairballs off the carpet on the floor of the cupboard and said disdainfully that some people were filthy, and what needed doing next?

They finished by seven, the place sparkling.

'Now what?' asked Dolly, turning her rubber gloves inside out, hanging them to dry over the tap.

'No Gosling?' asked Sadie, surprised.

'I'm a real-ale widow tonight,' said Dolly, winking. 'Gosling's gone to Wiltshire to see a brewery he saved from burning down. He used to work in Wiltshire. Anyway, he did something personal for the managing director, like saving his life, and since then they're booze brothers. Every year the whole lot of them have a booze-up on their own real ale. Gosling goes down, gets brain-damage drunk, is put to bed by someone's long-suffering wife and will come home tomorrow looking ghastly. He's warned me not to try to speak to him for a couple of days. What about Dougal?'

'Dougal and I will probably pass the evening bickering gently about why I keep on my flat.'

Dolly folded dusters. 'Domestic life,' she remarked dismissively. 'And you call that having fun!'

* * *

They sat on the step of the open patio doors, side by side, listening to birds calling from a sycamore tree in the next garden. From the flat above drifted a mouthwatering smell of bacon and frying onions.

'Let's go out,' suggested Dolly. 'Girls' night on the town.'

'Where?'

'There's this club over towards Hackney. Saturday is girls' night. It's a riot.'

'I can't go out looking like Mrs Mop.'

'Nobody'll be looking at *you*,' said Dolly, grinning. 'I'll lend you a top and a belt. One of my T-shirts on you will be as good as a dress.'

'What sort of club is it?' asked Sadie.

Dolly cackled.

'It's a mystery tour,' she said.

It was an early spring evening, warm enough for pubs to leave their doors open on to the pavements. A blackboard stood outside a pub on a corner, coarsely lettered in red and white chalk; GIRLS' NITE STRIPPERS. A hubbub of women's voices came from the open doors, and the smell of beer and cigarettes poured out. In a dark-brown earthy ethnic shift, Dolly looked rather, Sadie thought, like a Christmas pudding with a gleeful expression.

'*Strippers?*' bleated Sadie.

'They're a laugh and a half,' cried Dolly, dragging her inside.

The bar was packed to the rafters. The few men hovering looked either camp and eager, or uncertain and lonely. Bar staff pulled pints as if for a rugger team's night out, served a river of gin and tonic, Scotch and coke, to the more refined. Girls in denim and T-shirts brought mothers well dolled up, all blue eyeshadow and best frocks, cigarettes in pursed and painted mouths, blood-red nails clutched round glasses.

'It's a brave man who takes his knickers off in front

of this lot,' screeched Dolly through the racket, winking. Checkout girls, secretaries, typists and housewives out for a laugh, danced together, packed like sardines in front of the DJ's desk. Sadie elbowed her way through the crush, was pushed and shoved, trod hard on someone's foot.

'Sorry,' she mouthed.

The woman swore. She was small and dark-skinned, Spanish-looking, all flashing eyes and sneering mouth. She dived for a gap in the crowd, in front of the bar, cutting Sadie up so that she lost her place in the queue for two cold lagers. After a wait, Sadie and Dolly crammed on to the end of a table, putting their lager and limes into a sea of puddles on the table top.

'When do they come on?'

Nothing interesting was happening on the dance floor and Sadie was eager not to miss anything.

'When *we're* ready,' Dolly said, with a wicked grin.

The music changed pitch, deafening, to cheers and whistles.

'This is going to be good,' said Dolly.

Four heavies in black made a ring, holding thick, soft rope, keeping the excited audience back. The DJ cut the music, a microphone whined and clunked, came on with a screech. To screams and catcalls, a black man, topped and tailed and bow-tied, bounded into the rope ring, the microphone to his lips, looking round with calculating eyes.

'Birthdays,' he invited, eating the microphone, making it whistle and hum. 'Birthday girls . . . hen night . . . yes . . . come on, come on. What's your name, love?' Hands pushed a tousled girl into the ring, a length of net curtain clipped to her long hair with a silver comb. 'Let me guess,' the stripper said sardonically. 'Hen night.'

There was a breathless squeak.

'What's your name.'

He let the net fall over her face and grinned at the audience.

'Sandy. Is your party here tonight, Sandy?'

The net curtain nodded.

'Sandy's shy,' roared the microphone. 'Let's hear it for shy Sandy.'

A forest of white arms waved in the gloom, to screams and yells of excitement. He bent and kissed her cheek, found two more hen nights, a birthday and an anniversary. Then the show went on.

The strippers, thought Sadie, struggling to keep her feet in the crush, were beautiful. Young and muscular in jeans and braces, skin gleaming with oil, they bumped and ground their hips, thrusting, provoking, unbuttoning flies. Braces draped, jeans inched down to howls of encouragement. The men on the rope strained, keeping everyone back. The strippers got down to business and women's eyes gleamed in the flashing light, predatory, speculative, almost serious. Some of the shouting died a little, giving way to an intense animal interest in flesh.

As one of the men danced towards her part of the crowd, it pushed Sadie right to the front. A shocking-pink posing pouch wiggled and shook itself inches away, slender, sinewy thighs quivering. The man's intense eyes met hers, cool, mocking. Touch, don't touch, touch, don't touch. He danced back and forth on his heels, teasing. He mocked, advanced, stroked, danced away. The women went wild. The rope barrier strained and held. The pink posing pouch stayed in place.

'I thought they took them off,' cried Sadie, disappointed. The tall black man who had done the introductions strutted centre stage in naval officer whites. He took them off slowly, sensuously, keeping on the decorated peaked cap which even in such circumstances lent a curious air of devastating authority. The crowd surged with excitement and Sadie, crushed, clutched at a shoulder for balance, caught the Spanish woman's cheek with her fingernail. Her breath hissing, the woman lunged, nails clawing, drawing bloody lines down Sadie's face. The music pounded, the stripper twirled, displaying perfect buttocks, pouting over his shoulder. The rope barrier fought grimly back as the East End women got into the spirit of the thing, piled in merrily and the fight spread and got out of hand.

The police car was carrying a senior inspector away from a meeting at the Yard that had lasted all day. It was not on duty, but it heard the call go out, saw it was close, radioed in that it would answer. Tired, the senior man watched the streets of the East End speed by. After this, the driver could take him straight home rather than back to the office. Strange that the idea of going home was still comforting, for it was empty and silent, no one there.

The club was a riot. The crowd parted to let the uniformed man through, followed by a man in a dark suit. The black man stood looking down disdainfully, all but naked, his fine features cold, the music a soft growl. He picked up his trousers from the red velvet chair and began to put them on, indifferent. Women melted away as the plainclothes man bent down to a woman on the floor, his face expressionless.

'Are you all right?' he asked.

She looked up.

'*You?*' John Campling didn't touch her. '*Here? Brawling.*' There was blood on her forehead. With cold, professional detachment he stood up, looked down at her from what seemed a great height, as she lay on the floor, and said, 'It's only a couple of scratches. You'd better get a tetanus shot. Dirty fingernails. You'll be all right. You want to lay any charge of assault?' His neutral voice held no encouragement.

The Spanish woman had long disappeared, the rest drawn back into half dark, their backs to the scene, ordering drinks as if nothing had happened. Sadie, alone on the floor, shook her head. She wiped her face with her knuckles, awkwardly, like a little girl.

'Better off out of places like this,' John Campling said, as if to a stranger, and walked away. The DJ flicked a switch, dowsed the lights. The show went on.

Dolly didn't see her go, couldn't see her anywhere. She waited until the floor show finished, in case Sadie was there in the crowd. Outside, the little *deux chevaux* was gone. Dolly stood uncertainly on the pavement, in the light from the club. It was after eleven, not a time to chase round the East End looking for someone who obviously wanted to be on her own. She dithered, attracting interest, sick with worry, didn't know what to do. In the end, scared by the growing attention of several men hanging around, she went back inside and phoned for a cab to take her home.

In the flat they had cleaned earlier, showered, heavy wet hair scraped back from her face, wrapped in a bath towel, Sadie sat cross-legged in the middle of her bed, studying her reflection in her dressing-table mirror. The scratches stood out against her pale skin. They were not deep and would not scar. It was John Campling's words that would leave scars. The phone rang.

'*There* you are. Are you all right?' said Dolly's anxious voice. 'I looked all over for you.'

'I wanted to be on my own.'

'Are you OK?'

'I'll live,' said Sadie.

'What on earth did you do to make that woman go crazy like that?'

'I scratched her accidentally. It wasn't my fault.'

I lost John Campling tonight, she thought, as Dolly chattered on, excited and entertained by the drama in the club now they were both safe. Sadie's head felt very clear and light, her mind shadowless, replaying the expression on John's face as he'd said, '*You?*' Reason asserted itself. She had not lost John Campling; he wasn't hers to lose. Never had been, except for three long-ago days that were now like a dream. Eventually Dolly got tired of her monosyllabic answers, and got off the phone. Sadie went on sitting cross-legged on her bed for a long time, waiting for the pain to fade. She was as much in love with

John as ever, married to Dougal. There was nothing to be done about it, except make the best of what she had, which was a kind and loving man. Make the best of it.

Dougal answered the phone after a long time. He'd been fast asleep.

'Where are you?' he mumbled, barely awake.

'My flat. I'm OK. I'm on my way home.'

'You wake me to tell me you're on your way home?'

'No. I love you, Dougal. That's what I woke you up to tell you.'

Dougal's mind was foggy, but something niggled at him.

'I love you, too. Couldn't we have told each other in the morning?'

'I'll be home in half an hour.'

He put the receiver down and sank back into his warm pillow. Sliding back into sleep, he knew what it was. I'm on my way *home*. She always said, 'I'm on my way *back*.' In his sleep, Dougal smiled.

Chapter Thirty-Five

While Sadie got over her girls' nite out, swore never to go near a strip club again, resolved to work harder at being a good wife to Dougal, to sort out the misunderstanding with Maria, to straighten her life out and be unaccustomedly virtuous, Maria over in Barnsbury was crabby and moody, preoccupied with going into hospital to have her baby. She sat in her half-landscaped garden, a book folded over her bump, frustrating her mother-in-law's attempts to console and advise. She pushed a glass of water into the middle of the table between them, slapped the book about childbirth down after it, feeling, as she kept complaining, like a wheelchair-bound Tweedledee.

'I know I can't have a home delivery. It's obvious,' she snapped. 'But I can wish, can't I? Sheila Kitzinger makes natural childbirth sound heavenly. They put the baby straight on to your stomach and you can hold it the second it's born.'

'Messy and hideous,' answered her mother-in-law tartly. 'Next thing you know, all these natural birth women will be telling you to eat the afterbirth, the way they carry on. I like babies washed and wrapped and humanised and everything done nicely and discreetly.'

'I think that book is lovely. I just wish . . .'

'It's a matter of taste,' said Anne Howard, closing the subject.

Maria groaned, lifting herself in her chair, avoiding pressure for too long on any part of herself, a chore made more tiresome than ever by the weight of the baby.

'Look at me,' she complained, 'I've got shoulders like a prizefighter. So unfeminine.'

Anne didn't take the bait. Maria was so fretful and moody it was pointless to try to comfort her. She had good reason, for as she got heavier and heavier, sores and skin breaks a constant worry, the threat of having to go into hospital had hung daily over her head for months.

'I actually can't think why anyone wants natural birth. It's natural pain, so far as I can remember. And a lot of it,' added Anne Howard, for good measure, meaning to encourage. The remark was a dire mistake.

'I'd give *anything* to be able to feel myself enough to hurt that much,' said Maria.

There was a difficult silence. Anne tried to make it better and said had Maria remembered that Rosalie and Figgin were coming for supper, but made it worse because Maria sulked over the suggestion she might have forgotten.

Since the March housewarming party Rosalie and Figgin had rarely been apart. They got on together with such effortless ease that everyone said they must have been made for each other. Rosalie, unperturbed by Figgin's eccentricities, brought out a kind of reverent side in him which Anne Howard had long recognised was there. Whatever Figgin was seeking in ashrams and meditation, he seemed to find in Rosalie as well and he treated her with such tender respect, such sensual grace that he went straight to her warm and practical heart. Combined with his own practical good sense and an excellent income, Figgin's qualities as a lover (if you didn't mind knobbly knees and nose, and a distinct lack of height) took a lot of beating. Rosalie surveyed her choices, eyed her dainty but very plump figure in the mirror, told herself neither of them were spring chickens and at their age they could do as they liked. They welcomed each other into their respective lives, houses and beds and were totally and utterly happy.

Knowledgeable in things Indian, Figgin did a delicious chicken tandoori. He took charge of the barbecue and soon spicy smoke rose straight up in windless, humid air.

Rosalie chopped salad in a big wooden bowl, Philip poured beer and uncorked wine. Figgin wiped his smarting eyes, left his chicken to cook, and got into a deep discussion about gardens with Anne.

'Gardens are spiritual oases,' he was saying. 'Can be – *should* be – magical places.'

'We're trying to be practical, economical *and* magical,' said Anne, who adored her plumber's imagination. She and Rosalie both absolutely understood that a man could have love affairs with central-heating systems, the high reaches of the Mother Ganges, and the woman in his life, without offence to any of them.

'A nice challenge,' said Figgin.

'It's a blind and disabled garden,' Anne explained, running her hand over a piece of smooth grey rock waiting to become part of a small waterfall course. 'We're raising the ponds and flower beds to wheelchair height, so Maria can look after it.'

'What's a blind garden?'

'Oh, lovely. Texture, scent, shape to feel with your hands. Sound. Running water, things that rustle. Plants, like herbs, that scent your fingers when you handle them. A very, very sensuous garden,' she said. 'Exciting and soothing. Infinite variety.'

'Sounds like a woman,' said Figgin earnestly, nodding his knobbly little head, meaning every word of it.

Rosalie blushed.

'Exactly like a woman,' said Anne.

Philip lit citronella candles. A moth, up early, hovered dangerously, drawn by the flame, repelled by the smell. They sat, contented, sipping beer and cold white wine, watching the chicken blacken over charcoal.

'I'll go,' said Rosalie, when the phone rang.

'A surprise,' she said, coming back. 'It's Sadie with an olive branch. What shall I say?'

Maria caught her husband's eye. He nodded.

'Ask her to come over,' she said casually. 'Say we're having a barbecue and I'm having a baby the day after tomorrow, so she'd better come quick because it's her last chance to see an elephant in a wheelchair.'

'Put the rest of the chicken on, Figgs, and put another bottle in the fridge,' ordered Rosalie.

'Let's hope,' remarked Philip through a mouthful of salad, 'that the end of this absurd feuding between you two is in sight.'

'Look at that poor silly thing,' muttered Rosalie.

The moth lay frizzled in the citronella dish, its wings charred, while several more were well on the way to following it.

The Monroes arrived. Chairs were pushed back, room made around the table, the first moments of tension covered with busy servings of charred chicken and cold white wine.

'I'm sorry . . .' began Sadie hesitantly.

'Least said, soonest mended,' Rosalie said it a way that meant there was no need to go on and in no time at all, things were back to normal, as though they had never fallen out.

By the time they'd finished eating and catching up on each other's news, the dying barbecue glowed red in the dusk. A red late-August moon hung low in the sky, pitted and pocked like some vast, over-ripe orange, sinking below the horizon. A patio light threw the garden into deepening shadows. Dougal, Philip, Figgin and Anne played cards at the cleared table. Rosalie and Sadie washed up. Standing at Maria's low sink, uncomfortably bending over dishes, they heard Maria laughing.

'What?' asked Sadie, turning round with soapy hands.

'If anything ever made me glad I'm sitting in this thing, it's those.'

Three pairs of eyes took in Sadie's feet.

'Platforms,' she said, sounding pleased. 'Dolly made me get them. She's got some.'

Rosalie said could she try them on and staggered round the kitchen on two-inch soles. Figgin called from the patio that they'd go with a sari, so Rosalie hastily took them off again. When the washing-up was done they sat with Maria watching the sun sink slowly over the rooftops of London, quiet in August, everyone away, holiday time. But not for them. No one in the Giangelli family went away when Maria's baby was on its way.

'This is perfect,' sighed Sadie, happier than she had been in a long, long time, leaving the absurd sandals under the kitchen table, enjoying the cool flagstones under her feet.

'It's so perfect, I get scared it can't last,' answered Maria.

Rosalie looked up sharply.

Maria looked over at her husband. 'I sometimes wonder, why me? I wonder what I've done to deserve all this.'

Rosalie and Sadie sat speechless.

'I get scared,' Maria went on in a low voice, 'because there were about twelve girls in the ward in the unit, when I was there, who were engaged or married. When they got paralysed, none of them lasted. The ones who were engaged got broken, and the ones who were married got divorced. Men don't want to look after women.'

'Philip doesn't look after you,' said Rosalie, recovering from the idea that Maria saw herself as *lucky*. 'You look after you.'

The others were absorbed in their game.

Maria lowered her voice to a whisper. 'What if I can't manage the baby? What if I get sores? What if I get a bladder infection? What if I have to go into hospital and leave Phil with the baby.'

'We'll manage, between us,' said Sadie.

'They're all things that happen easily,' Maria said despondently.

Philip studied his cards, his big ears apparently swivelling like antennae, for he fanned out his cards and said casually, 'The motto in this family is, anything can be done. *Anything*.' He slapped a card on the table and said to Dougal, 'Your go.'

Maria bit her lip, stroked her kicking baby and stared at him, absorbed again in his cards. Sadie looked up into the navy sky, the tropical moon leaving a crimson glow. 'I don't think it's what might happen, and whether Phil can look after a baby that's scary,' she said.

'What is, then?' asked Maria.

'I think it's love that is scary,' said Sadie.

They fell quiet, sat in darkness, feeling the warmth from the dying barbecue, seeing the stars come out, thinking over what they had said.

Chapter Thirty-Six

Maria's son bounced into the world, by prior arrangement with her surgeon, at just over seven pounds. He didn't cry, he wasn't hideous. He lay bundled in a cotton blanket, gazing quietly at his mother. It wasn't natural, but it was a very happy birth.

'I had a very natural Caesarean,' joked Maria, sitting up in a low hospital bed, 'as Caesareans go. Sheila Kitzinger would have been proud of us. Phil did his breathing and rubbed my back, like the book says, so we got as near as we could to a feeling kind of birth. He felt it, anyway.' She giggled. 'Actually, he overdid it and hyperventilated and went funny. I think it was a bit much, really, and he was glad when they took me away. Then he could get on with pacing, and do things properly, that men are meant to do.'

Her cubicle, off the main maternity ward, was stuffy, heavy with the scent of summer flowers. Outside, it was muggy, the sun glaring behind low clouds, weather for headaches and storms. A good storm would clear the air, but none were forecast that day.

'Did you?' asked Sadie, speaking to Philip, gazing at James Anthony Howard stirring in his plastic bassinet, swaddled in white hospital baby blankets.

'Pace? Of course, I paced splendidly. I like traditions.'

His demeanour belied his cheery words. Philip, Sadie thought, looked tired, his jaunty air subdued. Along with the feeling of storms coming outside, there was change in the air indoors. The arrival of the baby brought an era to an end. They'd all waited, put off going anywhere, closed ranks around Maria in case she needed them. Now it was over, the baby safe. Life would move on again, Maria no longer its centre, which, on the night of the barbecue, had been mainly what she feared. She had an uneasy feeling that being a mother could turn out rather lonely.

Anne Howard frowned, gazing at her grandchild's fuzzy head. She wanted to stay, enjoy the early days, get to know him, but the time she spent with Phil and Maria was showing in the accounts. Business demanded her full attention and a trip to the United States. Going to Los Angeles for a long spell just after the birth of a first grandchild was bad timing, but couldn't be helped. And maybe it would be for the best. It would give Maria a chance to do things her way with no anxious grandmother clucking in the background.

The baby snuffled and grunted. With the bassinet at the end of her bed, her baby was out of Maria's reach. She looked anxiously at her chair, propped against the wall, also out of reach.

'I wish they wouldn't take it away,' she said.

Her wheelchair was Maria's lifeline, her safety. Anne knew she had nightmares about not being able to get to it. Very especially she was afraid of fire, of being trapped, unable to save herself, burning to death. She dreamed that often, waking in terrible panic, sobbing.

'Put Maria's chair where she can get it,' she told Philip. 'And on my way out, I'll speak to Sister. I'll ask her to tell her nurses not to tidy it away.'

'Do you think Jamie's hungry?' Maria asked hopefully, relaxing about the chair. She adored feeding him, couldn't wait for him to wake up.

'He looks very fast asleep, to me,' said Anne.

'Why is he twitching, then?'

'They all do that. Babies are noisy twitchers and they snore.'

Jamie Howard lay under the gaze of several pairs of eyes, oblivious to all the rapt attention.

'What if I don't know what to do when I go home?' asked Maria.

'Hardly anybody does,' said Sadie. 'You learn as you go along, if my clients are anything to go by.'

I hope they do better than your clients, thought Anne Howard. She quelled her guilt again, at going away. She had a business to run and they would have to do what other young parents did, and manage on their own.

It was Dougal who got really worried. Managing on their own, when Maria was back home again and absorbed in the baby, seemed to be taking it out of Philip.

'It's just as well we're not all having babies. Phil is taking a lot of time out of the office,' Dougal complained. As little Jamie Howard grew and flourished, his father's business seemed on the verge of a decline. Dougal looked depressed, worried, said business was down, the market suffering from political uncertainty, loss of business confidence and the dire consequences of going into the EEC.

'Do you know,' he read the paper with a frown, not finding the story funny at all, 'that we're not allowed to buy beef from anywhere in the world while those bureaucratic idiots in Brussels have a beef mountain no one can afford. It says here they're selling it off cheap to the Russians, who subsidise it and get fat on our steak we can't afford to eat. How can we compete in a world run by prats?'

'Your business is doing OK, isn't it?' asked Sadie. 'We seem fine.'

'Computers are a growth area. We're the lucky ones.'

'Then what are you fussing about? Philip never seems to worry.'

'Phil worries all right. He handles it well,' said Dougal.

They visited the Barnsbury house a lot, especially after Anne Howard went away.

'I wish we'd got one, don't you?'

Driving home through London streets damp after a heavy shower of rain, she wished it were her, sitting as Maria had, her baby at her breast.

'He's pretty ugly,' answered Dougal lightly.

'You don't think they're ugly when they're yours,' she said wistfully.

'That's a case of beauty being strictly in the eye of the beholder.' He drove through a deep puddle, sending a sheet of water over two hurrying pedestrians, looked at them staring after the car with outrage on their faces.

'It is a long time since I threw away my pills,' she said in a noncommittal kind of way, looking at their victims over the back of her seat.

'I didn't see that puddle until I was in it. How long?'

'Too long.'

She waited for an answer, but he seemed to concentrate on driving. It was the first time they had said anything, acknowledged that she wasn't getting pregnant. She longed to talk about it, now they'd made the first step, but Dougal was very quiet the rest of the way home and showed no inclination at all to pursue it.

Chapter Thirty-Seven

Once Philip and Maria were settled down with their new baby and Philip took less time away from the office, Dougal and Sadie took a holiday, a late fortnight in the Lake District. They drove up at a leisurely pace, enjoying early autumn colours, trees just on the turn. Dougal had booked good hotels. They walked, climbed, swam in indoor pools, ate, talked, made love, unwound from their usual frenetic pace.

'I do love you. We should get away more often. Spend more time together, relax,' she said. Around them a hotel dining room, discreetly and softly lit, buzzed with low conversation. They ate fresh trout and home-made ice cream, appetites sharpened by long walks.

'Why don't we, then? We could take weekend breaks,' he said idly.

A gardener had been raking leaves all afternoon, and they could see the pile busily spreading itself back over the grass in a rising, whipping wind.

'You are too busy turning a buck, and running a company should be a job, not a life's work, particularly when it isn't your own,' she said.

Dougal snorted and poured the last of the wine. 'Try getting you away from the office.'

She tensed. It was a familiar argument, and one that led nowhere. Even at moments like this, if she tested it, the thin fabric of their relationship tore too readily, showing discord behind it. Their waiter took away their plates, covering the moment.

'Do you think they're right,' he asked suddenly, 'when they say women don't get pregnant if they're tense?'

She was shocked that he could bring that up, spoil their pleasant evening with prejudice. She was instantly wary, tried to hide it.

'See what I mean? You're uptight.'

'I am not uptight,' she said stiffly.

'OK,' he spread his big hands comically, denying his own words, 'you're not uptight.'

A pianist whom she had barely noticed tinkled in the background. A table of diners got up to go, wiping their mouths on thick white linen napkins, looking sleek and satisfied. A waiter danced attendance, pulling out chairs. The pianist straightened his shoulders, woke up and launched into 'Lara's Theme'. She and Dougal had seen *Dr Zhivago* together and it had made her cry.

'I just meant, let's not worry about it,' said Dougal.

'Lara's Theme' rose and swelled and her eyes glittered with unshed tears.

'You are too emotional. No wonder we've got problems,' said Dougal casually, not intending to hurt, setting the seal on the evening. The joy gone out of it, she followed him to their room later. It doesn't work like that, she thought, lying beside him in the enormous hotel bed. We may not be getting pregnant, but I'm no tenser than a million other women. It really doesn't work like that.

'You've got an awful lot thinner,' she said, meeting Dolly on her first day back at the office.

'I have,' Dolly agreed coolly.

'Dieting?' It was hard to imagine Dolly on a diet, she liked her food too much and herself just the way she was.

'No.'

Dolly was being hard work. Sadie frowned. Dolly was never hard work, so something must be wrong. Her Ribena-coloured hair was scraped back into a comb and her make-up was wobbly, as though a child had drawn it, or Dolly had put it on after she'd been crying. Red platform shoes, instead of looking daft and wacky, today looked sad and made her ankles heavy. Dolly without her sparkle looked something she'd never looked before – her age. It didn't suit her.

'We enjoyed the Lakes,' said Sadie, trying again. 'It didn't rain and the hotels were lovely.'

'Good,' snapped Dolly, snatching the receiver off her phone at its first ping, making it clear she was too busy to chat.

'Sorry I spoke,' said Sadie, astonished and rebuffed. For Dolly to be that unfriendly, whatever was wrong was *dire*.

The fact that it was Monday didn't help, and also that it was turning out to be one of those days. They were both on reception, dealt with a stream of boring money complaints that they rerouted to Social Security, a hysterical teenage girl wanting to leave home because she didn't get on with her mother, a recent young widow who felt like following her husband into the grave and needed a listening ear, and someone's hugely fat daughter wanting bath aids for her elderly parents. Sadie was taking the bath aid details, promising to send an occupational therapist round, when Dolly knocked and stuck her head round the door.

'Got to go out. The police have found a young woman in some derelict house with the DTs. She'd been trying to send a four-year-old girl to the off-licence for whisky. Everyone's out.'

'I'll cope,' said Sadie.

Dolly flew round there with police and ambulance, and had a terrible time.

'Ooooh,' she cried, her bad temper forgotten, 'it was enough to put you on the wagon for life. She had poisonous snakes coming out of the walls, and she went for us like a maniac every time we came near, screaming that we were monsters and devils. It's put me off booze, I can tell you. She's only twenty-four.'

'What about the four-year-old?'

'Daddy came to fetch her. A nice man. God knows what's gone wrong there.'

She sounded all at once tired and depressed again.

'Huh,' said Sadie. 'Something must drive her to it. What's the betting it's him? In secret.'

'How perspicacious you are,' jeered Dolly.

The penny dropped.

'How's Gosling?'

Dolly's face fell. 'How would I know?' she snapped.

'You should. He lives with you.'

'Only,' cried Dolly, with all the day's pent-up feeling, 'when he feels like it. It was fine at first, all lovey-dovey, but now it's now you see me, now you don't. Half the time I don't know where he is, and the other half, I do know, and it's not with me,' she added bitterly.

'Oh, oh,' said Sadie. 'Bad as that?'

'Worse. Don't ask. You don't want to know.'

'That's why you aren't eating.'

'Can't be bothered,' sniffed Dolly. Sadie noticed she'd only put mascara on one eye, which accounted for her slightly odd, Picasso-like appearance.

'I saw there's no knitting in your bag. That's a very bad sign,' observed Sadie. 'You've *always* got knitting.'

'I'm not doing anything,' yelped Dolly furiously, 'except crying my eyes out, and waiting for him to call, and making a complete *idiot* of myself. I sit and stare at the phone. Me, who never *ever* sits and stares at the phone. I sit and wait for it to ring and when the bastard strolls in in the morning, I don't say a word. He says it's all-night shift, but he's lying his socks off, I know he is.'

'I'm sorry about this,' quavered Sadie, her mouth trembling, 'but I'm going to have to laugh.'

'Well, thank *you*,' shouted Dolly, mortified. 'Now I know where to go when I want sympathy.'

'It serves you right for being so mean to Ali Baba and the rest. You've met your match, Mrs Fiske.'

'Ali Baba was small and meek and desperately well meaning and had a Turkish sense of humour,' snuffled Dolly. 'Gosling is six foot four and wears a sexy uniform, has my sense of humour, behaves like a bum and doesn't give a damn. I adore him. I want to marry him.'

Sadie grinned from ear to ear. The old Dolly was back.

'Does he want to marry you?'

'He says he does,' said Dolly dismally, 'but I don't believe him.'

'Men don't usually lie about it. They don't bother. They either marry you or just shove off.'

'He's shoved off on a training course in Birmingham.'

Sadie sensed they were getting to the heart of the matter.

'*Six months*,' screeched Dolly. 'No do you mind? or will you come with me? or what will you do on lonely evenings without me, darling? I should take up needlepoint, I suppose,' spat Dolly, working herself up. 'He told me to buy a knitting machine, occupy myself, would you believe it? A *machine*.'

'This,' pronounced Sadie solemnly, 'is a man without soul.'

Dolly's exquisite hand knits were works of art, but even so, it was terribly hard not to laugh.

'What does *he* do on lonely evenings? What, come to that, does anyone do in Birmingham?'

'He goes out with other women,' Dolly said, her eyebrows disappearing up into the Ribena fringe. 'Just like that. Doesn't even bother lying. Says it doesn't matter, it's me he loves, and he'll be home in six months' time. How about that?'

Sadie giggled.

'You're no help,' snapped Dolly. 'What do I do?'

'You take the advice you hand out to me in such liberal dollops. You know perfectly well what to do. You stop whingeing, put your best face on and get out and have a good time. Show him.'

To Sadie's amazement, a tear rose in Dolly's bloodshot eye, the one with no mascara.

'I can't. I miss him.'

'Then you'll have to wait and hope he means it and cry for six months.'

'I'm not crying miserable,' yelled Dolly. 'I'm crying *furious*. I *swore* I'd never do this over a man, ever again. And look at me. I don't *want* to be in love.'

Sadie remembered the look in John Campling's eyes when he recognised her in the strip club, before astonishment and contempt took over. Love. She stopped laughing.

'It's a mug's game,' she said, shrugging. 'All you can do is try to make what you've got work. Or give up and end up with nothing.' She'd gone back to Dougal. Whether or not she was making it work was another matter.

'You know?' Dolly went on with wry humour. 'You look yourself in the eye in the mirror, you wag your finger, and you say, Dolly Fiske, you're making an ass of yourself. He won't respect you for hanging on, and you'd better tell him to push off, before he tells you. I *swore* I'd never get involved like this, again. I could scream.'

'Swearing and screaming don't work,' said Sadie. 'I should know.'

'They do not,' agreed Dolly grimly.

They sat contemplating life, and men. All over the big, ugly building people packed up, went out into rush-hour traffic and late-night supermarkets, to get supper things to take home. A cleaner banged a broom out in the passage and hummed to herself. Dolly had her head on her arms, half lying on her desk, depressed. Neither of them could be bothered to move.

'You never know,' observed Sadie after a while. 'Figgin's teaching Rosalie transcendental meditation and she's talking about going to Rikikesh with him. He bought her a bright-red sari with gold spangles from that shop in Tottenham Court Road, for her birthday. She won't wear it, but she goes and strokes the silk in the wrapping paper. Maria told me Rosalie told her, and said to keep it a secret. So of course Maria promptly told me. If Rosalie and Figgin can make it work, anyone can. You might be in with a chance.'

'I suppose Gosling *might* mean it,' Dolly remarked grudgingly. 'He *might* be just having a good time, but not cheating.'

'You don't *have* to jump to conclusions,' Sadie agreed.

'Pigs *might* fly,' said Dolly quizzically.

They exchanged knowing, philosophical half-smiles. Dolly cheered up.

'Make us a coffee, before we go home,' she said.

Sadie plugged the kettle in and found a mug which didn't have mould at the bottom of it.

'There's only dried,' she said, putting a carton of soured milk in a wastepaper bin for the cleaner to find and get angry about.

'Dried'll do, pet.' Dolly stuck her short stout legs out and put her feet together, wiggled the bright-red shoes. 'I got these in the market. D'you like them?'

'They are appalling and they suit you down to the ground,' said Sadie, grinning affectionately. The old Dolly was back.

Chapter Thirty-Eight

Maria threw Dr Spock in the bin. First she read his book from end to end, then she concluded that unless Jamie read Dr Spock, too, so that the baby knew exactly what was expected of him, it was of rather doubtful use. She also began to read some of the feminist books coming from America, and to think about things. She found, without meaning to, that she objected to the kind doctor, however amiable and clever, thinking he knew better than she did. In particular, he said nothing useful whatsoever about wheelchairs. She'd looked it up in the index, under C for chair, W for wheelchair and D for disabled. Nothing. It was as if no disabled woman ever had a baby. Fuming, she chucked all her baby books away except for her well-thumbed Sheila Kitzinger, and resolved to go it alone.

'Alone,' she muttered one morning, 'is the right word.'

It was lonely, on her own all day with the baby, and she was tired all the time. Her arms ached fiercely from doing all the things the rest of her body couldn't. Jamie fed like a glutton, a health visitor's dream. He slept a lot, was enchanting and jolly when he woke up. At six weeks he produced a gummy grin that stole everyone's hearts. He did everything a baby is supposed to do, and gained weight and grew. Maria found this a doubtful blessing.

'Baby's doing splendidly,' was the health visitor's verdict. She packed her scales away in her car and came back in to say goodbye.

'Baby may be doing splendidly, but I'm knackered,' said Maria. 'I'm scared I'll drop him. He's getting too big for me to manage.'

The health visitor tweaked Jamie's round cheek and avoided answering by chatting to the baby. Maria raced across the room when she left, parked her chair and watched the woman drive off. She felt such frustration, she was afraid she'd go crazy. At such moments Maria learned what it was to want something so much she'd kill for it. She beat the windowsill with her fists until the frustration poured out in tears, and in the exhausted calm afterwards she contemplated the paradox. She'd kill to have legs and then they'd be dead legs, like her own.

'That woman's got horrible legs, anyway. Puffy ankles like socks.'

That made her feel a little better. Jamie, woken by his mother's tears, lay watching, quite quiet. When she said the health visitor had puffy ankles he gave a radiant grin and crowed with delight.

'You don't understand a word of it,' said Maria, drying her eyes. 'But you're nicer about it than anyone except your dad.'

But none of it changed the fact that the bigger he got, the more she struggled with bathing and changing.

'What if I drop him?' she asked again.

'He'd probably bounce, he's so fat,' Philip said, admiring his plump baby son. 'Stop worrying.'

She tried. She had dreams of toppling out of her chair, not being able to get up from the floor, of hurting him and herself, of lying unable to reach him, of not being able to manage. All the old worries became everyday torment. Once, she dreamed she was dancing, waltzing and twirling, faster and faster, and the faster she danced towards the baby, the further he drifted away. When she looked down, her feet were rotting and rotting away, would never carry her anywhere.

* * *

'You're doing fine,' said Philip.

'I do it, but I'm so slow. You don't know how long it all takes,' she said, exhausted.

She'd thought housework in Anne's perfectly adapted house would be easy but she had no idea of the work a baby brings. Tired to death, she forgot things, adding to her work by endless wheeling back and forth. She dreaded visitors; even answering the door meant extra journeys to and fro.

Rosalie and Figgin were there on the Saturday afternoon Philip found a pile of mouldy shirts in the utility room, under some sheets waiting to be washed. He took them through to show her.

'I forgot to put them in the dryer,' she cried. 'I had the Milton to change, and nappies to put in soak, and the milkman wanted paying and I get in a muddle and forget things.'

'Eight shirts,' said Philip reproachfully.

Figgin suddenly remembered there was some pipework for the ponds that he needed to look at in the garden. Rosalie followed him out.

'There are cracks showing,' said Figgin. 'She's got a lot of stress.'

Stress was becoming the new disease and Figgin said it with a certain pride that he knew about such things.

'We all have the odd crack,' answered Rosalie. 'She's good at coping. Eight shirts are only eight shirts. It won't break their bank.'

'So long as cracks don't become chasms,' Figgin said.

'It's really up to them to work it out,' she answered.

'We've embarrassed them,' Maria told Philip. James lay in her lap, beaming. Philip watched Rosalie pull weeds from one of the raised flower beds.

'A few mouldy shirts don't matter,' he said, changing his tune.

'I think they do,' she answered sadly.

'Let me hang them out,' said Figgin, coming back indoors.

Philip went to hand them over.

'Leave them be,' cried Rosalie.

'It's no trouble,' said Figgin, taking the mildewing pile in his small arms, 'but they don't half pong.'

'Philip can cope with his own shirts,' said Rosalie in a stern voice that made them all turn and stare.

They left early, the atmosphere not good.

'A bit of help is what she needs,' argued Figgin in the car.

Rosalie was implacable. 'It is not. It won't take many mouldy shirts before he gets the message that she needs *his* help. It's up to them to sort it out. It takes a woman to understand this kind of thing.'

'I think I'm going to do a little meditation,' announced Figgin, lying back and closing his eyes. 'Wake me up when we get home.'

Rosalie put on the brake with a jolt fit to give him whiplash.

'Oh no you don't,' she cried. 'You've got to understand right now that if Maria starts depending on other people, she's finished.'

Figgin opened one cobalt eye and closed it again hurriedly. Placid Rosalie looked all het up.

'*She* has to be the one who copes. *That's* independence. *Wake up, Figgin, and listen.*'

Figgin looked at her from under his colourless lashes and sighed.

'You're lovely when you're angry. I never saw you so cross before.'

Rosalie looked at him with an expression he'd never seen before, either. Incredulity.

'That is the corniest load of twaddle I ever heard,' she snapped.

'Probably,' he said, 'but that doesn't mean it can't be true.'

She stared at him for a while, speechless, then started the car again.

'You're extraordinary, Figgs,' she said. 'You're something else, you know?'

'*Now* you're talking,' shouted Figgin joyously, waking up, the threatened storm averted.

Rosalie, still full of doubt and diffidence, wondered whether she might just try on the sari.

When Maria finally did drop Jamie and, being neither brain-damaged nor even hurt, he turned out none the worse for it, it was a relief. One wet afternoon, rain rattled at the windows at bathtime. She had the bath on its stand, and him in it, walking her fingers over him, tickling. He loved it. He shrieked and splashed.

'Careful,' she said to the baby, too late. His soapy arms slipped through her hands and the bathstand tipped its contents, baby, water and all, right into her lap. At first Jamie thought it a great game, and chuckled. As Maria sat speechless, listening to water dripping from her clothes and her chair, drenched with warm water she couldn't feel, a spreading puddle on the carpet, he got cold, kicked and began to grizzle.

'We're a mess,' she said flatly.

Jamie wailed. She hugged him close. He went red, hating being squashed against the wet, cold wool of her jumper, gave a great flail of his limbs and slid, still soapy, off her lap. On the floor, he stopped bawling and lay, apparently interested by the new turn of events.

'If I don't get some help,' Maria told him, leaning over to see him, 'something awful is going to happen.'

'I told you he'd bounce,' said Philip cheerfully. 'What sort of help do you want?'

'A cleaner. If I didn't have to clean the house, I could do the rest.'

She wondered why it took him a weekend to agree to it. They could afford it. It was only out of pride that she hadn't had a cleaner before.

'I'll get someone, but they don't do my den,' he said on the Sunday morning.

Maria shrugged. If Phil wanted to do his own housework upstairs, it was his business. But it did seem a bit strange; he never did anything downstairs, left it all to her.

'Have you got something hidden up there?' she joked.

'Of course not.'

Something in his voice made her glance at him, puzzled. Then Jamie woke up and started to cry, and she forgot all about it.

Philip was as good as his word. A cleaner arrived to do four mornings a week and life cheered up. Rosalie came for tea and reported back. Figgin was meticulously cleaning grease from under his nails with dabs of Swarfega after a mucky day's work.

'No sign of chasms,' said Rosalie with satisfaction.

'I told you so,' said Figgin.

'You did not. I told *you*.'

'Any way you like,' said Figgin agreeably and went back to scrubbing his nails.

The months flew by. Jamie learned to crawl, to pull himself up by the side of her chair, and before she knew it, he was toddling. They were playing hide-and-seek around the raised ponds and flower beds on a sunny spring day when the front door bell rang.

'In the garden,' Maria shouted.

They came round the side entrance and three heads appeared over the garden gate. Sadie came into the garden, looking all buttoned-up and pink and peculiar, followed by Figgin, looking nonchalant.

'What's Rosalie doing?' asked Maria.

Her stepmother was hanging back, behind the wooden gate, looking over with an odd expression.

'She's a bit nervous,' said Sadie, sounding strangled.

Maria pulled Jamie on to her lap, wheeled to the gate, pulling it wide. Hastily, she pulled herself together.

'Rosalie. You look . . . stunning,' she gasped.

Resplendent in red spangled silk, Rosalie tugged at her midriff self-consciously and said in a stifled voice, 'It's lovely and cool.'

'Hot weather,' said Maria, on a very average spring day. 'Prickly heat. Definitely.'

'It's hot in India,' gasped Rosalie.

A strange sound came from behind one of the ponds. Sadie stuffed her hands into her mouth and cracked up with laughter.

'What are you laughing at, Sadie?' snapped Maria.

'She's coming unravelled,' shrieked Sadie hysterically.

Rosalie twisted round to look. In the short trip from the car, her sari had come loose, hanging down behind, knickers for all the neighbourhood to see.

'Oh, God,' gasped Sadie, 'she looks just like a parcel come all unstuck.'

Figgin took charge, his small body ramrod-straight with indignation that they were laughing.

'You need a little re-tucking,' he said kindly, solemnly ushering Rosalie in. He closed the gate behind her, spun her like a top and whipped the spangles off. Rosalie stood, scarlet with embarrassment, plump pale thighs tapering to shapely knees, in stretched pink St Michael cotton smalls.

'Now then, let's start again, and do it properly. You'll soon get the hang of it,' said Figgin, ignoring their hysteria. He rewound her, tucking her in carefully. Fooka, sitting on a table in his cage, to get some sun, eyed the performance. Apparently put out by the competition with his own splendour, he began to preen furiously.

'There,' said Figgin proudly.

'You're actually going to wear it?' cried Maria. 'You're awfully brave.'

'Om, om, om,' cackled Rosalie, getting the giggles herself. 'I've got a mantra and an Indian frock and all I need now is one of those red dots over my nose. Go on Figgs, where is it?'

'Om,' screeched Fooka. Even out of doors he made Sadie's skin prickle. She rubbed her arms.

'Not yet, you can't have one of those. One thing at a time,' said Figgin.

'Oh, go on . . .' she begged, laughing, pulling a face. 'Don't be mean, Figgin.'

Eventually, when they all calmed down, Rosalie asked anxiously, 'Do you think I look *completely* ridiculous?'

Maria and Sadie were spared an answer as Figgin pointed out she'd look like everyone else in Rikikesh. Rosalie patted her ash-blonde hair and looked only slightly reassured.

'Well, nearly like everyone else in Rikikesh,' he added, a truthful man.

'You're going to India?' demanded Maria, the meaning of their words sinking in.

Figgin faltered for once. This was family. Serious. He looked at Rosalie hopefully.

'We are getting married,' she said obligingly, when he was too cowardly to speak. 'In India.'

Fooka, feeling sudden tension in the air, cocked his head.

'You don't mind, do you? We only just decided,' asked Rosalie anxiously.

'Mind?' cried Maria. 'I'm *thrilled* and so will Phil be.'

'There you are, we set a precedent, getting married by ourselves,' said Sadie, feeling vindicated at long last. 'No one will be able to come to a wedding in India.'

Jamie slid off his mother's lap. Rosalie picked him up and hugged him much too tightly, beaming.

'Bugger my bunions,' snapped Fooka from his place in the sun, very put out at such good vibrations. They all turned to look. He snapped his beak angrily, and they ruined his moment by laughing until they cried.

Chapter Thirty-Nine

The second half of 1976, then, brought Rosalie and Figgin home from Rikikesh as man and wife, and when they'd been to the Islington registry office, to make it all proper, Philip and Maria, not wanting to steal their thunder by announcing it at the same time as the wedding, said they were to have a second baby. Philip had been in Berlin a lot that summer, leaving Dougal in charge at the office. When he'd come back for good, Dougal and Sadie snatched two weeks in Cyprus and came back tanned and fit. Nonna paid a brief visit to Maria when Philip was in Europe, to keep her company. Michelangelo and Jove took Mags, Sissy and the children off to Rome for a return visit. For the Giangellis it had been a very good year indeed.

'It's been a good year all round,' Dougal echoed the general feeling, sitting in Maria's garden.

'Not half bad,' agreed Figgin. Anne Howard's business was thriving, and he had more work than he could handle. She'd suggested he might have to go to sites outside London, and he and Rosalie were wondering about letting both their houses and travelling around a bit.

Gathered on Maria's patio once more, the now-completed garden humming with insects, they enjoyed the splash of the fountain and the sweet scent of night stock as they talked and talked and talked. There was so much to talk about, so many photographs and slides to look at, so many stories to share, they sat until the early hours while the barbecue died once more. Unable to tear themselves away, Dougal and Sadie got home at half past two in the morning.

* * *

Dougal sat in the car, rubbing his eyes. Sadie's new Golf soft-top was parked in front of them, reminding them they had to go to work that same day.

'Christ, I'm tired. We're going to feel a bit grim tomorrow,' remarked Dougal, stretching, opening his door.

'Dougal.' Sadie sounded absolutely at the end of her tether. 'I feel grim all the time.'

He stopped, the driver's door half open. 'I noticed you didn't say much.'

Her face was drawn and colourless under the sodium streetlight.

'Not just this evening. I get desperate every month now. I hope and hope, and I touch wood and pray and I try to will it to have happened. And it doesn't, and . . . I feel . . .'

'It often takes a couple of years,' he said uneasily.

She put her head on his shoulder. 'Dougal, it's been a lot more than a couple of years.'

'Has it really?'

He tried to sound surprised, light-hearted, and realised guiltily he sounded merely indifferent.

'Do you think I should go and see a doctor?'

She wanted to say *we*, but her courage failed her.

'I don't know. I haven't thought about it. I suppose I just assumed that if we keep on, we'll end up making a baby.'

'We're not making a baby,' she persisted, sensing his distaste for her despair, having to go on.

Dougal looked at his watch, unconsciously rubbed the scar on his cheek.

'It's twenty to three. Let's talk about it tomorrow.'

You won't, she thought, you'll try to forget about it, and look daggers if I try to make you listen. They got out and locked up the car.

'Promise you'll make time to talk about it,' she said, going into the dark and empty house.

He yawned, exhausted.

'I tell you what, why don't you go and talk to the doctor about it, and let me know what he says. He'll probably just tell you not to worry.'

She gave in. Three o'clock in the morning; her timing was terrible.

'All right. I'll do that,' she said.

She lay sleepless, feeling the memory of little Jamie's small arms around her neck, his fine hair on her cheek, the warm weight of him on her knee. She got up at six, gritty-eyed, sat drinking coffee, watching birds wake in a pearly dawn.

Dougal woke to the alarm at seven, bad-tempered, still tired.

'I have decided,' she told him, ignoring his mood, 'to do two things.'

'Have you?' he asked, fumbling with shirt buttons. He held out his wrists like a little boy, for her to do them up.

'I'm going to apply for secondment, to get a proper training at poly, and I'm going to ask for fertility investigations,' she said, fastening his cuffs.

Dougal looked sharp. 'I shouldn't tell them that. You won't get them to pay for training if they know you're trying to get pregnant. You'd be a lousy investment if you gave up half-way through to have a baby.'

'Trust you to see it like that,' she snapped. 'I don't have to broadcast my private life, do I? Why should I tell them that?'

'I'm relieved to hear it,' he said coolly.

She felt sorry for him. Dougal was afraid someone would find something wrong with him, the big rugger player, bold businessman who wasn't scared of the world. He had a Hampstead house and two cars and a working wife and stocks and shares to prove it.

'I wish you were as easy to cuddle and comfort as little Jamie,' she said, straightening his tie, handing him his jacket. She put her arms round him, heard herself repeat the same dishonest argument she'd rejected long ago in the Lake District. She realised she was trying to comfort him.

'If I went to college, it'd take pressure off. Perhaps if I relaxed it'd be all right.'

He accepted her kindness wordlessly by kissing the top of her curly head.

'Things are tough at work. Philip is being difficult. He likes to control and it clips my wings. Not a good delegator. We're working on sensitive stuff, as well.'

'I thought you liked working together. What sort of sensitive stuff?'

He stood with his hands in his pockets, staring at the floor. They were both going to be very late for work.

'Control systems,' he said slowly. 'Defence stuff. They have ruthless specifications and you can't always get the right staff.'

'I didn't know you did defence work,' she said in surprise. She thought his distaste for the arms race as strong as her own.

'Some,' he said. 'We solve problems and find solutions for anyone who pays us. It's only part of what we do.'

'Oh,' she said, who had once belonged to CND, nonplussed.

'Don't let's let this baby thing get out of hand,' he said. 'Babies are nice, but we have a good life, why spoil it?'

She drew away.

'Nothing is out of hand,' she said evenly, keeping her temper.

'OK.' He paused, and she thought for a moment he was going to come to her, hold her, say, what shall we do, together?

'Look, you do whatever you want to do, let's agree on that,' he said, smiling kindly. 'OK? Got to go, I'm late.'

'You look like something the cat brought in,' accused Dolly, dropping in at lunchtime from a series of visits.

'I've been to the training officer. She says they'll probably offer me secondment for a full-time course, if I can get an application in, like yesterday. There are still places, even though term has started.'

'Good grief. That's unusually helpful,' Dolly observed sardonically. 'They must want to keep you badly.'

'I've been here a long time, and I'll have to come back

if I get secondment. I'm an investment, Dougal said, and she seemed to think so, too.'

'Makes you sound vulgarly gilt-edged, pet. But I know what you mean.'

'I'm tired of having a job. I want a career.'

If I can't have a baby, I'll have *something*.

'Bully for you,' said Dolly.

Chapter Forty

Having left school without a great deal in the way of qualifications, Sadie thought she would be intimidated by the idea of study, but her place at polytechnic was arranged so fast, for a course that had already started, that she found herself there before she had time to worry and took to it with enormous enjoyment. Studying, after a first few uncertain weeks, came easily. She had a natural aptitude for it, and plenty of practical knowledge. After several years in everyday social work practice she found the theory of social work sometimes fascinating, quite often silly, always stimulating, as was the new social life. At college she caught up on the freedom she had missed because of Maria's accident and Giovanni's death. For the first time, she began to have fun.

In stark contrast, the investigations she'd started, into why she wasn't getting pregnant, were very depressing indeed, and so was Dougal's attitude.

'I'm glad you find something stimulating,' snarled Dougal, towards the end of her first year. He stood holding a little brown sterile pot between finger and thumb, scowling. 'As far as I'm concerned this is the kiss of death to stimulation.'

He stared into the little pot with loathing, the scar on his cheek looking raised, quite white with distress.

'I'm sorry it's awful,' she said.

He marched into the bathroom and banged the door. It promptly flew open again. He stood holding the little pot, a flower spray half filled with iced water, and a couple of pairs of St Michael boxer shorts.

'Baggy knickers, cold showers on the balls and *pots*,' he said bitterly, 'and I was fool enough to think that making a baby might be *fun*.' He threw the shorts on to their bed and retreated back into the bathroom. 'Just doing my marital duty, darling,' he said through gritted teeth as he banged the door once more.

'If this goes on we won't have a relationship left to have a baby *in*,' Sadie said to the closed door. 'Please, Dougal, it's not *that bad*.'

There was silence from the bathroom.

They rushed Dougal's offering to the lab and waited for the experts' verdict on his sperm count. Again. They'd rushed to the lab again and again as investigations went on, given it their all, with a sad lack of any results. Sadie still didn't get pregnant.

It all started with high hopes. When she signed on for investigations, she had a new clinic card. Her old card was for Family Planning and was number XS77569. Her new one was for Subfertility, number 2061. A smaller and more select little group, Subfertility patients waited for miracles on hard yellow plastic chairs in a long corridor of brown doors. It was quiet in the corridor and the cream-painted walls were bare. In Family Planning it was busy and noisy. Women chatted, knitted, looked after restless children who delved into a boxful of toys. Family Planning was in the same place as Antenatal, had posters about breastfeeding, vaccination and childbirth classes. In Subfertility there was no box of toys, women looked anxious, studied their temperature charts before handing them over, were lost in their thoughts. If they chatted, it was about treatments and tests. Quite often, someone was crying. Sometimes it was Sadie.

'It's like being on a roller-coaster,' she said to Dolly during a rare visit to her East End house. 'One minute I'm up, having a good time, the next minute I'm so down I just cry.'

College had changed the way Sadie dressed. Flared denim jeans and a skimpy sweater made her look thinner, younger, more vulnerable than the social worker who wore court shoes and sensible grey coats. She'd grown her hair and it flared round her small face like an overgrown Afro. It began to dawn upon Dolly that Sadie had grown up too quickly after that accident, had missed something that Dolly had in abundance despite being more than ten years older. Youth.

'College is OK? You look good on it.'

'College is great,' said Sadie.

Something in the way she said it made Dolly wary. 'But?'

Sadie took a deep breath. 'I couldn't tell anyone else,' she admitted, unhappily, 'but I find myself looking into prams.'

'Oh, oh,' said Dolly, seeing awful implications, baby-snatcher headlines, tearful appeals on the telly from distraught mothers.

'You see, it's that bad,' said Sadie, relieved to get the secret nightmare longings off her chest. 'I have criminal thoughts. I look at other people's babies and wonder if I just picked them up and ran . . .'

'You absolutely must do nothing whatsoever about that,' said Dolly, full of alarm, 'except *think* it. No one can blame you for that. Just don't *do* it, whatever you do.'

'No, I know. I tell myself I'd never actually reach out and . . . but I can't help imagining.'

'*That* stays strictly imaginary stuff,' snapped Dolly, scared stiff.

'You've no idea what it's like,' said Sadie. 'But I don't think I'd ever do it; I'm too scared.'

'They'd put you in hospital or prison or both,' warned Dolly.

'There's a crèche at the poly,' Sadie said wretchedly, 'and I see women leaving babies, and going off to classes, and part of me knows they've a right to be doing it, and another part of me could *kill* them for leaving them.'

'Are these odd moments of delirium?' asked Dolly, hoping that was all it would be.

Sadie looked dreadful. 'It's almost all the time. I'm obsessed, I only stop thinking about it when I'm working so hard my mind is full of other things.'

'You'd better work harder than ever, then, until you get over it,' said Dolly sternly.

It was the loneliest thing in the world, being without a child in a world full of babies. She couldn't explain to anyone, not even Dolly or Dougal, least of all to Maria, she thought, what it was like to want a baby so much you could die. The people who understood were the other women on the hard yellow chairs in the subfertility clinic, and they had problems of their own. She'd cried the very first time she went there, in front of the doctor. Tears poured down her cheeks; she was racked by pain, deeply shocked by the violence of her longing for a child, shocked that the doctor, a matter-of-fact woman, should see it. Sadie, used to being in control of her feelings, was stunned by their force. After that first visit, she was braver and more in control again, so that she only cried later, when the doctors were done. It became a habit to contain it all until she was walking to the tube station to go home. Then she'd be blinded by tears so that passers-by stared at such a display of sorrow and grief. It never crossed her mind that Maria, who had daily to do without the use of her legs, would have known *exactly* how she felt.

As months went by she passed her tests at college, wrote good essays, sat her first exams and passed with flying colours. In the hospital clinic they did physical tests, counted sperm, said, with measured judgement, there were about enough. Dougal was mortified at the slur. They said the sperm could swim; he brightened up, indignant.

'Of course my sperm can swim,' he muttered furiously.

'*Dougal, please*,' she hissed back. 'You'll get their backs up.'

He didn't care, sat and watched morosely as they studied

her cervical mucus after she and Dougal had made love, pronounced it not brilliant; not too tacky, either. Tacky. Did tacky mean she was producing something shoddy, no good? They meant sticky, but tacky made her feel cheap.

'Your body isn't hostile to your husband's sperm, so far as we can tell, though it's not a hundred per cent, either,' pronounced the woman doctor, looking at scrapings from Sadie's cervix, under a microscope.

Nothing was quite wrong, nor quite right. The doctors' tests consigned her and Dougal to a reproductive no-man's land where all the necessary bits appeared in working order, but not *quite* working enough. Sadie suffered creeping anxieties that it was the combination they'd got wrong; that with other people, they'd both be all right.

'Then why don't we conceive?'

'We don't know. His sperm could swim a bit better, be a little more motile, and there could be more of them, ideally,' she said thoughtfully, as if passing judgement on applicants for the Olympic team, 'but they wiggle quite nicely. They should be doing their stuff.'

Sadie brooded. Her body *was* hostile. It was refusing to conceive. His sperm were not doing their stuff. They were failing each other. She and Dougal stopped talking about babies and children. Their minds got stuck at conception, a goal in itself. Talking diffidently to other women, getting to recognise old hands in the clinic, as month followed month, she found it was generally the same; your mind got stuck on conception.

'We'll give the ovaries a bit of a boost,' said the doctor briskly.

They'd blown gas through her tubes, pronounced them clear.

'All right, give me a bit of a boost,' she said, trying to cheer herself up. 'Perhaps it'll make me have twins.'

The fertility drug made her body ache, made her feel ill. When her period came, she felt better.

'In a funny kind of way, your treatment did me good. I

was glad to bleed. It made me feel better. Usually I feel awful, and cry,' she confided.

The doctor frowned and didn't seem pleased.

The more she failed to get pregnant, failed the clinic, failed as a wife, the harder she worked. It took her mind off conceiving. Her marks were high, her commitment outstanding. 'You'll go far,' said her tutors, pleased. 'Why not think about doing a degree?'

'They say I could do a degree,' she told Dougal.

'Mrs Monroe, B.Sc. I like the sound of that,' he said.

Everyone thought them a golden couple, with brilliant careers. No room for a child. Selfish, perhaps, but that's how they are, absorbed in themselves and each other.

'People envy us,' said Sadie ironically. 'If only they knew.'

They didn't. If she'd told them, she realised afterwards, things just might have been a great deal better.

Chapter Forty-One

That year, 1976, brought the hottest summer in ages. For months on end the sun blazed, bringing drought, standpipes, dead gardens and a small rash of prosecutions for using hoses. The paths over Hampstead Heath were cracked and dusty, grass yellow and shrivelled. Sadie swam in the Ladies' Pond most evenings, the sun burning still, until the water level dropped too low. In her Barnsbury garden, Maria's fountain fell silent, her little raised ponds stagnant, finally turning into puddles and dry dustbowls streaked with brown roots and remains of waterlilies.

Philip took them to Cornwall for a fortnight in August. The hotel coped with wheelchair life effortlessly, and on scorching afternoons, sunblock on her nose, her black hair tied up in a red and white bandanna, Maria was pushed determinedly by Philip over soft, cloying sand into the sea, far enough for her to swim. He stayed close, and she floated free on her back, her face to the sun, salt water on her lips, riding the swell of the waves, in heaven. It was an idyll. Each evening, as silver insects danced in the falling dusk and the sun sank over the curving line of the ocean, they fell in love all over again, sitting on the hotel terrace after the children went to bed, gazing quietly across darkening water, watching the moon come up, hand in hand like newly-weds. Maria looked into the uncertain future and prayed it would never end.

Back in London the drought went on. At night the children fussed, complained and grizzled, scratched with prickly heat, got her out of bed, exhausted her. Philip, constantly woken, took to sleeping upstairs in his study where he claimed it was cooler, all the dormers wide open for a breath of air. But Maria heard him pacing in the night, and when he came down, haggard, in the morning, he complained he had not slept. Their euphoria, stifled by city noise and haste and heat, died away, became a dream. The enchantment went out of long hot days, sunbathing lost its delight and they longed for rain and wind and mellow autumn mists.

Dougal took over at the office while Maria and Philip went away. Sadie, on holiday from college, lay in the garden reading, and got very, very brown, walked the parched and colourless heath, stirred the tepid sludgy waters of the ponds with her painted toes and wandered the traffic-choked Hampstead lanes aimlessly, passing time, day-dreaming.

By the Round Pond one afternoon, she stopped to watch children sailing boats. Two nannies sat on a bench with prams, and a young father in cut-off denims squatted at the side of the pond, supervising. A little girl in a yellow dress pulled a Snoopy on a bit of string, her wheat-coloured hair damp on her brown cheeks. Traffic roared nearby, stopping at a junction, then pulling away up past Jack Straw's Castle or left to go around the heath. Snoopy edged dangerously close to the kerb. The young father was tying down a flapping sail and didn't watch. The nannies started up, ran to pull her away. Snoopy spun on the end of his string, and jerked to safety. Left for a moment alone, one of the prams started to cry. Inside, Sadie saw a newborn baby, its crumpled face red, eyes screwed tight with effort, lightly covered with a lacy shawl. Its nanny was holding Snoopy, telling the child to go over by her daddy, not to go by the road again. The father got up and came over, smiling, frowning, shaking his head at his child, thanking the nannies. Sadie's hands sweated with terror. They inched towards the baby of their own accord, to pick it up . . .

'Hullo,' said the taller of the two nannies.

Sadie jumped out of her skin, took a horrified look at the girl's suspicious face and fled, her sandals slapping the pavement as loud as her pounding heart banging in her ribs. The nanny stared after the slight figure in cotton shorts, thick hair in two bunches, a child with haunted eyes. The nannies sat back on their bench and watched the little boats again, their hands protectively on their pram handles.

She sat in a thicket of dry grass by a bramble bush, tiny green blackberries just showing underneath half-withered flowers, waiting for someone to chase after her, accuse her. A lark sang, a pinpoint in the brilliant sky, high above the heath. No-one came.

'There has to be an end to this,' she said aloud, her throat hoarse. 'I can't go on and on.'

But they were in the middle of an intensive series of visits to the clinic. She could not imagine how to make that choice, to give up. Call it a day. Say, we won't go on.

That night Dougal lay bathed in sweat. Beside him Sadie lay naked, curled on the crumpled sheet. She turned away, longing for air through the open window. Beyond it, in the night, London sweltered.

'I'm sorry,' she whispered.

'I can't do it to order,' Dougal mumbled. 'I have to *feel* like it, not have some doctor telling me. It makes me feel used.'

She felt empty, too exhausted even to cry.

'I'm going to sit in the garden,' he said. 'It might be a bit cooler.'

'It's midnight.'

'Sure it's midnight. So what?'

He dragged on the hated boxer shorts and went out, wandered to the end of a yellow patch that had been a lawn, feeling its dry, coarse stubble beneath his feet. He came to a wall that hid the incinerator and a weedy compost heap, skirted round it to a shady alcove right at the end of the garden. Surrounded by drooping honeysuckle, overshadowed by an apple tree, the alcove held a stone seat. In the luminous London night, he could see clearly the stone-lined oval sandpit he'd dug. It had a stone bottom, carefully laid, smooth and cool, so as not to catch and scrape a child's fingers, not to be full of worms. Last summer's project, for a child who never was. He sat down, the stone bench cool on his damp skin. Looking through his fingers at the empty sandpit, which he had come to believe in his heart no child of his would ever use, he wept.

'We have come to the end,' she said, standing in the half dark like a ghost, 'haven't we?'

Dougal's fingers were wet with tears, a big, defeated man weeping as though his heart would break. She sat down on the stone bench beside him. Now she knew how the choice was made.

'It's over now,' was all she said.

Chapter Forty-Two

They had gone back to bed and lain not touching each other, slept fitfully and got up to a sun already burning off a thin early-morning mist lying like gauze across the heath. Still red-eyed from silent crying, Sadie made coffee which Dougal drank just to please her, bits of tissue glued to his chin by blood where he had cut himself shaving. When he'd gone she went and stood in a tepid shower, trying to freshen up and cheer up. She took the hated flower spray from the bathroom shelf, the loathed St Michael boxer shorts from Dougal's cupboard and threw them into the kitchen bin. Then she made fresh coffee, fetched *The Times* from where it had dropped through the letterbox, and watched the clock with one eye. At nine o'clock, before she could lose last night's determination, she rang the clinic and cancelled all their appointments. 'I'll ring back,' she said when the clerk protested she'd have to come and discuss it with the doctor. Then she put down the phone and wandered through the house with nothing to do and nowhere to go. A part of her life was ending, and she had no sense of new beginnings, just a dull sense of dread.

'You look like something the cat brought in.' Dougal's secretary, Pauline Cookham, stopped clacking her keyboard for a few moments and surveyed his ravaged face. She frowned and started clacking again at tremendous speed with perfectly painted shell-pink fingernails. Pauline was shell-pink all over, with a true English-rose complexion and glossy, straight blonde hair, worn like a schoolgirl's, parted to the side, with a pink Alice band. Widely spaced grey eyes completed the illusion of schoolgirl innocence. It was an illusion. Pauline's superspeeds in shorthand and typing were merely a starting point for her office skills, as more than one executive would have testified. She had never made a play for Dougal because she had never thought it worth her while. She was happy working for him and careful whom she got involved with, didn't want to spoil a good working relationship. He thought her pretty and sophisticated and treated her with absolute correctness. So far as Pauline was concerned, Dougal Monroe was out of court because he was a very happy man. She looked, despite the early heat of another scorching day, fresh and composed, smelled deliciously of flowers.

'Had a rotten night. Too hot. How on earth do you do it?' demanded Dougal grumpily, picking up his post on his way past her desk.

'I do it at one hundred and eighty a minute,' she said demurely.

He grinned. 'How do you look like you do, when everyone else is wilting before they start?'

'How is Sarah?' asked Pauline, side-stepping the question.

'I think she's going over to Maria for the day. They're taking the kids for a picnic somewhere by a stream that I gather isn't completely dried up. Epping, I think she said.'

'Is Maria all right, picnicking by streams?'

'Maria is always all right,' he snapped, going into his office, next door to Philip's.

He stuck his head out again.

'Phil in?'

'Not yet.'

He frowned. Philip had been travelling a lot that spring and summer, in Europe and the States. Several trips to West Berlin had left Dougal vaguely dissatisfied, not briefed fully on the outcome. And he seemed to be out of the office a lot in general. But they were doing well in tough times and Dougal told himself he wasn't Phil's keeper. Dougal shrugged and settled down to read his post, propped against his open diary. He sweated under his shirt and tie, pulled off the tie and undid his shirt. The computer room had air-conditioning; the offices did not.

He spent the morning on the telephone, had lunch in the pub, squashed back to back with a sweating horde of grey-suited clones, guzzling beer and ploughman's in the garden.

'Wife's gone down to Cornwall with the kids. I go next week,' bawled one grey suit to someone he knew, holding lager in one hand, a plate of shepherd's pie in the other. 'Where can I put this down?'

'Here,' said Dougal, inching up his picnic bench, clearing a space among the glasses.

'Cheers.' The grey suit began to eat rapidly, leaving his lager under Dougal's nose. He put his plate down, half eaten, and grinned. 'That's enough. Taking someone out this evening. Meal.'

'While the wife's in Cornwall,' remarked Dougal.

The man snickered. 'Near St Ives. Got a cottage. Let it out rest of the time. Pays for itself.'

'Nice for the summer,' said Dougal obligingly.

'We get three weeks. She takes the kids. I get a week in, if I'm lucky.'

'Sounds nice,' repeated Dougal, getting up to order a second pint.

'*This* is nice,' simpered the middle-aged man.

Pauline pushed through the crowd, a glass of white wine and ice clinking in her hand, her peach linen dress standing out like a flower on wasteland against all the crumpled grey suits.

'Do you know each other?' she said, putting her hand on Dougal's neighbour's arm, kissing his cheek briefly.

'No. What would you like?' asked Dougal, surprised.

'Pint of lager,' said Pauline's friend promptly.

The three of them squeezed on to the bench as people got up to go. Pauline's hand rested on her friend's sleeve, casually. You had to know someone quite well to sit like that, thought Dougal.

'This is Marcus,' she said. 'Marcus Wallgrace, Dougal Monroe, my boss.'

'Pauline's my secretary,' said Dougal. 'I take it she's the meal,' he added, jealously, under his breath. Marcus retreated from over-familiarity, and accepted the second lager when Dougal came back from the bar. Dougal studied them covertly, intrigued. St Ives is a long way away from London, on a boiling day in late August. No wonder Marcus Wallgrace's mind ran on fantasies, for Pauline was a city woman, bare arms in pale linen, brown legs, painted toenails, light, sweet scent, left behind while wives and children went away. Temptation incarnate, thought Dougal, nearly nodding off. In the heat, midday beer went straight to the head. The sandpit seemed a fevered dream. Sleepy and vaguely sad, he got up to go.

'See you later,' he told Pauline, meaning, watch your lunch hour.

'Cheers, man,' said Marcus.

She came back exactly on time, and he realised irritably that he had been waiting for her anxiously.

'What on *earth* are you doing with a creep like that?' he demanded.

Pauline tapped one perfect nail against her pretty rosebud lip and said he *was* a creep, wasn't he? She seemed to think it funny. Dougal's voice came out of its own accord. He listened to it in amazement, not having meant to say a word of what he now knew he was about to say, and it appalled him. First he protested, very distinctly, 'And he's married. With kids.'

'The world is full of married men,' she said. 'It's my business, what I do in my own time, if you don't mind, Dougal.'

He leaned on her desk and the words he'd only just discovered he wanted to say came out despite a frantic last-minute effort to stop them. He sounded, in consequence, squeaky and breathless, as though his voice was breaking. 'I do mind.'

'What?'

'I mind. What you do. If you're going to have business outside the office, I want it to be me.'

Pauline's eyes widened. She leaned back in her swivel chair. One of several beige phones on her desk rang and she picked it up and put it on hold. 'And I thought you were one of the few,' she said, innocent grey eyes looking straight into his.

'Few what?' he asked anxiously.

'Few happily married men who were faithful to their wives. You're a terrible disappointment.'

'I'm sorry I'm a disappointment,' he said stiffly, embarrassed.

'It seems a shame,' she said lightly. 'That's all.'

'Of course. You're right. Will you bring in the files I asked you for, please.'

He retreated behind a pile of work, angry with himself, knowing he was no better than the creep.

His door not quite shut, he could hear her keyboard clacking, her quick, slightly clipped voice as she answered the phone. She sounded efficient and cool and pleasant as a good secretary should.

Philip still did not come into the office. There was no answer from his number at home. They had things to discuss. Frustrated, Dougal idly watched pigeons on a roof across the road, mentally writing Phil a memo about absence and poor communication. It was nearly six. His door opened.

'I've put him off,' said Pauline. 'He was only a whim. I don't know him, really. He looked better sitting behind a paper in the tube. Not my type, really.'

'What is your type?'

Her grey eyes wandered up and down. 'About six foot, untidy dark hair, the odd scar, mature, cuddly . . .'

'*Cuddly?*'

'Hm.' She moistened her full lower lip.

'Solid muscle,' he said indignantly. 'Rugger muscle.'

'What about Sarah?' she demanded bluntly.

He found it difficult to look at her. 'We haven't been happy for quite a while.'

Pauline's eyes narrowed, but she didn't persist.

'She won't come home from Maria's until late. They put the kids to bed and gossip for hours and hours. I wondered if you'd like to go out, have a drink somewhere.'

'Where do you want to go?'

To bed, thought Dougal urgently. Like it used to be.

'Anywhere you 'specially like?' he asked casually.

'I like The Inn on the Park.'

Prices, he thought. *Jesus*. She stood in his office doorway in her perfect dress, smiling, a living, breathing invitation. She was adorable. He couldn't believe he'd never really noticed before. The Inn on the Park was an investment.

'Let's go,' said Dougal.

'I rent my spare room out. She's on holiday,' Pauline chattered, perched on a bar stool. Outside, it was dark. Traffic raced and roared down Park Lane towards Hyde Park Corner, leaving acrid fumes, blue-grey smoke, foul London air. The bar was cool, voices low. He wondered what the rules were of this new game, adultery. Would she expect romance, a stroll in the park?

'Would you like to go and look at the Serpentine in moonlight?'

'What moonlight?' she demanded derisively. 'You won't get much moonlight in central London.'

He felt deflated, embarrassed. 'All right. Serpentine by streetlight.'

'*That's* not romantic,' she said dismissively.

'Did you want to be romantic?' he asked cautiously.

Pauline sighed. 'Aren't men dense?'

'This man is scared.'

Pauline looked into the bottom of her wine glass and shook her head, half smiling. He grew desperate to know where he stood, to fend off what could be a terrible humiliation.

'Shall we go to your flat?' he blurted.

'Do you need everything spelled out?' she asked softly.

'I think I probably do,' he said. 'Is that a yes or a no?'

'Are you boring?' she demanded, deliberately teasing him.

He wanted to deny it, saw it would mean falling into that very trap of sounding pathetic, pedestrian, not suave at all. Instead, he nodded for his bill, glanced at it and shuddered. He put a credit card in the dish.

'Where's your flatmate gone on holiday?'

'Italy.'

That'll do. Can't come back suddenly from Italy in the middle of proceedings.

Pauline slid off her stool. 'Shall we go, then?' she asked, schoolgirl face innocent of all expression.

'You're sure?' Dougal asked, feeling an ass. What if she only meant a peck on the cheek at the door, or worse, a perishing coffee . . .

'You are being boring,' she warned languidly and kissed him, running her lips along the scar. Dougal shivered, the barman smiled, handed back the credit card and flimsy.

'Good night, sir.'

Dougal met the man's knowing grin unflinchingly, now he had the invitation he'd been longing for.

Much later, she said urgently, 'You'll have to use something. I'm not on the pill.'

Dougal buried his face in her neck and muttered, 'It's all right. I can't have children.' He was suddenly crestfallen.

'Is that the trouble with Sarah?' she asked gently.

He nodded, feeling himself losing interest, despair creeping back. 'I'm sorry.'

'Why be sorry? It's not me who wants babies.'

'I'm using you.'

Pauline giggled and wriggled. Her face fell. 'You're not using me, you know.'

Dougal flushed, was about to give up.

'Stop that,' she ordered, 'and turn over. Here . . . Let me.'

Pink nails and silky blonde hair, full, painted lips and the innocent face of a schoolgirl. Dougal thanked his guardian angel and did as he was told.

Chapter Forty-Three

Christmas Day was a low point in the year Sadie gave up trying to have a child. A time for families, above all a time for children, for her it was a day of mourning. She remembered the little fair-haired mite in the yellow dress, pulling her Snoopy by the Round Pond, and imagined a daughter of her own just like that. The only thing to be said for having a fantasy child, instead of the real thing, she thought wryly, was that fantasies could be perfect and need never grow up. But then she watched Maria's children, their small dark heads in oversized, slippery paper crowns out of crackers, side by side at the crowded table, little Alison's nose just level with the tablecloth, as she perched on a pile of cushions. They were sheer delight. She picked at the turkey on her plate, admired the expensive watch Dougal had given her, and tried to cheer herself up.

The thoughts drifted round her head while the Giangellis did what they did best; enjoyed themselves. Jove and Michelangelo had frozen a feast, adding to it for weeks, then ferried it all to Islington, to Rosalie's house. She and Figgin pushed tables together, squeezed everyone in. The six cousins sat together at two card tables, the grown-ups around Rosalie's dining table. Coloured lights flashed on and off on the tree in the hall beyond the dining-room door where once Maria had had her bedroom. The living-room floor was still strewn with wrapping paper in which one of Figgin's cats gambolled. Jove brought in a flaming Christmas pudding, topped with holly, full of old silver coins. The children's faces were bright with wonder and everyone clapped until the flames went out.

* * *

After the Queen's speech, they argued good-naturedly over James Bond or *The African Queen*.

'*African Queen*,' said Rosalie, opening a box of chocolates. They dozed in front of it, almost knowing it by heart from many previous Christmas afternoons, half watching, half asleep. Sadie sat cross-legged on a floor cushion, Alison in her lap. The child had jet-black curls, eyelashes that swept her cheeks, a miniature Maria. Dougal got bored, turned his back on *The African Queen*, started telling jokes, being the life and soul of the party, determinedly cheerful. They were steadily drifting apart. He'd long since reclaimed his favourite Y-fronts, been open about his relief that the investigations could be considered over, and plainly thought the matter closed.

Dolly came to Hampstead for New Year's Eve, Gosling in tow, finally home from Birmingham. Despite Dolly's dramas and feeling that they knew him already, it was the first time they had all met. He stood in their hall, taking off his coat, so tall he had to duck to avoid a hanging lampshade. Dolly caught Sadie's eye and grinned self-consciously; Gosling was everything she'd claimed, tall, broad-shouldered, dark wavy hair and a wide, ready grin. He stepped, thought Sadie, amused, straight from the pages of Mills & Boon.

'You've been a mystery for a very long time,' said Sadie, shaking his hand. 'I'd begun to wonder if you were real.'

'I've been on a training course in Birmingham almost since I met Dolly,' he said.

'Shiftwork, unsocial hours, and being down the boozer with the lads when he's off don't make for a brilliant social life,' said Dolly acidly. She'd lost more weight, sported an imitation-tiger-skin jump suit, with silver heels, which should have looked appalling, and didn't. The pale-Ribena pink hair had been deepened by henna to a glossy purple. Against all odds, Dolly looked stunning.

'She gives me a hard time,' he said, grinning, towering over all of them.

Dougal was a bit offhand; he didn't like being dwarfed and wasn't too keen on Dolly. She perplexed and awed him and made him feel inadequate in ways he couldn't quite catch.

'He's gorgeous. You lucky thing,' whispered Sadie in the kitchen, after they'd finished eating, waiting for the coffee maker to make coffee and finish going plop, plop, plop.

'He wants us to move in together. Said he wants us to buy a flat, and talks about commitment,' Dolly whispered back.

'You can't give your house up,' whispered Sadie, shocked.

'He doesn't want to live in my place. Wants to start afresh in a new place of our own.'

'Is he talking about getting married?'

'He calls it commitment,' said Dolly defiantly. 'It's almost as good as.'

Sadie was appalled. 'You're selling out,' she hissed. 'You *love* your house, it's you. You *can't* do that.'

'Not selling out, just selling,' said Dolly.

The coffee was ready.

'You know, that's the worst idea you ever had,' said Sadie.

They put golden oldies on the hi-fi. Dougal thawed, full of venison stew and apple pudding, and became quite affable. Gosling told funny fireman stories. Dougal poured glasses of wine and kept filling them up. The coffee went cold. On the television people threw coloured streamers and popped party poppers and shrieked at one another.

'Did you hear they had a suicide in Claybury on Christmas Day? Hung himself,' said Dolly, turning round to see if Sadie already knew. She was fetching a bottle of chilled champagne because it was nearly midnight.

'Social work talk is forbidden. It's five minutes to midnight,' ordered Gosling.

'Anyone we knew?' asked Sadie, taking no notice.

'Darren Barnard.'

'The boy in the canal?'

'They were all inside for Christmas,' explained Dolly. 'They generally get really depressed and voice-ridden at Christmas. His mother's voices apparently told him to go hang himself, so he did. In the lavatories. Gave one of the cleaners a frightful shock.'

Dougal fiddled with the wire on the champagne bottle.

'Glasses, Sadie? Ready to kiss the old year out, and the new one in? Nineteen seventy-seven here we come, and may it be a damn sight better than the last year,' he said cheerfully.

'You reckon?' said Sadie, staring into the bottom of her empty wine glass. 'Why should it get better?'

'Are you sure you want champagne?' observed Dougal.

'Don't patronise me. Why should it get better?' she persisted tipsily.

He popped the cork and started filling glasses with golden bubbles.

'You're a bastard,' she said clearly.

Dolly and Gosling looked away and studied the squawking television screen with sudden concentration. Cameras showed densely milling crowds in Trafalgar Square, zooming in on half a dozen youths climbing into the fountains and several policemen standing by, eyeing them. Then it showed the face of Big Ben. Dougal looked at his watch.

'Half a minute.'

'He thinks I don't know,' Sadie said. They all stared at the screen fixedly.

'Ten seconds,' announced Dougal.

'Who is she?' demanded his wife.

'Sadie,' said Dougal patiently, 'you're tight.'

'Who is she?'

Dolly's gaze was on Dougal's face, curious.

'Who is who?' he asked, humouring a child.

'The woman you're having an affair with.'

Big Ben began to chime, the crowds in Trafalgar Square

went crazy, and Gosling turned the sound up on the television, so it drowned their squabbling.

'I'm not having an affair with anyone,' hissed Dougal in his wife's ear, trying to kiss her against the rowdy background of 'Auld Lang Syne'.

'I won't kiss and pretend,' she cried shrilly, twisting free.

Dolly and Gosling stopped trying to kiss each other and sat down again.

'I wanted a baby,' she cried, 'I wanted a baby. I can't.'

'Sadie . . .'

'Now you don't even touch me. I *hurt* and you don't care.'

'Sadie,' said Dougal in a very tight voice, 'now is not the time . . .'

Just for that moment she stopped loving him and hated him completely.

She fled upstairs. They could hear her sobbing. They sat in dreadfully embarrassed silence, pretending to watch the remains of the night's television.

'I think we should either go home, or go up to her,' said Dolly.

'You won't get anywhere,' Dougal said, depressed.

'It's been terribly tough on her,' Dolly added.

And on me, he told her silently. What about tough on me?

'She'll have to come to terms with it, sooner or later. We've done everything,' he said aloud.

Sounds of sobbing eased off from upstairs.

'Have you thought about adopting?'

The champagne loosened his anger.

'No, not that it's frankly any business of yours.'

'What about Sadie?'

'She wanted to go into it,' he admitted reluctantly. 'But I would find a child that wasn't mine very hard to take to. We agreed to call it a day.'

'You'd stop her having a child?'

Dougal looked ragged with fury at her impertinence.
'Dolly, it's time to go,' muttered Gosling.
'And a happy New Year to you both,' snarled Dougal.

'I'm sorry.' She lay in a sprawl on their bed, scarlet with crying.
'It doesn't matter,' he said, taking off his shirt, 'Not with those two.'
She lay with her eyes closed. 'Do you want a divorce?' she asked.
He was stunned.
'That has never crossed my mind,' he said.
'You want both of us? I don't think I can live with that.'
There was silence from the bathroom where he cleaned his teeth. When he came back he said, 'I haven't the faintest idea what you are talking about.' He nudged her gently, making her move over so that he could get into bed.
Sadie lay quite still, her head spinning. Maybe she had it all wrong.
'I'm sorry,' she whispered.
Anger and resentment drained out of him. 'Look,' he said, 'we can't go on like this. Would trying to adopt really make you happy?'
'It wouldn't make you happy. They'd never let us adopt if you are half-hearted, and you would be. You don't really want to do it.'
He withdrew as though she had slapped him. 'Remember I offered,' he told her.

He got out of bed again and put on his dressing gown, vented his feelings by angrily tidying away downstairs until she was asleep. Then he went back to bed and lay beside her feeling sad, slightly hungover and sorely misused. He dreamed, restless, fragmented dreams, and then of travelling in a train, on a long, long journey, with a woman dressed in rich furs, diamonds around her neck glimpsed when she moved to look out of the window, her face hidden by a veil. He longed to see her, to see if he knew her, because he felt he did. As they drew out of a station, in some land he did not recognise, she lifted the heavy veil aside, and he saw, with extraordinary relief, that it was Pauline.

Chapter Forty-Four

'I made an ass of myself. I'm sorry,' said Sadie mournfully, calling round on Dolly two days later, finding her with her feet up on the fender of a log fire, knitting something long and gorgeous with a lot of gold thread in it.

'I don't mind. I quite often make an ass of *my*self,' said Dolly cheerfully.

'You look so cosy,' Sadie said wistfully. 'And I do owe you an apology, so please take it or I'll go on feeling embarrassed to death.'

'I was a cow and cried on your shoulder when I thought Gosling was playing around. Why should you be any different?' Dolly said cheerfully.

'I had too much wine. I was awful.'

'Oh, only so-so awful,' corrected Dolly. 'I've seen a lot worse than that.'

'Does Gosling think I'm appalling?'

'Actually,' grinned Dolly, turning her needles round to start a new row, 'he's rather intrigued. Do you *really* think your old man's got a bit on the side? I always thought he was besotted with you.'

'Huh,' said Sadie, 'he's not besotted lately. There's been too much strain.'

'It's tough, but it's not necessarily terminal.'

'I wanted a child too much.'

'I didn't mean that. I meant, one of you having an affair.'

Sadie took a deep breath. 'I came to ask you to help me find out whether he is, or not.'

Dolly finished her row, went out to her kitchen and brought back a tray of tea and crumpets which she put down on the floor in front of the fire. A quarter of an hour later they were rolling about with laughter.

'I *have* to know,' gasped Sadie. 'I may be laughing now, but it's really no joke.'

'You called a private eye to snoop on Dougal?' Dolly absolutely chortled, incredulous.

'I looked in the Yellow Pages,' said Sadie stoutly. 'I rang him up and said I was sure my husband was having an affair, and I wanted to know who with.'

'You must have felt an absolute *berk*.'

'Not when we got talking. He was nice. He said if he thought his wife was cheating on him, he'd want to know, as well, and he thought I was being very sensible.'

'Money,' retorted Dolly. 'That's what that's about.'

'No. If you give me a chance . . .'

The fire fell in the grate with a crackle, sending out a puff of fragrant wood-smoke, and began to flame afresh. Dolly reached into a wicker basket, threw on a log.

'Isn't Hackney a clean-air zone? Are you meant to burn those?'

'Probably not,' Dolly said indifferently, 'but I like it. Go on, what does Sherlock Holmes do, then?'

'Nothing. You're wrong about money. He said if I wanted to meet him one evening, he'd tell me what to do. Said, why pay him, when I could do a job like that myself?'

Dolly picked up her knitting. 'Are you going to?'

'I have.'

Dolly counted stitches aloud, came to the end of the row. 'And?'

Sadie began to laugh again. 'Do you fancy a white wig, or a black wig, or a red wig? We don't have to put stockings over our heads.'

Dolly put her knitting down in astonishment. 'What?'

'He said to take a car Dougal doesn't recognise, and disguise ourselves so he won't spot us driving it, and when we're suspicious he's up to something, we follow him.'

'What if you get lost in the traffic?' demanded Dolly, her interest caught.

'You go home and try again another time. You just have to keep trying.'

'You want to play cops and robbers round Hampstead in this freezing weather? You're crazily obsessed. It's unhealthy.' Dolly kicked a log back into place on the fire, sending flames up the chimney.

'I'm all those things,' agreed Sadie, 'and I'm going to do it anyway, because I have to know.'

'And then what? When you know?'

Sadie stared into the flames.

'Nothing, probably. I'd know, and this kind of itching in my head would stop. I'd know where I was.'

'I wouldn't bank on that,' Dolly warned. 'You might have to tell him you know, and there's no saying where it'll end.'

'Dougal knows my car,' Sadie said blandly. 'We'll have to take yours.'

'We? My car?' squeaked Dolly. 'Hang on a minute . . .'

'You'll have to drive, and I can stay low in the passenger seat. He won't spot us, especially in wigs and in the dark.'

Dolly put her knitting down in her lap and stared. 'Now I know you're crazy,' she snapped.

'Yes,' said Sadie humbly. 'I am crazy. I don't think I care.'

'But, well . . . I suppose it wouldn't half be a laugh,' Dolly added, beginning to give in.

'Wherever he goes,' Sadie went on, 'he goes from his office, so that's where we wait.'

Outside, a wet, raw wind rattled leafless twigs against the kitchen window, blew rotting leaves along the guttering, the damp giving a dismal sheen to tarmac roads underneath streetlamps. An owl hooted from over by the canal running through Victoria Park. It was a distant, eerie sound.

'I suppose someone has to protect you from yourself,' Dolly sighed.

'You'll do it,' cried Sadie.

'Bagsy I have the black wig. And definitely no stockings.

I get claustrophobia in a stocking and it wrecks your make-up.'

'Absolutely no stockings.'

'Oh, God, what lunatics,' cried Dolly. 'Can Gosling come? Do we need muscle and a big pair of hands?'

'No muscle, no big hands, no hangers-on. This is a lean, mean operation,' said Sadie, getting the giggles again.

'I hope him and me never come to this. Where do you get wigs from?'

'Mail order. The nylon sort aren't expensive. I thought I'd send off for them. I don't fancy someone else's dandruff.'

'You've even done your homework. My God, you mean it.'

'I mean it.'

The fire crackled cosily. They talked through half a dozen plans and in the end, they cried with laughter.

They got to first base on their first attempt, which was just as well, because it was farcical. They followed Dougal from his director's parking slot below the office block off the Finchley Road. It was a very short chase. Dougal made only a small detour from his usual route home, to stop at a florist's. Then he looked for a moment as though he *was* heading for home and for a few moments Sadie felt a complete idiot, that she had got it all absolutely out of proportion and wrong. Then he turned in the unfamiliar direction. He wasn't going home at all. It was a bad choice of evening to follow a car; rain and wind lashed leafless branches, and home-going traffic choked the narrow roads of NW3. Dolly had a hard time keeping Dougal's car in sight. Their disguises were reassuring but not exactly necessary, since no one could see further than their noses in the appalling weather. They stopped when Dougal stopped. The first time was to get flowers. The second time was outside Pauline Cookham's flat.

'The rat,' screeched Sadie, about to dive from the moving car into driving rain, splashing off tarmac, running down the gutters of Fitzjohn's Avenue in torrents.

'Shut up and come back, you ass,' hissed Dolly, swerving into the kerb. 'He'll see you. He damn near saw you at the florist's.'

Dolly could scarcely drive for laughing. On the way from his office to Pauline's flat, Dougal had stopped, left his car with the engine running on triple yellow lines and run with his jacket over his head into a florist's, still open at eight. Screeching to a halt in the wet, Dolly gritted her teeth, observed that it would be just their luck to have a police crawler spot that a maniac was driving her car, and tried to restrain Sadie from having hysterics when she realised the bouquet Dougal was picking up, all of a rush, must have been pre-ordered and pre-paid, since he certainly didn't stop to do either.

'They're for her,' Sadie howled, scraping sopping blonde nylon tresses from her wet cheeks, half in, half out of the car. 'Let me get my hands on him . . .'

'We'll lose him. Quick,' yelled Dolly, revving her engine. 'Of course they're for her. We're on the trail.' She dragged Sadie back into the car where she slumped damply into the passenger seat. Yellow lights winked, Dougal was about to pull out and move on.

'I don't think I want to go any further,' said Sadie in a small voice.

The black-haired vision in the driver's seat pushed its coiffure up its forehead, where it kept slipping down, and snarled, 'Don't you *dare* change your mind now.'

Sadie sat sulking. 'Glads,' she muttered, above the swish, swish, swish of the wipers. 'Did you see? They were glads.'

'Glad? I thought you'd had enough. Make your blasted mind up, Monroe.'

Dolly shot away from the kerb after Dougal. They drew up behind him at red traffic lights.

'Glads. He's got her *glads*. They must cost a *fortune*, this time of year, flown from somewhere. Israel, or South Africa or somewhere. *Damn*.'

'Oh, gladioli,' said Dolly, following Dougal down a long hill, peering beneath her crooked wig. She scratched, careering after Dougal, not letting other cars pull between them. 'This damn thing itches like hell,' she complained.

'He can't see us. He can't see a thing. It's stupid,' cried Sadie resentfully.

'Shut up,' Dolly snapped. 'I'm concentrating.'

They whizzed round two sharp corners in showers of spray from puddles, and began going uphill again.

'Fitzjohn's Avenue. Flat-land,' cried Dolly triumphantly. 'I bet this is it.'

'It's not five minutes from home,' muttered Sadie furiously. 'How *can* he?'

Dougal slowed and crawled along, looking for somewhere to park. He pulled in, turned off his lights. Sadie and Dolly drove past and pulled over at the first space.

'I'm going to see which flat,' yelped Sadie, bundling out of the door, immediately getting soaked, trying to hide and pry at the same time.

'Idiot, he'll see you,' hissed Dolly.

It didn't matter any more if he did. She ran through the cold downpour, feet splashing, strangely elated at finally knowing the truth. A little way down the hill, Dougal locked his car, the long spray of hothouse gladioli, wrapped in transparent cellophane, beaded with rain, rain running down his neck, soaking his shoulders. It was a wild night.

A woman walked quickly towards him, looking distraught. Pulling up his collar, he hurried over the streaming road, up the steps of a very large house. At the door, he pressed one of a row of bells, stood waiting, looking back over his shoulder. The woman had stopped. There was something very familiar about her. Sodden pale-blonde hair streaked her dark winter coat to the waist, her eyes were hidden in shadow. She seemed to be staring at him, standing quite still under a streetlamp. He wondered if she were all right, whether she needed help. But the rain teemed down and Pauline answered his ring on the intercom before he could move. 'Dougal,' he said, his hair dripping down his neck as he bent to speak into the intercom grille. The door swung open, and closed behind him with a heavy, homecoming thud.

Sadie crossed the road, went up the steps, looked at the list of names against the numbers of the flats.

'Cookham,' she read.

Pauline. Fresh-faced little Pauline with the Alice bands and a mouth that wouldn't melt butter. His secretary. A cliché.

'I should have known it would be something banal.' She stood looking up at lighted windows, wondering which were Pauline's. Curtains drawn against the winter looked softly inviting, secure. She slopped slowly back to the car.

Dolly tossed her wig in the back and said, 'Well, do you know her?'

'Of course. It's obvious.'

'His secretary?'

'How did you guess?'

They sat in the car, steaming up, the heater blasting away, burning their ankles.

'Shall we go now?' asked Dolly. 'Let's get dry and have something to eat.'

'Can we go back to your house? I couldn't bear to go back to mine right now.'

'Gosling's coming home. He won't mind, he'll think it's a joke. But you might mind because he'll laugh,' Dolly warned.

'I need someone to tell me it's funny,' muttered Sadie ominously. 'It would be good for Pauline Cookham, if someone can make me laugh about her. Otherwise I might take a meat cleaver to her sweet little skull.'

'Please don't do that,' said Dolly, starting off up the hill, leaving Dougal's parked, locked car behind. 'Murder with meat cleavers is frightfully messy.'

'You asked for it,' pronounced Gosling, grinning. 'Eavesdroppers never hear any good of themselves,' he added inconsequentially. 'What business is it of yours?'

'He's my husband,' Sadie answered furiously. 'His lying and cheating is my business.'

'That's why I don't get married. You have to lie and cheat if you want to do your own thing,' he said, watching Dolly go glum out of the corner of his eye. He fetched a bottle out of the fridge, polished three glasses.

'This is the toad I'm sharing my life with?' demanded Dolly, arms akimbo, a red pinny over her skirt. She'd been rinsing spaghetti.

'I'd never go running round in drag,' he said affably, 'trying to catch you out.'

'She cares about him,' snapped Dolly.

'If you care about him, why not let him do what he wants?' asked Gosling lazily.

'He's already doing what he wants,' Sadie pointed out crossly. 'The question is, whether I can stand it or not.'

Dolly put garlic bread on the table in a basket and said, 'And can you?'

'When I saw him going into her flat with those stupid flowers, I could have killed him.'

'At least he wasn't taking glads to a curly-haired *boy*,' remarked Dolly. 'Like mine was.'

'That would be worse, I suppose,' agreed Sadie, staring Gosling's amused look down.

'You can stop grinning,' snapped Dolly, banging his supper in front of him, 'and eat that.'

They ate in offended silence.

'People shouldn't use each other,' remarked Gosling, sharing the last of the bottle equally between them.

'I thought I was just trying to stay married,' said Sadie, banging her chair away from Dolly's little dining table. 'I think I'll go home,' she said stiffly.

Their wigs hung askew on the back of a kitchen chair, drying out. Gosling picked one up and perched it on top of his head, grinning.

'Stop that,' snapped Dolly.

'Thanks for helping.' Sadie, refusing to find him amusing, stalked out before Dolly could get up from the table.

'Now she's really hurt,' Dolly shouted, hearing her front door close in a hurry.

Gosling put the wig back on the chair to finish drying.

'Know what I did today?' he said calmly.

'Played cards down the station and dossed?' she snapped sarcastically.

'I pulled a four-year-old out of a fourth-storey flat with fifty per cent burns. *That's* being hurt.'

'That's your job. Why couldn't you be nice to Sadie?'

'I don't like her spying. I'd hate to be Dougal.'

'I've been there,' Dolly said evenly, picking bits of French bread off the table top, 'and I know I couldn't stand it again. That kind of betrayal is like a hundred per cent burns. If you think it wouldn't matter, doing that to me, I don't want to live with you.'

'Then you'll have to live without me.'

She felt giddy. The fire fell softly. The nylon wigs hung limp, softened by its heat, sad remains of a desperate joke.

'I mean it,' he said. 'No guarantees. I'm not planning on another woman in my life, but I won't lie to you.'

Dolly looked weary, middle-aged, her fingers rubbing the crumbs slowly.

'Why do I fall for bastards?'

'I'm not.'

'I suppose I'd rather be miserable with you than without you,' she said heavily. 'That way, at least I'll be happy some of the time. The rest of the time . . . I don't know.'

Gosling stretched his long legs and contemplated the low ceiling.

'I want a bit of security,' she went on. 'I want to know where I am. Like Maria Howard. Whatever the secret is, she's found it.'

Gosling closed his eyes.

'You don't think so?' demanded Dolly, mystified.

Gosling yawned. 'How would I know what Maria Howard has? I don't know her. But I do know that mostly marriage is compromise. It's what most people have. They just don't think much about it.'

Dolly folded her arms, ready to pursue it.

He yawned again, shaking his head. 'Neither of us is much good at that, Doll. We make lousy compromisers and we'd only make each other miserable. Let's like what we've got, eh?'

'I don't know . . .' she began.

He shook his head. 'I do. It's time for bed,' he said firmly, and went on up.

Chapter Forty-Five

1981 was half over and life appeared normal. Dougal, and Sadie, a fully qualified senior social worker in her old office, were drinking coffee in the garden on a bright July day.

'Look,' said Sadie, spreading *The Sunday Times* open. 'The world's first test-tube baby is three.' Pictures of Louise Brown gazed back at her. 'She's sweet,' she said.

'All three-year-olds are sweet. You wait till they're thirteen, then they're horrors,' answered Dougal.

She read the article, sat staring at the photograph. He knew that expression on her face and tried to distract her train of thought. Babies.

'Let's count our blessings,' he said. 'We can afford the mortgage, two holidays a year and two cars and your clothes. We are lucky.'

Gladioli in winter, thought Sadie acidly, and the odd trip for two on 'business'. Lying and cheating in comfort. We can afford those, too, and you think I don't know what the real price is of counting my blessings. Huh, she thought, and went back to the article in the paper. 'I bet they've come a long way since Louise was born. Got better at it, this *in vitro* treatment.'

The thoughtful note in her voice made Dougal look up, wary.

'No,' he said, 'I will not even talk about it. We are not going to go back to the clinic, ever.'

'I might.'

'I think they only take committed couples for *in vitro* fertilisation. And I'm not committed, Sadie. I thought we'd agreed ages ago to call it a day.'

The sun shone in a cornflower-blue sky, leaves hung dark and full on the trees, an adolescent thrush banged a snail ineffectually against a stone in the rockery Dougal had built where there had once been a sandpit and seat. He sat drinking coffee, tanned from two weeks in Greece, the scar standing out against brown, stubbled skin, as he squinted at newsprint in sunshine. Sadie poured herself more coffee, caught herself admiring the bright gleam of nail polish against her own carefully tanned skin. They *had* had a good time in Greece, eating and drinking and sleeping and swimming, lying spread out in the sun on the beach, carefully oiling the other's familiar body, making greasy fingerprints on paperback rubbish brought out as a jolly good holiday read. They got along well provided nothing serious ever came along to disturb the peace.

'We get along fine, so long as I never bring it up, don't we?' some demon drove her to say.

Dougal put down his paper.

'Lawn needs a mow,' he observed. 'I'll get it out in a minute.'

'There you are, that's just what I mean,' she said. 'You walk off when you can't cope.'

Dougal fetched the Flymo from the garage, marched up and down, cutting straight lines.

'One thing I'd do differently,' Sadie told his back. 'I'd tell people. I wouldn't keep it a secret, like we did.'

'What did you say?' He paused, a bit puffed.

'I said, I'd tell people next time that we couldn't have children. Once people knew we weren't spoilt yuppies, they got much nicer.'

'Nobody else's damned business,' muttered Dougal.

'It's made it easier with Maria. She was so kind when I finally told her, I wished and wished I'd told her before.'

Sadie's thoughts wandered over the black-haired children of black-haired Maria, granite-coloured eyes in porcelain faces, small white teeth, piercing, eager voices.

'Maria is nice,' agreed Dougal, reaching for the Flymo switch. She watched the thrush give up on its snail.

'I'm not as bitter as I used to be,' she said, knowing he couldn't hear her. 'Jamie and Alison *are* nice kids. You don't have to own children to love them.'

Dolly, she thought, would retort that you *never* own children. Sadie looked at Louise Brown's smiling picture again. Dolly was right and one day, maybe, the ache would go away. Maybe, one day, so would Pauline Cookham.

On the same lovely summer Sunday, Pauline Cookham ached. She sat in her third-floor flat, not far away from where the Monroes sat in their garden, her back bathed in hot sun streaming in through open Victorian windows. She got up, moved away from the sun, its heat making her itchy and cross. The ache quickened to nausea, she got to the bathroom just in time.

'I read in your magazine that bright-red toenails are a real turn-on.' Pauline's flatmate, Deirdre, put polish on her toenails with deft strokes. She sat back to admire the result, glanced up. Pauline's hair was sticky and sweaty, her skin pallid.

'You look awful,' said Deirdre.

'I feel awful. I keep being sick.'

'Not pregnant, are you?' asked the other girl casually. 'By dear Dougal.' Deirdre disapproved of Dougal, being a married man who showed no sign of leaving his wife to make Pauline an honest woman. She thought the affair would end in tears. Pauline's.

'No. I can't possibly be pregnant,' said Pauline.

'I can't be pregnant,' she said to Dougal, walking in Regent's Park. The sunshine had turned to rain, falling softly on green, green grass. 'Can I?'

They turned and took a path that led towards the zoo, striding along, her arm in his. She lagged behind, slowing him down, feeling bloated and sick.

'What have you been doing behind my back?' He felt alarmed and angry, possessive, betrayed . . . and laughed shamefacedly. 'Who am I to talk?' he admitted. 'Sorry.'

'I haven't done anything behind your back. There isn't anyone else.'

They came to the entrance to the zoo.

'Shall we go in?' he asked, putting his hand in his pocket for his wallet.

'Yes.'

They stood looking at the signposts inside, wondering which animals to see.

'Can't you go to the doctor? Get a test or something. All our tests were because we were not getting pregnant; I don't know what you do if you are.'

'Let's look at the gibbons.'

They watched monkeys grooming, picking fleas off each other. They lingered, arm in arm, the rain letting up, a break in the clouds bringing brief moments of sun.

'I went to the doctor,' she said.

He went very still, his eyes on the monkey enclosure as if completely absorbed.

'I'm going to have a baby.'

He was silent so long, she wondered if he'd understood.

'You could get rid of it,' he said neutrally.

'I could.' She tried not to sound shocked.

'Is that what you want to do?' he asked.

'No. I've already made up my mind to have it, so I'd be glad if you didn't try to persuade me to do anything different. If you want to leave me, I'll understand, but,' she looked up at him, straight in the eye, 'I won't forgive you.'

They walked on, sat huddled together on a bench by the tiger enclosure. The tigers dozed in a striped bundle of furry bodies. One had one eye half open, keeping watch. Two little girls with clear plastic see-through umbrellas stopped to look.

'One day, perhaps we'll bring our son to see the tigers, and say, here is where your mum and dad decided to get married, right in the middle of London Zoo,' said Dougal enigmatically, his expression bland.

Pauline laced her fingers together. 'What about your wife?'

Dougal still didn't look at her. He stared at the tigers, who rolled lazily on to their backs, under the trees, out of the rain.

'My wife will be hurt and angry and scared,' he said. 'She won't be surprised about you, but she will be about the baby. The worst thing will be the baby. She'll hate me, and she'll hate you, but she won't hate the baby. She'll want it and it will tear her to pieces.'

'That sounds a bit sinister,' she said uneasily.

'I'm not leaving her because I don't love her,' he said bleakly. 'You have to understand that. If you don't, it won't work.'

'Do you love me?'

'In all sorts of ways.'

'Not like Sarah?'

'It's different.'

The rain came down faster again.

'No,' he said more decidedly. 'It's been the end of the road for a long time,' he went on, half talking to himself. 'I remember how much I *did* love her.'

'You'll have to sack me,' she said.

'You'll have to resign. So will I.'

'Won't you hate me for that?'

'I'd been thinking about it anyway. It wouldn't necessarily have been anything to do with you. You've just made me make up my mind.'

'Philip relies on you.'

'Phil never made me a partner. If he had, it might be different. I don't want to be someone else's man all my life.'

'An awful lot of change,' she said quietly.

'It's going to be hell,' said Dougal, 'on every count.'

'You will lose a lot. Your house?'

'Probably. We'll have pneumonia if we stay here.'

Rain splashed through the thick leaves of the chestnut tree above them, making them run for shelter into the twilight of the insect house.

'We'll be all right.'

He peered into a lighted glass cage, trying to find the

stick insects the label claimed it contained, hoping to God that he'd soon feel as much conviction as he'd put into his words. She slipped her arms around him and pointed.

'Look, it's there.'

He could finally make out the insect's twiggy legs, and in the twilit place concluded that against all the jumble, the meaning of life was just about as difficult to make out as a stick insect's body against a bush. He said this to Pauline, feeling quite profound, but she simply smiled in the gloom and moved on to the bats hanging upside down in a cage at the very end of the insect house. Upside down, thought Dougal, beginning to feel a bit hysterical. He who was sterile was going to have a child. Upside down, inside out, the world was turning too fast. The bats seemed happy enough in their upside down state; perhaps there was a moral in the bats, as well. Then the rain stopped and they spent the rest of the afternoon outside, wandering the zoo hand in hand like a pair of bemused children, trying to get over their shock, trying to make plans.

Chapter Forty-Six

Not long after Dougal and Pauline realised their gentle affair had been changed forever and that they had, whether they liked it or not, to face a lot of pain and an uncertain future, Gosling was on night shift. They'd been busy. They'd barely got back from a call when they had another shout, just after one o'clock in the morning. As the engine raced out of the open doors, screaming over red lights and down near-deserted night-time streets, Gosling sweated profusely in slickers. He'd been wearing breathing apparatus and would have to put it on again in a hurry if there were persons reported and he had to go in to find them. He always sweated. It wasn't fear – he was not afraid – but a high surge of adrenalin, an intense excitement, a peaking of something that left him restless and sometimes mildly depressed at the end of a shift, like a junkie coming down from a high. He loved his job, hated fire and pain and death, never got used to them. Fire was a personal enemy, hand-to-hand combat every time. Gosling grinned; nor did he ever get used to the sight of women in skimpy nightdresses standing in the road, staring open-mouthed at fire engines screaming up in the night, flashing lights playing and flickering over their faces. There were always women there, every time.

'Is there anyone in there?' shouted the officer, jumping down. *There* was a small end-of-terrace house with a high hedge in front of it and several milk bottles standing on the front step. Smoke poured from a half-open upstairs window.

'Who lives here?' yelled the officer, going towards the women at a run.

'There's people in there,' shouted a woman in a gauzy dressing gown, her hair in pink plastic rollers.

The officer stood in the middle of the road, peering at her intently, trying to hurry her and not frighten her. 'Who? Who lives here?'

Behind him, Gosling and his partner were back in breathing apparatus, moving towards the burning house, waiting to know from the crowd if there were people inside . . . where . . . who. Flames caught round the edge of downstairs curtains, brilliant and greedy and red.

'There's three, I think. Sometimes he goes away,' the woman in curlers mumbled, her hand over her mouth, uncertain. An elderly man in pyjamas and a dark dressing gown pushed forwards, lipless without his teeth. He munched his gums for a moment, then said, 'Mum, dad and baby. Small baby.'

'Where's the kid's bedroom?' yelled the officer, waving his arms at Gosling – his foot on the front step by the milk bottles, ready to dash – telling him to wait. The old man shook his head, didn't know.

'In the front,' said a neighbour frantically, running up. 'Their bedroom is at the front.'

The officer was gone. 'Persons reported,' he shouted, running alongside Gosling, barging through the front door. 'Front bedroom. Two adults and baby.' Fire licked at the windows, glass exploded. Behind them the second team had the hoses ready, waiting for people to come out before they turned the water on. Water in there would fill the place with steam and burn everybody worse than the fire. They waited.

Gosling was in at top speed, sprinting, shutting doors as he ran, his second behind him. They charged up stairs licked by fire, into smoke as thick as soot. The lamp on Gosling's helmet showed a door ahead, half open. Front bedroom. They charged in, leaving the door wide, drawing more and more smoke into a room where no one could breathe, playing the lamps on the bed at the far side of the room. Footsteps pounded up behind them. Four in the room. Big men in slickers and breathing apparatus filled the small room, nimbly dodged to keep out of one another's way. The two who had arrived last pulled bodies from the bed. Gosling nudged his partner, held up two fingers, then a third, and shook his head. Two people. Flashlights played round the room briefly. No cot, no baby. Gosling pointed at the ceiling with a fist covered in anti-flash glove. Then he ran. The two people dragged out of bed didn't move. Impossible to take pulses in anti-flash gloves, to check, expose them any longer to smoke. The firemen would carry them out as fast as they could, knew they were probably dead. They worked with incredible speed; snatch and run. They tried not to crowd and hamper, they grabbed bodies and let Gosling get out fast to look for the baby. He raced down a narrow landing, narrow steps ahead, a tightly closed door. A loft conversion in the small, steep roof-space of a small, steep house. He swore aloud, charged the steps, flung back the door, was cannoned into by his partner, coming up at top speed out of dense smoke from behind, was reaching for the baby in the cot before he was half-way into the room. Snatching it up, he ran like hell, pushing and barging, shouting like mad, almost falling, clutching the baby against his slickers, jumping and swerving, yelling and roaring. Everyone got out of his way. Nothing mattered but getting the child out of the smoke. Down burning stairs, through the front door, and he was on the pavement, his heart thundering, the baby squealing frantically in his arms.

'Give her here,' cried the woman in curlers, holding out her arms, 'while you get your breath.'

He took his breathing apparatus off, holding the baby. 'No, thanks. Where's the paramedic?' An ambulance stood, its doors open. No one hurried. They were dead.

'They're all out,' said the officer, coming up to Gosling. A woman from the ambulance took the baby and it stopped screaming, firelight playing on its slanting dark eyes. Water arched into the building. With a series of cracks, windows popped and blackened.

'I wish,' he roared, 'that people would understand

about *smoke* and not put babies into illegally converted attics.'

'They're dead,' said the officer, turning away so the woman wouldn't hear.

The baby cried in the ambulance, which drew away in a hurry, flashing its lights.

'*Fuck*,' snarled Gosling.

Hoses dripped on tarmac, the flames going out.

'It wasn't even a big bloody fire,' he said to the little crowd, talking to himself, really. 'If they'd woken up, they could've stopped it or got out.' The crowd stared, regarding his rage with curiosity and anxiety.

'What's he swearing about?' muttered the woman in gauze.

He was a hero. Heroes didn't lose their rag after behaving like heroes.

'*Smoke*,' he snarled. 'When will you listen?'

They backed off, scared, feeling accused. The fire was none of their fault.

'Swan,' roared his officer.

Gosling left the little crowd disappointed by his un-hero-like attitude, and went to get on with his job.

The fire, and the hospital to which the baby was taken, were on Sadie's territory. She was fast asleep in bed when someone rang at half past two in the morning. There's a baby, someone said. Both parents are dead. There are no relatives nearby, you must come. The voice gave the hospital, and the name of the doctor looking after the baby in the baby unit. Puzzled, she put down the phone and only then woke up enough to realise she wasn't on call. The caller had not left a name. It was odder and odder. She lay and wondered what to do, then got up and dressed. Without waking Dougal, she crept out and went to the hospital.

Not knowing her name, the nurses had called the baby Eve. It was written on her cot. She lay dozing, monitors on her chest because of the smoke.

'Why call me?' Sadie asked the doctor crossly. 'There's nothing I can do. She's safe. You're not planning to operate or anything. Why call me out at this time of night?'

'I didn't,' answered the paediatrician, looking tired and surprised.

Sadie's shoulders slumped. She was tired, too. 'Someone's got crossed wires,' she said. 'The hospital social workers will deal with it in the morning.'

They gazed down at the baby. She'd fallen asleep.

'Down's syndrome,' said the doctor. 'Can be prone to chest problems. Vulnerable. We'll probably keep her a few days, for observation.'

'She's a Down's baby?' asked Sadie, bending down to look more closely at Eve. 'How old is she?'

'Yes. She's about eight weeks.'

Eve's eyelids were curved just the slightest bit, thought Sadie, looking into the cot. You'd never know. Perhaps when they were open, she had more of that almond-eyed look. The baby had fine silky hair, little wisps that might become curls. They'd washed the smoke smudges off her, put a little angel top on her, and covered her with a little white blanket. She snuffled in her sleep, and woke, opening small almond-shaped eyes, looking straight at Sadie, who was leaning over her.

'She's sweet.'

'If you'll excuse me,' answered the doctor, her bleeper going off in her pocket. She left Sadie alone in the nursery. She and Eve stared at each other and then it came to Sadie. The caller had been a man.

'Gosling,' she said to the baby. 'I think that call came from Gosling.'

Why would he pull a hoax like this? Eve coughed and mouthed at her fingers.

'Are you hungry?' asked Sadie. 'I expect they'll bring you a bottle in a minute.'

Eve's gaze wandered, came back to Sadie's face and focused. Night pressed upon the brightly lit nursery, on its big, dark, uncurtained windows. Monitors and machines in the next nursery beyond Eve's cubicle hummed and clicked and buzzed. Through glass partitions Sadie could see green-gowned nurses busy around the incubator of some very sick baby. Eve still stared.

'Your mummy and daddy are dead. I'm sorry. Have you got aunties or uncles or cousins or grannies to look after you? Because if you haven't, little girl, your future is grim.'

Eve stared unwinkingly.

'Or, if you haven't . . .'

The baby sucked her fingers hungrily. Sadie knew why Gosling had called.

'If you haven't got any family to look after you, there's always me,' she said.

Chapter Forty-Seven

Dougal's birthday that year coincided with the last night of the Proms. Knowing how he'd love it, Sadie had made an effort to get tickets, booked a table for two for dinner afterwards, and looked forward to giving him a treat.

'He's still fun to do things with, even though he's a toad. He'll adore singing "Jerusalem" and throwing streamers,' she remarked wistfully, shortly before the outing.

'If you leave telling him to the last moment and don't fix something, he'll look in his diary and say "sorry, I've got business things to do",' warned Dolly. 'The wretch will be too busy to come, and we know what *sort* of busy, don't we?'

'He wouldn't dare,' answered Sadie. 'Would he?'

Dolly's expression spoke volumes.

'All right.' Sadie smiled maliciously. 'I'll get sweet little Pauline to fix him, and she'll fix herself at the same time, because if the boss's wife has said to keep his diary free for his birthday, because she's taking him out, neither of them will dare to do differently.'

Sadie picked up the phone on her desk and dialled Dougal's office.

'Don't you ever feel like shouting at her that you know she's messing around with your husband and you'll be over with an axe right away?' asked Dolly curiously, from within a cloud of menthol cigarette smoke.

'Of course I do. Sometimes I can't think about anything else. But why should I give her the satisfaction of knowing I know, and turning my life into a crisis I'm not ready for?'

The phone kept on ringing.

'That's what you *think*,' observed Dolly. 'I'm amazed you can actually *do* it, though. I'd freak and lose my cool and spill the beans.'

'There's no-one there. It doesn't make a good impression for the business,' said Sadie, waiting, 'having to hang on and on, as though no-one can be bothered to answer the phone.'

'The girl's probably in the loo,' remarked Dolly, picking up a file and leafing through it idly.

Sadie held up a finger to indicate that she was through.

'Could you put me through to Pauline, please?'

Dolly put the folder down and listened unabashedly.

'Sarah Monroe,' said Sadie.

Dolly was near enough to hear a male voice faintly.

'No, I don't want to speak to Dougal, just Pauline,' said Sadie. 'Well, when will she be in the office?'

There was a brief pause as the male voice spoke, and Dolly saw the colour drain from Sadie's face until she looked the ghastly colour of something that's been too long in the water.

'No message. Thank you.'

Dolly could hear the dialling tone, but Sadie sat with the receiver in her hand like a waxwork.

'What's happened?' asked Dolly, knowing that only something *horribly* wrong could bring that expression to someone's face.

'The girl had gone to the loo,' Sadie whispered. 'Someone passing picked the phone up.'

Dolly waited.

'Dougal's there, but whoever it was couldn't put me through to Pauline because she's got the afternoon off.'

Dolly watched Sadie trying to get the words out and her heart sank.

'He thought – he wasn't sure – but he thought she wouldn't be in again until tomorrow because she's gone to the antenatal clinic and she'd mentioned that it takes all afternoon. He said I could ring back about five, in case she returns to the office.'

'Ah,' breathed Dolly, perceiving the enormous implications and ramifications of that in a flash.

Dolly got up and filled the kettle, plugged it in, and made coffee, wondering how she could prevent anyone else who might come back to the office, from marching in on the dreadful moment. She couldn't. She couldn't protect Sadie from anything at all. 'How do we know it's Dougal's?' she started, going straight to the heart of the matter.

Sadie made a visible effort to think, and admitted they didn't. 'Then before we get into a state, we should find out,' said Dolly decidedly. 'Where do you go to have babies around your end of the woods?'

'How would I know? I've never had one. So far as I know, you can go where you like, to have babies.'

'But she lives and works in Hampstead. She'd go locally,' said Dolly, with more certainty than she felt, pulling the telephone directory towards her. 'Start naming hospitals, Sadie.'

'It's a needle in a haystack.'

'Names,' snapped Dolly, pencil poised, prepared to make a list.

'No,' said Sadie, coming out of her shock, pulling the phone towards her, pushing it away again as she realised Dolly had to make the call. 'Let's do it the easy way. The girl will be back from the loo, by now, and I bet she knows where Pauline's gone. If the men in the office know that much, I bet the women know more. You ring and say you're a friend of Pauline's and when they say she's out for the afternoon, say you wanted to go to the clinic with her and can they tell you which hospital she's gone to, so you can pop along and find her. That girl hasn't got much brain. She'll swallow it.'

'You could ask Dougal and have it out with him,' suggested Dolly.

'I can't ask Dougal because I want Eve. If I ask Dougal, it's all over because everything will come out and that will be that. We'll have to divorce, and I won't be allowed to have Eve.' Sadie stared fixedly at her desk, seeing the intractability of the trap she was in, closed round her like a vice. Lying and being lied to were the only choices left. Dolly made the call. It was easy.

Pauline had not gone locally. She was sitting in Gower Street in the basement clinic of a big teaching hospital, seeking anonymity. But she had not been discreet enough. Dolly and Sadie skulked into the clinic later that afternoon and it was simple to get a friend of Dolly's, in the hospital social work department, to take a quick look at Pauline's file as it lay with a dozen others, waiting for the doctor.

'This is unprofessional behaviour,' said Sadie, pale and frightened of what they were doing and of how fast things were happening, full of terror that once they had done it, and found out that Dougal was the father of Pauline's baby, there would be no going back.

'Do you want to know, or not?' demanded Dolly.

She nodded.

While Dolly sat in her friend's office and waited for results, Sadie crept down to the antenatal clinic to look. It was a big room full of women in varying stages of pregnancy, big enough and busy enough for Sadie to stand behind a pillar, staring at Pauline Cookham, sitting, demure and composed, waiting her turn with the doctor.

'Hey,' hissed Dolly in her ear, arriving with bad news and making her jump. 'Is that her?'

'That's her.'

They stood like the conspirators they were, peering around the pillar.

'I'm afraid it's Dougal's,' whispered Dolly. 'She's put his name in the file. I'm awfully sorry.'

Sadie leaned on the pillar and closed her eyes. When she opened them Pauline had gone.

'You all right?' asked Dolly anxiously.

Sadie looked round at the bustling nurses, the chattering women, the long row of cubicles into which Pauline had gone, and she shivered. 'No, I'm not all right. Let's get out of this place before someone asks us what we're doing.'

'I'm awfully sorry,' repeated Dolly.

Going up the stairs to street level, Sadie scared her by rounding on her furiously.

'I could *kill* her,' she hissed. 'Right now, I could kill her. And him.' She shook with barely controlled rage. 'Pauline Cookham can take my husband away, and my home, and, and, and . . . she isn't taking Eve.'

'You can stand it? Not saying anything?' asked Dolly, thinking of the months ahead, of staying silent, of pretending she didn't know things that would eat into her, of the nightmare it would be.

'I can, to get Eve,' Sadie said grimly, climbing the stairs again. 'But God help those two if I don't. I'll kill them.'

She spoke with such intense anger a woman coming up behind them stared in amazement and hung back, half afraid.

'You'll have to race me to it,' said Dolly, feebly trying to joke, thinking that if Dougal let Sadie down now, over adopting Eve, she'd murder him herself.

Unsmiling, Sadie nodded. They turned out into the street, towards the tube station, and Sadie hung on to Dolly's arm like a drowning woman, as Dolly took her home.

Chapter Forty-Eight

Eve had no family. She was discharged from hospital into the care of foster parents, and Sadie had immediately applied for adoption. She and Dougal barely spoke about it. Her mind was made up, and she was prepared to take whatever consequences there might be from bulldozing him into it. He was too guilty about other things to dare to say anything. The application proceeded with silence between them, though she knew that when the social workers came to interview them, they'd have to put on a better front than this, or they wouldn't be allowed to go ahead.

'Anything you say. We'll take it as it comes,' muttered Dougal, giving in all along the line. What else could he do? he wanted to know, pacing Pauline's flat.

'She's snookered me,' he snarled.

He paced up and down, up and down. Pauline's flatmate complained she felt dizzy and went and sat in her room in a huff.

'She's fed up,' said Pauline. 'She's got to find somewhere to go when you move in. We're barely speaking.'

'She thinks *she's* got problems.'

He looked out of the window, his hands behind his back, perspiring in his dark suit. He'd come straight from working late and Pauline had been home a while already. She looked cool and composed and calm when even the weather conspired to make him miserable. He hated overcast, humid late-summer days with the sun behind low cloud, turning the city into a greenhouse. The evening dragged towards darkness, streetlights coming on all up the hill.

'Tell me again.'

Sitting on her windowsill, he went over it all over again.

'She's found a child whose parents died in a fire, with no other family. The baby's three months old and has Down's syndrome and won't be easy to place for adoption, and Sadie's offered. There's every chance we'll get her.'

'There would be.'

'Of course, she goes for this like a homing pigeon,' remarked Dougal reflectively, 'because it's practically what happened to her as a kid. If I let her down, I'm reopening old wounds. I can't do that.'

'There has to be a way round this,' Pauline said.

'If there is, I can't see it.'

'No family at all? Are they sure?'

'None anyone can find. She's in a foster home, but they don't want to keep her forever because she's a mongol.'

'Down's,' said Pauline softly. 'Even I know better than *mongol.*'

'Sadie saw her just after the fire, fell in love, and says it's fate. You try arguing with that.'

'Would you have adopted Eve if you didn't know about our baby?'

Dougal squirmed wretchedly on his windowsill.

'Probably. For Sadie's sake. I wouldn't have been keen, but I'd have done it.'

He read her expression. She wanted him to do exactly what Sadie wanted him to do, adopt. He felt eerily that his wife and his mistress were in collusion against him. He wondered vaguely if he shouldn't run away and disappear, like Reggie Perrin. In *The Fall and Rise of Reginald Perrin* the hero pretended to drown, left his clothes on the beach and vanished; left his troubles behind him and afterwards went from strength to strength. Lucky sod, thought Dougal, who hated swimming except for the occasional lounge in warm Mediterranean waters. He watched traffic climbing Fitzjohn's Avenue towards Hampstead and sighed. No Reggie Perrin for him. No one would ever believe it. Unwillingly he dragged himself back to reality.

'I'm sure they'll see through me in no time. I won't ring true. They're ruthless, those social workers. You can have a dozen kids of your own and beat them all up, and no one suggests you shouldn't have had them. But you try to adopt, and it's why do you want a child, why did you get married, why are you breathing? You've no idea what they put you through. The Inquisition were amateurs by comparison.'

Pauline waited until he'd run out of steam. 'You lie to perfection when you put your mind to it,' she answered sweetly. 'You do it all the time. You know you do.'

Dougal bridled, and then laughed shortly.

'You're getting worse than my wife.'

'I know you, like she does.'

'It would put off you and me. Adopting a baby takes months. No divorce, no getting married before our baby's born. Our baby would be illegitimate. How would you like that?'

'Parents who get married after they've had a baby can adopt their own child and make it unillegitimate. And it'd give me time,' she said, astonishing him with her calm. 'I'll get the flat ready to sell, work out my notice, house-hunt for us and half of the chores will be done by the time I have our baby and you get your divorce.'

'I'm planning to leave my wife with a newly adopted handicapped baby.' Dougal sounded as though he were trying to wake from a tasteless dream. 'This is crazy.'

'You were going to leave anyway, and as a single person, trying to adopt, it'll be an awful lot harder.'

'I'd have to give her the house.' Dougal looked deeply depressed by the thought. 'I love my house and I'm not used to being poor.'

'You are each entitled to half of the house. It's worth a fortune so neither of you will be poor.'

'Half of the house and money for the child. That's the least I can do.'

'I don't like what we're doing, either,' said Pauline, 'and

I wish it had all turned out some other way. But I can't see how we can help it. Unless you stay with Sarah and leave me, instead.'

He looked at her sharply. In most women that would have been an insincere threat. In Pauline it was genuine. She had the confidence of one to whom nothing serious had ever been denied. That should have made her selfish and spoiled, he supposed, but she had instead unshakeable composure. And she had his child. *Touché*.

'I won't leave you,' he said, knowing it was true. 'None of this is anyone's *fault*. No one meant it to happen.'

'No one ever does,' said Pauline.

Dougal sighed.

'Cheer up. You can do it, darling,' she said.

By closing time, Dougal was well away, in his local. He kept considering going back to Pauline for the night. They had a rule that he almost never stayed the night. He kept forgetting what he'd decided, tried to focus on the problem all over again and figure out what he'd decided last time. It was a tiresome, drunken process and the publican resolved the whole question by calling him a cab and telling the cabbie Dougal's address.

Sadie was used to evenings alone. She tucked herself up in front of the television with some reports to write. Dougal had phoned to say he was taking visiting Americans out to dinner, would be back very late. Sadie snorted and wondered why they played the game so strictly to rules that had never been acknowledged. Tired to death by ten o'clock, not feeling well, she went to bed.

Dougal woke at four in the morning with a raging headache, his mouth dry as bone. He staggered out onto the landing, padded into the bathroom, had a long drink of water and peed. He looked down to fasten his pyjamas and gaped. He was streaked with blood. His head buzzed and reeled. Perhaps he was still tight? He looked again.

* * *

'Sadie,' he yelped, jumbled images of knives and worse tumbling through his throbbing head. He stumbled back and shook her, lying looking quite as usual, fast asleep.

'What?' she said, coming awake. 'Whatever time did you get in?'

'Sit up,' he cried, sounding frightened. 'There's something wrong.'

She moved, and knew instantly, feeling the hot gush on her leg.

'It's OK. Time of the month.'

Dougal collapsed on her side of the bed, holding his head.

'Whatever kind of time of the month do you call this?'

He pulled his pyjamas straight.

'I'm sorry. I'll change the sheets.'

'Sadie,' he began, afraid he'd start crying, sob it all out in a horrible, maudlin dumping. Give her the problem. She and Pauline, they were the strong ones, not him. He fought self-pity grimly, seeing her standing there, holding the blood-soaked bedclothes, turned towards him, waiting.

'Nothing,' he mumbled. 'You are going to see a doctor tomorrow. How long has it been like this?'

'A while. It looks worse than it is.'

He ran a hand exhaustedly through his hair. He listened as she ran the shower. While she showered he got up and remade their bed, stuffing the soiled sheets into the basket, sobered.

'I'm sorry. You must find it unpleasant.'

She looked wan, damp from the shower, dandelion hair flattened with water, terribly vulnerable.

'It scares me.'

She nodded. 'I don't suppose I've got cancer,' she said, deliberately bringing the word up bluntly, not tiptoeing around it. 'I don't want to say anything to anyone about it until we've got Eve. If they get the idea that I'm ill, they'll put it off and put it off, and we can't really afford to wait, can we?'

Dougal stared at her standing there, at half past four in the morning, wrapped in a long nightgown. *Can't really afford to wait*. How much did she know? He began to wonder which of them was the cat and which the mouse, and whether he was the one being made an ass of.

'Oh, Lord, what a mess,' he groaned.

'Yes,' she said softly, 'but we're going to do it anyway. Never mind the reasons.'

Sadie turned out the light and lay on her back, wondering how long dawn would take to show in the windows. She cared too much about Eve to examine Dougal's motives for doing what he was doing. Whatever he was up to hardly mattered any more. She was already certain in her own mind that she'd have to have a hysterectomy. If she was ever to have a child, Eve was her only chance.

In the morning she got up early, made breakfast, leaned over Dougal, boyish as ever in his sleep, darkly stubbled, breathing lightly.

'Here, I've brought you coffee and a paracetamol if you need it.'

He groaned and woke up. 'I do love you,' he said, on impulse, his head clear and weightless, as though his troubles had vanished in the night. She smiled and put down the coffee, put the paracetamol by his hand.

'I know you do,' she said, and left him to it.

Chapter Forty-Nine

Sadie kept her problems to herself and Dougal behaved impeccably. To the world they presented a united front, united in their desire to have Eve. They passed their interviews, filed the papers, went to court, and five months after the fire, Eve Anne Maria Monroe became their legal daughter. They kept the name Eve, as she had been christened by the nurses, because Sadie loved it, and had always thought of her as Eve. Maria couldn't be godmother, being Catholic, and Rosalie said since she was probably going to become a Buddhist, she didn't think she'd be much good. Anne Howard said she'd be delighted, so they named the baby after her, and Eve was duly christened. Dolly was second godmother and undertook to love and watch over Eve, even though she never went to church. Finding a godfather was more of a problem, the Giangellis being Catholics. In the end, the vicar stood godfather himself.

'I wanted to ask Phil,' she told Maria, 'but Dougal went a bit funny about it.'

'Did he?'

'Is something the matter?'

'I don't know. Perhaps Dougal knows more than I do. Perhaps he didn't want to give Phil extra responsibility.'

Sadie looked at her narrowly, puzzled.

'He's been a bit strange lately,' admitted Maria.

'How?'

'Well,' she said, 'perhaps strange isn't the right word. Strained. Not with us. He spends so much time up in that office, upstairs, we hardly see him. He's gone all *quiet*.'

'Dougal goes quiet when he's telling lies,' said Sadie acidly, 'and when there's trouble in the office. Is the business in trouble?'

'Does Dougal say so?'

'No.'

'I have a feeling,' said Maria, 'that I wouldn't tell anyone except you.'

'Lies?'

Maria shook her head. 'I think he's worried nearly to death about something. I don't know what.'

In the next room, the children were watching BBC children's programmes on television, listening to Jemima and Little Ted. Eve slept in her pram outside on the patio. The washing machine sloshed to itself in Maria's utility room, where she let Phil's shirts get mouldy, so long ago. An ageing Fooka sat on his perch, motionless, minding his Ps and Qs. It all felt normal, everyday, ordinary.

'Money?' suggested Sadie.

'We don't have to worry any more than anyone else about that. Not enough to send him into a permanent funk.'

'It's as bad as that?' asked Sadie, surprised.

Maria fiddled with her cushion.

'This is going to sound really stupid . . .'

Sadie waited.

'Well,' said Maria, 'I started thinking he was a bit odd at the end of last November. D'you remember they caught Blunt out – he confessed he was a spy?'

'I remember,' said Sadie.

'If Phil read the interviews and things with Blunt once, he read them fifty times. He went over and over them. When I asked him why, he mumbled and kept disappearing upstairs.'

'What on earth does Phil have to do with Blunt?' cried Sadie, baffled.

'I don't know.'

'Pictures and computers. They've never met, or anything, have they?'

Maria gave her a look which said, don't be daft.

'It was only an idea,' said Sadie. 'After all, they were all at Cambridge.'

'About a hundred years apart,' snapped Maria. 'Anyway, he reads that book, as well. But he stopped reading it in front of me, since I realised he was going over and over that, too.'

'What book?'

'*Climate of Treason.*'

'Never heard of it,' said Sadie.

'It came out at the time they caught Blunt. Andrew Boyle wrote it.'

'I never heard of him, either. Have you read it? Could you see what was so interesting?'

'He'd underlined bits,' Maria said, her face suddenly looking worn and frightened and sad. 'About there being twenty-five other people in the conspiracy, whose names they knew. Phil hasn't been himself since then.'

The two women stared at each other.

'What do you make out of that, then?' asked Sadie cautiously.

Maria hesitated for a long moment, conflicting feelings ravaging her face. Then she seemed to lose courage. 'Nothing at all,' she said with a deprecating laugh. 'I'm being silly.'

Sadie sensed an abyss without shape or form and knew that, this time, they would side-step delicately around it.

'They all have their little ways,' she said encouragingly, 'and their funny moments. I should take no notice, and get him to go for a check-up if he doesn't sort himself out in a few months.'

'Right,' cried Maria brightly, as though they'd solved the problem.

You are a poor liar, thought Sadie grimly. We're all hiding awful secrets, and all lying, and sooner or later, it will all come out.

Chapter Fifty

With Eve safely her own, Sadie faced the fact that her body had the bit between its gynaecological teeth and needed seeing to. She made the necessary appointment and when the day came, left Eve with Rosalie and went to see her doctor. After he had examined her, she lay on her back on his narrow couch, her head turned to one side, watching her GP write notes.

'Where would you like to go?' he asked. 'Back to old friends?' He meant the hospital with the Family Planning and Subfertility clinics she attended for so long.

'No,' she said, 'if you wouldn't mind, and the NHS can arrange it, I'd rather never go to that clinic, or that hospital, again. Can you send me somewhere where they'll start from scratch, where no one will think of me as a failed subfertility experiment who wasn't very cooperative? I'm sure I've got a black mark against my name.'

He knew her well, and smiled. 'Choose, then,' he offered.

She stared at a little crack in his white ceiling, just over the couch. 'I don't know. Somewhere where there are good surgeons who'll do it right, where people are kind, and where my family can visit easily from Barnsbury, Islington and . . .' She was going to say Hampstead, but instead thought of Dolly and Gosling, realised that when she was feeling ghastly in some hospital bed, there would be no one she'd rather have near her than them. '. . . my friends can get to from the East End,' she finished, feeling she was asking the earth.

'St Martha's,' said her GP promptly. 'There's a very good chap there. It's old and shabby, but the care is unbeatable, so I hear. It meets your logistical requirements, being not far from Old Street. That's near Hoxton. Very rough area coming up in the world. That do?'

'Make it St Martha's,' said Sadie. 'Can I get up?'

She dressed and sat on the hard chair at the side of his desk. He was almost the same age as her father would have been, perhaps a little older. He was stooped and grey and lined, looked more than his middle years, had seen everything that life and death had to offer, and was staunchly kind. They'd got on from the start and he'd guided her compassionately and caringly through the barren years of treatments.

'Have I got cancer, do you think?' she asked bravely.

'I very much doubt it. I think you've grown some very splendid fibroids, which will probably have to come out. They'll take you in for a day first, for a quick look, to check for just that. Then if the diagnosis suggests it, I'm afraid they'll probably suggest a hysterectomy.'

'That's what I thought.'

He tried to second-guess her, to comfort. 'You won't get fat, you won't grow a beard and you won't feel any less sexy,' he said. 'Old wives' tales.'

'No children.'

'Ah, I'm afraid not.'

'Not that it ever looked like there would be. But one does go on hoping – just in the back of one's mind, vaguely. But I've grown lumps instead of babies. Do you think there's some significance in that?'

He rubbed the tips of his fine fingers gently together.

'I doubt it. Could be a disturbing thought, for a woman, I should think. You're welcome to come and talk it over. Are you still seeing that therapist you had?'

'That ended years ago.'

'Didn't help?'

'I don't mean to imply that – she helped me get where I wanted to be. I never wanted to examine the inside of my head for the sake of it.'

He smiled. She realised the appointment was over, she'd had her time.

'You'll get an appointment for the day surgery quite quickly. A month or so, I should think.'

She looked him in the eye, frowning.

'That's jolly quick for the NHS. Does that mean I'm urgent?'

'Moderately, I'm guessing. The consultant will be able to say much better than I, when he's had a good look.'

'Good,' she said briskly. 'I've got things to do, and this gets in the way. The quicker it's all over, the better, providing I come out in one piece.'

'Only a small bit missing.' He smiled, falling into her tone, liking her, wishing they'd been able to do something about the baby problem. No miracles there.

Sadie stood up to leave.

'St Martha's it is, then,' she said, and within a couple of months, after a preliminary investigation that confirmed everything her GP had said, into St Martha's she went.

'Wake up,' said Blossom. 'You gave up on that jigsaw hours ago, and you've been sitting there, miles and miles away. I'm honorary tea-lady while the staff sit on beds and chatter,' she shouted suddenly, making sure the nurse who had been pushing the trolley heard her. She looked up from the side of someone's bed and grinned. 'Do you want a last request before starvation sets in?' Blossom demanded, turning her attention back to Sadie. 'I've got tea, chocolate or Horlicks. I should warn you that the Horlicks is disgusting and has lumps in it.'

'Like me,' said Sadie.

'Don't get morbid. We've all been very considerate and tippy-toed round you while you day-dreamed.'

'Chocolate, please,' said Sadie.

Gales of laughter came from Sister's office at the far end of the ward.

'Glad someone finds something funny,' remarked Alice, slurping her tea.

'The night shift are playing What's My Line?,' called an auxiliary nurse from the end of Gabriella's bed. 'It's report,' she explained, beginning to laugh. 'They are telling the night staff what's the matter with you and what you're all having done tomorrow. They have to mime it, like they do on the telly.' She stood in the centre of the ward to demonstrate. 'You know the female reproductive system looks like a sort of square with two wiggly tubes off its two top corners, with little bulges at the ends. That's the ovaries. Well, they do this.' She bent at the waist, put her arms up behind her, for fallopian tubes, and her fists clenched for ovaries. 'If they're taking an ovary out, you put one arm behind your back. A uterus with only one fallopian tube, see? The day staff mime and the night staff have to guess the diagnosis and what surgery you're having.'

Howls of laughter came from the office.

'Mad as hatters,' Daphne Salmon's nose twitched in outrage. 'And to think we put our lives in their hands.'

'I wonder how they mime, Don't Know What's Wrong But It Might Be Awful,' said Gabriella.

Unseen by her, the auxiliary put her hands together and cast her eyes heavenwards. No one found that funny. The auxiliary got the message, and went round hanging *nil by mouth* notices at the heads of their beds.

'Not so much as a mouthful, ladies,' she called.

'What if we did?' asked Blossom.

'They'd send you home,' threatened the auxiliary. 'Or you'd be sick under the anaesthetic and die,' she added with relish.

Daphne clucked irritably. She rummaged in the chemist's shop on top of her locker, found setting lotion and began to wind stiff, lustreless hair on to small grey curlers.

'Good grief, you're never going to go down with curlers.'

Daphne refused to take the bait, ignoring Blossom's sniggers. Sadie caught sight of Gabriella's pinched face, fear written all over at the words *going down*, conjuring white-tiled walls, gleaming lights on scalpels and surgeon's glasses.

'I love your balloons,' Sadie said. They bobbed and

strained on their long ribbons. 'They make a lovely change from boring old cards. They might last long enough for you to take them home, mightn't they? They're so pretty.'

The laughter had stopped at the far end of the ward. It was bedtime. The drugs trolley rattled round.

'Something to help you sleep, Miss Miller?'

Gabriella held out her hand for the little glass tumbler with two green capsules.

'Something to help you sleep?' The trolley arrived at Sadie's bed. She watched Gabriella swallow the pills. The image of Cherie, lying in evening light the colour of dried blood with her bottle of pills, came into her head. Depression ran like hemlock through her veins, making her cold and heavy. 'Don't be afraid to ask if you'd like them. A lot of people can't sleep in hospital. No point in lying awake.' The nurse's tone was kind. She was used to frightened people.

Sadie brought herself back with an effort of will.

'I'll try to sleep without, if you don't mind.'

'Let us know if you want anything a bit later.'

The trolley continued on its round, and at the very end of the ward, the auxiliary turned out most of the lights. Over each bed a lamp glowed. One by one the occupants turned them off. Gabriella lay like Juliet in her trance, face to the ceiling, marble-skinned in the gloom. Alice began to snore softly. Daphne turned restlessly on her porcupine head. Blossom read a paperback. Sadie listened to her turning her pages, the soft sound of paper. Resigned to her own thoughts, she let terrible images run their course, of her parents dancing to their deaths on the ice, of the Sangster twins tied into their cots, of her own death. Hospital brings on such thoughts; she held the terror until it faded away of its own accord, as Eva had taught her to do a long time ago. As Blossom put away her book and turned out her lamp, Sadie drifted into calmer waters, dreaming strange, vivid dreams, and soon was deeply asleep.

Chapter Fifty-One

After lunch the long ward was quiet, beds full of dozing women, visiting time not yet started. The office was quiet, too, the phone not ringing, no doctors due to do rounds, no recent emergency admissions. Outside the ward doors, lift gates clanked as a couple of cleaners arrived. A slack spot in the day. Bridges decided the time was right to make her little speech. She went soundlessly down the polished floor to the beds of her recuperating ladies and raised her voice so that the whole dozing ward heard her mortifying advice.

Molly Bridges didn't bother mincing words. Major surgery was a great leveller and put patients in touch with basics. Some coped better than others and experience taught her that bluntness was best.

'Ladies, you are going to break wind like elephants, after major abdominal surgery,' she beamed, 'and there's no point in hanging on, straining away, being embarrassed. It's better out than in, so let go, my dears.' She stood in the middle of the circle of beds and surveyed her patients, three days into their recovery. Daphne's mouselike features first twitched in puzzlement, followed by consternation. Blossom, having had quite a bad time in the operating theatre, had been looking like a pale and beautiful youth, almost as white as her well-laundered pillows. She now livened up for the first time and grinned delightedly. Sadie wondered if she'd heard quite right, and saw from Daphne's outraged whisker-twitching that she had. Alice looked straight at Bridges, unmoved. Bridges, seeing her impassive face, wondered if all the tension at home with

Mr Penn gave her problems down there, anyway, a touch of irritable bowel. She resolved to ask some other time. Jean Hargreaves smiled faintly and Gabriella's waxen face took on a faint tinge of pink. She was embarrassed. Bridges wondered how and when they'd break the diagnosis to her, and sailed back to her office on a tidal wave of their astonishment.

They all still hurt. The registrar who had operated on Sadie leaned over her as she lay, exhausted, on a pile of pillows.

'How do you feel?' the tall, elegant woman asked, her hands in the pockets of an immaculate white coat. Sadie's gaze slid over the green and brown curtains that hung around her bed, while her mind, slowed by painkillers, rejected the ruder replies that wandered into it; it wasn't a good idea to offend doctors.

'As though you've taken a chainsaw to my middle,' she said.

The classically lovely face of the registrar broke into a smile.

'I'm glad you're pleased,' whispered Sadie weakly, offended.

The registrar beamed. 'If it feels like a chainsaw, we've done a good job. If you had no pain, I'd worry we'd short-changed you.'

'Well, now, isn't success a wonderful thing,' snapped Sadie feebly, wishing the doctor would go away, leave her to sleep. She did.

The doctor moved off down the ward to check on other patients. Sadie closed her eyes in relief. They snapped open again. Three nurses chorused that they'd come to help her out of bed, to sit in a chair. Clutching a drainage bottle partly full of something she didn't care to examine too closely, attached to some part of herself she hadn't fully liked to explore, Sadie wilted resentfully in a green easy chair, longing for peace. She managed to look so dreadful that they took pity, allowed her back into bed. She slept.

She woke. No one came to see her during the afternoon. Grateful, she slept again. At evening visiting time, she looked forward to seeing Maria, who knew more than most about being in hospital. It gave them a lot of new experiences in common.

'However do you stand spending months in somewhere like this. I'm sorry I haven't been so sympathetic before. I had no idea,' Sadie whispered. Maria, looking totally at home, leaned forward in her wheelchair and said anxiously, 'Why, aren't they kind?'

Out of the corner of her eye Sadie could see Daphne, lying feebly back against her pillows, suffering in ear-splitting silence, languidly clutching her leonine husband's refined and clerical hand. They seemed equally unable to find anything at all to say, but stared furtively at Maria in her wheelchair as if she were sitting on a magic carpet. Sadie knew Daphne had sprayed perfume in her armpits and backcombed her hair before visiting, and before that had been several times around the ward accepting chocolates. Now she looked as though she hovered between life and death. Sadie laughed aloud and winced. Laughing hurt.

'They couldn't be kinder.' She turned back to Maria. 'But it's a ruthless sort of kindness, isn't it? They drag you out of bed and push you around when you'd rather be left to die quietly in peace, thank you very much.'

'They have to be ruthless,' answered Maria wisely, 'otherwise none of you would want to get better and get out. You'd enjoy yourselves too much, being babies all over again. And talking of babies, Eve is splendid, and Rosalie says to give her love, she can't get in because she doesn't want to leave her with a babysitter.'

Back to babyhood? Half incontinent, dependent, passive. Funny places, hospitals, thought Sadie. Maria should know. Sadie admitted to herself that she *wasn't* too keen on getting out, facing what waited for her, adjusting to a weak and painful body that would take weeks to get back on its feet and wasn't at all the way it used to be. Nice to stay and be looked after, not to be responsible for any of the problems gathering like storm clouds on her horizon. Maria was quite right.

Dougal came every evening, said little. He sat on an orange chair looking preoccupied. Sadie got tired of staring at the top of his very slightly balding head. There were cracks on the peeling green paint on the wall opposite and she began making them into patterns and pictures to pass the time, like a child. It was all very boring.

One evening he made a thing of going and watering the plant he'd brought the day she came in. He seemed anxious to be there, anxious to be gone. Every visit was the same. Sadie brooded until Blossom told her that in *her* place, *she'd* say her piece and get it over with.

'Say what?' asked Sadie.

Blossom's sharp little face went thoughtful as she rubbed her stomach very gently, easing its ache.

'Whatever it is that's eating you up.'

'Worry is what's eating me up,' said Sadie. 'He's going to leave me and I've a child to look after. What shall I do?'

'Shoot him?' suggested Blossom blandly.

Sadie looked thoughtful but that evening's visiting came and went with no shootings, and no confessions, either.

The next day, after teatime, a loud crack broke the ward's late-afternoon stupor, followed by someone blowing a raspberry. Stunned, they stared open-mouthed at Daphne.

'Bravo,' cried Blossom meanly. 'Let it all hang out, darling, like our Molly said.'

Daphne stared straight at the ceiling, mortified into emotional rigor mortis. After a bit, the ward lost interest, went back to its doze. She began mentally to pray, trying to ask forgiveness for evil and wicked thoughts. Blossom's grinning face came between her and her devotions, bringing feelings of pure hatred. Distracted, she began to panic. What if she went off during visiting? How *could* He?

Daphne felt a lifelong relationship with God beginning to slip ominously; the beginnings of a spiritual estrangement which could lead to a divorce. She was *furious*.

'You should hear what goes on when you're all asleep,' said Alice later, feeling sorry for Daphne. 'And I don't mean just the snoring.'

Gabriella hid under her bedclothes. They were old and loud and coarse and knowing. They had neither shame nor modesty. They frightened her.

Visiting time brought the usual little queue waiting just beyond the ward doors. Daphne could see her husband's dog collar. She lay back and squirted L'Air du Temps down her cleavage. She sniffed appreciatively, then stiffened under her tidy counterpane. She fought grimly. She clenched desperately. She'd rather die. With a sense of doom mixed with exquisite relief, she lost the battle. They laughed. They laughed and gasped and groaned. It hurts, they gasped, don't make us laugh, we'll split our stitches, oh, don't look like that, it can't be helped, Bridges did warn us. Daphne lay in dread. It was going to happen again. She felt wind rolling and rattling around inside her, like a gutful of marbles. In here, nothing matters, Alice said kindly, scowling at all the laughing women. Cheer up, Daph. Visiting time came round. Appalled, Daphne saw the ward doors open.

Sadie told Dougal about poor Daphne, in a whisper, to make him smile, cheer them both up. He didn't. He looked nervous, picking at his thumbnail, like a little boy.

'Dougal,' began Sadie, turning close to him, on the edge of her bed, her pink counterpane clutched in her fists, speaking very low.

'Sadie,' began Dougal in the same breath.

They stopped, each waiting for the other to go on.

'I . . .' said Sadie.

'I . . .' he echoed.

She leaned against her pillows, already worn out.

'I'm sorry,' she said, 'I haven't the energy to play games.'

He spoke very slowly, plodding. 'I've heard that before; about getting wind after operations.'

'No,' she cried, but Dougal had his bulldog look. He'd finally got to the point and nothing now would stop him. 'Because,' he plodded on, 'there is a woman in the postnatal ward with Pauline, who had a Caesarean, and they were talking about it yesterday. She said it was like stones rolling around inside her. Painful.' His expression begged her not to make a scene.

'That's why you don't visit in the afternoons?' she said calmly, the secret out at last. You go to the postnatal ward to visit your secretary.'

Dougal looked stunned.

'You know?' he cried.

'That you've been having an affair with your secretary? For ages, yes.'

'She isn't my secretary. I mean, she was, but she's worked her notice. She's left.'

She wondered why men resorted to pedantic attention to *facts* in awful situations.

'I take it,' she said clearly, 'that Pauline Cookham and you have just had your baby. Congratulations.' She wanted to laugh and laugh and laugh until she cried.

'Thank you,' said Dougal, nonplussed. He'd dreaded her reaction, was put out because there wasn't one. She *knew*. At that moment Mr Penn came lurching and banging through the doors at the far end, holding a paper bag. Bright-red jelly oozed from half a dozen doughnuts.

'You're taking it awfully well,' he muttered, turning back.

Mr Penn licked jelly off his thumb and went to the wrong bed. He forgot every time where Alice was. He bellowed with fright until Alice sat up and waved and he saw her.

'I take it you'll divorce me,' said Dougal.

'You planned all this,' she said flatly. 'You planned to leave me with Eve.' You were so stupid you thought I wouldn't know.

'No,' he protested.

Sadie looked straight through him.

'Yes,' he said.

'I'll get a lawyer,' she said, 'when I've got the energy. Right now, go away.'

Dougal felt indignant. He could have handled a tantrum but she behaved as though it didn't really matter.

'Look, I want you to understand . . .' he began. She opened her eyes and gave him such a look that the words shrivelled on his tongue.

The minutes ticked by interminably. Sadie seemed to have dozed off and Dougal sat, unable to get up and go, outraged by her indifference. He needed to make her see . . . She shot up in bed, wakened by Mr Penn shouting, frustrated by his sister-in-law's efforts to tell him it was time to go. He wanted to stay. He roared like an angry moose, holding the side of Alice's hospital bed.

'Come *on*,' cried his sister-in-law, exasperated. 'You can come back tomorrow.'

He bellowed miserably. Alice prised his fingers off and patted his cheek. 'There, there,' she soothed.

Asia and Blossom held hands and watched. Dougal made one last effort to get his point of view across. 'I want to explain . . .' he began once more.

Sadie, galvanised, scrambled to her knees and shrieked, '*Get out*.'

The whole ward turned as one and boggled.

'*Get out and don't come back*,' yelled Sadie, finally and absolutely having had enough.

Hurt and rejected, Dougal backed off and embarked on the longest walk of his life, head lowered, down the whole length of the ward, between endless pairs of pitiless, curious eyes. He got to the doors like a dying man coming out of the Sahara, and fled. A pair of hands clapped slowly, joined diffidently by another. Blossom and Jean Hargreaves were grinning from ear to ear.

'You finally gave him his marching orders. Bravo,' cried Blossom, and blew her a great big kiss.

Chapter Fifty-Two

Shocked by the sudden ending with Dougal, when Sadie's hormones took a nosedive, so did her spirits.

'Baby blues, only no baby. No nothing,' she sobbed, sitting in the bathroom, on a cork-topped stool, away from the ward and its host of interested eyes. Blossom, overhearing, beckoned Bridges as she was passing.

'I think Mrs Monroe is upset,' she whispered.

'People don't always want interference,' snorted Bridges brusquely. 'But I'll go and see she's all right.' She bore off towards the bathrooms.

'You can interfere with me any time,' sighed Blossom enviously.

Bridges perched on the side of the bath and contemplated her patient scrubbing at her eyes, embarrassed.

'Sorry. Silly,' mumbled Sadie.

'Do you find it hard to let go and cry?' Bridges asked. 'A lot of people do. It's like the wind, though, better out than in. Poor Mrs Salmon finds it very hard to bear, doesn't she? But it can't be helped. Any more than you can help wanting to cry, my dear.'

'I'd never have had a baby anyway.' Sadie scrubbed furiously at her face and cried afresh.

'You've lost hope. It's painful,' said Bridges, meaning to comfort.

Sadie sat up straight on her cork stool and snarled, taking Bridges aback. 'What I've lost hope about is for Pauline Cookham to *fry*. My husband's gone off with her. She's sitting in some hospital somewhere with their baby, doubtless deliriously happy, and I'm sitting in this one losing everything.'

Bridges put an arm like a ham around her. Sadie thought involuntarily that Blossom would give *anything* to be in her shoes, and began to laugh. Misinterpreting her quivering shoulders, Bridges drew her closer and said like a comforting nanny, 'What toads. There now, just you have a jolly good cry.'

The ward made a tactful show of unconcern at Sadie's red and swollen face when she emerged from the bathroom after Bridges. Alice Penn shuffled around in a flowered dressing gown, arranging her fruit bowl, then went to the day room to watch telly. Daphne hobbled after her, urine bag and stand in one hand like some monstrous handbag, her hair done up in unyielding waves, denying the sadly disordered patchwork of her other parts.

'We are a sight, aren't we?' sighed Sadie, blowing her nose. 'Put us all together and you'd barely come up with a couple of fully equipped women.'

Daphne looked down, twitched, and passed on by as if she hadn't heard. Gabriella sat beneath her bright balloons, a fragile waif with an unopened Mills & Boon in her lap, wearing a pure silk nightgown, her hair in plaits, looking about twelve years old.

'Your hair all falls out when you have chemotherapy,' she bleated in a small-girl voice.

Jean Hargreaves looked at her sharply. 'Have they said you need that?'

'No one tells me anything,' Gabriella said petulantly, 'but I know. My mother was crying the other day. She thinks I didn't notice, but of course I did.'

'You shouldn't jump to conclusions,' said Mrs Hargreaves.

'You'll see,' murmured Gabriella.

If you just sit back and drift into dying, you will, thought Jean Hargreaves crossly. A houseman wandered down the ward and veered right, pulling curtains around someone's bed with a squeaky rattle of rings. He stopped the conversation.

Blossom peeled an orange. 'Want a bit of this?' she asked. No one did.

'I live in Epping. In a cottage,' said Jean Hargreaves, folding her hands in her lap, looking as though she'd just made up her mind about something. They looked across their beds at her politely.

'It's nice out there,' said Blossom pleasantly. 'We go for walks in the forest sometimes.'

'I'm going to New Zealand to stay with my daughter,' continued Mrs Hargreaves, 'so my cottage will be empty for six months.'

There was a pause, since no one knew why she was telling them this. 'You could take tenants,' suggested Sadie, finding something to say.

'I don't want tenants,' said the elderly woman testily.

They fell silent, nonplussed.

'What about you?' she said, looking at Sadie. Blossom and Sadie glanced at each other across the ends of their beds, the same thought in both their minds. She was wandering.

'Bring your baby and look after my cottage,' Mrs Hargreaves went on. 'If it would suit you for a bit.'

'But you don't know me,' blurted Sadie, astonished.

'I know enough. If you don't want it, it's all right by me.'

Sadie thought rapidly, of the big house in Hampstead, full of Dougal and Dougal's things. Even if he moved out at once into Pauline's flat, there would still be all the sorting and agreeing and dividing to do. Estate agents' boards; letters from solicitors; enough paperwork to drive you batty. Divorce was paperwork and high drama and exhaustion. She'd seen enough clients in the throes of it to know she'd be better off away from Hampstead, dealing with it all at a distance. Her mind made itself up.

'That's a marvellous idea. Thank you.'

Jean Hargreaves grunted and said she could come when

she wanted, straight out of hospital if she wanted. They'd look after each other, and the baby.

'Not the baby,' said Sadie. 'Rosalie has promised to keep Eve for a few weeks because I won't be able to lift her. I was going to get someone to help, but now I'll take Rosalie's offer.'

'You want a babysitter, ask Asia,' called Blossom. 'She's studying art and quite often she's got time on her hands. She's sweet with kids and she'd fancy the money. Wouldn't ask much.'

Sadie looked from one to the other. 'I don't know what to say.'

They went vague.

'Sure,' said Blossom offhandedly.

'It suits me,' said Jean Hargreaves brusquely.

A burst of laughter came from the day room, and loud music from the television. Daphne appeared, walking extremely upright, with dignity, urine bag held in one rigid hand.

'Oh dear,' said Alice Penn, following after her, 'it's 'appened again, poor soul.'

Blossom winked. 'Some problems are easier solved than others, aren't they, Daph? Just give it time and it'll go away.'

Daph. How dared they? It was impossible to *stalk* effectively, with a proper show of hauteurs thought Daphne grimly, when you'd had your poor tired undercarriage repaired and you felt humiliated and lonely and jealous of the way they all seemed to get on. She retreated into the bathroom and sat on the cork-topped stool until her complete mortification had faded to simple, tired indignation.

'Oh, Lord, why me?' she said.

Why not you? answered the Lord, unmoved.

'We get our stitches out tomorrow,' observed Jean Hargreaves.

'Perhaps that will help Daphne.'

Alice Penn chose a pear from the pile of fruit on her locker and bit into it noisily. She ate like PacMan, thought Sadie, and never had so much as a burp. Daphne picked and fussed and dabbed at her food, and went off like a blown-up balloon.

'Nothing in life is fair,' said Blossom, reading her thoughts, grinning.

'Life,' said Sadie resignedly, 'is nothing more than a joke.'

Chapter Fifty-Three

Sadie and Blossom and Jean trundled around after tea, passing time, afternoon visitors gone. One pair of pink pom-poms, one pair of canvas slip-ons and Blossom's man's leather slippers stopped in a row, as something registered with them.

'Hang about. Her curtains have been drawn for *ages*.'

They stood at the end of Gabriella's bed, which was shrouded in green curtains and silence.

'Doctor. Since before tea,' mouthed Alice.

The sound of laughter and clapping from the television in the day room was suddenly incongruous. A woman who had nearly died from an ectopic pregnancy groaned in a bed further down. Sadie's skin prickled. She leaned on the side of a stranger's bed, exhausted.

'You can't go poking in there, Blossom,' whispered Jean Hargreaves. 'It's not our business.'

Sadie found the edge of Gabriella's curtain, peeped in with one eye. Gabriella lay face-down on top of her bedclothes, motionless and alone.

'Are you all right?' whispered Sadie.

Gabriella burrowed her head further into her pillows. Sadie slipped inside the curtain, leaving the other two straining their ears. She sat on the edge of the bed.

'Would you like to talk about it?'

Gabriella froze.

'Have they told you bad news?' asked Sadie.

The girl raised a pinched little face a couple of inches and nodded.

'A growth, like you thought?'

'Cancer,' mumbled Gabriella. 'I'm going to die.'

'Did someone tell you you are going to die?'

Gabriella didn't answer.

'You're jumping to conclusions,' said Sadie.

Enraged at the criticism, Gabriella sat up with a furious bounce on her bed. 'It's in my bowel,' she threatened. 'I *will* probably die.'

'That's better, now you're sitting up and cross,' remarked Sadie. 'Did they say what they would do?'

'Are you a doctor?' demanded Gabriella sullenly.

'No, just someone who likes you.'

Gabriella's slate-coloured eyes filled. 'My mother says I'm going to die.'

Sadie thought, I *knew* it. That woman's got negativity written all over her. 'Mothers aren't always right,' she said, 'and sometimes they can't see the wood for the trees. They're too involved, and they panic. It might be better to talk it over with other people.'

'There's nothing to talk about,' muttered Gabriella ungraciously.

'Why don't you go and ask Mrs Hargreaves to explain what it was like?' Sadie persisted. 'She's had surgery and chemotherapy. She's a lovely, kind, steady person. She won't get upset if you ask her and she might know better how you feel than the doctors or your mum.'

'I feel awful,' mumbled Gabriella. 'My mother wants to tell me how awful *she* feels and she doesn't want to listen to me.'

'Shall I quietly ask Mrs Hargreaves to pop in, while your curtains are drawn?' suggested Sadie. Gabriella scowled, but didn't say no. Sadie leaned over and took her shoulders gently. 'This is a good place to find friends. Blossom and Mrs Penn and even poor Daphne . . . we all care about you.'

Gabriella sniffled. Sadie slid her hand down her back and handed her a wad of tissues from a box. 'Here,' she said, rubbing the small of Gabriella's back absently, 'blow your nose and try to cheer up.'

'You're giving me pins and needles,' snuffled Gabriella.

Sadie remembered as if it were happening now, a bird

running in circles, broken wing trailing in sand, beak snapping under hot coppery sky. Her bare feet covered in sand, a faded blue dress wet round the hem from the sea. Queenie standing throwing black shadows, tall on the dunes above, shading her eyes with her hands, calling.

Sadie's hand where it stroked the girl's back grew hot.

'Ouch,' cried Gabriella, pulling away, 'you're hurting me.'

The bird had flown away. 'She's got it,' Queenie had said to Victoria, looking sly. Victoria had been cross and hushed her.

Sadie took her hand away. The burning died.

'What did you do that for?' demanded Gabriella childishly.

Embarrassed, Sadie drew right away. Around them the sounds of a modern surgical ward, disconnected voices, the television news; not a place for ancient gifts, mysteries.

'It's probably something to do with the drugs we've all been taking. They do funny things. Take no notice.'

'Are you a witch?' asked Gabriella, looking at Sadie closely, not so stupid as she sometimes liked to make out.

Sadie began to laugh. 'No, but I had a great-aunt who used to say she was. She was a very old woman with a face like a turtle. She knew a lot of things. She did potions.' Potions had caught Maria's interest years before, sitting on the bench at school, overlooking the silver sea.

Gabriella perked up. 'Did she have a broomstick?'

'For sweeping the yard,' said Sadie, smiling. 'Perhaps she flew on it at night, when I was asleep.'

Gabriella had colour in her cheeks.

'Would you like a cup of tea?' Sadie suggested. 'I could go down and ask someone to make one for you.'

For the first time in days, the girl smiled, and asked her to open her curtains.

As Gabriella drank her tea and ate a pile of biscuits, sitting cross-legged on her bed, Blossom frowned, puzzled.

'She isn't giving out all those tragic vibes,' she hissed. 'What on earth did you say to her?'

'Nothing much,' Sadie said truthfully.

'Well, something's happened to cheer her up,' said Blossom suspiciously. She stared at Sadie, found her face inscrutable. 'Hm,' muttered Blossom.

And she had no choice but to leave it at that.

Two days later there was a commotion around Gabriella's bed. Mrs Miller burst into noisy tears and clutched the registrar's arm hysterically. 'You are lying,' she shrieked.

The doctor shook her hand off and retreated to the far side of the bed. The ward watched, round-eyed.

'The scan shows no tumour,' the registrar repeated, her flawless face calm. 'I can't explain it. I can only tell you that that is what we have found. We'll do another scan in a couple of days, and keep checking and double-checking.'

'It's a miracle,' screeched Mrs Miller, appealing to the ward, 'isn't it?' She began crawling over her daughter in her eagerness to get at the registrar, to make her confirm it.

'I don't know,' answered the doctor.

Gabriella sat between them, looking from one to the other.

'Shut up, Mummy,' she said loudly. '*Shut up*.'

Mrs Miller gasped. The balloons wavered on their moorings, wilting slightly, still screaming their fluorescent *Get Well Soon*.

'You can stop making such a fuss,' said Gabriella firmly. Her mother crumpled, took out a small embroidered hanky and sniffed into it.

'Shall we finish our talk in the office?' suggested the registrar.

Gabriella watched her mother totter, unsteady in very high heels and shock, in the doctor's wake.

'*Well*,' said Blossom, fascinated.

'You don't all have to stare,' snapped Gabriella.

'Hey,' murmured Sadie.

Gabriella shot her a very odd look and subsided.

Blossom narrowed her eyes.

'I don't suppose anyone is going to let on what's been going on here,' she demanded.

Gabriella and Sadie suddenly both wanted to go and watch the television in the day room. Blossom watched them go. She was right; no one was going to say a word. Gabriella seemed to be better and no one knew why. There was nothing Blossom hated more than mysteries, but this time there was no solution.

Chapter Fifty-Four

After they had been ten days in hospital, it was time to go home. They sat by their beds, fully dressed, waiting for people to come with cars to take them away. Mrs Miller came just after lunch, fussing and clacking and flapping, insisting on taking away the wilted balloons. Gabriella kissed Sadie and whispered, 'Thank you.' Then she kissed Jean Hargreaves, who gave her her address and telephone number, in case she should ever need it.

'Miracles aren't all that reliable, are they?' said Blossom acidly when she had gone, fishing to know what had happened.

Sadie wasn't saying anything.

Asia came for Blossom. Mrs Penn's sister came in a cab with a long face, because Mr Penn was already back home and playing up. Alice, her holiday over, looked tired and depressed, her locker scattered with empty fruit bags and finished chocolate boxes. She shuffled out, her bounce all gone.

'That is such a shame,' said Sadie.

'My friend said she'd be here by now,' said Jean Hargreaves, looking at the clock. There was a stifled whickering noise from over the way. 'Good heavens, she's crying,' whispered Jean Hargreaves. Daphne sat ramrod-straight on a chair by the side of her bed, dressed in tweed that had seen better days, squeaking, more mouselike than ever.

'Shall I call someone?' asked Sadie, concerned. 'Are you in pain?'

'No,' yelped Daphne, scraping tears from her freshly

rouged cheeks. 'I don't want us to go. I'll miss you. I'll miss you all, dreadfully.'

Sadie and Jean Hargreaves looked at each other in consternation. It just went to show you never could tell what someone else was feeling, and that you should *never* go on appearances.

Chapter Fifty-Five

Jean Hargreaves' cottage was tucked away at the back of the common, just on the outskirts of Epping. Two old grey horses grazed a hummocky field behind it which in springtime would be full of baby rabbits. It was quiet, the main road a constant faint roar in the distance; the cottage was shielded from the road by banks of bushes and oaks, beyond which stretched outer fortifications of green and spiky gorse bushes.

'My great-aunts had a cottage in Norfolk,' said Sadie one afternoon. 'There you could hear the sound of the sea instead of the traffic.'

They sat in a sun porch, overlooking the field, their feet on stools, slowly getting better and stronger. Later they enjoyed a quiet walk down the lane that ran past the field into open Essex countryside. They leaned on a wooden fence, enjoying woods turning to yellow and bronze, wood-smoke drifting, a faint brown smudge across fields.

'Norfolk is flat, too,' Sadie went on, picking up threads. 'Do you know it?'

'No,' said Jean Hargreaves. 'We moved out here from the East End, during the war. We stopped put. We used to go fruit-picking in Kent. Not great ones for travel.'

'Your daughter's in New Zealand, and you're off, too, in three weeks. That's serious travel.'

Jean Hargreaves sighed, pushed herself off the fence and turned to walk home.

'She met her husband, and that was that. If I want to see her, I've got to up sticks and go. I'll probably die in New Zealand, my daughter knows that. She'll have the cottage when I'm gone, but I doubt she'll ever come back to see it. She'll sell it.'

'I'll miss you,' Sadie said shyly. 'It's funny how there are some people whom you meet and hardly know, but there's such a rapport you feel you've known them forever. And I wish you wouldn't talk about dying.'

'Why not?' the old woman said shortly. 'They've taken out another lump, but they always come back. May as well face it. And you won't miss me for long. You've too much to do. All those things to sort out in your young life, and that baby, they'll keep you going, my dear.'

Sadie took her arm and they walked back. They were still too weak to stay on their feet for more than an hour; even that meant creeping along. They led old-lady lives in an old-lady cottage. For the moment, it was just what they needed.

The day Jean Hargreaves left to go to New Zealand, Maria drove over with Jamie and Alison to spend the afternoon, to keep Sadie company. She found she couldn't get into the cottage. The steps by the front door were impassable, the old doorway too narrow for her wheelchair to go through. Steps to the sun porch at the back were equally impossible.

'I should have realised,' cried Sadie, 'when we arranged it. I don't think very clearly at the moment. I think all those drugs do funny things to you.'

'It doesn't matter,' said Maria. But it did. They sat in the garden, a breeze blowing the first fallen leaves over the grass.

'Have you seen Dougal at all?' asked Sadie, with careful neutrality.

'Yes.'

'And Pauline?'

Maria looked embarrassed.

'It doesn't matter,' said Sadie.

'I can't help it. Philip's terribly upset and angry because Dougal's left the company and taken Pauline with him. I suppose he feels Dougal's let him down terribly. Anyway, he asked them round to talk things over. I had to be polite.'

'And?'

'And nothing. Dougal's applied for a job teaching business studies in Swansea and it looks as though he'll get it. He says he wants to go back to Wales and make a fresh start.'

'He's going back to Wales?' cried Sadie incredulously.

'Yes. Having a child seems to have sent him running back to his roots. I suppose it easily could. And talking of roots, why don't you come to us, instead of isolating yourself here?' asked Maria. 'I wish you would.'

Sadie shaded her eyes and watched the children run round the corner, holding sticks they'd found in undergrowth in the field, pretending they were guns.

'I think a bit of isolation might be what I need, to think things over. Just for a little while.'

The children shrieked, 'bang, bang', and ran off out of sight.

'I've been wanting to ask you something,' said Maria. 'If anything happened to me and Phil, would you take them for me, Sadie?'

'Nothing will happen to you and Phil.'

'If it did,' she insisted.

'You're being morbid. But of course I would, if that's what you want.'

'I do, and I've put it in my will,' said Maria.

That evening Sadie sat alone, looking over the darkening field at the back of the cottage, and made some decisions. She wrote to her tenant, giving notice that she'd decided to sell the flat. She decided to tell her lawyer to push through a divorce from Dougal as fast as possible, and she decided to do everything she could not to hate him, or Pauline. She wrote to her lawyer, posted both letters, then she heated up some soup and had supper. Night fell. It was too quiet. Being alone turned into being lonely. She missed Jean acutely, missed Dougal worse and faced the fact that she would go on missing him for a long time, even though they hadn't been happy. She looked at the phone, thought of calling him, then several other people. She had resolved to cope on her own, and didn't call anyone.

When she looked back on that night, a long time later, she wondered if the horror of it was due to ESP, some kind of awareness of what had happened when Maria got home. Not normally afraid of the dark, the only other time she'd feared it so was the night Fooka sent Maria into hospital and she had run to Dougal. Even that moment of fear was a pale echo of the night in Epping. She became increasingly terrified, the dark bringing fears she did not know she had. Pitch-black windows full of darkness, the dark itself, stretching like a living menace, across the common, into the forest, where there were hiding-places, under the trees. The back of her neck prickled, as her hair stood on end. They found *things* in the forest, bodies and . . . Sometimes they didn't find things; things that should have been there. People went missing in the forest. There was something *there*. She panicked, tore curtains tightly shut all over the house, switched on lights, turned the telly right up. Then she sat down, trembling.

She thought of all the times she'd told clients, *ring the Samaritans*. She realised with a wry sense of the absurd that what stopped her was the dreadfulness of having to start at some beginning, to make sense of it all to a stranger. Ring someone you know, Dolly or Rosalie or Maria, said common sense. She tried, but her legs wouldn't take her to the phone. Like Maria, she was paralysed, but by dread. Her heart pounding, she strained to hear the smallest sound, a creak of a floorboard, the brush of a skirt, the intake of breath from something that *could not* be there. Hugging one of Jean Hargreaves' *petit point* cushions to her, like a child, in the small hours, exhausted by terror, she fell asleep. In the morning the sun came up over the yellowing trees of the forest, bringing a bright new autumn day with a chill in the air. She bathed and dressed, made coffee and decided to walk down to the town for the paper. Glad she had not rung anyone during the night and made a fool of herself, she turned on the radio for the morning news, listened with half an ear. Coffee spilled from the pot in her hand as she froze.

Chapter Fifty-Six

When she left Sadie, to go home, Maria felt headachy, edgy. James and Alison squabbled and fidgeted in the back of the car, making her tense. Being stuck in the front garden at Mrs Hargreaves' had annoyed and upset her. She tried and failed to argue herself out of it. There was no reason in the world why the old lady should live in a cottage fit for a wheelchair. The whole world lived in places wheelchairs couldn't get to. Maria usually refused to let it matter, but this afternoon it did, though she could not have said why. She snapped at the children to sit still. The sun was low in the sky and, driving west, it shone straight in her eyes. Her headache got worse; she was immensely relieved to get home.

It was suppertime. She was rummaging for fish fingers when there was a series of crashes from over her head. Maria froze at first like the contents of her freezer, dropped the fish fingers back in the basket and raced for the hall.

'Who is up there?' she shouted, thinking for a confused moment that maybe Philip was home, hadn't called down when they came in.

'Mummy,' cried Alison, appearing guiltily at the top of the flight of narrow stairs leading up to Philip's study, 'Fooka's got out.'

'What are you doing up there?' shrieked her mother.

Alison stood, looking down, a small version of Maria, scared.

'You know it's absolutely forbidden for you to go up there, where I can't get to you. *Don't you?*' screamed Maria. 'Come down here *at once.*'

Alison began to come down, hanging back, one stair at a time, when there was another crash.

'Fooka's got out,' she repeated, looking back up the stairs. 'He flew upstairs and he's flying around making an awful mess in Daddy's study.'

'You mean, you *let* him out,' screeched Maria.

Her daughter backed up the stairs. Mummy seldom lost her temper; when she did, you looked out.

'Come here,' shouted Maria, panicking. Philip, mildly allergic to Fooka, disliked the parrot's foul-mouthed ways and had more than once threatened to get rid of him. If Phil came home and found Fooka wrecking his study, it would be the excuse he needed to call the taxidermist in.

'Daddy always locks his door,' cried Maria. 'Wasn't it locked?'

Alison shook her head, unwillingly coming down the last of the stairs.

'Right,' cried Maria, grabbing her shoulders, 'what's that bird doing?'

'He flew up and got in Daddy's room, and he's flying around at top speed banging into things. I think he's a bit scared because he hasn't been up there before.'

'Droppings all over your father's papers,' groaned Maria. 'How *could* you let him out of his cage?'

'He's knocked Daddy's lamp over. I was giving him some water,' said Alison.

Maria stared with dread up the long, narrow, uncarpeted flight of stairs. They were highly polished with smooth, rounded edges, lethal for her to climb. But Phil was moody enough these days to have Fooka put down. She made up her mind.

'Stay here,' she ordered Alison, 'and wait by my chair. I'll try to climb up there and then you bring the cage up and I'll try to make Fooka get back in it. Then you can bring him down, and bring me up some cloths and stuff, and we'll try to clear up the mess before Daddy gets home.'

'You can't, Mummy,' Alison cried.

'I can,' said Maria, grabbing the newel post, sliding out of her chair to the second stair.

'Mummy . . .' Alison sounded scared.

'Fooka won't get back in for anyone else,' snapped Maria, beginning to drag herself on her bottom, from stair to stair, 'so don't start grizzling. Do as I say.'

Eventually Alison obeyed orders and went to fetch the cage.

Maria stopped half-way up, arms aching. Her legs dangled frighteningly over the stair treads, hanging. She pulled them up, dreading bruises and cuts. She put her hands behind her on the next stair up, took a deep breath and hauled. When she looked down, Alison had gone. She got to the top, dragged herself across the small landing, into the room she had never seen, where her husband spent so much time.

'Damn you,' she said wearily to her parrot. Fooka, perched on a low table by a sofa, stared straight back, barely six inches away, yellow-rimmed eyes alert. She pulled herself into the room. 'You like doing this and upsetting everyone, don't you?' she snarled, dragging herself towards him.

As Alison brought the cage in, he squawked and flew to the top of the curtain rail, where a white smear appeared, as if aimed deliberately.

'Fooka,' Maria screeched, 'get in. *Now*.'

He hopped guiltily from foot to foot, wouldn't obey.

Maria pulled the cage upright and planted it on the floor.

'*In*.'

He sidled mournfully from side to side.

She scraped seed up in her palm and held it out. He was overfed, didn't care.

'You *bloody* bird, get inside your cage,' yelled Maria.

Miserably, Fooka flew to Philip's desk, hopped to his chair, on to the carpet and into his cage. He sat disconsolately, listening to the rage in Maria's voice. She banged his door shut, ignored the chastened bird and surveyed the damage. It wasn't so bad. He'd upended a lamp and a vase lay broken. That must have been one of the crashes. He'd put droppings on the carpet and curtains, and disordered Phil's desk, where he'd scrabbled among papers, folders and books. Sending Alison for cleaning things, she took time to look from her place on the floor at her husband's study, where she had never been before.

The bungalow had a huge roof, and it made a very large, high, airy room, brightly lit by dormer windows on both sides. It was furnished with masculine colours they'd all chosen together, white and grey and soft duck-egg green. The thick carpet was palest grey. Around the walls were bookcases, a stereo stack, more bookcases and a low glass table with a drinks tray. Then more bookcases, filled with bound journals, and rows of photographs of school and university days. Photographs of his father and mother hung on one wall, and himself as a baby, then a small boy. In the full light from one of the dormers was a big mahogany desk, which had had to be winched in through the roof with one of the windows taken out. It had been an expensive palaver, but the desk had once been his father's.

Maria pulled herself over and leaned against it. Anne had shown her the plans, she had helped furnish this room, helped choose the sofa that was a fold-down bed, the easy chair and stool by the stereo. For all its Conran furniture and Sanderson fabrics, Philip's study was a monument to the past, to the time before he had known her. It was a single man's room, with not one trace of his family. To stand in Phil's study was not to know he had a wife, or children, or any other home. She waited for Alison, ignored Fooka's beak rubbing, which meant he wanted to make up and be friends, and tried to come to grips with her own bewilderment. What did he do in a room like this? She was filled with a mounting sense of dread.

* * *

Alison took her time. Maria, too tired by her climb to go back to the stairs and argue with her daughter, pulled herself up into the leather chair behind the desk and began to tidy Fooka's mess. Papers lay disordered, letters, bills, photographs, company papers, accounts, a couple of postcards. One from Venice, one from Scotland. Maria turned them idly over, not recognising the signatures. She picked up the photos. A woman of maybe thirty-something looked out with serious, slanting eyes from an oval face with a small, pointed chin. The photograph was black and white. She could have been perhaps blonde or red-haired; straight shoulder-length hair was held back from her face by a twisted scarf. What looked like fabric hung in the background, curtains perhaps, plain, untextured. Dull. It might have been taken in a booth, or against the furnishings of a cheap hotel.

She turned it over; there was nothing written or printed on the back. She began to sort feverishly through the desk, throwing aside bills and brown envelopes. A thin sheaf of airmail paper lay in the bottom of one of Philip's drawers, in which a key stood, unlocked. Maria read the halting, stilted English. Then she sat, the paper, evidence of something more, limp in her fingers, before her. She looked at the photo again, went through the rest of the drawers. In the last, she found a slim leather wallet, and inside a dozen or more colour photos of the woman, sitting on a beach in a one-piece bathing costume, laughing, her hands pelting the untanned, lean English body beside her with sand. Philip was laughing, too. Her hair was tied up in a ribbon and she was strawberry blonde, with long, slender legs. Maria looked at the letters again.

'Honor. What a funny name for my husband's mistress,' murmured Maria, the photographs slipping into her lap. She sat, quite stunned, light-headed, floating off into a make-believe world, imagining them together on some foreign, nameless beach. Imagining them together . . .

She turned at the sound of his voice.

'I see you've been prying.'

Philip stood, his briefcase in his hand, crumpled and tired.

'Fooka got out,' said Maria dully. 'I came to stop him making a mess of your things.'

'Fooka got out,' he repeated, as though it didn't mean anything.

'Alison let him out and he flew up here and she came up after him. I can't stop them, Phil, all the time. They are old enough to do what they will and I can't always stop them. I can't run after them.'

'Did I forget to lock the door?' he asked, as if that were something absolutely extraordinary.

'You must have. I have no key.'

She turned the photographs in her fingers.

'Who is this?'

'Honor. As you have already found out for yourself,' he added, looking at the letters spread before her.

'Who is Honor?'

'An East German.'

She waited. He rubbed his nose wearily.

'I met her several years ago, when I was in West Berlin on business.'

'Do you love her?'

He snorted with mirthless laughter.

'Why is that always the first question? Women think it's so important.'

'I'm not women,' said his wife. 'I would like to know.'

He put his briefcase down and went to a bookcase. He pulled out an atlas of the world, a heavy volume that seemed not to close properly when unwedged from the rest. He drew out several black-and-white prints, handed them silently to Maria. She examined them with great care, then looked at him, her face ashen.

'*Men* and women?' she said, dazed. 'You?'

'You see, love has nothing to do with it.'

'What has to do with it, then?' Her lips felt stiff and cold.

'They are good at making you want things you never would normally dream of. Because I was ashamed, and never wanted you to know, they could blackmail me. Now you have made a waste of it all, by seeing them anyway.'

Maria looked up at him.

'You can't claim *this* is my fault.'

'You have made it all worthless. So long as you didn't find out, there was a point to it.'

'A point to *what*?'

'Betraying my country, so as not to betray you any further. I did certain things, so that they wouldn't show you those photos. You've made everything I've done, to protect you, a mockery.'

Her head swam. He was an angry, desperate stranger, with twisted, crazy reasoning.

'You're a *spy*.' She began to laugh. He was teasing her. 'You? James Bond of Barnsbury? Honor Blackman. Oh, come *on*, tell me this is all a joke.'

Alison came in and put the dustpan on the floor beside her, and Maria pulled her quickly on to her lap, like a shield, still laughing.

'Daddy's telling jokes.'

The horrible photographs lay before her. Obscene. She snatched them up, hid them from Alison, stopped laughing.

'What are you going to do?' she asked Philip.

Alison wriggled off her lap and glared at Fooka.

'He messed up your room, Daddy,' she said virtuously.

'Go downstairs, Alison,' he ordered.

She hung around, pouting.

'Alison.'

'You sound tired to death,' Maria said. 'Whatever are we going to do?'

Alison stamped hard on every step as she went down, to protest at being sent away. Maria gathered her wits and tried to guess what would be best to do, how to give them both some time.

'Will you help me, carry me down? We'll tackle the mess in the morning.'

He didn't move.

'Please, Phil?'

'I tried to believe you'd never find out,' he told her in a deadly monotone. 'She's a whore. We spent the odd weekend on the Black Sea, during business trips.'

She pushed the glossies towards him. 'Did those happen on the *odd weekend* as well?'

'I got drunk. They pushed them at us. Maybe there were things in the drink. I don't know.'

'Us?'

Philip's mouth set in a line.

'Don't ask,' he said, and she knew it would be no good going any further.

'They knew you'd be weak,' she said sadly. 'Didn't they? You had a paralysed wife. You wanted more . . . *This* kind of more.'

She didn't want to look at the photographs, at tangles of limbs. Who was doing what? She shuddered.

'No, I told you, they set me up. I didn't go looking,' he said drearily.

'I think you did,' she said. 'Otherwise, why go back? Why go back for weekends?'

She saw his mind close off.

'I always loved you. No one else,' he said.

'It isn't hopeless,' she cried in terror, seeing utter despair in his face. 'Now I know, they can't blackmail you any more.'

'You don't understand. I've dug my own grave. I'm small fry, Maria,' he tried to explain wearily. 'I gave them a few odds and ends. Bits of control systems, computer solutions to things they could work out for themselves only they seem to prefer to get it by industrial spying.'

'I didn't know you were political,' she exclaimed. 'You never talked much about politics. The Eastern bloc, for goodness' sake? You always vote for the Tories.'

'I'm not *political*,' he snapped. It showed how little she grasped. 'I'm a small businessman who got caught up in it. It's nothing to do with what I *think*. No one ever bothered with what I *think*.' He had always known that if this moment came, he would be able to explain nothing.

'*Blunt*.'

'Blunt.' He laughed. 'I was terrified the book would lead them to me. It was a joke. I'm so insignificant, no one would bother. Being scared all the time makes you paranoid.'

She could not get up, go to him, love him, rescue them both.

He took a cigar from his breast pocket, struck a match. A curl of cigar smoke drifted across.

'Happiness is lighting up when all seems lost . . .' She tried to jolly him, and failed.

He threw the glossies into the waste-paper bin.

'These are copies. They have the negatives,' he said, setting a second match to them. They caught and flared.

'At least you won't have to look at them ever again,' he said softly, walking away, out of the room. The paper burned brightly.

'Philip,' she screamed, throwing herself to the floor in her terror, useless legs holding her back. 'Philip!'

Flames crackled in the bin. His footsteps went down the uncarpeted stairs, he said something to the children. She heard the door slam. She opened her mouth to scream, and not a sound came out. By the time the neighbours called the fire brigade it was much too late.

'A paralysed woman died in a fire in Barnsbury, North London, last night,' said the radio news reader. 'The police would like to interview her husband, who has been named as Philip Howard.'

Sadie was standing still, holding the coffee pot, stunned, when the phone rang.

'Yes,' she gasped, snatching the receiver.

An awful noise came from the other end, and someone said, 'Give it to me.'

'Who is this?' cried Sadie, terrified.

There was some kind of tussle and then Gosling said, 'Sadie?'

'*Gosling*.'

'You heard it on the news? I'm sorry no one rang you first. It's been such a night . . .'

He told someone to let him hold on to the phone a moment, and Sadie realised the terrible sounds were Rosalie's crying. Figgin was saying something faintly in the background.

'Maria died in the fire,' said Gosling.

Sadie swallowed, her throat suddenly dry as bone. 'And Philip?'

Gosling paused.

'Sit down,' he said gently, 'and have you got anyone there?'

'No. Yes. I mean, I'll sit down and there's no one here. Where's Philip, Gosling?'

He swallowed. She heard it quite clearly over the line.

'He's hanged himself.'

Blood roared in her head.

'Are you all right? Dolly is on her way over to you already. The children are safe, just shocked. They'll come out of hospital later today,' he said.

'Thank you,' she whispered and was suddenly so weak, she dropped the receiver.

She sat by Jean Hargreaves' old-fashioned black phone and was sitting there still when Dolly came pounding on the front door, calling her name.

They made hot sweet tea.

'Did Philip kill her?'

Dolly shook her head and they retreated from the unthinkable. It was hard to think of things to say.

'Mags and Sissy are taking it in turns to be with the children. Rosalie's in an awful state. Frances has been ringing and screaming at her from Los Angeles and Rosalie is threatening a breakdown if Frances comes here. Michelangelo tried to talk sense into Frances, said there was nothing she could do, but she's still threatening to get on a plane.'

'Eve,' said Sadie. 'I can't leave Eve with Rosalie five more minutes.'

'Gosling's got Eve under his arm like he's had six of his own. Don't you worry.'

Bright autumn sunlight played on the walls. The old grey mares grazed in the meadow beyond the gnarled garden fence. Maria, here yesterday, had drunk tea in the garden.

'Maria is *dead*?' said Sadie. 'Are you sure?'

The news just wouldn't sink in.

'I'm terribly, terribly sorry,' said Dolly.

Chapter Fifty-Seven

'Philip *era uno spione*!?' bleated Nonna, arriving post-haste from Rome. She wheeled her luggage towards the car park at Heathrow. Jove trotted behind, trying to get a word in edgeways.

'It seems so. Someone seems to have been making use of the poor chap. Not that anyone tells us anything.'

'They do the third degree in Rome,' snapped Nonna, her voice rising indignantly, '*un' interrogazione*. Two men in coats,' she snorted contemptuously.

'What's wrong with coats?' asked Jove, baffled.

'Did not take them off. Sat in my sitting room in coats asking questions. What was I supposed to know? No manners. Oafs.'

'Philip was being blackmailed.'

They stood in the car park while Jove found his keys.

'We have inquests, insurance people crawling all over us, security men, the police, the press. The neighbours are having the time of their lives,' said Jove grimly, climbing into the car.

Nonna stared out as he negotiated his way out of the airport, turning towards London.

'Do they say,' she hesitated, 'do they say he murdered Maria?'

'We'll never know what he *meant* to do, but he may have started the fire,' Jove said.

'He killed himself because he killed her,' muttered Nonna.

'I wouldn't fancy a prison sentence, in his shoes,' answered Jove. 'They'd have had to have put him in solitary for his own protection, once the others found out what he'd done to a woman who couldn't run away. The fire started in a waste-paper bin. Someone was burning photographs.'

'Maria?'

'I don't know. God knows what Maria was doing up there in that firetrap, anyway. Alison told the policewoman that Fooka got out and Maria went after him and Phil came home and they had some kind of a row.'

Nonna fingered her old black beads and tried to think, looking, in dense black mourning, much, much older.

'One thing I've learned,' said Jove, sad and angry, 'is that you can never, ever really know someone. I'd have staked my life on Phil as a decent, honest, right-thinking bloke, and look at what . . . and my sister . . .'

He had to pull over. Nonna waited until he'd stopped crying. They sat with the engine running, crushed by the enormity of it all.

'The children?'

'Quiet. It's very hard to know what to do for the best. Mags and Sissy are awfully put out. Maria left everything to the kids if she died, and named Sadie as guardian. It seems Sadie agreed to look after the children if anything happened to Phil and Maria. Well, it has.'

Nonna was silent for a long time.

'Is not time for taking offences,' she said at last.

When they arrived in Islington Anne Howard appeared in the doorway, pale and haggard, Eve in her arms. Figgin looked over her shoulder, very calm. Unnaturally calm, thought Jove angrily. Bloody Buddhist nonsense. Jove mopped his brow. Death, disgrace and catastrophe, all in one week, while good for publicity and his restaurant business, were altogether overwhelming.

'Could do with a bit of Buddhist cloud nine myself,' he muttered, pushing past to take Nonna's bags indoors.

Figgin nodded courteously.

'Oh, bugger off,' snapped Jove.

'All right, mate,' said Figgin gently, touching his arm.

'Sorry,' mumbled Jove.

* * *

When Dolly had to go home, leaving Sadie on her own again, the thought of Maria burning, trapped, unable to run, tormented her, an endless horror. She jumped again when the telephone rang, stared at it, dreading more bad news. Gabriella's childlike voice was on the other end, ringing to say she had been to the hospital again, and the scan had been clear.

'I'm glad,' said Sadie mechanically.

'My mother said someone she knows, who she was talking to about it, asked her if you'd cure her, too. There's this meeting, where people go to see faith healers, and she wondered if you'd go too.'

'No,' cried Sadie, appalled by the idea of getting into dark and murky areas of the unknown at a time like this. 'Absolutely not. You got better all by yourself.'

'Oh, no. It was you.'

'Look,' said Sadie, at her wits' end, 'Gabriella, there have been disasters since I saw you in hospital and I have too much to cope with. I couldn't heal anything, and I probably never did. Tell your mother I'm sorry, I couldn't possibly go to that kind of meeting.'

Gabriella, offended, put down the phone.

Sadie marched up and down. Even Gabriella Miller's whiny little voice was better than the silence, better than being completely alone in this horrible place. She made up her mind.

'It's time to arrange to go home,' she said bleakly. She would try to get her flat back.

She drove to Hackney, then, without meaning to, took a large detour, found herself standing opposite Maria's burned-out house. Blackened windows gaped, shockingly empty. She imagined orange flames, smoke, the awful screaming the neighbours had heard, described so vividly to the press. Maria, lying helpless, her worst dread come true; fire.

'They take my chair away, because it's a fire hazard in the gangway,' she'd complain if she went to the cinema, the theatre, any public place. 'But if there's a fire, *I'm* a hazard.'

'If I'm there, I'll carry you,' Sadie would promise. 'Don't worry, I'd get you out safely.'

Standing on the pavement, in tears, Sadie thought desolately that she hadn't been there, she hadn't got Maria out.

'You all right?' A woman came out of a nearby house and stood looking across the road. 'Did you know them?'

Sadie turned away, crying, went back to her car.

'Well, some people,' said the neighbour, going back indoors.

Pulling herself together, Sadie wondered whether to go round to Rosalie's. She ought to see Eve. Later. She'd first do what she'd come to do, see her tenant in Hackney, try to get her flat back, go home.

'You can't. It's in the agreement,' said the woman. 'I've got another four months.'

'I need it,' said Sadie wearily. 'I wrote you a letter. Surely you can understand. I've got a baby to look after, and my husband is selling our house. I've nowhere to take the baby, except here.'

'I can't help that,' retorted her tenant. 'I've got to find somewhere else, too, you know.'

'It is very hard, a woman on her own with a child.'

'Four months. I'll give you notice, if you like, and if I can find somewhere sooner, I will.'

'Please,' begged Sadie.

'I think I'm being very reasonable,' the woman said. 'A lot of people would stand on their rights.'

Places ran at random through her overwrought mind. Rosalie, stay in Epping until the notice was up, rent with the money she'd get when the house was sold, jump off a bridge.

'Please put it in writing, then,' she said.

'I'll do it now,' the woman said indignantly.

Sadie left with the scented pink envelope in her pocket, furious. She got in her car, shaking.

'Can't drive like this,' she muttered, pulling the key out of the ignition again. 'I'll cause an accident.'

Streetlamps shone on the shedding chestnut trees of the park, crisp leaves lay thick in the gutters. They reminded her of times when life was good. She would walk round the edge of the park, to Dolly, calm down in fresh air. Dolly would help her decide what to do.

Two youths watched her out of the corners of their eyes. The woman walked quite slowly, as if she were tired. She had a shoulder bag with a thin strap, flat shoes, good clothes. They stood beneath a streetlamp, seemingly uncertain which way to go. The park gate in front of them, they looked round, appearing to debate direction. Sadie noticed them, smart, well-groomed, one half-caste, face like an etching, all beautiful, sharp lines; one a good-looking blond boy, dressed in something made dirty-yellow by the sodium lamps. She passed them. Hair pricked the back of her neck. She wanted to turn, hurried on, instead. She felt them come up behind her. One ran round, looked her full in the face, barring her way. The half-caste grabbed at her neck, pulling her down into the crisp leaves in the gutter.

She was able to think quite clearly. She'd read that muggers didn't like noise, ran if their victims fought back. She opened her mouth to scream. Casually, calculatingly, they kicked her, winding her agonisingly tender stomach.

'Bitch,' whispered the half-caste, tugging her bag from her fists. The other stood over her, kicking her, almost disinterested. The strap on her bag broke and he stood on her wrist.

'Give,' he snarled.

She crawled after them, tearing her hands and knees on gravel, saw them leap into a car she had not noticed, around the corner, engine running. As they drove away with a squeal of tyres, she screamed, and people opened their doors, came running.

* * *

Someone made her hot, sweet tea in a steamy kitchen. The clock on an oven said ten o'clock. A policeman arrived after a while.

'We may catch them,' he said, 'but it's not very likely.'

'They didn't look like muggers,' cried Sadie.

'What do muggers look like?'

She knew he wanted to catch her out saying 'black'.

'Poor,' she said. 'I thought they'd look poor. They were smarter than me. That's what I noticed, how well they were dressed.'

'Women walking alone after dark give them plenty of practice. They sound very professional. I don't doubt they buy their gear in Next,' he said sourly. 'Will you come down to the station tomorrow and make a full statement.'

'Yes,' she said.

'Someone coming to take you home?' he asked.

The woman whose house they were in said she was welcome to use the phone.

'I'll be there straightaway,' cried Rosalie, not stopping to ask questions. Sadie sighed with relief. She was going back to Islington at last, going home.

Chapter Fifty-Eight

'Would you go to court and give evidence, if we catch them?' asked the detective, taking her statement in the police station the following day.

'Definitely,' she said, touching her sore wrist.

'Good. They'll go on assaulting women until we do.'

'They'd obviously had plenty of practice. They attacked me as though they'd choreographed it. They must have done it a lot of times to get that good at it.'

'Yes,' he said, writing things down. 'Can you tell me what was in your bag?'

'Purse.'

'Much in it?'

'About thirty pounds.'

He pulled a face.

'Uninsured cash.'

'Cheque book, credit card, banker's card, keys and my wedding ring.'

He glanced automatically at her ringless left hand.

'It isn't valid any more, so I kept it in my purse,' she said lightly, trying to ward him off asking questions.

'Keys to your house? Car?'

'Keys to the house I'm living in, a house I no longer live in, and my car, yes.'

'You should get your locks changed at once. If they find your address, which is presumably on things in your bag, you could have a visit.'

She looked desperately weary, he thought. Battered.

'It's hard work, isn't it, getting mugged?' she said. 'By the time you've run round cancelling everything and changing locks . . . I hope you catch them.'

There was a knock on the door of the shabby interview room.

'Yes,' he shouted.

A hand pushed the door open, and someone asked her interviewer for a moment.

'I'll be a minute,' he said, getting up. 'I'll be right back. We're nearly finished.'

'I . . .' stammered Sadie.

He went out of the door and closed it behind him.

John Campling came back, instead.

'I saw your name in the book. I told him I'd take over. Are you all right?'

She shook her head. If she started crying, she wouldn't be able to stop, and he'd go away again in disgust. Remembering, her face flamed. They stood, warily waiting for the other to say something. He began.

'That day in the club, I was hasty and clumsy. I've regretted it more than I can tell you.'

'So have I,' she said, her throat tight.

'I didn't know how to put it right, or I would have done so. I thought you might not want to see me again.'

'I never felt that at all.'

He folded his arms and sat back, tipping his chair.

'My wife had just died. I was touchy and tactless.'

'I'm sorry,' she said mechanically.

'It was a relief. I was relieved and heartbroken at the same time and for a long while I didn't handle things too well.'

'Yes,' she said simply.

'I heard about Maria Howard. I wanted to see if there was anything I could do, but I didn't know where you were. I went to your flat but there was someone else there, and she wasn't helpful.'

'No one can do anything. Do you want me to finish my statement?'

He pulled a biro out of his breast pocket.

'We'll finish the police statement here, and then I'm going to take you somewhere quiet, to finish the rest of it.'

'Finish what rest of it?' she asked stupidly.

'Us,' he said brusquely. He looked at the closely written sheet of paper. 'What is an invalid wedding ring?'

'My husband left me. I took off my ring and it was in the purse they stole. We'll be divorced soon. It was a joke to say it was invalid. That other man must have taken me seriously.'

'We're a literal lot,' he remarked, unsmiling.

Sadie gave a sickly smile. 'I do better than this, most of the time,' she joked feebly.

'Let's get the formalities over,' he said.

'Nonna is waiting outside for me,' she told him, as she signed each page of her statement. 'Maria's grandmother.'

'Can I meet Maria's grandmother?' he asked gravely.

She hesitated.

'Or not,' he said. 'Perhaps this is not a good time. Too soon. Not appropriate.'

'Aren't you on duty?'

'This is duty. Follow-up of a mugging.'

She glanced at his well-cut suit and discreet tie.

'You wouldn't usually do mundane things like this, would you?'

'I can be as mundane as I like,' he said. 'It's one of the privileges of a little bit of seniority.'

She signed the last page of her statement. Nonna was waiting. She sat, unable to move, didn't want to leave him.

He was a good man, good, ordinary and decent. He would be at home with them, and they with him. She saw him in her mind's eye, with Rosalie and Figgin, Nonna, Dolly and Gosling, with all of them. She'd never thought of it before, seen their ordinary goodness, their marvellous, everyday, unstated kindness, their unpretentious good-heartedness that made almost a virtue of their many faults.

'What are you thinking?'

'You just made me think,' she said, confused.

John Campling smiled, opened the door, waited.

'Come and meet Nonna,' said Sadie.

Chapter Fifty-Nine

With profound relief Sadie locked up Jean Hargreaves' cottage and moved in with Rosalie and Figgin, Nonna and little Eve.

'We keep talking about moving, but I don't suppose we will. Figgin's putting his up for sale,' Rosalie said, making up the room next to Nonna.

'It's one of the things about second times around, isn't it? Having two homes, I mean. Which one do you leave?'

Eve lay on her back on her mother's bed, pulling sleepy faces.

'You've been wonderful,' Sadie went on. 'I couldn't have coped if you hadn't had her.'

'She helped me cope,' answered Rosalie. 'There were moments when having to get up for her was the only thing that made me get up at all.'

Mourning-black didn't suit Rosalie, Sadie thought, made her look washed out and a little bit brassy. She'd looked like that after Giovanni died.

'Figgin believes Maria will come back, reincarnated. Do you believe that?' asked Sadie, curiously.

Rosalie grimaced.

'If it keeps him happy, he's welcome to think whatever he likes. I don't mind the trips, ashrams and gurus. I quite like saris occasionally. But I don't care for the idea of coming back as a cat or a rat, or being a baby of someone I don't know. Makes me feel funny. So I let him get on with it.'

'I thought it might help when people die, thinking like that. Figgin always seems so calm.'

'Whatever you think, it doesn't change the fact that she's

gone. Anyway it'd mean Philip's coming back, after what he did, and where's the justice in that?' finished Rosalie indignantly.

'I have nightmares about it,' said Sadie.

'We all have nightmares,' said Rosalie shortly.

Sadie put a pile of underwear into a chest of drawers and closed her empty case.

'Whatever am I going to do about the children?' she asked.

'There's no rush,' said Rosalie.

'They need to be settled. And there's school to think about.'

Eve gurgled and turned on her stomach, dozing fitfully.

'She needs to be settled, too. So do I.'

'Mags will keep them, if you want. We'll all muck in.'

'Dougal's had a very good offer on our house. He's been so decent, and I've made him take some of the money, but there's still a lot left. And I'll sell the flat for a good price as well. Hackney is an area where prices are shooting up.'

'You won't be short of pennies, then,' said Rosalie.

'No.'

Rosalie wrinkled her nose thoughtfully.

'Why not buy a house there, then? Stay near us.'

'I'll never live in the East End again,' Sadie said decidedly. 'It's a frightening place.'

'Sounds like you need a desert island,' Rosalie observed, with a tired attempt at humour.

'What we need is somewhere right away from the scandal, from people pointing and awful memories.'

'You can't take those children far,' cried Rosalie, alarmed. 'They've got to stay part of the family.'

'They need somewhere safe, tucked away, but near . . .'

'What?' demanded Rosalie, pushing Eve back into the middle of Sadie's bed, stopping her rolling off. 'What have you got your mouth open like that for?'

'I've got it,' said Sadie.

'Got what?'

'The answer to the problem of where to live.'

'What?' demanded Rosalie, frustrated.

'Let me think. Can I use the phone?'

Rosalie picked Eve up.

'If you're going downstairs, I'll put her in her cot.'

Sadie left her holding the baby.

Old Mary Llewellyn listened carefully.

'I'll have it unlocked and swept out,' she said, 'but you couldn't possibly live in it. It's fit only for pigs.'

'Not as it is,' said Sadie. 'But I could live in it if we rebuilt it. I'll bring someone with me who is an architect. Do you think I could build on to it?'

'Plenty of people do. There's holiday homes going up all over the place.'

'This wouldn't be a holiday home. I'd move back to stay. With the children I've been left by Maria to look after.'

'I'll see to it, then,' promised Mary Llewellyn.

On a raw March day, just after midday, they walked across the dyke to the great-aunts' cottage, standing untouched and unchanged on the edge of the salt marshes, swept by winter winds from the grey North Sea.

'Can it be extended and done up and turned into a family house?' Sadie asked anxiously.

Anne Howard walked around it very slowly, examining walls and roofs and boundaries.

'There's plenty of room. If we get planning permission, yes. I'll draw you some plans.'

'What do you think?' Sadie asked the others, who had not been there before.

'You'll have to lay a proper road,' said Figgin, eyeing the mud.

'With a car, you are not too far away,' remarked Nonna, huddled in winter woollies, so well wrapped up she bizarrely resembled a black toilet roll. 'We come for summer holidays. Buckets and spades. Lots of *bambini* and picnics. *Sì*.'

It was the seal of approval.

John Campling came back from inspecting the overgrown garden, waist-high in brambles. 'We'll have to start from scratch,' he remarked. Sadie bit her lip at the *we*, and he smiled.

Figgin strolled around with his hands in his pockets, studied the landscape with brilliant blue eyes and said it was a magical place, and what about solar panels. Rosalie held Eve on her hip, remarked, 'She'll be able to run about safely here. No traffic.'

'The village school is closed,' said Mary. 'They'll have to go into Hunstanton.'

'It's no distance by car,' said Sadie. 'We'll have to rely on cars, and buses when there are any. Country people do.'

'It will be exciting to build for my grandchildren,' said Anne Howard. 'Something I can do for them, after . . .'

Eve crowed in Rosalie's arms, wanting to get down.

'The village'll take her under its wing,' said Mary Llewellyn.

'She'll be no village idiot,' said Sadie sharply. 'She'll have a normal life, go to school. There are degrees of Down's, and they think she isn't too bad.'

'I meant, people will help,' said Mary softly. 'They keep themselves to themselves round here, and they're not quick to come forward, but you belong here already.'

'John's a foreigner, from Norwich,' said Sadie, taking Eve from Rosalie.

'Perhaps I'll get them to transfer me back there. Go back to being a country cop.'

'I doubt that, somehow,' said Sadie, smiling.

'There's no hurry to make decisions,' he answered. 'It'll take ages to get this place into shape.'

'I haven't got ages,' said Sadie. 'The children need to settle down.'

'There's a cottage to rent in the village, near mine,' suggested Mary Llewellyn.

'If you are going to do it, do it,' ordered Nonna, muffled by scarves, bored with skirting the issue.

'If we leave my grandchildren with Mags until this is ready, we are talking about not less than six months, and that'll be asking for miracles. Maybe closer to a year. It'll be much harder for them to move by then,' said Anne Howard.

'The cottage to let is the other end of the village. We could walk there in fifteen minutes,' urged Mary Llewellyn.

'Talk, talk, talk,' sighed Nonna.

'Let's go and see this cottage,' said Sadie.

'Yes,' crowed Nonna, setting off at speed. Parked on the main road was a little convoy of cars, which had brought them down to Norfolk, headed by the racing-green Morgan. Nonna clutched the keys in her fist and trotted back. Despite a terrible row with Her Lady about the means by which it had come to fall into her hands, and a nagging conscience, she had driven it all the way to Norfolk in a state of ecstatic delight.

Chapter Sixty

Sadie took the cottage in Ditchwell and was busy with plans to move. Her divorce was well on its way, the house in Hampstead nearly sold. Dougal got his job in Swansea, and he and Pauline and their baby daughter left London. The flat in Hackney sold the minute it went on the estate agent's books. Very gradually, life began to return to some kind of normality; at least there was the hope of it, after all the tragedy and doubt.

Dolly was thinking about it, and about her own future, as she poked her fire several weeks after the trip to Ditchwell and fitted a crumpet on to a toasting fork. An April wind wailed round the chimney and hooted eerily down to where coals glowed. Gosling's long legs stretched either side of her as she sat on the floor, leaning back against his chair.

'I've decided something,' she said, pushing the butter closer to the fire to soften.

'Good. When are we going to move to a place of our own?'

'This *is* my own,' she said quietly.

'*Our* own.'

'That's what I've been making decisions about. I had a long talk with Sadie, and I'm going to Norfolk with her.'

He sat up in astonishment. 'You are joking.'

'I am not joking. I've given in my notice. I'm getting out of social work. I'm going to stop running round after people who aren't in the least bit interested, and I'm going to make beautiful sweaters for people who are interested, and who'll enjoy them. I'm going into business.'

'What about me?' he demanded, stunned.

'What about you?' she asked calmly.

He stared at her, nonplussed. This wasn't the Dolly he knew.

'I thought,' she said, buttering the crumpet, 'if you care about me, you'll either come with me, or get a transfer, or take up something different, or whatever. If you want to, we can make it work. But only if you want to. I'll make it work because it's what I want, and I finally realised that that's all that matters. That I live my own life.'

'I'm a fireman,' he protested. 'I have a job. I can't just drop it.'

'You don't have to drop anything. They need firemen in Norfolk.'

'That isn't the same.'

'I thought it wouldn't be,' said Dolly. 'You could come and see me, then, when you've got time off.'

'I thought we were going to live together.' Gosling almost whined, caught himself, and coughed to cover it up.

'I'll be living in Norfolk. Where you'll be living, and whether it's with me, is what I'm saying is up to you to decide.'

He cast around for dampeners to put upon her plan. 'You don't know anything about running a business.'

'Then I'll learn. I'll take some courses and go to evening classes. I'll learn accounts and book-keeping and things like that. I'll enjoy it.'

'It takes capital.' He seized upon another problem. 'Money.'

'Property in London has rocketed. Norfolk's much cheaper. A little one-bedroom place will suit me. The difference between selling here and buying there will help me start up.'

'East Anglia's depressed,' he said. 'Like me.'

'Quite,' she said cheerfully. 'It's cheap at the moment. And there'll be plenty of outworkers.'

'You're serious.'

Dolly handed him a cooling crumpet.

'Absolutely.'

He pondered, looking at her with a very strange expression.

'Is this going to be the end of us?' he asked diffidently.

Dolly wanted to laugh.

'Only if you want it to be. You can live in a flat if you want, in a concrete tower. I'll knit in my little cottage, and we can visit. I think we could be very happy that way. I've never been good at domestic stuff, or at really living with other people. I'm better on my own.'

'Well, I'm blowed,' he said, his world temporarily upside down. He was silent for ages.

'Doll?'

'Hum?'

He leaned and slid his arms around her.

'Will you come and see me? In my concrete tower? It wouldn't be all one way?'

'I'll come and see you and you can come and see me.'

'No Norfolk farmers?' He tried to keep anxiety out of his voice, and failed.

She laughed.

'I'll be as faithful as you. How about that?'

He grinned. It was cosy sitting there with her in his arms, the wind moaning outside.

'All right,' he announced, leaning back again. 'It's a funny arrangement, but let's give it our best. We'll suck it and see.'

Dolly lay back on her elbows, watching the fire dying down, dreaming of a little place by the sea, a shop of her own in King's Lynn, visiting craft fairs all round the country, selling beautiful hand-knits, orders, maybe, from Harrods one day. Bliss.

'You know, I think this could work,' she said.

Gosling sighed.

'You're a remarkable woman, Doll,' he said.

'I know,' said Dolly. They both smiled, liking each other immensely.

Chapter Sixty-One

The stone Norfolk cottage Sadie rented was cramped after the big London houses they were all used to. They moved, helped by Jove, Nonna, Rosalie and a rented van, one damp Saturday and the rain outside did nothing to lift their spirits as they all picnicked uncomfortably on bread and cheese and pickle and strong tea, trying to cheer each other up. The children sat very quietly, subdued and withdrawn. Even Eve seemed to feel despondent.

'I'm beginning to wonder if I've done the right thing, making them come here. They'd got used to Mags and now it's another big upheaval and losing people again,' Sadie muttered anxiously to Rosalie and Nonna as the others got ready to go back to London. For the first time, she felt frightened at being left alone with three children and the future to face, all of it unknown. Neither offered an opinion, aware of too many uncertainties, and the moment passed in kisses and hugs and goodbyes and a hasty departure before any more was said.

Sadie closed her front door on the rain, which was coming down harder than ever, and turned to find the children in a little row at the bottom of the stairs, watching her with guarded, wary eyes.

'Hey, you guys,' she said, trying to joke, 'we're on the same side.'

The children simply stood, unnervingly silent, almost hostile. Sadie went into the living room and began to put matches to fire lighters in the prepared grate, to bring some life to the place, brighten it up. Rain rattled and ran in torrents down window panes and she realised that she had forgotten how savagely weather can sweep the Norfolk coast. She blew on the coals and after a while they caught and began to glow.

'Look,' she called into the hallway. 'Come and get warm by the fire.'

Eve forgot her gloom and played happily enough with wrapping paper and odds and ends, but Jamie and Alison sat on the bottom step and looked daggers; the next time Sadie went to look, they'd gone upstairs, where she could hear nothing but profound silence and the gurgling of rain in the guttering.

'All right,' she said to Eve. 'If that's how they want to play it, we'll just have to sit it out until they thaw, won't we? But don't let's you and me go to war, or I don't think I'll cope.' Little Eve climbed into her lap and sucked her thumb contentedly, watching the leaping flames in the fire, while Sadie hung on to her for dear life, overcome by loneliness and the silent, hostile presences upstairs that would somehow have to be won over, though she wasn't at all sure how. She looked longingly at the telephone, wondered about making a call.

Rosalie answered, her voice critical. 'So soon?' she said. 'Can't you stay anywhere five minutes, Sadie?'

Stung, Sadie defended herself. 'I'm sorry. Send them to Mags, where they won't be angry. Tell them to come downstairs, downstairs, downstairs. Maria couldn't come downstairs . . .' Sadie heard herself begin to weep.

'"If anything happens to me and Phil, will you take my children,"' asked Maria reproachfully, haloed by flame. '"You'll take my children, my children, my children . . ."'

'No,' gasped Sadie and woke up with a jolt, dozing over Eve's head, lulled for a moment by the heat from the fire. The chintz cushions in old-fashioned rose patterns were scratchy on her cheek, unfamiliar. She sat in a half stupor, tired and low, wishing the phone would ring, or Mary Llewellyn call round, but everyone was leaving her alone, tactfully letting her get on in her own way. Even Dolly. Sadie's spirits sank even further and in the grey light from rain-lashed windows and the glow of firelight, she saw difficult and discouraging times ahead.

* * *

'Alison and Jamie are *abominable*,' she told old Mary two months later. 'They hate everything and everyone, and me in particular.'

'Of course.' Mary knew about children, having taught them for forty years. 'After losing their mother and father, they hate everyone who isn't their mother and father. And then, they are angry with their mother and father for leaving them. So who do you expect them to trust? What else do you expect?'

'Fewer tantrums and threats to walk back to London and screaming matches and sulks would do for a start,' snapped Sadie, battle weary. 'And a few nights' uninterrupted sleep.'

'Nightmares?'

'Worse. Night terrors,' answered Sadie. 'I can't even have people to stay, they are so awful. It's embarrassing. Someone'll have the NSPCC round if they go on the way they are because it sounds as if I'm doing something dreadful to them. They scare poor Eve to death sometimes.'

'It's grief,' said Mary equably. 'They'll come out of it when they're ready. It isn't getting bottled up, and you're doing all the right things.'

'Am I?' said Sadie doubtfully.

'Yes,' said the old woman firmly.

But the pitched battles went on, and outwardly calm, inwardly she raged, wondering if she had made a promise to Maria that Maria's children would never let her keep.

Moonlight spilled across Eve's cot and made bars on the carpet at the foot of Sadie's bed. It was a huge, old fashioned mahogany bed with a feather mattress, all billows and hummocks into which she disappeared beneath a pile of woollen blankets. The winter nights were long and freezing and bright with stars and tonight a full moon shone.

Alison shifted from one frozen foot to the other and pinched Jamie hard. He burst into tears of shock and surprise.

'What . . . ?' Sadie scrambled out of her deep sleep and deep mound of feathers and found two shivering children standing in bright pools of light, Jamie's tears silver on his cheeks.

'He was crying for Mummy and so I brought him to you, to make him shut up,' said Alison.

'I was *not*.'

Eve stirred in her cot and woke, pressing her face against the side of the bars.

'He was, and he wants to get in your bed,' said Alison, pushing him forwards. 'Go on.'

Sadie put on the light on her bedtable.

'I *don't*,' yelped Jamie, fully awake and indignant.

His sister glowered and Sadie saw her eyes red-rimmed with crying, her small face a mask of determination. It had been she who had wept, come looking for comfort, marching Jamie before her to save face.

'He wants you,' Alison said, her gaze on the floor.

Sadie eyed her shrewdly. 'You look as though you could do with getting in and warming up, too,' she offered, holding the blankets up so they could creep under.

'Brothers . . .' sniffed Alison, crawling in, wiping her nose on her pyjama sleeve.

'I was asleep until you came and woke me up,' protested Jamie, his teeth chattering.

Sadie said it really didn't matter who woke who up, because they could all get warmed up together and go back to sleep. 'Shall we?' she asked, moving over to make room. Jamie sighed and climbed in. Sadie put off the light.

'Me,' said little Eve, looking through her bars.

'And Eve,' said Alison in a muffled kind of voice.

Sadie obediently lifted Eve from her cot and wedged her between Alison and Jamie.

'You look after her,' she said, turning the light off again, 'and let's all go to sleep.'

'I miss Mummy,' said Alison, snug in her feathers.

'I know,' said Sadie, 'and it's quite all right.'

It was all that needed to be said, and as the moon moved through the bars of the empty cot, they slept deeply and safely. Sadie, lying for a while awake, listening to their breathing, knew that her promise, in spirit and letter, would be kept.

Chapter Sixty-Two

Eighteen months later, a brilliant August sun shone over the salt marshes, bouncing off freshly washed windows, heating stone walls and the solar panels Figgin had installed with meticulous care in Sadie's roof. Stacks of builders' rubble waited to be carted away down an access road, freshly tarmacked, with a stout gate at the end. The garden for which John Campling had plans was still a desert, a mix of sand and cement and poor soil trampled flat by boots and equipment. A cement mixer stood on a rusty orange stand, its barrel drooping downwards forlornly, half blocking the entrance to the small annexe Anne Howard had built on to the main house for herself, so that she could stay with her grandchildren without imposing on Sadie. She had been in there all afternoon, making business arrangements by phone. She'd agreed to go down to the beach at four.

'Are they all down there?' she asked, coming out into the sun, shading her eyes.

Sadie came across the dusty yard, holding a heap of beach towels.

'They all went swimming. I'm just going down. Have you finished?'

'I booked my flights. The time difference means I can't ring the Los Angeles office until later.'

'It will be so nice to have you working from here.'

'I'll be away more than here.'

They strolled across the half-laid terrace that had once been the great-aunts' vegetable patch, just outside where the scullery had been. Sandy beach-shoes lay scattered among mats and a beachball game.

'I'll always look forward to coming back, though, however much I'm away,' Anne continued as they took a path across the marshes, crossed hot sand to the beach, where Dolly lay in enormous red sunglasses and a tiny orange bikini, watching the children play. Jove watched Dolly's tiny bikini. Mags nudged him sharply and put sun-tan oil in his hand.

'You want me to do her back?' he asked, making to get up.

Mags scowled and smacked his hand.

'Mine,' she snapped. 'Gosling'll be down later on. You leave her be.'

Jove grinned and oiled his wife's ample brown curves. Jamie and Alison swam in the shallows, their cousins' snorkels dipping and bobbing a bit further out. Mary Llewellyn sat in a beach chair, fast asleep, a handkerchief over her face.

'We are the only people on this beach,' sighed Sadie. 'I sometimes have to pinch myself to see if this paradise is real.'

'It won't be so glamorous when you're snowed up and the schools close and you can't get to the shops,' said Mags, quick to remember Maria and puncture the bubble of bliss. 'Rural life isn't all picnics.'

Sadie smiled. It was all right, really. Photographs of Maria and Philip hung in the hall and on the children's bedroom walls. They knew their roots, and were firmly attached to them, and to each and every Giangelli.

'Mummy.' Little Eve saw Sadie watching, toddled over the sand to clutch her around her knees.

'Carry. Carry me.'

Sadie stooped and picked her up. Eve's speech was slow, mostly she gave orders for her simple needs; food, cuddles, endless love.

'She's coming on, isn't she,' remarked Mags.

'The speech therapist in King's Lynn says there's no reason why she shouldn't speak quite well. The Portage lady will come when the others go back to school.'

'What's a Portage lady?'

'A woman who teaches us some exercises to help her develop as much as she can. I learn them, and do them with her.'

'Will you be happy,' asked Mags, 'staying at home? You were always such a career girl.'

'I am happier than I've ever been in my life,' said Sadie, 'even though it has all come about in a terrible way.'

'You live, and move on,' said Anne quietly.

'Dougal wants to come and see Eve,' Sadie told her. 'I had a letter a few days ago.'

'Will you let him?' asked Mags.

'Why not? He's her adopted father. Pauline's having a second child and I have a houseful of children. It didn't happen the way I would have wished, but I have everything I ever longed for.'

'Maria's children,' puffed Nonna from behind her, arriving from the house where she'd had her afternoon siesta.

'If wishing could bring Maria back, I'd wish it, with all my heart,' said Sadie.

They all knew it was true, but that life had to be lived the way it was, not the way they wished it might have been. The women began to settle themselves on the beach, taking off their sandals, unrolling mats, opening tubes of sun-tan cream.

'We are going to be very squashed,' Sadie said. 'John is bringing Blossom and Asia down with him, for the long weekend. They'll stay with Mary. Rosalie and Figgin will squeeze in with Anne.

'Everyone's here,' said Nonna contentedly, 'except Michelangelo and Sissy.'

'Can't close the restaurant on August bank holiday. We tossed for it and they got the short straw,' said Jove, mixing his metaphors cheerfully.

They lay in the sun with closed eyes, listening to the children's treble voices and the calling of gulls. Sadie sat up, began to dig with a little spade, to make a sand pie for Eve. Alison flopped down, shaking water from her hair, black and curly as her mother's.

'I'm starving. Is there anything to eat?'

'Apples in that bag,' said Sadie, pointing to the shade underneath Mary Llewellyn's deckchair. 'And some biscuits. Take them out carefully, don't crumble them up.'

'Yum,' shouted Alison, grabbing the packet, racing off down the beach. The four children shared them, sitting at the edge of the water, bronzed shoulders gleaming. Anne shaded her eyes, leaning on her elbow, watching them. The children finished their biscuits, lay in the shallows, splashing. Seaspray glittered. Behind them, across the dunes, Sadie's windows caught the sun, blinding, like some squat marshland lighthouse, beckoning them home. She finished the little sand pie and watched Eve knock it down again. A timeless game in a timeless place, which was home once more. Surrounded by her family, waiting for the man she loved to join her on the beach, Sadie lay back on the warm sand, utterly content.